"Finder has become a master of the modern thriller. There are twists and deceptions packed in here . . . once again, Finder has managed to update the claustrophobic thriller into something that resonates with our times . . . Joseph Finder has secured his niche as a master of the contemporary corporate thriller, a smart plotter in touch with our new century's soft spots." —*The Boston Globe*

"Propulsive . . . should cement Finder's reputation as a reliable chronicler of the perils lurking in e-mail and the executive suite." —*Entertainment Weekly*

PARANOIA
"A high-octane thrill ride." —*San Francisco Chronicle*

"The most entertaining thriller of the year." —*Publishers Weekly*

"Jet-propelled . . . this twisting, stealthily plotted story . . . weaves a tangled and ingeniously enveloping web . . . [with a] killer twist for the end." —*The New York Times*

"Last year belonged to Dan Brown's *The Da Vinci Code* . . . this year's first contender for Page-Turner of the Year is Joseph Finder's *Paranoia*." —*USA Today*

"Riveting . . . perhaps the finest of the contemporary thriller novelists, Finder is reminiscent of Michael Crichton, only with more character development and less slavish attention to detail . . . in the case of *Paranoia*, he's an expert on suspenseful storytelling that is at once slick and substantive . . . you may think you've read one mystery too many. Find Finder and you'll think again."
—*Pittsburgh Post-Gazette*

P9-CFD-593

"Kudos to Joseph Finder . . . in Finder's lively prose, even his thumbnail sketches come alive . . . it may go without saying that in a thriller of this quality, just about everyone has a story that's other than it first appears. What sets *Paranoia* apart from others of its genre is not only Finder's fun, chatty prose, but also his command of the setting. A former Sovietologist, the author knows his spy stuff—and has researched well the ins and outs of post-Enron corporate security . . . in a way, it's an intellectual puzzle that he has shaped into a thriller."

—*Boston Globe*

"Combining nail-biting suspense with state-of-the-art technology, it's sure to become one of the hotter books this year . . . Finder excels in keeping the reader guessing until the last sentence, literally." —*Dallas Morning News*

"*Paranoia* is a cleverly nuanced suspense story. It builds slowly and relentlessly, developing character and plot, creating intrigue . . . fresh, original, and without cliché, this is a cerebral, contemporary thriller that ends with a wrenching twist followed by a supple extra turn."

—*Boston Herald*

"A superbly edgy read . . . fraught action scenes worthy of the best heist movies . . . in *Paranoia*, Finder mines a rich vein of scary entertainment . . . grab[s] readers by their throats the way *The Da Vinci Code* did." —*New York Daily News*

"Page-turning perfection . . . dead-on dialogue . . . palpable tension . . . Finder has that rare knack for instantly pulling the reader into the story and then tops that with surprises within surprises." —*Cleveland Plain Dealer*

Praise for *New York Times* bestselling author
Joseph Finder and his novels

KILLER INSTINCT

"Unstoppable." —*USA Today*

"Masterful." —*Houston Chronicle*

"Explosive . . . wickedly fun." —*Entertainment Weekly*

"Master of a complex suspense formula . . . flawlessly executed violence, crisp dialogue, and taut pacing."
—*The New York Times Book Review*

"A first-rate thrill ride." —*Pittsburgh Post-Gazette*

"A roller coaster of a read." —*Cosmopolitan*

"Clear your schedule before you start reading this one. It's one of those books that once you start reading, you won't be able to put down." —*The Boston Globe*

"The best book of its kind since Michael Crichton's *Disclosure*."
—*The Providence Journal-Bulletin*

"Truly frightening." —*Chicago Tribune*

"A crowd-pleaser." —*Fortune* magazine

"This is fun stuff, with lots of plot twists. Finder once again proves adept at genre conventions and inventive in applying an action-movie sensibility." —*San Francisco Chronicle*

"Rich territory . . . an entertaining read."
—*The Wall Street Journal*

MORE . . .

"Readers who enjoy movies where you have to fight the urge to shout, 'Stop! Don't open that door!' will love this one."
— *Publishers Weekly* (starred review)

COMPANY MAN

"At long last someone has done for executives what John Grisham did for lawyers: create fictional ones sufficiently three-dimensional to care about . . . the book doesn't slow down for a second."
— *Fortune*

"Compelling . . . *Company Man* confirms what *Paranoia* made clear: [Finder] has unusually keen instincts for back-stabbing in the business world . . . as much a novel about the chicanery of the business world as it is a mystery story . . . Finder weaves these prospects menacingly throughout the story."—*The New York Times*

"Sharply created characters . . . makes the workplace as duplicitous a world as any in the Cold War. *Company Man* resonates with anyone who has seen corporate politics at its worst."
— *Sun-Sentinel* (South Florida)

"It's everything a thriller should be: suspenseful, entertaining—and, above all, thrilling."
— *Chicago Sun-Times*

"Finder (who last mined corporate culture in 2004's *Paranoia*) expertly keeps the pages turning as he ups the stakes chapter after chapter in Conover's professional and personal life. He is equally confident in portraying the small stuff involving family conflicts, marriages in turmoil and especially the telling details of corporate life . . . it more than achieves its main goal of entertaining the reader—as a good thriller is supposed to do."
— *Baltimore Sun*

"Once again, Finder has produced a page-turning corporate thriller with enough twists and turns for any reader."
— *The Denver Post*

"Terrific . . . riveting . . . practically redefines the high-stakes, high-tech thriller. It's the best novel of its kind since Michael Crichton's *Disclosure*."   —*Providence Journal-Bulletin*

"Fast, funny, and very, very topical."—*Toronto Globe and Mail*

"A terrific thriller . . . expertly paced and full of suspense and surprises."   —*San Jose Mercury-News*

"This novel is the real deal: a thriller that actually will keep readers up way past their bedtimes . . . relentless suspense . . . a first-rate surprise ending packs a wallop . . . the most entertaining thriller of 2004."   —*Publishers Weekly*, starred review

"The archetype of the thriller in its contemporary form . . . late in the book we discover how completely we have been fooled, and with real escapist pleasure."   —*The New Yorker*

"Edge-of-your-seat action . . . you'll think twice about who's watching you at work!"   —*Washington Post*

"Fun . . . movie-ready . . . twists aplenty . . . the fear of seeing Cassidy exposed as a spy . . . provides more chills than any ghoul with a chain saw."   —*Entertainment Weekly*

"*Paranoia* is a built-for-speed thrill ride. What raises it above . . . is its author's verbal and satirical flair."

—*Wall Street Journal*

"Imaginative and original, this is a gripping thriller with three characteristics too rare in the genre: humor, heart, and good writing."   —*Detroit Free Press*

ALSO BY JOSEPH FINDER

POWER PLAY

JOSEPH FINDER

St. Martin's Paperbacks

NOTE: If you purchased this book without a cover you should be aware that this book is stolen property. It was reported as "unsold and destroyed" to the publisher, and neither the author nor the publisher has received any payment for this "stripped book."

This is a work of fiction. All of the characters, organizations, and events portrayed in this novel are either products of the author's imagination or are used fictitiously.

POWER PLAY

Copyright © 2007 by Joseph Finder.

Cover illustration by Tom Hallman based on a photograph from Corbis

All rights reserved. No part of this book may be used or reproduced in any manner whatsoever without written permission except in the case of brief quotations embodied in critical articles or reviews. For information address St. Martin's Press, 175 Fifth Avenue, New York, NY 10010.

Library of Congress Catalog Card Number: 2007016178

ISBN: 0-312-34750-2
EAN: 978-0-312-34750-5

Printed in the United States of America

St. Martin's Press hardcover edition / August 2007
St. Martin's Paperbacks edition / March 2008

St. Martin's Paperbacks are published by St. Martin's Press, 175 Fifth Avenue, New York, NY 10010.

10 9 8 7 6 5 4 3 2 1

For my editor, Keith Kahla—the best

Knowing your own darkness is the best method for dealing with the darknesses of other people.

— CARL JUNG

BEFORE

IF YOU'VE NEVER killed someone, you really can't imagine what it's like. You don't want to know. It leaves you with something hard and leaden in the pit of your stomach, something that never dissolves.

Most of us, I'm convinced, just aren't wired to take a human life. I'm not talking about some stone-cold sniper with a thousand-yard stare, or one of those psychos who come back from the war and tell you that killing guys was like squishing ants. I'm talking about normal people.

I remember reading once how, during World War II—the Good War, right?—maybe 85 percent of the soldiers never even fired at the enemy. These were heroes, not cowards, yet they couldn't bring themselves to aim at a fellow human being and pull the trigger.

I understand that now.

But what if you don't have a choice?

I was standing at the end of a splintery wooden dock in the pale moonlight, the turbulent ocean at my back, blue-black and flecked with gray foam. On either side of me was rock-strewn beach.

And less than ten feet away, a man was pointing a gun at me, a matte black SIG-Sauer nine millimeter.

"Boy, you're full of surprises, aren't you?" he said.

I just looked at him.

He shook his head slowly. "Nowhere to run, you know."

He was right, of course. There really was nowhere to run. There was nowhere to swim, either. And I had no doubt that, the moment I made a move to jump, he'd pull the trigger.

I took a long, slow breath. "Who says I want to run?"

I could smell the seaweed, the tang of salt in the air, the faint rot of dead fish.

"Just put your hands up, Jake," he said, "and come back inside. I don't want to hurt you. I really don't."

I was surprised he knew my name, and I was even more surprised by the gentleness in his voice, almost an intimacy.

But I simply looked at him, didn't answer, didn't move.

"Come on, now, let's go," he said. "Hands up, Jake, and you won't get hurt. I promise." The crash of the waves on the shore was so loud I had to strain to make out his words.

I nodded, but I knew he was lying. My eyes strayed to the left, and then I saw the crumpled body on the sand. I felt a jolt, felt my chest constrict, but I tried to conceal it. I knew he'd killed the guy, and that if it were up to him, I'd be next.

It wasn't up to him, though.

I don't want to do this, I thought. *Don't make me do this.*

He saw my eyes move. There was no point in trying to stall for time anymore: He knew what I'd just seen. And he knew I didn't believe him.

Don't make me kill you.

"Jake," he said, in his lulling reasonable voice. "You see, you really don't have a choice."

"No," I agreed, and I felt that hard lump forming in the pit of my stomach. "I really don't."

PART ONE

1

"WE GOT TROUBLE."

I recognized Zoë's voice, but I didn't turn around from my computer. I was too absorbed in a news report on the website AviationNow.com. A competitor's new plane had crashed a couple of days ago, at the Paris Air Show. I wasn't there, but my boss was, and so were all the other honchos at my company, so I'd heard all about it. At least no one was killed.

And at least it wasn't one of ours.

I picked up my big black coffee mug—THE HAMMOND SKYCRUISER: THE FUTURE OF FLIGHT—and took a sip. The coffee was cold and bitter.

"You hear me, Landry? This is serious."

I swiveled slowly around in my chair. Zoë Robichaux was my boss's admin. She had dyed copper hair and a ghostly pallor. She was in her mid-twenties and lived in El Segundo not too far from me, but she did a lot of club-hopping in L.A. at night. If the dress code at Hammond allowed, I suspected she'd have worn studded black leather every day, black fingernail polish, probably gotten everything pierced. Even parts of the body you don't want to think about getting pierced. Then again, maybe she already did. I didn't want to know.

"Does this mean you didn't get me a bagel?" I said.

"I was on my way down there when Mike called. From Mumbai."

"What's he doing in India? He told me he'd be back in the office today for a couple of hours before he leaves for the offsite."

"Yeah, well, Eurospatiale's losing orders all over the place since their plane crashed."

"So Mike's lined up meetings at Air India instead of coming back here," I said. "Nice of him to tell me."

Mike Zorn was an executive vice president and the program manager in charge of building our brand-new wide-bodied passenger jet, the H-880, which we called the SkyCruiser. Four VPs and hundreds of people reported to him—engineers and designers and stress analysts and marketing and finance people. But Mike was always selling the hell out of the 880, which meant he was out of the office far more than he was in.

So he'd hired a chief assistant—me—to make sure everything ran smoothly. Crack the whip if necessary. His jack-of-all-trades and U.N. translator, since I have enough of an engineering background to talk to the engineers in their own geeky language, talk finance with the money people, talk to the shop floor guys in the assembly plant who distrust the lardasses who sit in the office and keep revising and revising the damned drawings.

Zoë looked uneasy. "Sorry, he wanted me to tell you, but I kind of forgot. Anyway, the point is, he wants you to get over to Fab."

"When?"

"Like an hour ago."

The fabrication plant was the enormous factory where we were building part of the SkyCruiser. "Why?" I said. "What's going on?"

"I didn't quite get it, but the head QA guy found something wrong with the vertical tail? And he just like shut down the whole production line? Like, pulled the switch?"

I groaned. "That's got to be Marty Kluza. Marty the one-man party." The lead Quality Assurance inspector at the assembly plant was a famous pain in the ass. But he'd been at Hammond for fifteen years, and he was awfully good at his job, and if he wouldn't let a part leave the factory, there was usually a good reason for it.

"I don't know. Anyway, like everyone at headquarters is totally freaking, and Mike wants you to deal with it. Now."

"Shit."

"You still want that bagel?" Zoë said.

2

I RACED OVER in my Jeep. The fabrication plant was only a five-minute walk from the office building, but it was so immense—a quarter of a mile long—you could spend twenty minutes walking around to the right entrance.

Whenever I walked across the factory floor—I came here maybe every couple of weeks—I was awestruck by the sheer scale. It was an enormous hangar big enough to contain ten football fields. The vaulted ceiling was a hundred feet high. There were miles of catwalks and crane rails.

The whole place was like the set of some futuristic sci-fi movie where robots run the world. There were more machines than people. The robotic Automated Guided Vehicle forklift zoomed around silently, carrying huge pallets of equipment and parts in its jaws. The autoclave, basically a pressure cooker, was thirty feet in diameter and a hundred feet long, as big as some traffic tunnels. The automated tape layers were as tall as two men, with spidery legs like the extraterrestrial creature in *Alien,* extruding yards of shiny black tape.

Visitors were always surprised by how quiet it was

here. That's because we rarely used metal anymore—
no more clanging and riveting. The SkyCruiser, you
see, was 80 percent plastic. Well, not plastic, really. We
used composites—layers of carbon-fiber tape soaked in
epoxy glue, then baked at high temperature and pressure. Like Boeing and Airbus and Eurospatiale, we used
as much composite as we could get away with because
it's a lot lighter than metal, and the lighter a plane is, the
less fuel it's going to use. Everyone likes to save money
on fuel.

Unfortunately, the whole process of making planes
out of this stuff is sort of a black art. We basically ex-
periment, see what works and what doesn't.

This doesn't sound too reassuring, I know. If you're a
nervous flyer, this is already probably more than you
want to know.

Also like Boeing and Airbus and the others, we don't
really build our own planes anymore. We mostly assem-
ble them, screw and glue them together from parts built
all over the world.

But here in Fab, we made exactly one part of the
SkyCruiser: an incredibly important part called the vertical stabilizer—what you'd call the tail. It was five stories high.

One of them was suspended from a gantry crane and
surrounded by scaffolding. And underneath it I found
Martin Kluza, moving a handheld device slowly along
the black skin. He looked up with an expression of annoyance.

"What's this, I get the kid? Where's Mike?"

"Out of town, so you get me. Your lucky day."

"Oh, great." He liked to give me a hard time.

Kluza was heavyset, around fifty, with a pink face and

a small white goatee on his double chin. He had safety glasses on, like me, but instead of a yellow safety helmet, he was wearing an L.A. Dodgers cap. No one dared tell him what to do, not even the director of the plant.

"Hey, didn't you once tell me I was the smartest guy in the SkyCruiser Program?"

"Correction: excluding myself," Marty said.

"I stand corrected. So I hear we've got a problem."

"I believe the word is 'catastrophe.' Check this out." He led me over to a video display terminal on a rolling cart, tapped quickly at the keys. A green blob danced across the screen, then a jagged red line slashed through it.

"See that red line?" he said. "That's the bond line between the skin and the spars, okay? About a quarter of an inch in."

"Cool," I said. "This is better than Xbox 360. Looks like you got a disbond, huh?"

"That's not a disbond," he said. "It's a kissing bond."

"Kissing bond," I said. "Gotta love that phrase." That referred to when two pieces of composite were right next to each other, no space between, but weren't stuck together. In my line of work, we say they're in "intimate contact" but haven't "bonded." Is that a metaphor or what?

"The C-scan didn't pick up any disbonds or delaminations, but for some crazy reason I decided to put one of them through a shake-table vibe test to check out the flutter and the flex/rigid dynamics, and that's when I discovered a discrepancy in the frequency signature."

"If you're trying to snow me with all this technical gobbledygook, it's not going to work."

He looked at me sternly for a few seconds, then realized I was giving him shit right back. "Fortunately, this new laser-shot peening diagnostic found the glitch. We're going to have to scrap every single one."

"You can't do that, Marty."

"You want these vertical stabilizers flying apart at thirty-five thousand feet with three hundred people aboard? I don't think so."

"There's no fix?"

"If I could figure out where the defect is, yeah. But I can't."

"Maybe they were overbaked? Or underbaked?"

"Landry."

"Contaminants?"

"Landry, you could eat off the floor here."

"Remember when some numbskull used that Loctite silicone spray inside the clean room and ruined a whole day's production?"

"That guy hasn't worked here in two years, Landry."

"Maybe you got a bad lot of Hexocyte." That was the epoxy adhesive film they used to bond the composite skin to the understructure.

"The supplier's got a perfect record on that."

"So maybe someone left the backing paper on."

"On every single piece of adhesive? No one's *that* brain-dead. Not even in this place."

"Will you scan this bar code? I want to check the inventory log."

I handed him a tag I'd taken from a roll of Hexocyte adhesive film. He brought it over to another console, scanned it. The screen filled up with a series of dates and temperatures.

I walked over to the screen and studied it for a minute or so.

"Marty," I said. "I'll be back in a few. I'm going to take a walk down to Shipping and Receiving."

"You're wasting your time," he said.

I FOUND THE shipping clerk smoking a cigarette in the outside loading area. He was a kid around twenty, with a wispy blond beard, wearing a blue knit beanie, even though it had to be ninety degrees out here. He wore Oakley mirrored sunglasses, baggy jeans, and a black T-shirt that said NO FEAR in white gothic lettering.

The kid looked like he couldn't decide whether he wanted to be surfer dude or gangsta. I felt for him. During the eighteen months I'd once spent in juvie—the Glenview Residential Center in upstate New York—I'd known kids far tougher than he was pretending to be.

"You Kevin?" I said, introducing myself.

"Sorry, dude, I didn't know you weren't supposed to smoke back here." He threw his cigarette to the asphalt and stamped it out.

My cell phone rang, but I ignored it. "I don't care about that. You signed for this shipment of Hexocyte on Friday at one thirty-six." I showed him a printout of the inventory log with his scrawled signature. He took off his sunglasses, studied it with a dense, incurious expression, as if it were Sanskrit. My phone finally stopped ringing, went to voice mail.

"Yeah, so?"

"You left early last Friday afternoon?"

"But my boss said it was cool!" he protested. "Me and my buddies went down to Topanga to do some shredding—"

"It rained all weekend."

"Friday it was looking awesome, dude—"

"You signed for it and you pulled the temperature recorder and logged it in, like you're supposed to. But you didn't put the stuff in the freezer, did you?"

He looked at me for a few seconds. My cell started ringing again.

"You picked a lousy weekend to screw up, Kevin. Heat and humidity—they just kill this stuff. There's a reason it's shipped packed in dry ice, right from the Hexocyte factory to here. That's also why they ship it with a temperature sensor, so the customer knows it was kept cold from the minute it leaves the factory. That's an entire week's work down the tubes. Dude." The cell finally stopped ringing.

The sullen diffidence had suddenly vanished. "Oh, shit."

"Do you know what would have happened if Marty Kluza hadn't caught the defect? We might have built six planes with defective tails. And you have any idea what happens to a plane if the tail comes apart in flight?"

"Oh, shit, man. Oh, shit."

"Don't ever let this happen again." My cell started ringing for a third time.

He gave me a confused look. "You're not telling my boss?"

"No."

"Why—why not?"

"Because he'd fire you. But I'm thinking that you'll never forget this as long as you live. Am I right?"

Tears came to the kid's eyes. "Listen, dude—"

I turned away and answered my cell phone.

It was Zoë. "Where are you?"

"Oahu. Where do you think I am? Fab."

"Hank Bodine wants to see you."

"Hank Bodine?"

Bodine, an executive vice president of Hammond Aerospace and the President of the Commercial Airplanes Division, was not just my boss. He was, to be precise, my boss's boss's boss. "What for?"

"How the hell do I know, Landry? Gloria, his admin, just called. He says he wants to see you now. It's important."

"But—I don't even have a tie."

"Yeah, you do," she said. "In your bottom drawer. It's in there with all those packages of instant oatmeal and ramen noodles."

"You've been in my desk, Zoë?"

"Landry," she said, "you'd better move it."

3

I'D MET HANK Bodine a number of times, but I'd never actually been to his office before, on the top floor of the Hammond Tower in downtown Los Angeles. Usually I saw him when he came out to El Segundo, the division where I worked.

I waited outside Bodine's office for a good twenty minutes, flipping through old copies of *Fortune* and *Aviation Week & Space Technology,* wondering why he wanted to see me. I kept adjusting my rumpled tie and thinking how stupid it looked with my denim shirt and wishing I'd taken a couple of minutes to change out of my jeans and into a suit. Everyone here at Hammond world headquarters was wearing a suit.

Finally, Bodine's admin, Gloria Morales, showed me in to Bodine's office, a vast expanse of chrome and glass, blindingly bright. It was bigger than my apartment. I'm not exaggerating. There was even a wood-burning fireplace, which he'd had installed at enormous expense, though there was no fire burning in it just then.

He didn't get up to shake my hand or anything. He sat in a high-backed leather desk chair behind the huge slab of glass that served as his desk. There was nothing on it except for a row of scale models of all the great Hammond airplanes—the wide-bodied 818, the best-selling 808, the flop that was the 828, and of course my plane, the 880.

Bodine was around sixty, with silver hair, deep-set eyes beneath heavy black brows, a high forehead, a big square jaw. If you'd met him only briefly, you might call him distinguished-looking. Spend more than two minutes with him, though, and you'd realize there was nothing distinguished about the guy. He was a bully, most people said—a big, swaggering man with a sharp tongue who was given to explosive tirades. Yet at the same time, he had a big, bluff charisma—a kind of Jack Welch thing going on.

Bodine leaned back, folding his arms, as I sat in one of the low chairs in front of his desk. I'm not short—just over six feet—but I found myself looking up at him as if he were Darth Vader. I had a feeling the setup was deliberate, one of Bodine's tricks to intimidate his visitors. Sunlight blazed in through the floor-to-ceiling glass behind him so I could barely make out his face.

"What's the holdup at Fab?"

"No big deal," I said. "A bonding problem in the vertical stabilizer, but it's taken care of."

Was that why he'd called me here? I braced myself for a barrage of questions, but he just nodded. "All right. Pack your bags," he said. "You're going to Canada."

"Canada?" I said.

"The offsite. The company jet's leaving from Van Nuys in five hours."

"I don't understand." The annual leadership retreat, at some famously luxurious fishing lodge in British Columbia, was only for the top guys at Hammond—the twelve or so members of the "leadership team." Certainly not for the likes of me.

"Yeah, well, sorry about the short notice, but there you have it. Should be plenty of time for you to pack a suitcase. Make sure you bring outdoor gear. Don't tell me you're not the outdoors type."

"I do okay. But why me?"

His eyes bored into me. Then the ends of his broad mouth turned up in an approximation of a smile. "You complaining?"

"I'm asking."

"Jesus Christ, guy, didn't you hear about the Eurospatiale disaster?"

The crash at the Paris Air Show, he meant. "What about it?"

"Right in the middle of the aerial demonstration, the pilot was forced to make an emergency crash landing. An aileron ripped off a wing at thirty thousand feet and smashed into the fuselage."

"An inboard flap, actually," I said.

He looked annoyed. "Whatever. The piece landed smack-dab on the runway at Le Bourget about six feet from Mr. Deepak Gupta, the chairman and managing director of Air India. Almost killed the guy."

"Okay." That I hadn't heard.

"Mr. Gupta didn't even wait for the plane to crash," he went on. "Pulled out his mobile phone and called Mike and said he was about to cancel his order for thirty-four Eurospatiale E-336 planes. Said those guys weren't ready for prime time. Wanted to talk business as soon as the show was over."

"That's about eight billion dollars' worth of business," I said, nodding. "Give or take."

"Right. I told Mike not to leave Mumbai until he gets Mr. Gupta's signature on the LOI." An LOI was a letter of intent. "I don't care how sick of curry he gets."

"Okay."

He pointed at me with a big, meaty index finger. "Lemme tell you something. It wasn't just one damned E-336 that crashed at Le Bourget. It was Eurospatiale's whole program. And Air India's just the first penny to drop. This is a no-brainer."

"Okay, but the offsite—"

"Cheryl wants someone who can talk knowledgeably about the 880."

Cheryl Tobin was our new CEO and his boss. She was the first female CEO in the sixty-year history of Hammond Aerospace and, in fact, our first female top executive. She'd been named to the job four months before, after the legendary James Rawlings had dropped dead on the golf course at Pebble Beach. Bodine must have been as stunned as everyone else when the board of directors voted to hire not just an outsider—from Boeing, yet, our biggest competitor—but a *woman.* Ouch. Because everyone thought the next CEO was going to be Hank Bodine. Hell, he even *looked* like a CEO.

"What about Fred?"

"Fred's doctors won't let him travel yet." Fred Madigan, the chief engineer on the SkyCruiser, had recently had a triple bypass.

"But there's plenty of others." Granted, I probably knew more about the plane, overall, than anyone else in the company, but that didn't make any difference: I wasn't a member of the executive team. I was a peon.

Bodine came forward in his chair, his eyes lasering

into mine. "You're right. But Cheryl wanted you." He
paused, lowered his voice. "Any idea why that might be?"

"I've never talked to Cheryl Tobin in my life," I said.
"She doesn't even know who I am."

"Well, for some reason, you've been asked to go."

"Asked or ordered?"

I thought he'd smile, but he didn't. "It's not optional," he said.

"Then I'm flattered to be invited." A long weekend in
a remote lodge in British Columbia with the twelve or
thirteen top executives of Hammond Aerospace? I
would have preferred a root canal. Anesthesia optional.

His phone buzzed, and he picked it up. "Yeah. I'm
on my way," he said into the mouthpiece. He stood up.
"Walk with me. I'm late for a meeting."

He bounded out of his office with the stride of an ex-
athlete—he'd played football at Purdue years ago, I'd
heard—and I lengthened my stride to keep up with him.
He gave Gloria a quick wave as we hurtled through his
outer office.

"One more thing," he said. "Before we reach the
lodge, I want you to find out why that plane crashed in
Paris. I want Mike to have every last bit of ammo we can
get to trash Eurospatiale and sell some SkyCruisers."

The executive corridor was hushed and carpeted, the
walls mahogany and lined with vintage airplane blue-
prints in black frames.

"I'll do what I can."

"Not good enough. I want the facts before we get to
Canada."

Some other executive I didn't recognize passed by, and
said, "How's it going, Hank?" Bodine flashed a smile and

touched two fingers to his forehead in a kind of salute but didn't slow down.

"I doubt I can call Eurospatiale and ask them, Hank."

"Are you always this insubordinate?"

"Only with people I'm trying to impress."

He laughed once, a seal's bark. "You're ballsy. I like that."

"No, you don't."

He smiled, flashing big, too-white teeth. "You got me there." Then his smile vanished as quickly as it had appeared.

We stopped right outside the executive conference room. I sneaked a glance inside. One entire side of the room was a floor-to-ceiling window overlooking downtown L.A. On one wall was a giant screen on which was projected the Hammond Aerospace logo, which looked like some 1960s corporate designer's vision of the future.

Ten or twelve people were sitting in tall leather chairs at a huge O-shaped conference table made of burnished black wood. The only woman among them was Cheryl Tobin, an attractive blonde in her early fifties wearing a crisp lavender suit with crisp white lapels. Everything about her seemed crisp and composed and efficient.

Bodine looked down at me. He was a good four inches taller than I and probably seventy pounds heavier. He narrowed his eyes. "I'll be honest with you. You weren't my choice to fill in for Mike."

Like I want to go? I thought. "I'm getting that feeling."

"Cheryl's going to ask you all sorts of questions about the SkyCruiser. She seems determined to shake things up, so she's going to want to get involved in every little detail—the weight issue, the software glitches, the quality testing on the fuselage section, all that crap. And I just want to make sure you're going to give her the right answers."

I nodded. *The right answers.* What the hell did that mean?

"Look, I don't want any trouble from you this weekend. We clear?"

"Of course."

"Good," he said, putting his hand on my shoulder. "Just keep your head down and stay in your own lane, and everything should work out okay."

I wondered what he was talking about, what kind of "trouble" he was referring to.

Then again, I don't think Hank Bodine had any idea, either.

4

RIGHT AFTER LEAVING Hank Bodine's office, I drove the twenty miles to my apartment in El Segundo to grab some clothes. I don't travel much for work—unlike my bosses, who are constantly flying somewhere to meet with customers—but my dog, Gerty, understood at once what the black suitcase meant. She put her head down between her paws and watched me gather my clothes with a stricken, panicked look.

When I broke up with Ali a year or so ago, the first thing I did was get a dog. I guess I'd gotten used to having someone else around, and so I went to the animal shelter and adopted a golden retriever. For no good reason I named her Gertrude. Gerty for short.

Gerty was all skin and bones when she first moved in, but she was beautiful, and she took to me right away. To be honest, if her new owner was a serial killer and rapist, she'd have bonded with him instantly, too. She's a golden.

She was also sort of a head case: She followed me everywhere I went in the apartment, couldn't be more than two or three feet away at any time. She'd follow me into the bathroom if I didn't close the door; when I came out, she'd be right there, waiting. Gerty was needy, and extremely clingy, but no more so than some of the women I'd gone out with since Alison Hillman.

Sometimes I wondered whether her last owner had abandoned her because she was so clingy or whether she got that way because she'd been abandoned. Whatever the reason, her separation anxiety wasn't in the range of normal. She was like a Vietnam vet with post-traumatic stress syndrome who hears a lawn mower and thinks it's the last chopper out of Saigon taking off from the roof of the American embassy.

"Chill," I said.

Dogs are underrated as girlfriend-substitutes, I think. Gerty never complained when I came home late from work; if anything, she was even happier to see me. She didn't mind eating the same thing day after day. She never insisted on watching *Desperate Housewives* when I wanted to watch football, and she never asked me if I thought she looked fat.

At least, that's what I keep telling myself ever since I screwed up my relationship with Ali. Call it rationalization. Whatever works, right?

And whatever kept me from dwelling on the first time I saw her.

"JAKE LANDRY?"

I turned around in my cubicle, almost did a double take. A beautiful woman was standing there, looking angry.

"Yes?"

Did I mention she was beautiful? Big green eyes, auburn hair. Small and slender. Really cute. Her arms were folded across her chest.

"I'm Alison Hillman. From HR."

"Oh—right. I thought you wanted me to—"

"I had to be here anyway, and I thought I'd track you down."

I spun my chair around. Stood up, trying to be polite.

An Alison Hillman from HR had sent me an irate e-mail, told me to come see her in the headquarters building immediately. I hadn't expected her just to show up.

I also hadn't expected her to look like this. "You wanted to see me for something?"

She looked up at me, her head cocked to one side. The light caught her eyes. Golden flecks in her irises. *Sunflowers,* I thought. *They look like sunflowers.*

"Your name is on Ken Spivak's ERT form as the hiring manager." An accusation, not an observation.

I hesitated for a second. "Oh, right, the transfer form." I usually didn't do that kind of paperwork, was unfamiliar with the acronyms. "There a problem?"

"A *problem*?" She looked incredulous. "I don't know what you're trying to pull off, but a Cat C ERT has to be filed with the Hourly Workforce Administration as well as the QTTP and LTD administrators."

"Do you speak any English?"

She stared at me for a few seconds, shook her head. I wasn't sure, but it looked to me like she was trying to suppress a smile, a real one. "You put through a lateral transfer on this machinist, from the Palmdale plant to the El Segundo assembly plant, is that correct?"

"Yeah, so?"

"You can't do that. It doesn't work that way."

I tried to look innocent. "What doesn't work that way?"

"You're kidding, right? You don't have the power to just—just move an hourly employee from one division to another. You can't hire outside the candidate pool. There's a whole posting process that's mandated by the union collective bargaining agreement. There are extensive protocols that have to be followed. So, I'm sorry, but I have to cancel this transfer. He's going back to Palmdale."

"Moment of candor, please?"

She looked puzzled. "Yes?"

"You and I both know that we're about to sell the Palmdale division to some buyout firm, only the news hasn't been made public yet. Which means this guy's going to be laid off."

"Along with everyone else who works at the Palmdale plant," she said, folding her arms across her chest. "And most of those workers will find other jobs."

"Not him. He's too old. He's fifty-seven, he's been with Hammond for almost forty years, and he's a good man and a hard worker."

A half smile. "Moment of candor? We make it hard for a reason, Mr. Landry. It's about doing things the right way."

"Yeah, well, Ken Spivak has five kids, and his wife died last year, and he's all they've got. And it's Jake."

She seemed to be avoiding my eyes. "I—I appreciate what you're trying to do, but I really don't have a choice here. Do you realize what kind of legal nightmare we're going to face when the word gets out in Palmdale that one lucky guy got a transfer and everyone else gets laid off—including people with higher performance ratings? The union's going to be all over us."

I said quietly, "You know what kind of legal trouble you're going to be in if you revoke his job?"

She stared at me for a few seconds, didn't reply. She knew I was right.

I went on: "Don't transfer him back. Don't you do it."

"It's about doing things the right way," she repeated quietly. "I'm sorry."

"No," I said. "It's about doing the right thing."

She didn't say anything.

"You have lunch yet?" I asked.

I DIDN'T KNOW what to pack. "Outdoor gear," Hank Bodine had said, whatever that meant. I collected a couple of pairs of jeans, my old Carhartt hunting jacket, a pair of boots. Then I went online and looked up the resort, saw how high-end it was, and threw in a pair of khakis and a blazer and a fancy pair of shoes for dinner, just in case. I quickly changed into a blazer and tie to wear on the corporate jet.

Then there was the question of what to do with Gerty for the four days I'd be gone. Someone had to feed her and take her out two or three times a day. I called one of my neighbors in the apartment building, a widowed older woman. She had a black Lab and loved Gerty and had taken care of her a few times. Her phone rang and rang. Called a bunch of my friends, who all begged off.

They knew about Gerty.

This could be a major problem, I realized, because I really didn't want to board Gerty at a kennel, even assuming I could find one at this point. I glanced at my watch, realized I had about two hours before I had to be at the Van Nuys airport. Just enough time to race over to the office and download the latest files on the 880 and try to find out what caused the crash of that plane in Paris.

As long as I got Hank Bodine what he wanted, I figured, everything would go fine.

5

ON THE SHORT drive over to the office, I kept thinking about that strange meeting with Hank Bodine and wondering the same thing that he'd asked me: Why had the CEO of the Hammond Aerospace Corporation, who didn't even know who I was, put me on the "guest list" for the offsite? And what was Bodine so concerned about—what trouble was he afraid I might cause? If he wanted to make sure I gave her the "right answers," then what were the *wrong* ones?

As soon as I got to my cubicle, I shifted into multi-tasking mode—plowed through my e-mail while copying files onto a flash drive. Most of my e-mail stack I could safely ignore. One was from the Office of the CEO, concerning the importance of ethics and a "culture of accountability" at Hammond. I saved that one to read later. Meaning: probably never.

Zoë was watching me. "So what'd Bodine want?"

"I thought you knew everything."

"Sometimes the admin gossip network is slow. Let's hear it."

"He told me I'm going to the offsite in Canada."

"Get out! For what, to carry their luggage?"

I gave her a look, then went back to copying files. "Cheryl Tobin specifically requested me," I said with a straight face. "To stand in for Mike."

"Uh-huh. Like she even knows who you are."

"Not by name, exactly," I admitted. "She wanted someone who could talk knowledgeably about the 880."

"And you're the best they could come up with?"

This was why Zoë and I got along so well. Since she worked for Mike, not for me, she could pretty much say whatever she wanted to me without fear of getting fired.

"Don't you have work to do?" I said.

"So you actually agreed to do it."

I gave her another look. "Think I had a choice? It wasn't a request. It was an order."

She shrugged. "Like that ever made a difference to you. 'Kick up, kiss down'—that's your MO, right? Piss off as many people above you as you can."

"I still have a job, don't I?"

"Yeah. For now. Shouldn't you be at Van Nuys already?"

"The jet leaves in about an hour and a half," I said. "I gotta ask you a huge favor."

She looked at me warily.

"Would you mind taking my dog?" I said.

"Gerty? I'd love to. It's like rent-a-dog. I get a dog for a couple of days, then return it when it stops being fun."

"You're the best." I handed her the keys to my apartment. "Don't let her hump you," I said.

"What?"

"She likes to hump people's legs."

"Isn't she a female?"

"It's a dominance thing. Don't let her do it."

"No one dominates me," she said.

"It's the same way wolves establish the hierarchy in their pack."

"Wolves? Are we still talking about Gerty the Emo Dog?"

"Dogs and wolves are genetically the same species, you know."

"What do you know about wolves, Landry?"

More than you know. "Don't you watch the Dog Shrink on TV?"

"Don't need to. I do my own field research. All men are dogs—even the ones who act like wolves."

"Forget it," I said. "One more favor?"

Her look was even more suspicious. She had this great cold stare that she must have perfected at the clubs when she wanted guys to stop hitting on her.

"Bodine wants to know how the Eurospatiale crash happened."

"The wing fell off or something."

"A little piece of the wing, Zoë, called the inboard flap. The question is why. It's a brand-new plane."

"You want *me* to find out?"

"E-mail some of the journalists on the good aviation websites—ask them if they've heard anything. Rumors, whatever—stuff they might not have reported. And try to grab some photos."

"Of the plane?"

"If you can. Pictures of the inboard flap would be even better. Gotta be a couple somewhere—there were a bunch of photographers in the crowd taking pictures of the aerial demo. I'll bet you when that piece hit the tarmac, someone shot some close-ups. I'd love to get some high-res photos if you can find any."

"Why does Bodine care?"

"He says he wants Mike to have all the dirt on Eurospatiale he can get."

"It's not enough that their freakin' plane crashed?"

I shrugged.

"When do you need it? By the time you get back from Canada?"

"Actually, Bodine wants the info before we get there."

"That doesn't give me much time, Landry. Mike needs me to do a spreadsheet for him, and theoretically I do work for him, you know. I could get to it in a couple of hours."

"That should work if there's Internet access on the company plane."

"There is. Wireless, too. Just make sure you do it before you get to the lodge."

"Why?"

"The place is off the grid. No cell phones, no Black-Berrys, no e-mail, nothing."

"You're kidding."

"Uh-uh. Mike was dreading it. You know how addicted he is to his e-mail."

"I thought this was real high-end. You're making it sound like some kind of shack with no indoor plumbing."

"It's totally high-end. But it's so remote they don't have landline phones. This year, Cheryl's not letting anyone use the Internet or the manager's satellite phone. She wants everyone to be off-line."

"Sounds great to me. But those guys are all going to go apeshit."

"And you're actually going to have to talk to them."

"Not if I can help it."

"You don't get it, do you? That's the whole *point* of these stupid offsites. Team-building exercises and

morale-building and all that? A lot of outdoor sports?
Even ropes courses, I hear."

I groaned. "Not ropes courses."

"Well, maybe fancier than that. I don't know. But it's
all about breaking down barriers and getting people
who don't like each other to become friends."

Going kayaking together was supposed to make all
those EVPs into friends? All those supercompetitive
Type A personalities? They were far more likely to gar-
rote each other.

"Somehow I don't think it's going to make Bodine
like Cheryl Tobin any better."

Zoë gave me a long, cryptic look, then moved closer.
"Listen, Jake. Not to be repeated, okay?"

I looked up. "Okay."

"So, there's this chick, Sophie, works at headquarters in Corporate Security?"

"Yeah?"

"I ran into her at the Darkroom on North Vine last
night, and she told me she'd just finished doing this
huge, totally top-secret job for the general counsel's
office."

She paused, as if she was unsure whether to keep going. I almost said, *Couldn't be all that top-secret if you
know.* But instead, I nodded, said, "Okay."

"Going into people's e-mail accounts and archiving
their e-mail and sending it to some law firm in Washington, D.C."

"For what?"

"She didn't know. They just told her to do it. Kind of
creeped her out. She knew it meant something serious
was going on. Some kind of witch-hunt, maybe."

"Everyone's e-mail?"

She shook her head. "Just a few of the top officers'."
She waited a few seconds. "Including Hank Bodine."

"Really?" That *was* interesting. "You think Cheryl
Tobin ordered it?"

"Wouldn't surprise me."

I thought for a few seconds. I'd heard that one of the
reasons the board of directors had brought in an outsider to run Hammond was to clean house. There were
all sorts of rumors of corruption, of bribes and slush
funds, but to be honest, our business is sort of known
for that. "No wonder Bodine wanted to know if I was a
buddy of Cheryl Tobin's."

"If I were you, I'd be careful," Zoë said.

"Careful? What, I might get rope burn?"

Zoë grimaced. She seemed a little pissed off that I
seemed to be dismissing her hot gossip with a stupid
quip. But I figured that whatever was going on between
Hank Bodine and the CEO had nothing to do with me.

"No," she said. "Four days of all that face time with
the corporate bigwigs, I'm afraid you might speak your
mind and lose your job. Those guys aren't going to take
crap from you."

"No?"

"No. You may know dogs, Landry, but you don't know
the first thing about wolves. It's a dominance thing."

6

AS I CRUISED down the 405 Freeway to Van Nuys, making unusually good time, a police cruiser came out of nowhere: blue strobe lights whirling, siren whooping. My stomach clenched. *Damn it, was I speeding? Sure; who wasn't?*

But then the cop raced on past me, chasing down some other poor sucker, leaving me with only an afterimage burned on my retina and a memory of a time I rarely thought about anymore.

THE BAILIFF TOOK me into the courtroom in handcuffs.

I wore a white button-down dress shirt, which was too big on me—sixteen years old, lanky, not yet broadshouldered—and the label made my neck itch. The bailiff, a squat, potbellied man who reminded me of a frog, took me over to the long wooden table next to the public defender who'd been assigned to me. He waited until I sat down before he removed the cuffs, then took a seat behind me.

The courtroom was stuffy and overheated, smelled of mildew and perspiration and cleaning fluid. I glanced

at the attorney, a well-meaning but scattered woman
with a tangle of frizzy brown hair. She gave me a quick,
sympathetic look that told me she wasn't hopeful. I noticed the file on the table in front of her wasn't my case:
She'd already moved on to the next one.

My heart was pounding. The judge was a fearsome
black woman who wore tortoiseshell reading glasses on
a chain around her neck. She was whispering to the
clerk. I stared at the plastic woodgrain nameplate in
front of her: THE HONORABLE FLORENCE ALTON-
WILLIAMS engraved in white block letters.

One of the fluorescent lights was buzzing, flickering.
The huge radiators were making knocking sounds.
Voices echoed from the hall outside the courtroom.

Finally, the judge turned toward me, peered over the
tops of her half glasses. She cleared her throat. "Mr.
Landry," she said. "There's an old Cherokee legend
about a young man who keeps getting into trouble because of his aggressive tendencies." She spoke in a
stern contralto. "The young man goes to see his grandfather, and says, 'Sometimes I feel such anger that I
can't help it—I can't stop myself.' And his grandfather,
who's a tribal elder and a wise man, says, 'I understand.
I used to be the same way. You see, inside of you are
two wolves. One is good and kind and peaceful, and the
other is evil and mean and angry. The mean wolf is always fighting the good wolf.' The boy thought about it
for a moment, then said, 'But Grandfather, which wolf
will win?' And the old man said, 'The one you feed.' "

She picked up a manila folder, flipped it open.
Cleared her throat. A minute went by. My mouth had
gone dry, and I was finding it hard to swallow.

"Mr. Landry, I have found you guilty of criminally

negligent homicide." She stared at me over her glasses. The public defender next to me inhaled slowly. "You should thank your lucky stars that you weren't tried as an adult. I'm remanding you to a limited-secure residential facility—that is, juvenile detention—for eighteen months. And I can only hope that by the time you've completed your sentence, you'll have learned which wolf to feed."

The radiators knocked and the fluorescent light buzzed and somewhere out in the hall a woman's laugh echoed.

7

HAMMOND AEROSPACE HAD four corporate jets, all of which were kept at the company's own hangar at Van Nuys Airport, in the San Fernando Valley, about twenty-five miles northwest of downtown L.A. "Van Noise," as the locals grumpily called it, was farther from Hammond world headquarters than LAX, but since it didn't service commercial flights, it was quicker and easier to get in and out.

Not that I'd ever flown on the corporate jet before—whenever I traveled for work, I flew commercial. The company planes were only for the elite.

I parked my Jeep in front of the low-slung terminal building, grabbed my suitcase from the back, and looked around. The jet was parked on the tarmac, very close by. This was the biggest and fanciest plane in our corporate fleet, a brand-new Hammond Business Jet with the space-age Hammond logo painted on the tail. It glinted in the sun as if it had just been washed. It was a thing of beauty.

No one had told me where I was supposed to go when I got there—whether I should go directly to the plane or not. I knew you could drive right up to the aircraft and board. But I could see, through the plate-glass windows of our "executive terminal," a cluster of guys who looked like Hammond execs, so I rolled my suitcase up to the building and walked in.

The passenger lounge was designed to resemble a 1930s airport, with marble-tiled floors and low-slung leather couches. It reminded me of one of those fancy airport "clubs" just for the first-class passengers, the kind of place you sometimes catch a fleeting glimpse of as you trundle by, before the door slams shut to the likes of you. Out there in the overcrowded airport, you're dodging speeding electric passenger carts that beep at you hostilely, and being jostled on the moving walkway by overweight women clutching Cinnabons, while inside the hushed silence of the Ambassadors' Club or the Emperors' Club, rich, well-dressed passengers are clinking flutes of champagne and scarfing down beluga on toast points.

I looked around. There were ten or so men here. Not a woman among them. There were no women at the top of Hammond Aerospace. Except for the new boss, of course.

They all resembled one another, too. Their ages ranged from early forties to maybe sixty, but they all looked vigorously middle-aged, virile, and prosperous. They all had a certain gladiatorial swagger. They could have been relatives at some jocky family reunion.

Also, unlike me, none of them was wearing a tie. Or even a blazer. They were all dressed casually in sportswear or outdoor gear—cargo shorts and pants, golf shirts, Patagonia shells, North Face performance tees. Brand names all over the place.

I sure hadn't gotten the memo.

A couple of them were wandering around, talking to themselves, wearing Bluetooth earpieces that looked like silver Tootsie Rolls with flashing blue lights on them. Hank Bodine was standing near the entrance. He was wearing a navy short-sleeved knit shirt and talking to someone I didn't recognize.

Since he was the only one here I knew, I figured I should go up to him and say hi. I didn't want to break in on anyone's conversation, but I also didn't want to stand around like a mannequin. I may not be the most outgoing guy you'll ever meet, but I'm not socially stunted, either. Still, I couldn't help feeling like the new kid in grade school, peering around the cafeteria at lunch, holding my tray, looking for a familiar face so I could sit down. The same way I'd felt when I'd arrived at Glenview, when I was sixteen.

So I left my suitcase near the door and tentatively approached him. "Hey, Hank," I said.

Before Hank had a chance to reply, a tall, wiry guy came up and clapped him on the shoulder. This was Kevin Bross, the EVP of Sales in the Commercial Airplanes Division. He had a long, narrow face and a nose that looked like it had been broken a few times. Probably playing football: Bross was another Big Ten football jock—he'd played at Michigan State.

"There he is," Bross said to Hank Bodine.

Bross didn't even seem to notice me standing there. "You read that bullshit e-mail Cheryl sent around this morning?" he said in a low voice. He wore a black Under Armour T-shirt, tight against his broad, flat torso like a superhero's costume. "All that crap about 'guiding principles' and 'a culture of accountability'?" He stared at Bodine, appalled. I couldn't believe he was dissing the CEO so brazenly, and within earshot of the others.

Hank Bodine smiled, shook his head, unreadable.

Bross went on, "Like she's our den mother or something?"

Bodine just winked, and said, "Guess we didn't have any guiding principles before. You know Jake Landry?"

"How's it going?" Bross said without interest. He gave me a quick, perfunctory glance before turning back to Bodine. "Where's Hugo?"

"He should be here any second," Bodine said. "Flying in from D.C."

"So Cheryl didn't fire him yet, huh?"

"Cheryl's not going to fire Hugo," Bodine said quietly. "Though by the time she gets done with him, he'll probably *wish* he got fired."

They didn't explain, of course, but I knew they were talking about Hugo Lummis, the Senior VP of Hammond's Washington, D.C., Operations. In plain English, he was our chief lobbyist. Hugo was a Southern good ol' boy, a real Capitol Hill creature. Before Hammond hired him, he'd been a deputy secretary of defense under George W. Bush, and before that he'd been chief of staff for some important Republican congressman. He was on back-slapping terms with just about everyone in Congress who counted.

There were rumors around the company that he'd done something funky, possibly illegal, to land Hammond a big Air Force contract a few months ago. But just rumors—there'd been no charges, nothing concrete. Now I wondered whether that was why the girl from Corporate Security to whom Zoë had talked had been ordered to search through Bodine's e-mails.

"She's just gonna let him twist slowly in the wind, huh?" Bross said.

Bodine leaned close to Bross and spoke in a low voice. "What I hear, she's hired one of those big Washington law firms to do an internal corporate investigation."

Bross stared. "You're shittin' me."

Bodine just looked back.

"You got to stop this," Bross said.

"Too late. It's already wheels up."

"Hank, you're the only one who can persuade this chick you don't shit where you eat."

I was sort of embarrassed to be standing there listening to their conversation. But I guessed that, to these guys, I was just some functionary so far down the totem pole I might as well have been below ground. Since Bodine had reassured himself that I wasn't part of Cheryl's faction, I clearly wasn't a threat. He hadn't even bothered to explain to Kevin Bross who I was or why I was here.

"Well, my daddy taught me never to talk that way to a lady," Bodine said. He smiled and winked again. "Anyway, what I have in mind doesn't involve persuasion."

My cell phone rang. I took it out of my pocket and excused myself, though the two men barely realized I was leaving.

"Hey," Zoë said. "You having fun yet? Let me guess. You're kissing butt all over the place, sucking up a storm, and you're already the new golden boy."

"Something like that." I stepped outside the terminal building and stood in the sun, admiring the gleaming Hammond plane.

"Are you talking to anyone, or are you standing by yourself, too proud to hang with your superiors?"

"You got something for me, Zoë?"

"I just talked to a reporter from *Aviation Daily* about that plane crash. He said it was a composites problem that caused the whatchamacallit to break off."

"The inboard flap. What kind of composites problem, did he say? A joint?" I felt the sunshine warm my face.

"Do I look like an engineer to you? I can't even figure out my TiVo. Anyway, I took notes and put it in an e-mail to you. I also attached some close-up shots of that piece of the wing."

"Great, Zo. I'll download them after we board. Thanks."

"*De nada.* Oh, and, Jake?"

"Yeah?"

"The *Aviation Daily* guy also told me that Singapore Airlines just canceled their deal with Eurospatiale. Like, they totally freaked out over the crash."

"Really?" That was a major contract. Almost as big as the Air India deal. "Is that public information?"

"Not yet. The reporter just got the news himself, and he's about to put it on their website. So no one else knows yet. You're, like, fifteen minutes ahead of the curve."

"Hank Bodine's gonna squeal like a pig in shit."

"Hey, Jake, you know—you might want to tell him yourself. Break the good news."

"Maybe."

"You're hesitating. You don't want to look like you're sucking up. Yeah, well, you might want to start making friends with all the big dogs. Especially since you're about to spend a long weekend with them. You're probably going to be doing 'trust falls,' you know."

"In that case, I'm likely to get a concussion."

"I hear you."

"Okay, I'll break the news to Bodine. And thanks again. I owe you one."

"One?" Zoë said. "One *squared,* more like."

"That's still one, Zoë."

"Whatever."

I clicked off and headed back inside.

8

A BIG, ROTUND bald man with large jug-handle ears pushed through the glass doors of the terminal right in front of me. Someone called out to him, and he replied in a booming voice with a Southern accent, erupting in a big, rolling laugh. He started hailing people as if this was a frat party, and he was the rush chairman. His double chin jiggled. He wore a silvery gray golf shirt stretched tight over an ample potbelly.

This had to be the famous Hugo Lummis, our chief lobbyist. The man Cheryl Tobin was hanging out to dry, according to Kevin Bross.

He went right up to Bodine and Bross. I hung back a bit. Lummis checked his watch, a huge, extravagant-looking silver thing not much smaller than a Frisbee. Then Bross checked his watch, too, a gold thing just as big. They seemed to be concerned about the time, which I didn't quite get. Who cared what time we got to the offsite?

As I came over to Bodine's rat pack, Bross, who had a Klaxon voice you could pretty much hear anywhere, said, "IWC Destriero."

Lummis rumbled something, and Bross went on,

"Got it in Zurich in December. World's most complicated wristwatch. Seven hundred fifty mechanical
parts, seventy-six rubies. Perpetual calendar with day,
month, year, decade, and century."

So they were comparing wristwatches. "In case you
forget which century you're living in, that it?" Lummis
shot back. "Twenty-first, last time I checked, unless that
watch of yours knows different."

"The moon phase display is the most precise ever
made," Bross said. "Split-second chronograph. The tour-
billon has an eight-beat-per-second escapement. Take
a listen—the minute repeater chimes every quarter
hour."

"Excuse me," I said. I tried to catch Bodine's eye, but
he didn't see.

"That would drive me crazy," Bodine said.

Lummis held up his own watch, and announced:
"Jules Audemars Equation of Time skeleton. Grand
Complication."

"How the hell can you tell time on that thing?" Bodine said. "I just want to know what time we're going to
leave already."

"No one's going anywhere until Cheryl shows up,"
Lummis said. He looked at his wrist Frisbee. "I guess
Cheryl's gotta make an *entrance*. Fashionably late. Be-
ing the CEO and all."

"Nah," said Bross, "women are always running late.
Like my wife—it's always hurry up and wait."

Bodine was smiling faintly, neither joining in their
mocking nor disapproving of it. "Well, the plane's not
gonna leave till she gets here," he said.

Hugo Lummis noticed me, and said, "Wheels up?"

"Excuse me?" I said.

"We about ready to leave?"

"I—I don't know."

He squinted at me, then guffawed. "Sorry, young man, I thought you were a flight attendant." The men around him laughed, too. "It's the tie."

I stuck out my hand. "Jake Landry," I said. "And I'm not a pilot, either."

He shook my hand without introducing himself, looked down at my watch. "But you got yourself a nice pilot's watch there, I see. That an IWC, young fella?"

"This?" I said. "It's a Timex, I think. No, Casio, actually. Twenty-five bucks."

Lummis chortled heartily, turned back to the others. "And I was about to ask the young man to carry my bag onto the plane for me." Peering at me, he said, "You a new hire?"

"I work for Mike Zorn."

"Cheryl wanted an expert on the 880," Bodine explained.

"Hell, I've got *hemorrhoids* older than him," Lummis said to the others, then added to me, mock-sternly: "Remember, young fella, what happens in Rivers Inlet stays in Rivers Inlet." Everyone laughed uproariously, as if this were some kind of inside joke.

"Hank," I finally said to Bodine. "Singapore Airlines is in play."

It took him a minute to realize I was talking to him, but then his eyes narrowed. "Excellent. *Excellent.* How do you know this?"

"Guy at *Aviation Daily.*"

He nodded, rubbed his hands together briskly.

By then they were all staring at me. Kevin Bross said, "They had eighteen 336s on order from Eurospatiale.

That's five billion dollars up for grabs. I gotta call George."

"He's in Tokyo, isn't he?" Bodine said. George Easter was the Senior Vice President for Asia-Pacific Sales.

"Yeah," Bross said. "They're seventeen hours ahead of us." He stared at his watch. "What time is it, anyway?"

Bodine laughed, then they all did. "Three thirty in the afternoon. Makes it, let's see, seven thirty in the morning in Tokyo." He turned to me, flashed his watch. "Good old-fashioned Rolex Submariner," he said with a wink. "Nothin' fancy."

"Comes in handy when you're diving at four thousand feet, I bet."

Bodine didn't seem to hear me. He said to Bross, "Tell George to touch skin with Japan Air and All Nippon, too, while he's at it. This is our big chance. A no-brainer. Get to 'em with a bid before the other guys move in."

Bross nodded, then whipped out a handheld from its holster, a quick-draw BlackBerry cowboy. He punched in numbers as he turned away.

I was about to tell Bodine about the suspected cause of the crash, but then I decided to read Zoë's e-mail first so at least I knew what I was talking about.

"Let's get this show on the road," Bodine muttered, while Kevin Bross talked on his cell loud enough for everyone to hear. "There's billions to be made in the next couple of weeks, and she's got us playing games in the woods."

"Speak of the she-devil," Lummis said, and we all turned to the door.

Cheryl Tobin, wearing the same lavender suit I'd seen

her in earlier, entered the lounge. She bestowed a be-
atific smile on the assembled.

Right behind her came another woman, who I assumed was her administrative assistant or something.
An elegant, auburn-haired beauty in a navy polo shirt
and khaki slacks, holding a clipboard and moving with
a dancer's grace.

It took me a few seconds to realize that I knew her. I
drew a sharp breath.

My stomach flipped upside down and turned inside
out.

Ali Hillman.

9

HER APARTMENT, IN an old Art Deco building in Westwood, was like Ali: the unexpected corners, the skewed lines, stylish and a little mysterious and glamorous and sort of exotic.

"The rumor is that this apartment used to belong to Howard Hughes," she said as she led me inside the first time. We'd been spending nights at my apartment, so coming here felt like a new stage, like I'd passed some sort of test.

"He used it as a love nest for his girlfriends. That's what the landlord says."

"Either that, or he needed another place to store his mason jars." It was on the second floor, and you could hear traffic noise from the street, trucks roaring by, car horns.

"But I need to move. Too noisy. I can't sleep at night."

"Move in with me."

"El Segundo? It's a commute."

"I'm worth it."

"We'll see."

She put her mouth on mine, ending the conversation.

"Mmm," she said after a couple of minutes. "Yeah, I'm thinking you just might make the cut."

SHE DIDN'T SEE me. She was immersed in conversation with Cheryl Tobin as the two of them swept into the room, parting a Red Sea of middle-aged men. An electric force field seemed to surround them, crackling and radiating through the room. Like it or not, this was the boss.

And—what?—her assistant? Was Ali working for the CEO now? If so, when had this happened?

I felt the electrical charge, too, but of a different sort. It was the voltage generated by all sorts of little switches going off in my brain, circuits closing, thoughts colliding. I hadn't seen her in months, had assumed she was still in HR. But I'd lost track of what she was doing, exactly. Another guy might have kept tabs on her on the company intranet, asked after her. Googled her. She was the kind of woman who could turn men into stalkers.

I wish I could say I'd moved on, had the coldhearted ability to shift over to the next woman without looking back. The truth is, I knew that if I allowed myself to mope or obsess, I'd never get over her. I wasn't sure I ever would anyway. So as much as I thought about her after the breakup, I didn't let myself wallow in the sweet misery of tracking her from afar.

And now Ali was working with, or for, Cheryl—you could tell from the body language—and she was probably going on the offsite, too.

For a moment it felt as if I were inside a freeze-frame: I couldn't hear or see anyone around me except for Ali. The loud chatter and laughter dissolved into meaningless babble.

Ali.

I knew now who'd put me on the guest list for the off-site. One mystery solved. But it only created a new one.

Why?

YET BEFORE I could go up to her, she was gone. She said something to Cheryl and, holding a cell phone to her ear, disappeared down a side corridor.

Gradually, I returned to the room, became more aware, more present. I heard Bodine mutter to Bross, "Notice she said no staff, no assistants, no admins. Yet she brought one of hers."

Ali wouldn't be Cheryl Tobin's administrative assistant, of course; she was a rising executive in HR. But was it possible that she'd become an assistant to the CEO of some kind?

Cheryl worked the room like a master politician. She circulated among the twelve or so guys, smiling and touching them on the shoulders in a way that was warm but not too intimate.

Most of the men responded the way you'd expect. They gave her smiles that were too wide and too bright. They shifted their stances so they could watch her out of the corners of their eyes while she talked to others. They tried to suck up without being too transparent about it.

Not all of the guys, though. Hank Bodine's little clique seemed to be making a point of ignoring her. Kevin Bross said something under his breath to Bodine, who nodded, his eyes alert but unrevealing. Then Bross turned and headed toward Cheryl. Not right toward her, but meandering in her general direction. As he got

close, she must have said something—I couldn't hear—
because he turned and smiled right at her.

"I admired your e-mail this morning," he said, his
voice louder than he no doubt intended.

Bodine and Lummis were watching the exchange
from across the room.

I could see Cheryl's pleased smile. She said something else.

"No, I was really impressed," Bross said. "People
need to be reminded about the culture of accountability.
We all do."

Cheryl smiled and touched his shoulder. Bross nodded, gave a sort of contorted, embarrassed smile. His
face was flushed. Then he turned and looked at Bodine
and gave him a wink.

NOT UNTIL WE all began boarding the plane did Ali
see me.

She was at the top of the metal stairs leading into the
jet, just behind Cheryl Tobin, as I started to climb the
steps. She turned around, looked down as if she'd forgotten something, and her eyes raked mine.

Then, abruptly, she looked away.

"Ali?" I said.

But she pretended not to hear me and entered the
cabin without turning back.

10

BY THE TIME I boarded, Ali was nowhere to be found, and I was left feeling as if I'd been kicked in the solar plexus. Or someplace a little lower.

She'd seen me: No question about that. And whether she'd put me on the guest list or not, she had to know I'd be here.

Why, then, the cold shoulder?

I've always thought that living with a woman is like visiting a foreign country where no one speaks English and the signs are all in some strange alphabet that almost looks like English, but not quite. If you want to buy coffee or order dinner or get a seat on a bus, you have to learn a few basic phrases of the local dialect.

So in the year and a half that Ali and I went out, I learned to read the nuances in her voice. I became reasonably fluent. I stopped needing to consult the Berlitz book. And I still hadn't lost the ability to speak Ali.

But her reaction was baffling.

I assumed she'd gone off to work with Cheryl in the CEO's private lounge. It took all the restraint I could summon to keep from walking down there and asking her what was going on.

Instead, I took a seat in the main salon. Most of the seats were taken by the time I got there, but I found a chair off by itself, next to where Hank Bodine was holding court with Hugo Lummis, Kevin Bross, and someone else. I was close enough to hear them talking, but I'd sort of lost interest in hearing them compare watches, as fun as that was, so I tuned out.

Anyway, my mind had been derailed. As much as I tried not to, I couldn't stop thinking about Ali. And it wasn't just her strange behavior. It was simply seeing her after so long. I was like a parched man lost in the desert for weeks who'd just been given a thimbleful of water. My thirst hadn't been slaked; it had been whetted.

I thought about Ali, presumably sitting with Cheryl Tobin in the executive lounge, which included a private office, bedroom suite, exercise studio, personal kitchen, even a shower. Even among the superprivileged who got to fly on private corporate jets, there was first class. I loved that. You finally claw your way to the top only to discover there's still one more rung above you, a rarefied VIP echelon you'd never even heard of.

The rest of us weren't exactly in steerage, though. The main salon looked like an English gentlemen's club, not that I'd ever actually seen such a thing. It certainly didn't look like any airplane I'd ever been in before. The cabin walls were paneled in Brazilian mahogany. The floors were covered with antique-looking Oriental rugs. Huge, cushy, black leather club chairs were arranged in little "conversation groups" around marble-topped tables. There was a burlwood standalone bar.

Two beautiful blondes were circulating with trays of little Pellegrino bottles, taking drink orders. I wanted a real drink, but I was at work, after all, so I decided I'd better just get a Pepsi.

My chair swiveled and tilted. All around me was wide-open space. There was no seat six inches in front of mine that would tip back into my knees. Very nice. I could get used to this.

Granted, the furnishings were a little much—all that dark wood and antique rugs and black leather—but the plane was pretty great. The Hammond Business Jet was far and away the best on the market. It left the Gulfstream G450 and the Boeing Business Jet and the Airbus Corporate Jetliner in the dust. The Hammond had the widest body and the largest cabin of any private corporate jet on the market. Even configured as luxuriously as it was, it easily held twenty-five people.

The pitch we used to convince companies to spend fifty million bucks for one of our planes was that it wasn't simply a means of transportation. Oh, no. It was a productivity tool. It allowed an executive to make good use of his travel time. And a relaxed and refreshed executive could seal a deal much more effectively than his travel-worn counterpart.

Yeah, right. You can always justify any obscene luxury on the grounds of productivity, I've found.

In addition to the CEO's executive suite and the main salon, this plane also had a conference room (with videoconferencing capabilities), a small office suite, and three lavatories with showers. People sometimes called it the "flying penthouse" or the "flying boudoir." Or the "mile-high palace." The décor, someone once told me, was the legacy of our previous CEO, James Rawlings. The story was that he and his wife had flown on some other company's jet as the guests of the CEO and were both blown away by the way the cabin was outfitted, which made Hammond's jets look shabby by comparison. Mrs. Rawlings hounded her husband until he gave in and let her hire her favorite interior designer to overhaul one of the Hammond jets, the same designer who'd also done their house and their yacht.

While I waited for the waitresses, or the flight attendants, or whatever they were called, to take my drink order, I took out my laptop and powered it on. I had work to do—I had to download the files Zoë had sent so I could try to get Bodine the answers he wanted—but I was finding it hard to concentrate.

My computer located the wireless Internet signal, and I logged on to my e-mail. Opened Zoë's e-mail and read it over twice. Then I opened the zipped folder containing the *Aviation Daily* photos, eight high-resolution close-ups of the Eurospatiale crash, including the part that had ripped off, the inboard flap. They were big files and took a while to download.

Meanwhile, I could hear Hugo Lummis saying to the others, in his booming voice and mellow Southern accent: "You gonna tell me that's a level playing field? Uh-uh, no *sir*. So I'm having dinner at Cafe Milano with the Secretary of the Air Force just last week, and he keeps talking about 'the Great White Arab Tribe' and I finally say to him, 'What in God's name are you talking about?' And he says, 'Oh, that's just our nickname for *Boeing*.' So how does Cheryl think we're supposed to compete with that kinda favoritism if we *don't* grease the skids a little?"

I looked at him, without meaning to, and Kevin Bross

noticed my glance. He made some kind of a quick, subtle hand gesture, and then Lummis's voice suddenly died down.

After a while, I started smelling cigar smoke, and I looked over and saw Bodine and Lummis smoking a couple of big ugly stogies. Thick white tendrils of smoke wreathed their heads. I guessed this wasn't a no-smoking flight.

When one of the beautiful blond flight attendants finally came over to me, I decided to order a Scotch. Seeing Ali had set me back, I realized; I really did need a drink. So I asked for a single-malt Scotch, and she wanted to know what kind. Apparently I could get whatever brand I wanted. I said Macallan. She asked me how old. I asked what my choices were.

"Would you like the eighteen?" she said.

I told her I would.

Just then, someone made an announcement over the speakers that we'd be taking off momentarily and asked us to fasten our seat belts. It was a polite, almost apologetic request, not the sort of imperious demand they make when you fly commercial. No one ordered me to turn off all electronic equipment. No one said anything about stowing our bags in any overhead compartments. Not that there were any overhead compartments to jam our stuff into.

The flight attendant apologized profusely that I'd have to wait for my drink until after takeoff. She asked me to fasten my seat belt, then excused herself so she could do the same.

I could feel the idling engines roar to life—two Rolls-Royce Trent 1000 turbofan engines, with a three-shaft layout—and we began the takeoff roll. Seventy-five thousand pounds of thrust lifted us off the ground; but for all that power, you could barely hear any noise. One of the reasons it was so quiet is that the big fan in the engine moves a lot of air around the turbine, and that acts like a muffler. Plus, the engine nacelle inlet is lined with a one-piece acoustic barrel to absorb sound.

Airplane geek: who, me?

That baby could go Mach 0.89, and even when it was up against the barber pole—cruising at max speed—it was so solidly built that nothing ever squeaked or rattled. It had a range of almost seven thousand miles, partly because it was so light. The airframe was made of lightweight improved aluminum alloy, and the engine cowlings and all the control surfaces, the rudders and ailerons and elevator, were made out of advanced composites.

I learned to fly when I was in college, wanted to be a pilot but was disqualified because my vision wasn't totally perfect. But at least I got to work with planes, and when I'm a passenger on a well-built plane, I'm always watching and listening, noticing things most people don't.

Once we started our ascent—we'd be cruising at forty-five thousand feet, I knew, well above commercial airline traffic—I turned back to my laptop and began studying the photos. Which was when something caught my attention. I enlarged the photo to the full size of my computer screen, then zoomed in on one small area of the picture. A piece of the plane's wing was lying on the asphalt. The inboard flap, I could tell right away.

I zoomed in still closer. I could see where the aluminum hinge had ripped out. It was pretty dramatic looking, and sort of surprising, too.

The wings and the wing flaps on the Eurospatiale E-336 were made out of composite materials, just like our own SkyCruiser. But the hinges that attach the flaps to the wings are made of a high-grade 7075 aluminum.

And somehow those aluminum hinges had just ripped clean off the wing flap. How, I had no idea. I needed to study the pictures some more. Maybe do some more research.

My Scotch arrived, in a cut-glass crystal tumbler on a silver tray, with a dish of warm mixed nuts under a linen napkin. Next to it was a small envelope.

A bill? The Hammond private jet didn't exactly have a cash bar. So what could it be?

The envelope was made from very thick, expensive-looking stock. It was blank on the outside. Inside was a folded note, on a matching sheet of paper.

I recognized the handwriting at once. It said, simply:

Landry—
  Please come to the executive lounge as soon as you get this. BE SUBTLE.

                                                                    —A

I closed my laptop and got right up.

11

THE INNER SANCTUM—the CEOs' private lounge—was even more opulent than the main salon.

If I'd just come from an English gentlemen's club, then this was the club's private library. The walls here were paneled in a rich, antique wood, though I knew they had to be veneers, since real wainscoting would be too heavy. The lighting was indirect, from tiny ceiling pinpoints trained against the paneling, and gave the cabin an amber glow. The antique carpets were even finer. There were cabinets that looked like family heirlooms (though not my family, of course, whose oldest piece of furniture had been Dad's Barcalounger). A flat-screen TV hung on one wall, tuned to CNBC. A steel-clad galley kitchen with an espresso machine. A couple of overstuffed couches, upholstered in an off-white brocade.

And sunk down in the middle of one of the couches, facing the door, was Ali. She was reading a folder, but she put it down when I entered.

"Landry."

"There you are," I said, as casually as I could manage,

walking up to her. "A private summons, huh? And I thought you'd forgotten who I was."

"I'm so sorry about that. I really am. It's just really important for us to be discreet." She got up off the sofa and put her arms around me. She had to stand on tiptoes to do it. "Hey, I've missed you."

She spoke with a slight Southern twang, the residue of her years living in Fort Benning, Georgia, and Fort Bragg, North Carolina.

"Me, too." If I was perplexed before, by this time I was even more confused. She looked great, of course. Even more beautiful, which I found disconcerting. Ali was petite and slender—people tended to call her "pert" or "perky" or "spunky," words she hated, because she thought they were all basically synonyms for "short." When we were going out, she wore her hair short. Now it was long and flowing, down to her shoulders, and looked like she spent a lot of money getting it cut in some fancy salon. She'd done something to her eyebrows, too, made them sort of arched. She wore glossy lipstick with lip liner. The old Ali didn't wear much makeup; she didn't need it. She was beautiful, but you'd never call her stylish. She was like a tomboy who'd grown up. The new Ali was willowy, elegant, polished.

I liked the old Ali better, even if the new one was more striking.

"You look good," I said.

"Thanks. I like your jacket."

"You got it for me."

"I remember."

"It's the only decent blazer I own."

"No argument there. You did have the worst clothes."

"I haven't changed."

"That doesn't surprise me, Landry. You never liked change."

"That hasn't changed either," I said.

"IT'S TIME," I said, clicking on the remote.

Sunday nights at nine; we never missed it. My favorite TV show. *The Dog Shrink*: an Australian canine therapist who specialized in helping troubled dogs, invariably with a happy ending.

This week's show was about a vicious Presa Canario/Cane Corso/pit bull mix owned by a frail-looking old lady. The dog was highly territorial and fiercely protective and was about to be put down after horribly mauling a neighbor boy.

The Dog Shrink called Missy—that was the dog's name—a "red-zone dog" and said, "Missy was not born a killer. Monsters are made, not born. Her aggressive behavior was created by her caretakers. I'm sure Missy was abused at an early age."

Ali lay on the couch doing paperwork, manila folders arrayed on the old steamer trunk that served as my coffee table. "I always wanted a dog," she said. "But my dad wouldn't allow it. He liked everything to be 'trig,' as he called it. Totally clean and neat and squared away. He said dog hairs get all over everything, and you never ever get them out."

She was an Army brat: Her dad had been a drill instructor, then a master sergeant. My father had been a Marine, so we had that military-family thing in common, too. She used to tell me all about her dad, how she loved shining his shoes and polishing his belt buckle and ironing his handkerchiefs and his uniform and all that. How proud she was of him. And yet how distant he was. If you're not an Army brat, she once told me, you'll never really understand. She liked to talk all about her background, her childhood, her brothers, her parents' lousy marriage. I never talked about that stuff at all.

"Don't forget the poop," I said.

"How come you don't have a dog, if you love dogs so much?"

"I'd consider it if they'd take turns picking up *my* poop."

"Seriously."

"It's a real commitment."

"Right. They just take and take and take, don't they?"

I shrugged, admiring her dry sarcasm but not taking the bait. "Someday I'll get one."

"Did you have a dog, growing up?"

I shook my head. "My dad didn't like them."

"Why not?"

"Who knows? Probably because dogs didn't like him. They're really good judges of character."

"And what did they see in him?"

"Remember the dad on *The Brady Bunch*?"

"Vaguely. What about him?"

"Well, my dad was kinda the opposite."

On the TV, the Dog Shrink said, "Missy is a very protective dog. Anytime she thinks her owner is being threatened, she'll attack." There was scary footage of Missy frothing and baring her fangs.

The Dog Shrink said, "Missy just needed to understand that not everyone is a threat to her owner. She had to learn not to be so protective. And do you know what her secret was—the real secret of her aggressiveness?" He stroked the dog under her chin. "She was frightened!

That's what made her overcompensate. That's what made her so aggressive. So I had to show her there was no reason to be so afraid."

Cut to Missy after six weeks of intensive dog therapy, lying on her back, puppylike, licking the Dog Shrink's hand. "Now we see her in a state of calm submission," said the Dog Shrink.

"Aw, look at her," said Ali. "How cute is that?"

"Yeah," I said. "Look at that dog the wrong way, and I bet she still rips your throat out."

Ali laughed.

"Let me tell you something. Nobody ever really changes."

She laughed again, gave my face a playful slap. "Landry, no one makes me laugh the way you do."

She thought I was kidding.

"WHAT'S GOING ON?" I said. "You don't want these guys to figure out we used to be involved, is that it?"

"Yes."

"But so what?"

"Sit down, Landry. We need to talk."

"Words a guy never wants to hear."

She didn't seem to be in a lighthearted mood, though. She didn't laugh the way she normally might have.

"It's important," she said.

I sat next to her on the couch.

"How long have you been working for Cheryl Tobin?" I said.

"Since about a month after she started. So, almost three months."

"How'd that happen? I thought you were in HR."

"Only we call it People now," she said. "Cheryl heard

about how I brought in this fancy new information-systems program to keep track of payroll and benefits, and she invited me to her office to talk. We just hit it off. She asked me to join the Office of the Chief Executive Officer. As her Executive Assistant in charge of Internal Governance, Internal Audit, and Ethics."

I could understand why Cheryl Tobin would have been impressed by Ali. She was not just smart but whip-smart, *Jeopardy!*-contestant-smart. She had what my dad used to call a "smart mouth," only when it came from him, it was never a compliment. She was quick-witted; her mind cycled a lot faster than most. She always said that came from growing up the only girl in a family with four brothers: she learned to talk fast and to the point in order to get what she wanted. As a guy who tends to be better at listening than at speaking, I always admired her ability to express herself at such lightning speed. If I'd been another kind of guy, we could have had the sort of verbal-sparring relationship that Spencer Tracy had with Katharine Hepburn. Instead, it was more like Katharine Hepburn doing a one-woman stage show.

"Last time I checked, we already have an Office of Internal Governance." I was never sure what the Office of Internal Governance did exactly—I imagined it as sort of like Internal Affairs in a police department. Checking up on the company to make sure all the procedures are followed, maybe.

"Sure. And an Office of Internal Audit. But she wanted me to directly oversee them."

"Meaning she didn't trust them to do their job right without supervision."

"You said it, not me."

I nodded. She smelled great. She always smelled great. At least her perfume hadn't changed—something by Clinique, I remembered. I'm not a guy who remembers the names of perfumes, but I once went out with a woman briefly who smelled just like Ali. It messed with my head, and I'd asked her what it was called. Then I asked her to stop using it. That pretty much ended that relationship.

"Where's your boss?" I said.

She pointed at a set of leather-covered double doors a few feet away. Cheryl's private office, I assumed. "On a call."

"Can she hear us?"

Ali shook her head.

The door to the outside corridor opened, and a flight attendant peered in, a beautiful Asian woman. "May I get you or your guest anything, Ms. Hillman?"

"Landry?" Ali said.

I shook my head.

"We're fine, Ming," she said. "Thank you." Ming nodded and shut the door.

"You like working for Cheryl?"

"I do."

"Would you tell me if you didn't?"

"Landry," she said. She tipped her head to one side, an expression I knew well, which meant: *How can you even ask?*

Ali never lied to me. I don't think she even knew how to be less than honest. Even if it risked offending me or hurting my feelings. Which was another thing I liked about her. "Sorry."

"If I didn't like it, I wouldn't do it," she said. "Cheryl's one of the most impressive women I've ever met. One of the most impressive *people* I've ever met. I think she's amazing."

I nodded. I wasn't going to ask her at that point if Cheryl was really as much of a bitch as everyone said. Probably wasn't the best time.

"And yes, I know how all these guys talk about her." She waved in the general direction of the main salon. "You think *she* doesn't know?"

"It's just grumbling," I said. "They're probably freaked out by having a woman running the show for the first time. Plus, they're nervous they'll get canned, too."

She lowered her voice, leaned in closer to me. "What makes you think she has that power?"

"She's the CEO."

"The board of directors won't let her fire any more senior or executive vice presidents without consulting them. And believe me, all these guys know that."

"You're kidding."

"After her first round of management changes, riots almost broke out on the thirty-third floor. Hank Bodine went to one of his buddies on the board and had a little talk, and the board met in emergency session to limit her hiring-and-firing authority. It's practically unprecedented. And it's outrageous."

"If Bodine has so many buddies on the board, why didn't they make him CEO instead of Cheryl?"

She shrugged. "You can bet he wonders the same thing. Maybe he didn't have enough supporters on the board. Maybe they thought he'd be too much of a bully—a bull in a china shop. Or maybe they wanted to bring in someone new, an outsider, to try to clean up the mess here. But whatever the reason, it wasn't a unanimous vote, I know that. Plus, they all know how valuable Bodine is to Hammond, and they don't want to lose him. Which was a real risk when they passed him over. So a fair number of board members are watching closely to see if she screws up. And if and when she does, they'll get rid of her, believe me."

"Does any of this have to do with why I'm here? Why *am* I here?"

"Well, Mike Zorn said no one knows more about the SkyCruiser than you. He said you're—how'd he put it?—a 'diamond in the rough.' "

Just then I was feeling more like a golf ball in the rough. "But he didn't recommend me as his stand-in, did he?"

Ali hesitated. "He did say you might be a little . . . junior."

"Hank Bodine was convinced that Cheryl put me on the list herself," I said. "She didn't, did she?"

"No, of course not," said a voice from behind us. The leather-clad double doors had opened, and Cheryl Tobin emerged. "I'd never even heard your name before. But Alison Hillman tells me you can be trusted, and I hope she's right."

12

SHE EXTENDED A hand. I stood and shook it. Her handshake was excessively firm, her hand icy cold.

"Cheryl Tobin," she said. She didn't smile.

"Nice to meet you. Jake Landry."

I'd never seen her up close. She was better-looking from a distance. Up close, she seemed all artifice. Her face was smooth and unlined, but unnaturally so, as if she'd had a lot of roadwork—Botox or plastic surgery. Her makeup was a little too thick, masklike, and it cracked around her eyes. She gave me a steady, appraising look. "Alison tells me good things about you."

"All lies," I said.

"Oh, Alison knows better than to lie to me. Sit, please."

I sat down, more obedient than my golden retriever. She took a seat on the couch facing us, and said to Ali, "That was Hamilton Wender."

"And?" Ali said.

Cheryl lifted her head. "We'll talk." Then she turned to me. "I'll get right to the point. I'm sure you read my e-mail."

"Which one?"

She widened her eyes a bit. She was probably trying

to raise her eyebrows, too, but Botox had frozen her forehead. "This morning."

"Oh, that. About the ethics. Yeah, it sounded nice."

"Sounded nice," she echoed, her voice as frosty as her handshake. You could almost see the icicles hanging down from her words. "Hmph."

"I always thought that Enron had the finest code of ethics I ever heard," I said, and immediately wished I'd kept my mouth shut.

She looked at me for a few seconds as if she wanted to scratch my eyes out. Then she smiled with her mouth, though not the rest of her face. "Quite the brownnoser, I see."

"Not working, huh?"

"Not exactly."

I shrugged. "I guess that's the advantage to being a low-level flunky. I'm not a member of the team. You know what they say: The nail that sticks up gets hammered down."

"Ah. So you don't stick up. That way you can say whatever you want. Even when you're face-to-face with the CEO."

"Something like that."

She turned to look at Ali. "You didn't tell me what a charmer he is, Alison."

Ali rolled her eyes, and said to me warningly, "Landry."

Cheryl leaned forward and fixed me with an intense stare. "What I'm about to tell you, Jake, is not to be repeated."

"Okay."

"Absolutely no one must know what I'm about to tell you. Is that clear?"

I nodded.

"I have your word on this?"

"Yes." What next: a pinkie swear, maybe?

"Alison assured me you could be trusted, and I trust her judgment. A few months ago I hired a D.C. law firm, Craigie Blythe, to conduct an internal corporate investigation into Hammond Aerospace."

I nodded again. I didn't want her to know that I'd already overheard Bodine telling Bross about it. Or that Zoë's friend in Corporate Security had revealed how they'd been going through the e-mails of a few top officers in the company. I couldn't help thinking, though: For a brand-new CEO to launch an investigation of her own company—that was almost unheard of. No wonder everyone hated her.

"Do you remember the trouble that Boeing got into a few years ago with the Pentagon acquisitions office?"

"Sure." That was a huge scandal. Boeing's CFO had offered a high-paying job to the head of the Air Force acquisitions office if she'd throw a big tanker deal their way. The woman they'd co-opted, or bribed, or whatever you want to call it—everyone called her "the Dragon Lady"—had power over billions of dollars in government defense contracts. She decided which planes and helicopters and satellites and such the Air Force would buy. "Didn't he go to prison?"

"That's right. So did she. And Boeing's CEO was forced to resign. Boeing had to pay a massive settlement, lost a twenty-three-billion-dollar deal, and their reputation was damaged for years. I was at Boeing at the time, and I remember it well. So you can bet that I'm not going to let anything like that happen at Hammond—not on my watch."

I just looked at her, waited for her to go on, not sure why she was telling me all this. Ali was watching her, too, but it looked as if she was waiting for a cue to start speaking.

"I'm sure you've heard the rumors about something similar going on here," she said. "That *someone* at the Pentagon—presumably the current chief of acquisitions—was given a bribe by *someone* at Hammond."

"To lock in that big transport plane deal we signed a few months back," I said. "Yeah, I've heard that. Sounded to me like Boeing got a way better deal than us."

"How so?"

"All the lady at the Pentagon got from Boeing was a two-hundred-fifty-thousand-dollar job that she actually had to show up and do. But what I heard, Hammond gave her successor—I don't know, they say it was a million bucks."

"Be that as it may," Cheryl said, unamused. "At first I dismissed these reports as just sour grapes—you know, how in the world did a second-tier player like Hammond Aerospace beat out both Boeing and Lockheed? But after I got here, I was determined to make sure there was no truth in the rumors. Alison?"

Ali shifted on the couch so she could address both of us at the same time. "The investigators at Craigie Blythe have already turned up some interesting things," she said.

"Such as?"

"What looks like a pattern of improper payments, both here and abroad."

"We're talking bribes, right?"

"Basically."

"Who?"

"We don't have names yet. That's one of the problems."

"Hey, you've got the name of whoever the Air Force
acquisitions chief is now—why don't you just lean on
him—or her?"

Ali shook her head. "This is a private investigation.
We don't have subpoena power or anything like that."

"So why don't you tip off the government and have
them take over?"

"No," Cheryl broke in. "Absolutely not. Not until we
know who at Hammond was involved. And not until we
know we have prosecutable evidence."

"How come?"

"It's tricky," Ali said. "Once the word spreads at
Hammond, people will start destroying documents.
Deleting evidence. Covering their tracks."

Cheryl said, "And the moment you bring in the U.S.
Attorney's Office in a situation like this, it becomes a
media circus. I saw that with Boeing. Their investigation will go on forever and become front-page news,
and it'll do immeasurable harm to the company. No, I
want this inquiry completely nailed down. Only then
will we turn it over to the government—names, dates,
documents, everything."

"That's why this whole thing has to be done under
the radar," Ali said.

"Come on," I said, "you're telling me you have a
team of lawyers flying in from Washington and inter-
viewing people and combing through documents and
poking around the company and no one's going to find
out? I doubt it."

"So far, everything's been done remotely," Ali said. "They've got computer forensics examiners going through backup tapes of e-mail and financial records. Huge amount of stuff—*gigabytes* of data."

"Our in-house coordinator," said Cheryl, "is our general counsel, Geoff Latimer, and he's been tasked with keeping everything under wraps. He's one of only four people at Hammond who know. Well, five, now, counting you."

"Who else?" I said.

"Besides us and Latimer, just Ron Slattery." That was the new CFO, whom Cheryl had brought over from Boeing. He was generally considered to be her man, the only member of the executive council loyal to her. Which was another way of saying that he was her toady. Her hood ornament, some people called him. Her sock puppet.

"Oh, there's more than five who know about the investigation," I said.

Ali nodded. "The head of Corporate Security," she said, "and whoever he assigned to monitor e-mail. And probably Latimer's admin, too. So that makes eight people."

"More than that," I said.

"What's that supposed to mean?" Cheryl said.

"The word's out. I heard Hank Bodine tell Kevin Bross about the investigation."

"When was this?"

"This morning."

Cheryl gave Ali a penetrating look. "I suppose that explains why he's suddenly being so circumspect in his e-mails and phone calls."

He, I assumed, was Hank Bodine.

To me, she said: "You were in Hank Bodine's office?"
I nodded.

"Interesting. Do you go there often?"

"First time I've ever been there."

"What was the reason he asked you?"

"I think the real reason was to find out why you'd put me on the offsite list. He seemed awfully suspicious. He wanted to know if I knew you."

"Was he aware that you and Ali are acquainted?" Cheryl asked.

How much, I wondered, did she know? Had Ali told her about us?

I shook my head. "I don't think so. He would have said something."

For a few seconds she seemed to be watching the flat-screen TV. She wrinkled her nose, and said to Ali, "Do you smell cigars?"

Ali shook her head. "Cigars? I don't think so."

"The 'real reason,'" Cheryl repeated softly. "So there must have been an ostensible reason he asked to see you. A *cover* reason."

I was impressed: She was awfully smart. "He wanted me to find out why the E-336 crashed." I added, realizing she probably didn't know what I was talking about, "At the Paris Air Show, the—"

"I know all about it, believe me," she interrupted. "He wanted to know *why*, huh? That's also interesting. Did he tell you why he was so desperate to know?"

"Well, I wouldn't say he was desperate. He said he wanted to give Mike Zorn ammunition against Eurospatiale to help him 'trash' them."

"As if Mike needs that," she said, more to Ali than to me. "That's curious, isn't it?"

"How so?"

Cheryl glanced at Ali, then at me, obviously unwilling to answer my question. "Do you know who Clive Rylance is?"

"Of course." Clive Rylance was an Executive Vice President and the London-based chief of Hammond's international relations. That meant he oversaw all eighteen of our in-country operations around the world.

"Hank Bodine's planning to have a little chat with him at the lodge. To talk about some things he didn't want to put in an e-mail. I can't tell you how we know this." I had a pretty good idea, but I said nothing, waited for her to go on. "I want you to find out what they talk about."

I stared at her. "How?"

"Eavesdrop. Keep your eyes and ears open. Hang out at the bar with the rest of the guys. And feel free to bash me, if that helps you get in with them."

I smiled, didn't know what to say to that.

"I assume you get along with Hank, don't you? You seem to be a real guy's guy." She said it with obvious distaste, like I was an alcoholic or a pervert.

"Get along?" I said. "He barely notices me."

"Jake gets along with everyone," Ali said.

I gave her a raised-eyebrow look that I knew she got at once: *Everyone but you, maybe.* She shot me a playful scowl.

"If he doesn't notice you, that's actually a good thing," Cheryl said. "You're not a threat to him. You're invisible. He's not likely to be as careful around you as he might be with a member of the leadership team."

"You're asking me to spy," I said.

She shrugged. "Call it what you will. We need corroboration. We need to know where to point the investigators. Also, I want to know whether he mentions Craigie Blythe. Or Hamilton Wender, our lead attorney there."

I was momentarily confused. Hamilton Wender, Craigie Blythe—which was the law firm, and which was the lawyer? Finally, I said, "That's it?"

"Jake," Ali said, "it would be really helpful if you could find out whether Bodine or any of the other guys are talking about the Pentagon bribe thing. Even in some vague, indirect way. You know, sounding worried, warning each other, talking about deleting e-mails, like that. Because if we can narrow it down to certain individuals, the forensic investigators can use keywords and string searches and all that. Install applications that watch network traffic. Maybe we can speed things up."

"Anything that might indicate an illegal proffer of employment," Cheryl put in. "Any violation of policy that could conceivably get us in trouble. Any talk of 'gifts' offered as inducements to secure deals. Any mention of a 'special purpose entity.' Anything that strikes you as wrong. *Anything.*"

I thought about Lummis's remark about greasing the skids and the way Bross signaled him to shut up. But I said, instead: "Like, if someone removes a mattress tag?"

Ali glared at me, but I could see the flicker of a smile she was trying to suppress.

"I think we understand each other," Cheryl said, little dabs of red appearing on each cheek like cherry syrup on a sno-cone.

I didn't like this at all. What Cheryl was asking me to do sounded like nothing more than serving as her stool pigeon—finding out who was talking about her behind her back, who was disloyal. I was beginning to wonder if all this high-flown talk about law firms and internal corporate investigations was just a cover for turning me into her ratfink. I thought for a while, didn't speak.

Cheryl said to Ali, "I definitely smell a cigar."

"Do you want me to check it out?" Ali said.

"Oh, no," Cheryl said. "*I'll* take care of it."

"You know," I said, "there's a complete change of cabin air every two to three minutes."

Cheryl looked at me blankly. She didn't seem impressed. I guess I couldn't blame her. Then I said, "Is this spy stuff supposed to come before the team-building exercises or after?"

Now she gave me a look of seething contempt, or so it appeared. It sure wasn't love and admiration, anyway. I could tell she was regretting that she'd ever been introduced to me.

"You may not hear anything," Cheryl said. "Then again, you may overhear something that helps us crack the case."

I remained silent.

"I'm sensing reluctance on your part," she said.

Ali, I noticed, was avoiding my eyes.

"I'm a little uncomfortable with it, yes," I admitted.

"I understand. But this could be a very good thing for you. An *opportunity,* if you take my meaning." She probably would have arched her brows if her forehead still worked.

I didn't quite get what kind of "opportunity" she was hinting at, but I knew she was offering me her own kind of bribe. "I don't know," I said. "Being a spy isn't really a skill set I was hoping to develop."

"Are you saying you won't do this for me?"

"I didn't say that." I stood up. "I'll think about it."

"I'd like an answer now," Cheryl said.

"I'll think about it," I repeated, and walked out.

I RETURNED TO my seat and went back to inspecting the photos of the plane crash. Bodine and his buddies were still toking on their stogies. The cabin was dense with smoke. My eyes started to smart.

And I thought about Cheryl Tobin and Ali and what they'd just asked me to do. It wasn't as if I felt any loyalty to Bodine or Lummis or any of those guys, but I didn't much like being recruited as a spy. I didn't like knowing that this was the real reason Cheryl wanted me here. But I trusted Ali's judgment, just as Cheryl did, and I knew she wouldn't have asked me to do something that she didn't think was important.

Just then I saw someone stride into the lounge at top speed, like a heat-seeking missile. It was Cheryl Tobin, her face tight with anger. She went up to Bodine's circle. I could see her talking to the two men, but I couldn't hear what she was saying. Her head was inclined. She was speaking calmly, whatever she was saying. The anger had suddenly vanished from her face; instead she looked almost chummy. She smiled, lightly touched Hank Bodine's forearm, then turned and walked calmly back to her cabin.

Then I watched as Hank Bodine, a broad unperturbed smile on his face, extinguished his cigar in his single malt. I couldn't see Hugo Lummis's face, but I saw him crush his cigar out in the mixed nuts.

I smiled to myself, shook my head, and went back to mulling over that whole scene with Cheryl and Ali. I was willing to do what they wanted, but only because

Ali had asked. Still, I didn't like it. I was gradually becoming convinced that there was a lot more going on than anyone was telling me. By the time the plane landed, half an hour later, I'd gone from a low-level dread about the next four days to an uneasy suspicion that something bad was about to happen at the lodge.

I had no idea, of course.

13

THE LODGE WAS built on the side of a steep hill and rose above us, massive and rustic and beautiful. It was basically an overgrown log cabin, grand and primitive, probably a century old. It reminded me of one of those great old solidly constructed lodges you see in Yellowstone or the Adirondacks. The exterior was peeled logs, probably spruce, and the gaps between the logs were chinked not with cement mortar but creosote-treated rope. It was two stories, a steeply pitched roof shingled in salt-silvered cedar. A large front porch connected to a wooden plank walkway that wound down the hillside to a weathered dock.

The King Chinook Lodge was located on the shores of an isolated body of water called Shotbolt Bay, off Rivers Inlet, on the central coast of British Columbia, three hundred miles north of Vancouver. The only way to reach it was by private boat, helicopter, or chartered seaplane.

When they said the place was remote, that was an understatement. This was as close to the middle of nowhere as I'd ever been.

"Remote," to me, described the little town in upstate

New York where I grew up, fifty miles from Buffalo, in
rural Erie County. The nearest shopping mall was
twenty-five miles away, in West Seneca. The biggest
event all year was the Dairy Festival, I kid you not. The
most important event in the history of my town was
when a school bus was hit by a northbound B & O
freight train in 1934. No one was killed.

But my town was Manhattan compared to where
we'd arrived.

The Hammond jet had landed on the northwest tip of
Vancouver Island, at Port Hardy Airport, where we trans-
ferred to a couple of small seaplanes. After a quick flight,
we landed on the water in front of a simple dock. The sun
was low in the sky, a huge ochre globe, and it glittered on
the water. The setting was pretty spectacular.

We were met by a guy around my age, who introduced himself as Ryan. He was wearing a dun-colored
polo shirt with KING CHINOOK LODGE stitched on the
left breast. He greeted us with a big smile and ad-
dressed everyone but me by name: obviously he remembered them from the year before, or maybe he'd
brushed up. I almost expected him to hand us umbrella
drinks, like this was Club Med.

"How was your flight?" He was a slight, lanky fellow
with a thick thatch of sandy brown hair and clear blue
eyes.

"Flights," Kevin Bross corrected him brusquely as he
stepped onto the dock and walked past.

Hugo Lummis needed an assist onto the dock. He'd
donned a pair of Ray-Ban Wayfarers and needed only a
porkpie hat to look like one of the Blues Brothers.
"Fish biting?" he asked the guy.

"Timing couldn't be better," said Ryan. "The Chinook

are staging right now. I caught a forty-pounder yesterday, not two hundred feet from the lodge."

Another two dun-shirted guys, who looked Hispanic, were pulling crates of perishable foodstuffs from the back of the plane and unloading suitcases from the baggage hold.

Lummis said, "Last summer I caught a ninety-some-pounder with a Berkley four-point-nine test line. I do believe that was a line-class record."

"I remember," Ryan said, nodding. Something very subtle in his expression seemed to indicate skepticism. Maybe Lummis's memory was exaggerated, but Ryan wasn't going to set him straight.

"This is one of the best sports-fishing lodges in the world," Lummis told me. "World-class."

I nodded.

"You fish?"

"Some," I said.

"Well, it don't take a lot of skill out here. Nor patience. Just drop the line in the water. But reeling 'em in ain't for wussies. Chinooks—that's what they call the king salmon—they're monsters. They'll straighten out your hook, break your line, tow your boat sideways. Tough fighters. Am I right or am I right, Ryan?"

"Right, Mr. Lummis," Ryan said.

Lummis gave Ryan a pat on the arm and started waddling up the steps to the lodge.

"First time here?" Ryan said to me.

"Yep. Didn't bring any fishing gear, though."

"No worries. We provide everything. And if you're not a fisherman, there's plenty of other things to do when you're not in your meetings or doing your team-building exercises. There's hiking and kayaking, too. And if you're not the outdoors type, there's the sauna and the hot tub, and tomorrow night it's the Texas Hold'em Tournament. So it's not all fishing, don't worry."

"I like fishing," I said. "Never gone salmon-fishing, though."

"Oh, it's the best. Mr. Lummis is right. We've got incredible trophy king salmon fishing. Forty-pound salmon's average, but I've seen 'em fifty, sixty, even seventy pounds."

"Not ninety?"

"Never seen one that big," Ryan said. He didn't smile, but his clear eyes twinkled. "Not here."

14

THE LONG, DEEP porch was lined with rustic furniture—a long glider, a porch swing suspended by chains, a couple of Adirondack chairs—that all looked handmade, of logs and twigs. A different staff member held the screen door open for me as if he were a bell captain at a Ritz-Carlton, and I entered an enormous, dimly lit room.

I was immediately hit by the pleasant smells of woodsmoke and mulled apple cider. Once my eyes adjusted to the light, I realized I'd never seen a fishing lodge like this before.

I'm not the kind of guy who goes to hunting or fishing lodges. When my friends and I used to go hunting, we'd stay in someone's tumbledown shack. Or an outfitter's tent. Or a cheap motel. So it wasn't like I was an expert in lodges.

But I'd never seen anything like this. A fishing lodge? This was the kind of place you might see in some big photo spread in *Architectural Digest* titled "The World's Most Exclusive Rustic Hideaways" or something.

There wasn't any check-in desk that I could see. I was in a so-called great room with walls of rough-hewn timber. The floors were wide cedar planks, mellow and worn. At one end was a giant, three-tiered fireplace made from river stone almost twenty feet wide and thirty feet high. Above it was a giant rack of six-point elk antlers. On another wall was a huge bearskin, its arms outstretched like Jesus on the cross. More tree-branch furniture here, but the couches and chairs were plump and overstuffed and upholstered in kilim fabric.

Our luggage had been collected in the center of the room and was being carried off by staff. Obviously we weren't supposed to schlep our own suitcases. We were the last load of passengers to arrive. Everyone else seemed to have checked in to their rooms.

A man with a clipboard came up to me. He was middle-aged, balding, had reading glasses around his neck.

He shook my hand. "I'm Paul Fecher, the manager. You must be Mr. Landry."

"Good guess," I said.

"Process of elimination. I remember all our return-ing guests. But we've got three new people, and two of them are women. Welcome to King Chinook Lodge."

"Nice place you got here."

"Glad you like it. If there's anything at all I can get you, please let me or any of our staff know. I think you've already met my son, Ryan."

"Right." The kid down at the dock.

"Our motto here is, the only thing our guests ever have to lift is a fishing rod. Or a glass of whiskey. But the whiskey's optional."

"Later, maybe," I said.

He looked at his watch. It was a cheap plastic quartz diving watch. I'd never really noticed watches before.

"Well, you've got a couple of hours before you all get together for the cocktail party and the opening banquet. Some folks are taking naps. Couple of guys are working out in our gym downstairs. We've got a couple of cardio machines, a couple of treadmills, and free weights. Very well equipped. And if you just want to take it easy, we've got a traditional wood-fired cedar sauna." He gestured over to a bar at one end of the room, where Lummis was drinking with Clive Rylance. "And, of course, the bar's always open."

"I'll keep that in mind."

"Now, you're in the Vancouver Room with Mr. Latimer."

Geoffrey Latimer, the general counsel, was supposed to be a total stiff, straightlaced and humorless. He was also the one coordinating the internal investigation for Cheryl. That was an interesting choice. I doubted it was a coincidence.

"Roommates, huh?"

"There's twelve of you, and only seven guest rooms. You'll enjoy it. Take you back to summer camp." I never went to summer camp.

After I did the math, I said, "Twelve people and seven rooms, doesn't that mean not everyone gets a roommate?"

"Well, your new CEO, of course, gets her own suite."

"Of course." That meant that Ali got her own room, too.

Sharing a room with one of these guys. What a blast.

"Sounds like fun," I said.

15

YEAH, JUST LIKE summer camp. Except that some of the campers got suites with Jacuzzis.

As I climbed the stairs, I glanced into one of the suites. Its door was open, and I could see that the room was pretty big. Ali was in there, unpacking her suitcase. She looked up as I passed by, gave me a smile.

"Hey," she said. "Cool place, huh?"

"Not bad. So, you get your own room, huh?"

She shrugged. "Yeah, well, Cheryl—"

"And I thought you'd be sharing a room with Hank Bodine."

"Yeah, right. Why don't you come in for a second?"

I did, and she closed the door behind me. I felt that tingle of anticipation down below that I used to get when we were alone behind closed doors together, but of course I banished all those impure thoughts from my mind. As much as possible, anyway.

"Listen, could you sit down for a second?"

I shrugged, sat in a rustic, tree-branch chair with a tapestry cushion, and she sat in one just like it, next to me.

"You think it's safe?" I said.

"Safe?"

"My being in here, I mean. I thought you didn't want any of the guys to know we're friends."

"Just be careful when you leave. Make sure no one sees you walk out of here."

I liked the furtive thing. It was kind of sexy, actually. If only there were sex involved. "Gotcha." Then I added, with a straight face, "I sure wouldn't want anyone to think we were having an affair."

She gave a faint smile. "Listen, about that meeting with—on the plane. You seemed a little pissed off."

"A little put off, maybe. Being a ratfink for the boss isn't exactly the career path I had in mind at Hammond."

"But that's not what she's asking you to do," Ali said, looking uneasy. "Just keep your ears open, see what you hear. That's all."

"So why do I get the feeling Cheryl's got an ulterior motive?"

"What's that supposed to mean?"

"Can't really blame her. She's got the board of directors looking for an excuse to get rid of her, and Hank Bodine stirring up trouble like some deposed shah, right? But now he and his buddies suspect their e-mail is being monitored, so wouldn't it be convenient to press some junior guy into service as your own private informer—your double agent?"

I could see the flush in her porcelain skin, and I knew right away I'd struck a nerve. I'd forgotten how transparent her emotions were. She really couldn't hide what she was feeling; her face was like a mood ring. Or maybe a billboard. For her sake, I hoped she didn't have to do much negotiation in her new job: She had a lousy poker face.

She shook her head. "Boy, do you underestimate that

woman," she said. "She can handle any crap those guys throw at her, believe me. This is about flushing out evidence of a crime."

"Not about flushing Hank Bodine down the crapper?"

"It's about protecting the company from a huge legal nightmare, Landry." Her tone was peevish, even brittle.

"And if that ends up with Hank Bodine wearing an orange jumpsuit and handcuffs, doing the perp walk, so much the better."

"I wouldn't mind it. Admit it, you wouldn't, either."

"I don't really give a shit about the guy, frankly."

"The point is, if he or Hugo Lummis or Upton Barlow or anyone else in the company bribed a Pentagon official to get a contract, it's going to blow up in our faces. Just like it did at Boeing."

I paused. "Is this important to you?"

"Uh-uh, Landry. Don't do this for me."

"DON'T DO IT for me," she said.

Her voice was muffled, her head under the pillow.

"You've got that big meeting in the morning," I said. "Seven thirty, isn't it?"

She was right: Her apartment was noisy, and lately it had gotten even worse. A couple of gangbangers had begun to hang out on the street almost directly below her window, jeering and laughing and taunting each other, late into the night.

A cool night: the windows open. We lay, naked, under a goose-down duvet. We'd just made love, so I was groggy, but neither one of us could fall asleep now.

"I really need to move," she said.

"Move in with me."

She didn't reply.

"They're just kids, Ali. I'll go down there and tell them to shut up. For me, not for you."

She pulled the pillow off her head, stared at me. "You're serious? Landry, don't be crazy. They'll go after you."

"I can deal."

"No way."

I was silent.

"They're assholes, Landry. Never let an asshole rent space in your head." She got up, padded over to the bathroom, returned with some orange foam earplugs, handed me a couple. They looked like little nipples. She rolled the other pair into thin cylinders, put them in her ears.

In ten minutes, she was asleep. Not me.

A beer bottle smashed on the sidewalk. A shouted obscenity.

Inside me, the bad wolf was growling, wanting to be fed.

When I was sure she was deep asleep, I got up, dressed, went down to the street.

In the yellow streetlight, the two BGs—Baby Gangsters, as they were called—were laughing, punching each other, posturing. Shaved heads or backward baseball caps, sagging jeans. I walked up to them. One of them laughed, said something obscene; the other just looked at me. Maybe they were sixteen, seventeen. Aspiring members of some Latino street gang. I'd learned to handle kids like that at Glenview.

I said nothing. I just stared them down.

The two of them backed away, instinctively. They'd seen something in my face.

I slipped back between the cool sheets, my heart

thudding. A close call, I thought. Far too close. As long as I felt the need to protect her, I knew the bad wolf was going to win.

Ali mumbled in her sleep and turned over.

"OH, COME ON, Ali," I said. "You know that's why you brought me in. You knew I could never say no to you. Given our history."

She stared at me for a few very long seconds. "Given our history," she said softly, "I was taking a big risk you'd tell us both to go to hell." She saw me about to protest, and she quickly went on, "I suggested you to Cheryl because you're the only one I trust."

I didn't know what to say, so I said nothing. She looked down, then suddenly brushed her hand along my pant leg, down my outer thigh. "You've got dog hair all over your pants."

I felt a jolt, even though I knew she didn't mean anything by it. "I should probably buy a lint brush," I said.

"My dad always said—"

"I remember. But I don't mind. It's like smelling a woman's perfume on your sweater. A nice reminder."

She smiled as if secretly amused by something. "You still going out with that blonde with the big tits?"

"Which one?"

"The one who looks like a cheap slut."

"Which one?"

"The one I saw you out to dinner with at Sushi Masa."

"Oh, her. No, that's over." I tried not to show my surprise. I didn't know she'd seen me out on a date. Was I hearing some kind of vestigial jealousy in her voice?

She nodded. "I thought you hate sushi."

"I'm not really into blondes either."

"You seemed to be into both that night. You know how many times I tried to get you to go to that place?"

"You should take it as a sign of respect and intimacy that I didn't go with you. I felt safe enough with you to reveal my true, deep inner dislike of raw fish."

"That's nice," she said dubiously.

"So, are you in a relationship these days?"

"It's been too crazy at work. You?"

I nodded.

"But not a blonde."

"Oh, this one's a blonde too, actually."

"Huh. What's her name?"

"Gert."

"Gert?"

"Short for Gertrude."

"Sounds real sexy. What does she do?"

"Loves to run. And eat. Loves to eat. She'd never stop if I didn't limit her to two meals a day."

"Are we talking eating disorder here?"

"Nah, it goes with the breed."

She gave me a playful punch, but it landed hard. A strong girl. "So, you're still working for Mike Zorn."

"Of course."

"Yeah," she said, "you wouldn't want to move up or anything. Since a promotion is a kind of change, huh?"

"He's a nice guy. It's a good job."

"I bet you still have that junky old Jeep, don't you?"

"Still drives great."

"Probably didn't even replace that front right quarter panel, did you?"

"Doesn't affect the ride," I said.

"Looks like crap, though."

"Not from behind the steering wheel."

She smiled, conceded the point. Then she said, "You never congratulated me, by the way. On my new job."

I arched my eyebrows. I can do that. I haven't had Botox.

"Right," she said. "I'd forgotten about Jake-speak. No need to say what you know I know you know, right? Like, obviously you're happy for me, why should you say it out loud? Why waste words?"

"Talk's overrated," I said. "Of course I'm happy for you."

We fell silent for a few seconds. "Is this going to be—I don't know, complicated for us?"

"Complicated? You mean, you and me?"

I nodded.

"Because we used to sleep together?"

"Oh, right—we did, didn't we?"

"I don't think it'll be complicated, do you?"

I shook my head. Of course it would. How could it not? "Not at all," I said. "So, do we know each other?"

"Huh?"

"When we run into each other next couple of days. Are we supposed to pretend that we've never met?"

She dipped her head as if thinking. "Maybe we've seen each other around. But we don't know each other's names. We've never been introduced."

"Gotcha."

We sat there for a few seconds in silence. I didn't want to leave. I liked being around her. Looking at her. Being in her presence. Inhaling her smell. Then she stood up. "I should get back to work. I have to go over Cheryl's remarks with her. So, just be careful leaving here, okay?"

I nodded, got up, and went over to the door. I opened

it slowly, just a crack. I looked out, saw no one in the hall. Then I slipped out—and saw a couple of guys standing a few feet away at the top of the landing, whispering. On the other side of the door, where I hadn't seen them.

I recognized both of them, though I'd never met either. One was the corporate controller, John Danziger. He was tall and lean and broad-shouldered, around forty, with thinning blond hair and gray-blue eyes. He looked like an all-American preppy jock from an Abercrombie & Fitch catalogue. The other was the treasurer, Alan Grogan, around the same age and height, but slighter of build. He had thick, wavy dark brown hair touched with gray, hazel green eyes, a wide mouth, a sharp chin, and a prominent, aquiline nose.

As soon as Danziger noticed me, he stopped whispering. Grogan turned around, gave me a sharp look, and the two men parted abruptly, without another word, walking in separate directions.

Very strange.

16

THE DOOR TO the Vancouver Room was open. The
walls and ceiling were unpainted, rough-hewn pine
boards; the floorboards, smooth wideboard pine. All the
furniture—the two large beds, armoire, and desk—was
rustic and looked handmade. Big puffy down com-
forters on the beds. A window overlooked the ocean.

Geoffrey Latimer was already in there, unpacking.
He looked up as I entered. He looked around fifty. He
had warm, sincere brown eyes, the trusting eyes of a
child. Graying light brown hair, perfectly Brylcreemed
and combed into place and parted on the side. His face
was reddened and chafed, like he had psoriasis or
something. "I don't believe we've met," he said. "Geoff
Latimer."

He shook my hand, his grip firm and dry. His fingernails looked bitten. He was a worrier.

Latimer was thin and wore chinos and a navy-and-
gray-striped golf shirt. His clothes looked like they
came from the men's department at Sears. He also gave
off the faint whiff of Old Spice, which reminded me,
unpleasantly, of my father.

"Jake Landry. I'm filling in for Mike Zorn."

He nodded. "Those are big shoes to fill."

"Do my best."

"Just don't let the turkeys get you down."

"How so?"

"They're just middle-aged frat boys."

I gave him a blank look.

"Lummis and Bross and those guys. They're bullies, that's all. Take it with a grain of salt."

I was surprised he'd even noticed. "It's no big deal," I said.

He turned back to his suitcase, working methodically, like a surgeon, transferring impeccably folded clothes from a battered old suitcase to dresser drawers. Even his T-shirts and boxer shorts were folded into little squares.

"You'll see the same posturing when it comes to the silly team-building exercises," he said. "Those guys are always competing with each other. Who can climb higher or pull harder, that kind of thing. They don't want you showing them up."

"Show them up how?"

"Outdoing them. Climbing higher or pulling harder. You can't win either way. But you seem to take it well."

I smiled. Latimer was shrewder and more insightful than I'd expected. I knew he was coordinating the internal corporate investigation, but I wasn't sure whether he knew that I'd been told about it. Or that I'd been asked to help. So I decided I'd better not let on that I knew about it. Maybe wait for him to bring it up.

I unzipped my suitcase and started unpacking, too. My clothes were a jumbled mess. I'd tossed them in there in about five minutes. We unpacked in silence for a while. I noticed him take a handful of syringes out of the suitcase, an orange plastic kit, a couple of vials of something, and put them all in a dresser drawer. I didn't say anything. Either he was a heroin addict or a diabetic. Diabetic seemed a little more likely.

He looked over at me. "That all you brought?"

I nodded.

"Travel light, huh?" Latimer said.

"WHAT?" ALI SAID. "I travel light."

She'd started unpacking a duffel bag. Not her usual small overnight bag—a change of clothes, a toothbrush, the mysterious arsenal of cosmetics—but things that signified a longer stay.

"Not as light as usual," I said, keeping my tone casual.

She stopped, a couple of pairs of silk panties in her right hand. "Hey, Landry, correct me if I'm wrong here. But aren't you the one who keeps telling me to just move in?"

"Ah, okay." Spoken with more conviction this time. I gave her an encouraging, if forced, smile.

"Just the essentials," she said, putting the panties in an empty drawer in my dresser, patting them in place. "So I don't have to keep lugging all my stuff around, like a Gypsy."

"Great."

Her back was turned to me now, but she heard it in my voice. "You don't want me here, Landry, just say the word."

"Oh, come on," I said.

Later, in bed, her legs twined around mine: "How come you never talk about your childhood?"

"There's nothing to talk about," I said.

"Landry."

"It's not interesting."

"*I'm* interested."

"I'm not."

She made a quiet *hmmph* sound. "You're hiding something, aren't you?"

A jolt in my stomach, maybe more like a little twinge. I turned, a bit too quickly. Saw the playful gleam in her eye. "I'm in the Witness Protection Program."

"Mafia informer," she said, nodding sagely.

"Drug cartel," I said.

She ran her fingers along the bridge of my nose, down my lips, tracing a straight line to my chin. "The plastic surgeon did a nice job."

"Good enough for government work."

"Of course, for all I know, you really are in the Witness Protection Program." Her eyes told me she was no longer joking. "Given how little you talk about yourself. I feel like I don't know any more about you than what's on the surface."

"Maybe that's all there is." I started feeling uncomfortable. "Isn't it almost time for my dog show?"

"That's on Sunday nights, Landry."

I snapped my fingers. "Rats."

"You know what you remind me of? Remember when we went to Norman Lang Motors to buy your Jeep, and we saw that huge black SUV with those opaque tinted windows? Totally blacked out?"

"The Pimpmobile. Yeah, it was a Denali. What about it—I'm a pimp? I'm gangsta?"

"You see a car like that in traffic, and you turn to look at who's inside, but you can't see in. So you stare, longer than you usually might. For all you know, they're staring back at you. But you have no idea who's in there. That's you."

"Ali, I think you've been spending too much time watching *Pimp My Ride*," I said, suppressing a surge of annoyance. "I'd say I'm more like the sign they had on the Jeep's windshield. Remember what it said?"

She shook her head.

"It said AS IS. Okay? That's me. What you see is what you get. Don't go looking for hidden secrets. There aren't any."

"I think there's a lot more to you than you want me to see."

"Sorry," I said. "Deep down, I'm shallow." I clicked on the TV. "Today's Monday, right?"

"YOU MARRIED, JAKE?" Latimer said.

"Nope."

"Planning on it?"

"No danger of it happening anytime soon."

"Hope you don't mind me saying, but you should. You need a stable home life if you want to make it in business, I've always thought. Wife and kids—it anchors you. It's a safe place. A refuge when work gets stressful."

"I just drink," I said.

He looked at me keenly for a second.

"I'm kidding," I said. "You got kids?"

He nodded, smiled. "A daughter. Twelve."

"Nice age," I said, just because that seemed like the thing to say.

His smile turned rueful. "It's a terrible age, actually. In the course of a month I went from a guy who couldn't do anything wrong to a guy who can't do anything right. A loser. Uncool."

"Can't wait to have kids, myself," I said with a straight face.

WE CHANGED INTO dinner clothes. Latimer's boxer shorts were white with green Christmas trees and red candy canes on them. "Christmas gift from my daughter," he said sheepishly. He was scrawny, with a smooth, pale, hairless belly and spindly legs. His skin was milky white, like he'd never been in the sun.

He put on gray dress slacks, a white button-down shirt, a black belt with a shiny silver buckle. When he'd finished changing, he took out a BlackBerry from his briefcase. A few seconds later, he said, "Oh, right. I keep forgetting. No signal here. I'm addicted. You know what they call these things, right? Crack-Berries?"

I'd only heard that about a hundred thousand times. "That's good," I said, and smiled.

"Don't know if you're a gadget guy like me, but here's my latest toy," he said proudly, pulling out an iPod. "Ever see one of these?"

Not one that old, actually. "Sure."

"My daughter got it for me. I've even learned how to download music. You like show tunes?"

I shrugged. "Sure." I hate show tunes.

"Feel free to borrow it whenever. I've got *Music Man* and *Carousel* and *Guys and Dolls* and *Kismet*. And *Finian's Rainbow*—you ever see *Finian's Rainbow*?"

"I don't think I have, no."

"The best ever. Even better than *Man of La Mancha*. We love musicals at home. Well, mostly it's my wife

and I, nowadays. Carolyn only listens to bands with obscene names like The Strokes, I think they're called."

"Maybe I'll take a listen sometime."

"You know, I've always thought that so much of what
goes on in the business world is like a musical. A stage
play. A pageant."

"Never thought of it that way."

"Much of it's about perceptions. About how we per-
ceive things, more than what's really going on. So Hank
and Hugo and Kevin and all those guys look at you and
think you're a kid, you're too young to know anything.
Whereas in truth, you could be every bit as smart or
qualified as any of them."

"Yeah, maybe. So what happens tonight?"

"The opening-night banquet. Cheryl gives a talk.
The facilitator gives a rundown on the team-building
exercises tomorrow. I talk at dinner tomorrow night.
Lot of blabbing."

"What's your talk about?"

"Ethics and business."

"In general, or at Hammond?"

He compressed his lips, zipped up his suitcase, and
placed it neatly at the back of the clothes closet. "Hammond. There's a win-at-any-cost culture in this company. An ethical rottenness, sort of a hangover from Jim
Rawlings's hard-charging style. Cheryl's doing what
she can to clean it up, but . . ." He shook his head, never
finished his sentence.

Latimer was a real type: the clothes, the hair, the
packing, everything conservative and by the book. A
real rules-loving guy. I guess every company needs
people like that.

But I was a little surprised to hear him criticize our

old CEO. Rawlings had, after all, named Latimer general counsel. They were said to have been close.

"What's she doing to clean it up?" I said.

He hesitated, but only for a second or two. "Making it clear she won't tolerate any malfeasance."

"What sort of 'malfeasance' are you talking about?"

"Anything," he said, not very helpfully.

I didn't press it. "You think Rawlings encouraged that sort of stuff?"

"I do. Or he'd look the other way. There was always this feeling that, you know, there's Boeing and there's Lockheed; and then there's us. The predator and the prey. We were the little guy. We had to do whatever it took to survive. Even if we had to play dirty."

He was silent. He seemed to be staring out at the ocean.

"The big guys play dirty sometimes, too," I said.

"Lockheed cleaned up their act quite some time ago," Latimer said. "I know those guys. Boeing—well, who knows? But even if Boeing plays dirty, that doesn't justify our doing it. This is something Cheryl's really concerned about. She wants me to rattle some cages."

"That's not going to make you very popular around here."

He sighed. "A little late for that. I'm probably going to ruin some people's dinners tomorrow night. No one wants to hear doom-and-gloom stuff. But you've got to get their attention somehow. Like I always say, pigs get slaughtered."

He went quiet again. Then he said, "Look at this," and beckoned me to the window.

I crossed the room to the window. Off to the left, the sun was low on the horizon, a fat orange globe. The ocean shimmered. At first I didn't know what he was calling my attention to—the sunset, maybe? That seemed somehow, I don't know, sentimental for a guy like that. Then I noticed a dark shape moving in the sky. An immense bald eagle was dropping slowly toward the water. Its wingspan must have been six feet.

"Wow," I said.

"Watch."

With a sudden, swift movement, the eagle swooped down and snatched something up in its powerful talons: a glinting silver fish. *Predator and prey,* I almost said aloud, but that was just too self-evident to say without sounding like a moron.

We watched in silent admiration for a few seconds. "Boy," I finally said, "talk about symbolism."

Latimer turned to look at me, puzzled. "What do you mean?"

So maybe he wasn't all that insightful after all. "Then again, it's just a fish," I said.

17

GEOFF LATIMER ANNOUNCED that he was going downstairs and invited me to join him, but I told him, vaguely, that I had a couple of things to finish up. When he'd left the room, I pulled out my laptop to take another look at those photos of the crash that I'd downloaded on the flight over.

Theoretically, I guess, I was doing it because Hank Bodine had asked me to. But by then I'd become curious myself. A brand-new plane crashes—at an air show, of all places—you can't help wondering why.

And then there was Cheryl's remark, which was pretty much what Zoë had said: What difference did it make, really, what the reason for the crash was? We didn't need to know why it had gone down in order to sell more of our planes. It was, as Bodine liked to say, a no-brainer. Every airline in the world that had ordered the E-336 had to be a little freaked out by the crash.

So why *did* Hank Bodine want to know? I had a feeling, based on Cheryl's expression and the way she'd looked at Ali, that there had to be something else going on.

And, of course, I was determined to get to the bottom

of that crash. If for no other reason than to figure out what was *really* going on.

And here was the weird thing: According to one of the reports Zoë had sent me, the E-336 had made maybe twenty test flights before the Paris Air Show. That's the high-altitude equivalent of a new car. When you take delivery of a new car, it's always going to have a few miles on the odometer, from the test drive at the factory to the predelivery inspection at the dealership. Twenty test flights—that was nothing. That was brand-spanking-new.

So there had to be something wrong with the plane, and I knew that the Eurospatiale consortium sure as hell wasn't going to admit it. They'd blame the weather or pilot error or bad karma or whatever they could get away with claiming.

All I could tell from examining the photographs was that the hinges had ripped out of the composite skin of the flap. But why? The hinges were cut into the flap and glued on with a powerful epoxy adhesive. They sure as hell weren't supposed to rip out. After twenty years, maybe. Not after twenty short hops between Paris and London.

For a couple of minutes I stared at the damaged flap, until something itched at the back of my mind. A pattern was starting to emerge. A possible explanation.

I zoomed in as close as I could before the photograph disintegrated into pixels. Yes. At that resolution I could see quite clearly the cracks at the stress concentration points. And the telltale swelling in the composite skin. "Brooming," it was called. It happened when moisture somehow got into the graphite epoxy, which had a nasty habit of absorbing water—sucked it up like a sponge.

And that could happen for a number of reasons, none of them good.

Such as a design flaw in the plane itself. Which was the case here, I was convinced.

I knew now why the plane had gone down, and I was certain Hank Bodine wouldn't want to hear the explanation. He'd regret ever asking me to look into it.

Unless . . .

Unless, say, he already knew the cause and wanted me to find it out for myself. But that was too complex, too convoluted, and I couldn't see any possible logic in that. I wondered whether Cheryl knew more about the crash than she'd let on. Was it possible, I wondered, that she already knew what I'd just found out?

With a sinking feeling, I realized, too, that as much as I wanted to steer clear of the power struggle between Cheryl Tobin and Hank Bodine, I was already deeply embroiled in it.

I went downstairs to find Bodine and tell him what I'd learned.

18

AS I CAME down the stairs I heard loud voices and raucous laughter emanating from the bar. Hugo Lummis was clutching a tumbler of something brown and seemed to have a real buzz on. He was talking to a guy I recognized as Upton Barlow, the chief of Hammond's Defense Division. Barlow was tall, with sloped shoulders, looked like an athlete. Deep lines were etched around his mouth, a stack of parallel lines carved into his forehead. He had receding gray hair, little black eyes like raisins, a pursed mouth.

The two of them seemed to be trading travel horror stories. They were both members of the million-mile frequent flyer club, and it sounded like they didn't much like Europeans.

"Ever notice the crappy plastic toilet seats?" Lummis was saying. "Even in the good hotels? And the weird way they flush, like with metal plates on the wall or whatever?"

"No, it's the showers that are the worst," Barlow put in. "They're made for midgets."

I looked around the huge main room, saw Geoff

Latimer sitting by himself in a big overstuffed chair, reading the *Wall Street Journal.* I didn't see Hank Bodine, though, or Clive Rylance.

"Good luck finding an ice machine in your hotel," Lummis said. "Ask for Coke and you get it as warm as a bucket of spit. Must be some European Union law against ice."

"You can't even watch the news in your hotel room," Barlow said. "You put on CNN, and it's all *different.* You get, like, a forty-five-minute report on *Nairobi* or *Somaliland* or something."

I had a feeling the Europeans didn't like them much, either.

"Why don't you join us, fella?" Lummis said to me.

I hesitated for an instant. Having a drink with these old goats was just about the last thing I wanted to do. If Hank Bodine was going to have a talk with Clive Rylance, I should probably find some way to eavesdrop. If they weren't down here, maybe I could find Ali and pretend to introduce myself so I could spend some more time with her.

But then I reminded myself that if I was really going to help Ali uncover evidence about a bribe paid to the Pentagon, the two guys at the bar were exactly who I should be hanging out with. If a bribe had really been made to someone in the Pentagon, it would be surprising if these two *didn't* know about it. Both of them schemed night and day to sell planes to the Air Force and were willing to do anything to make the sale. If there was a conspiracy, they'd have to be two of the key players.

Upton Barlow picked up on my silence, and said, "Aw, he doesn't want to sit with us old farts."

"Sure, that would be great," I said, walking down the bar and sitting in the stool next to Upton Barlow. I introduced myself.

"I'm sure I've gotten e-mails from you," Barlow said, shaking my hand. "Mike Zorn's assistant, right?"

"That's right." I was surprised he remembered who I was.

"But Mike's not going to be here, is he?"

I started to answer, but Barlow turned away to greet someone else who'd just come down the stairs. It was Clive Rylance, an intense-looking, dark-haired, handsome man who looked as if he'd been carved out of a block of granite. He had an oblong head and a square jaw. He had a heavy beard that he probably had to shave twice a day. He should have been cast in the James Bond movies instead of the guy they have now.

"Well, if it isn't Clive Rylance, international man of mystery," Barlow said.

Rylance put one hand on Hugo's shoulder and, with the other, reached over and shook Barlow's. Actually, they seemed to be trying to crush each other's hands. "Gentlemen," he said.

"Speak for yourself," said Lummis. "You know everyone here, right? Don't know if you've met . . . Golly, what's your name again?"

"Jake Landry," I said, shaking with Rylance.

"Clive," Rylance said. "So are you a new member of the executive team?"

"Just filling in for Mike Zorn," I said.

"Good," he said. He looked around at the others and laughed. "Phew. I was starting to feel real old there for a second."

"You just fly in from Paris?" said Barlow.

"Yesterday," Rylance said. "I had a dinner in New York last night."

"Oh yeah? Where'd you eat?" Lummis said. I had a feeling Hugo Lummis dined out a lot, judging from his girth.

"Per Se."

"You actually got a table?" Barlow said.

Rylance shrugged. "Come on, man."

"Yeah, what am I saying? If anyone can wangle a reservation, it's you," Barlow said. "So you have that risotto with the truffles from Provence?"

"The Kobe beef with the marrow," Rylance said. "Fantastic."

"I don't know why everyone says it's not as good as French Laundry," Hugo Lummis said. "I think it's even better. But I think we're leaving our friend Jake out of the conversation, aren't we?"

"Not at all," I said. "Never heard of French Laundry, but I'd put it up against Roscoe's House of Chicken 'n Waffles any day."

"Chicken and waffles?" Rylance said, disgusted.

Lummis wheeled his stool around to look at me, and said, "Say, I *love* that place."

"Admit it," I said, "given a choice between some microscopic piece of beef at that Laundry place and Herb's special at Roscoe's, you wouldn't hesitate, would you?"

"Roscoe's, for sure," Lummis agreed. "Ever had their candied yams?"

But Rylance wasn't interested. "Anyone seen Hank around?" he said.

"Last I heard, he was hot on Cheryl's trail," Barlow said. "Had something he wanted to raise with her."

"Raise all the way up her ass, I suspect," said Lummis.

"So, Jake, you ready to be inspired and motivated by our fearless leader?" He fanned his hands in the air like a preacher rousing his flock. "The symbol of our company is the lion," he said in a falsetto, not a bad imitation of Cheryl Tobin. "And I'm here to make that lion *roar.*"

I laughed politely, and both Rylance and Barlow guffawed loudly, then Barlow leaned in close to the guys and muttered out of the side of his mouth, "It *is* a goddamned *gynocracy* around here these days."

The bartender took my order—another Macallan single-malt, only he didn't ask me how old—and Rylance pulled up a stool on Lummis's other side. Then Kevin Bross passed by, wearing black workout shorts and a black sleeveless shirt that showed off his sculpted physique. He was drenched with sweat. The watchband of his heart-rate monitor was beeping rapidly. Bross had broad shoulders and a narrow waist and looked like he spent a lot more hours in the gym than at the office. As he walked behind me, he bumped up against my only good shirt with his slick arm, dampening my shoulder.

"Good workout, Coach?" Clive Rylance said. "Hey, did someone strap a time bomb on you or something?"

"Huh?" Bross said.

"Sounds like you're about to explode."

"Oh, that," Bross said, and he reached under his shirt and tugged at a chest strap. It came off with a Velcro crunch. "Heart-rate monitor. What about you, big guy? Brits don't exercise?"

Rylance hoisted his tumbler of Scotch. "Just my left hand," he said.

"Guess your right hand doesn't need the exercise, huh?" Bross said.

They both laughed.

"We gonna do Zermatt again this year, Kev?" Barlow said. "I want to see you wipe out doing the slalom again. That was a blast."

"Cram it, Upton," Bross said jovially, "or I'll tell them what happened to you at the top of the Blauherd lift."

Barlow tipped his glass and laughed. "Touché. So, is the sauna coed this year?"

"Clothing optional, I hope," Rylance said, and everyone cracked up.

Just then I saw Hank Bodine—or, to be accurate, I *heard* him. He was standing in one of the alcoves on the other side of the room, hands on his hips, talking to someone.

No, actually, he was yelling at someone.

As soon as I realized that the person he was chewing out was Ali, I jumped up from my seat and, without thinking, bolted across the room.

19

ALI WAS SITTING in a chair while Bodine stood right in front of her, obviously trying to intimidate. She'd changed into a white skirt and a peach-colored silk blouse, cut just low enough to emphasize the swell of her breasts, and she looked stunning.

She also looked angry.

I could hear Bodine saying, "You want me to take this up with Cheryl, that it?" He was clearly holding back a great deal of anger and was on the verge of letting loose.

"Obviously I can't stop you from talking to Cheryl," she said. "You can do whatever you want. But not before the meeting starts. Sorry. She's busy."

I stopped a ways off, not wanting to barge in. Ali had put on a fresh coat of lipstick and lined her lips, too. She had gold bangles on her wrists and a necklace of tiny gold beads interspersed with large teardrops of polished green turquoise. Matching gold-and-turquoise earrings.

"This sure as hell isn't the offsite agenda I cleared," Bodine said.

"The agenda changed," Ali said. "You're not the CEO. You don't get to clear the agenda."

"Well, sweetheart, I never heard a single *goddamned* mention of anyone giving a speech here called 'Hammond and the Culture of Corruption.'"

Ali shrugged. "I'm sorry . . . Hank." I could tell she was about to counter that "sweetheart" with something acerbic but thought better of it. "That was a last-minute addition."

"You don't make last-minute additions without running them by me first. That's how it's always worked."

"I guess things have changed, Hank." Ali folded her legs. I thought I saw a ghost of a smile flit across her face, as if she were enjoying facing him down.

Bodine rocked back on his heels. He took his hands off his hips and folded them across his chest. "Correct me if I'm wrong, young lady, but isn't this your first year here? So I don't think you know the first thing about how things are supposed to work."

"I know what Cheryl asked me to—"

"Let me tell you something," Bodine said. "You are making a serious mistake. I'm going to do you a favor and pretend none of this ever happened. Because I am not going to have my team demoralized by unsubstantiated accusations and rumors about 'corruption' in this company. And if the board of directors gets wind of the fact that your goddamned boss is trying to throw mud and level charges that have no basis, heads are going to roll. And I don't just mean yours. You hear me?"

Ali gave him a long, styptic look. "I hear your threats loud and clear, Hank. But the agenda stands."

"That's *it*," Bodine said, raising his voice almost to a shout. "What room is she in?"

"Cheryl's preparing her remarks," Ali said. "She really doesn't want to be disturbed."

I could no longer hang back and watch Bodine talk to her that way. He was really starting to piss me off. I walked up to him, tapped him on the shoulder. "What's that your daddy always told you about how to talk to a lady?" I said lightly.

Bodine looked at me with fury. I said, "I got you the information you wanted. About the E-336."

"You," he said, jabbing his index finger into my chest. His voice rumbled, and his cheeks were flushed. "You might want to watch your ass." Then he strode away.

As soon as he was gone, I leaned forward and extended my hand to Ali. "I'm Jake Landry," I said.

20

"I GUESS HE'S just not that into you," I said.

"What'd you do that for?" I could tell she was secretly pleased but didn't want to let on.

"Because I don't like bullies."

"I didn't need your help, you know."

"Who says I was trying to help?"

"You butted in. You shouldn't have."

"I didn't like hearing him talk to you like that."

"Thanks, but I can handle Hank Bodine. I don't need a protector."

"That's obvious."

"What's that supposed to mean?"

"It's called a compliment. You handled him great. Way better than I could have."

She looked momentarily appeased. "Anyway, the idea was for you to get on his good side. Not alienate him."

"I don't think he has a good side. Plus, alienating him is more fun."

"He could get you fired."

"Your boss can overrule him."

"Not if she gets fired herself."

She had a point. "I could always move back to up-state New York and get a job with the cable company again. Maybe the vent-pipe factory."

"The factory's probably out of business by now. Just like every other company there."

"True."

She glanced at her watch. "I think Cheryl needs me. The reception's about to begin." She stood up. "Nice to meet you, Jake. It was really great."

IT WAS REALLY great, the note read. *I'm sorry.*

One of her cards—ALISON HILLMAN in engraved letters on thick cream stock—propped on the bathroom sink. Where she knew I'd see it when I got up.

It was only a couple of days after she'd first brought the big suitcase over to my apartment. Her toothbrush was missing, her silk panties, her extra set of work clothes.

When I finally reached her on her cell, later that morning, she sounded harried. She said she couldn't talk: She had someone about to come in for a meeting. She said she wasn't angry or anything, she just thought this was for the best. We wanted different things, that was all.

Then I heard her speak to someone in the room, a different Ali voice: welcoming and warm. I could hear her big radiant smile. When she got back on the phone with me, she was all business.

That night I called her again.

"I don't know, Landry," she said. "Sometimes I think there's something frozen inside you. I don't know. But now I get it about the 'As Is' sign."

I sent her a couple of long, heartfelt e-mails—I

found it easier to express myself through the impersonal machinery of the keyboard and the computer monitor. Her answers were polite but brief.

I figured that she'd seen something in me, something that didn't sit well with her. Over the years, since the nightmare of my teen years, I'd been building a tall privacy fence inside me, using the finest lumber, making sure the boards butted right up against each other so no one could see between the cracks.

But maybe she could. Or maybe she just didn't like my carpentry.

A month or so later I was at an Irish bar in downtown L.A. with some friends—the motto in the window, in pseudo-Gaelic lettering: "We pour, you score"—when I spotted Ali sitting by herself at a small table in the back. She was dressed in black, a tall glass of black liquid in front of her: Guinness stout. I sat down in the other chair.

"Hey," I said.

"Hey." A note of melancholy? Maybe I was imagining things.

Then I noticed the second glass, the bottle of Rolling Rock. "Oh, sorry—someone's sitting here."

"He's in the bathroom." She smiled. "He likes the mural."

There was a legendary mural in the men's room of a buxom nude blonde, laughing and pointing down toward the urinal. "In case he's not sure where to aim, huh?" I said. The old joke. "How long have you been going out?"

She shrugged. "We're not, really. This is, like, our second date."

"Huh." A long, awkward silence. "Band's not very good tonight, is it?"

"Pretty bad," she agreed.

Another beat of silence. I picked up her date's Rolling Rock bottle, turned it around. "Huh," I said.

"What?"

"It says, 'Latrobe Brewing Co., St. Louis, Missouri.' "

"So?"

"Used to say 'Latrobe Brewing Co., Latrobe, Pennsylvania.' But Budweiser makes it now. In Newark."

"That's pretty sneaky."

"Not really. Hell, if you're really interested, it's all there on the label, actually. Printed right on the glass. Everything you could ever want to know."

"Except it says St. Louis, not Newark," she said, a mysterious glint in her eyes.

The bar band launched into a post-punk rendition of "On the Street Where You Live." Or maybe it was Metallica's "Bleeding Me." It was kind of hard to tell with those guys.

"But who cares where it comes from anyway?" I said. "If you like the beer, isn't that enough?"

Ali gave me a funny look, tilted her head a few degrees. "You are talking about beer, right?"

I smiled and was about to reply, but then a tall, good-looking, black-haired guy came up to the table.

He cleared his throat. "Sorry, this seat's taken," he said.

21

THE PREDINNER COCKTAIL reception was held in a smaller room off the great room. A big banner hung from the low ceiling that said WELCOME HAMMOND AEROSPACE.

They were serving blender drinks and mojitos and flutes of champagne, and voices got steadily louder, the laughter more raucous, as the guys got increasingly soused. The exception seemed to be Hank Bodine, who was talking to Hugo Lummis, looking really pissed off. Ali had gone to Cheryl's suite to talk through the evening's schedule. I stood there holding a mojito and looking around when someone sidled up to me. One of the guys I'd seen whispering in the hall upstairs—*caught* whispering, I thought.

"You're Jake Landry, right?"

This was the blond one, which meant he was John Danziger, the corporate controller. The other one was Grogan.

"And you're John Danziger," I said. We shook hands, and I went through what was by then my standard pitch about how I was Mike Zorn's stand-in. But instead of giving me the expected response, about how big the shoes were that I had to fill and all that, Danziger said, "I'm sorry if I was rude to you upstairs."

"Rude?"

"That was you in the hall upstairs, right? When Grogan and I were talking?" He had a pleasant, smooth baritone voice, like an NPR radio announcer.

"Oh, was that you? Looked like an intense conversation." That meant he'd seen me coming out of Ali's room. If, that is, he knew it was Ali's room.

"Just work-related stuff," he said. "But sort of sensitive, which is why Alan overreacted."

"No worries." But it wasn't Alan Grogan who'd noticed me in the hall and suddenly broke off their conversation. It was Danziger. I couldn't figure out why he was making such a big deal out of something so trivial. Maybe he was afraid I'd overheard something. Whatever it was, he and Grogan had probably been too preoccupied to pay much attention to me or where I'd just come from. "So can I ask you something?"

Danziger gave me a wary look. "Sure."

"What does the corporate controller actually do, anyway?"

He looked to either side, then came closer. "No one actually knows," he said conspiratorially.

"Do you?"

He shook his head. "Don't tell anyone."

"Seriously," I said. "I have no idea what a controller does. Besides . . . controlling things."

"I wish I could tell you."

"You mean, if you told me, you'd have to kill me?"

"If I told you, I'd put us both to sleep," Danziger said. "It's too boring."

Someone tapped Danziger on the shoulder. It was

Ronald Slattery, the Chief Financial Officer. He was a small, compact man, bald on top, with prominent ears, wearing heavy black-framed glasses. Slattery was wearing a blue blazer and a white shirt. This was the first time I'd ever seen Slattery not wearing a gray suit. He was the sort of guy you could imagine going to bed in a gray suit. Danziger excused himself, and the two men turned away to talk.

"Hey, there, roomie." Geoff Latimer grabbed me by the elbow. "Having a good time?"

"Sure," I said.

He faltered for a few seconds, looked as if he was searching for something to say. Then: "Everyone already knows everyone else. It's kind of a tight circle in some ways. Would you like me to introduce you to some people?"

I was about to tell him thanks but no thanks, when there was a tink-tink-tink of silverware against glass, and the room quieted down. Cheryl Tobin stood under the banner with a broad smile. She was wearing a navy blue jacket over a long ivory silk skirt and big jewel-studded earrings. Ali stood close behind her, studying a binder.

"Ladies and gentlemen," Cheryl said. "Or maybe I should just say, gentlemen." Polite laughter.

Clive Rylance said loudly, "That rules out most of us," and there was a burst of laughter. Kevin Bross, standing next to Rylance, leaned over and said something mildly obscene to him about Ali. He probably meant to whisper, but his voice carried. I wanted to slam the guy against the peeled-log wall and impale him on a set of antlers, but instead I let the anger surge with a prickly heat and subside. Bodine and Lummis and Barlow were all standing together. I could see Bodine whisper something to Lummis, who nodded in reply.

"Well, you know me by now," Cheryl said smoothly. "I always expect the best. I'd like to welcome everyone to a Hammond tradition I'm proud to join. The annual leadership retreat at the remarkable King Chinook Lodge. It's great to be out of the L.A. smog, isn't it?"

She smiled, paused for the laugh. When it didn't come, she went on, "Well, I for one can't wait. From the minute I arrived at Hammond Aerospace I've heard stories about this place." She paused. "Some of which I can't repeat."

Some low chuckles.

"What's that you guys say—'What happens at King Chinook stays in King Chinook'? I guess I'm about to find out what *that's* all about, huh?"

"You know it," someone said.

"It's not too late to escape," someone else said.

"Not too late to escape, hmm?" she repeated. Her smile had grown thin. "Easier said than done. It's a long swim to the nearest airport."

She was making a good show of pretending to enjoy the testosterone-rich rowdiness, but at the same time you could sense the steel. As if she were willing to be a good sport, but there was a point beyond which she wouldn't go. You really didn't want to push this woman too far. She also looked as if she wanted to get the hell out of there. Back to corporate headquarters, back to her big office where she could sit behind her big desk and receive important visitors and be the CEO instead of one of two sorority girls at a frat party.

"And believe me, I've thought about it," she said. "Especially after hearing about the courses that Bo's about to take us through."

She looked across the room toward a giant of a man

with a shiny-bald head and a big black mustache. That had to be Bo Lampack, the team-building coordinator. He stood in the back corner with his arms folded across a great broad chest. His shoulders were the size of ham hocks. He looked like a cross between G. Gordon Liddy and Mr. Clean, only without the gold earring.

Lampack gave a conspiratorial grin. "We haven't lost anyone." He paused for dramatic effect, then added, "Yet."

A burst of raucous laughter, laced with cheers.

"What about Gandle?" Kevin Bross shouted.

"Come to think of it," Lampack said, "I don't see Gandle here this year."

More loud laughter. Larry Gandle was the old CFO, whom Cheryl had replaced with Ron Slattery. He'd gotten some huge golden parachute early retirement package and moved to Florida.

Cheryl held up her hands to quiet everyone down. "Well, we'll hear more from Bo at dinner. And tomorrow, you guys are all going to see that we women can keep up with men—not just in the office but on the ropes as well." She looked around, then held up an index finger. "I'm not just the first outsider to lead Hammond Aerospace, but I'm the first woman. And I know that makes some of you guys a little uncomfortable. I understand that. Change is always difficult. But that's one of the . . . challenges . . . I hope we'll get a chance to work through this weekend."

The room had gone quiet but for a few pockets of restless stirring. Both Bodine and Barlow stood watching her in identical poses: their right arms folded across their bellies, supporting their left elbows. Their left hands clutched tumblers of bourbon. Like babies holding bottles of formula.

"If not," she said, "I hope you're all strong swimmers."

She looked around for several seconds. No one laughed. So she continued, "You know, they say a general without an army is nothing. I need each and every one of you in there pulling—not for me, but for this great company. Let me remind you that the symbol of the Hammond Aerospace Corporation is the lion. And with your help, together we're going to make that lion roar."

Lummis elbowed Upton Barlow so hard that Barlow dropped his glass of bourbon. It crashed against the hard plank floor and shattered into a hundred shards.

A FEW MINUTES later, as we all filed into the great room for dinner, Hank Bodine put a hand on my shoulder. Upton Barlow was at his side. "So you have some information for me," Bodine said. He'd cooled off some, though his tone was curt.

"I'm pretty sure I've figured out why the E-336 crashed," I said.

"Well, let's hear it." His hand came off my shoulder. Barlow's raisin eyes regarded me curiously.

"Maybe we can talk in private, later on," I said.

"Nonsense. We have no secrets. Let's hear it." To Barlow, Bodine said, "Jake here says he knows why that Eurospatiale plane wiped out at Le Bourget." There was something smug, almost defiant in his tone, as if he didn't believe me, or was daring me, or something.

I paused. Cheryl and Ali were approaching from behind Bodine. "How about later?" I said.

"How about now?" said Cheryl. "I'd like to hear all about it." She extended her hand. "I don't believe we've met, actually. I'm Cheryl Tobin. Will you sit next to me at dinner?"

Bodine gave me a look of pure, unadulterated loathing.

22

A LONG TABLE had been set up in a bay of the great room that overlooked the ocean. Night had fallen, and the windowpanes had become polished obsidian, reflecting the amber glow of the room. You couldn't see the ocean, but you could hear the waves of Rivers Inlet lapping gently against the shore.

Cheryl Tobin was seated at the head of the table. I was at her immediate left. On my other side was Upton Barlow, then Hugo Lummis, whose potbelly was so big he had to push his chair way back from the table to make room for it.

Lummis was telling some long-winded anecdote to Barlow. Meanwhile, Cheryl was talking with her CFO, Ron Slattery. His bald head shone: oddly vulnerable, a baby's. He was saying, "I thought your speech was absolutely masterful."

The table was covered with a stiff white linen cloth and set with expensive-looking gold-rimmed china and gleaming silverware. An armada of cut-glass wine and water glasses. Next to each place setting was a narrow printed menu listing six courses. A white linen napkin, folded into a fan, on each plate. A little card with each person's name written in calligraphy.

There was nothing spontaneous about Cheryl's decision to seat me next to her. If she wanted me to spy for her, I really didn't get it.

I buttered a hot, crusty dinner roll that was studded with olives, and wolfed it down.

Hank Bodine was down near my end of the table, but in no-man's-land, if you believed in close readings of dinner-table placement. Ali was on the other side, between Kevin Bross and Clive Rylance. Both Alpha Males seemed to be putting the moves on her, double-teaming her. She smiled politely. I caught her eye, and she gave me a look that conveyed a lot: amusement, embarrassment, maybe even a secret enjoyment.

A couple of Mexican waiters ladled lobster bisque into everyone's bowls. Another waiter poured a French white wine. I took a sip. It tasted fine to me. Not that I had any idea.

Barlow took a sip, grunted in satisfaction, and pursed his moist red lips. He said out of the side of his mouth, "I don't have my reading glasses—this a Meursault or a Sancerre?"

I shrugged. "White wine, I think."

"Guess you're more the jug-wine-with-a-screwtop type."

"Me? Not at all. I like the gallon boxes, actually." Might as well give him what he wanted to hear.

He laughed politely, turned away.

Ron Slattery was keeping up his line of sock-puppet patter. "Well, you've got the entire division running scared, and that's a good thing." His mouth was a thin

slash, barely any lips. The small fringe around his shiny
dome was shaved close. His heavy black-framed eyeglasses might have looked funky, ironic, on someone
like Zoë, but on him they were just nerdy.

"Not too scared, I hope," Cheryl said. "Too much
fear is counterproductive."

"Don't forget, a jet won't fly unless its fuel is under
pressure and at high temperature," he replied.

"Ah, but without a cooling system, you get parts fail-
ure, right?"

"Good point," he chortled.

Then she turned to me, raised her voice. "Speaking
of which, why'd it crash?"

How had she put it before? *I know all about it, believe me.* She knew the reason; she had to. But she
wanted me to tell her in public, in front of everyone
else.

"An inboard flap ripped off the wing at cruise speed
and hit the fuselage."

"Explain, please." She really didn't need to speak so
loudly. Her eyes glittered.

"A three-hundred-pound projectile flying at three
hundred miles an hour is going to do some serious damage."

"Obviously." Exasperated. "But why'd it rip off?"

"Chicken rivets."

"*Chicken rivets,*" she repeated. "I don't follow." People around us were listening now.

Maybe she didn't know as much about the crash as
she'd claimed. But whether she did or not, she wanted
me to explain, which was tricky: even though she'd
been the EVP for Commercial Airplanes at Boeing before she came to Hammond, I had no idea how much

she actually knew about building airplanes. Lots of executives rely on their experts to tell them what to think. I didn't want to talk over her head, but I also didn't want to condescend.

"Well, so Eurospatiale's new plane is mostly made out of plastic, right?"

She gave me a look. "If you want to call carbon-fiber-reinforced polymer 'plastic' instead of composite."

You got me there, I thought. So she did know a thing or two. "Most of the senior guys still don't trust the stuff."

"The 'senior guys' at Hammond?"

"Everywhere."

She knew what I meant, I was pretty sure—the senior execs at all the airplane manufacturers were inevitably older, and what they knew was metal, not composites.

"So?"

"So all the flaps on the wings are made of composite, too," I said. "But the hinges are aluminum. On the wing side, they're bolted to the aluminum rib lattice, but on the flaps, they're cut in."

"The hinges are glued on?"

"No, they're co-cured—basically glued and baked together. A sort of metal sandwich on composite bread, I guess you could say. And obviously Eurospatiale's designers didn't quite trust the adhesive bond, so they also put rivets into the hinges, right through the composite skin."

"The 'chicken rivets,'" she repeated, unnecessarily loud, I thought. "Called that why?"

I glanced up and saw that more and more people

around the table were watching us. I tried not to smile. "Because you only do it if you're 'chicken'—scared the bond won't hold. Like wearing belts and suspenders."

"But why are 'chicken rivets' a problem?"

"When you put rivets through composites, you introduce micro-cracks. Means you run the risk of introducing moisture. Which is clearly what happened in Paris."

Barlow signaled one of the waiters over and told him he wanted to try whatever red wine they were pouring.

"How can you be so sure?" she said.

"The photographs. You can see cracks at the stress concentration points. You can also see the brooming, the—"

"Where the composites absorbed water," she said impatiently. "But the plane was new."

"It made maybe twenty test flights before the show. Flew out of warm, rainy London up to subzero temps at forty thousand feet. So the damage spread fast. Weakened the joints. Then the flap tore off its hinge and hit the fuselage."

"You're sure."

"I saw the pictures. Nothing else it can be." Ali looked at me, a glint of amusement in her eyes. Kevin Bross put his hand over hers, making some point, and she delicately slid hers away.

The younger of the two Mexican waiters poured red wine into Barlow's glass. It was deep red, almost blood-red, and even at a distance it gave off the smell of a horse barn. I guessed that meant it was good.

Then the waiter's hand slipped. The neck of the bottle struck the glass and tipped it over. Wine splashed on the tablecloth, speckling Barlow's starched white shirt.

"Hey, what the *hell*?" Barlow cried.

"I sorry," the waiter said, taking Barlow's napkin and daubing at his shirt. "I very sorry."

"For Christ's sake, you clumsy ox!"

The waiter kept blotting his shirt.

"Will you get the hell out of here?" Barlow snapped at the kid. "Get your goddamn hands off my stomach."

The waiter looked like he wanted to flee. "Upton," I said, "it's not his fault. I must have knocked into it with my elbow."

The waiter glanced quickly at me, not understanding. He couldn't have been twenty, had an olive complexion and close-cropped black hair.

The manager came out of the kitchen with a small stack of cloth napkins. "We're so sorry," he said, handing a few to Barlow and laying the others neatly over the stained tablecloth. "Pablo," he said, "please get Mr. Barlow a towel and that spray bottle of water."

"I don't need a towel," Barlow said. "I need a new shirt."

"Yes, of course, sir," the manager said.

As Pablo the waiter left, I said to the manager, "It wasn't Pablo's fault. I hit his glass with my elbow."

"I see," the manager said, and kept blotting.

Cheryl watched with shrewd eyes. After a minute, she said: "Well, at least Hammond would never do something so stupid as to use chicken rivets, of course."

I glanced at her quickly, then caught the sharp edge of Hank Bodine's menacing stare. "Well, actually, we did," I said.

"We did . . . what?"

"Put chicken rivets on all the wing control surfaces. Other places, too."

"Wait a second," she said. She sat forward, intent. If

this was performance art, she was Meryl Streep. "Are you telling me our SkyCruiser team didn't *know* this might cause a serious problem?"

The frightened waiter returned with a stack of neatly folded white towels and handed them to Barlow. "I said I don't *need* any damned towels."

"Excuse me," I said to Cheryl. Then I touched the waiter's arm. *"Mira, este tipo es un idiota,"* I said softly. *"Es solo un pendejo engreído. No voy a dejar que te meta en problemas."* The guy's a jerk, I told him. A pompous asshole. I'd make sure he didn't get blamed for it.

He had an open, trusting face, and he looked at me, surprised. Maybe even relieved.

"Gracias, señor. Muchas gracias."

"No te preocupes."

"You speak fluently," Cheryl said.

"Just high school Spanish," I said. I didn't think she needed to know that my "teachers" were a couple of cholos, or at least Latino gangstas-in-training, at a juvenile detention facility.

"But you've got the idiom down well," she said. "I spent a few years in Latin America for Boeing." She lowered her voice. "That was sweet, what you just did."

I shrugged. "Never liked bullies," I said quietly.

She raised her voice again. "You're not seriously telling me that we made the same stupid mistake, are you?"

"It's not a matter of being stupid," I said. "It was a judgment call. Remember a couple of years back when Lockheed built the X-33 launch vehicle for NASA?"

She shook her head.

"They made the liquid fuel tanks out of composite

instead of aluminum. To save some weight. And during the tests, the fuel tanks ripped apart at the seams. A very public disaster. So our people looked at that, and said, Man, throw in some rivets just in case the adhesive fails like it did with Lockheed."

" 'Our people.' Meaning who? Whose . . . 'judgment call' was it? Some low-level stress analyst?"

"I'm sure the decision must have been made at a higher level than that."

"How high a level? Was it Mike Zorn?"

"No," I said quickly.

"Surely you know who made the decision to put in the . . . chicken rivets?"

"I don't really recall."

"But the name of the engineer who signed off on it is a matter of record, isn't it?" she said. "I'll bet you've got the spreadsheet on your computer. With the CAD number, listing the employee number of the stress analyst who stamped and signed off on the chicken rivets." She smiled thinly. "Am I right?"

Man. She knew a hell of a lot more than she was letting on. The guy who signed off on all the wing drawings was a stress analyst who'd been with Hammond for more than fifteen years, a very smart engineer named Joe Hartlaub. I remembered how he argued, long and hard, against putting rivets through the composite skin. Remembered the e-mails between him and Mike Zorn. Zorn took Joe's side—then Bodine jumped in and overruled them.

Bodine, who'd been building metal airplanes for decades, considered composites "voodoo." And he had the power to overrule both Zorn and the stress analyst. Bodine was the boss. He always won.

"I'm sure one of our stress analysts stamped the drawings, but it couldn't have been his decision," I said. "It would have had to be made at a higher level."

"By whom?"

"I don't know."

"Surely you do."

"I don't want to speculate," I said.

"Meaning that you know and won't tell me?"

"No. Meaning I'm not sure."

"Probably an old-line metal guy, as you put it. Right? A senior executive?"

I shrugged again.

"Because now it's clear, based on what happened in Paris, that the wings are going to have to be scrapped and rebuilt from scratch. A design change, partial-scale integrated testing, tooling and fabrication and touch-and-gos. Which will delay the launch of the SkyCruiser by six months, even a year."

"That would be a disaster. A delay like that, we could lose billions of dollars."

"And if we sell planes that we know to be defective, we're criminally negligent. So we don't have a choice, do we? Which is why I want to know who made that id-iotic decision that's going to cost us so dearly."

My theory was right. She was determined to use the Eurospatiale crash to undermine Hank Bodine, then get rid of him. And I'd just gotten trapped in the maws of that battle.

I just nodded.

"Well, I intend to find out who it was," she said. "And when I do, I will cut him out like a cancer."

23

THE WAITERS CLEARED away the bowls and the gold-rimmed service plates and began setting out a battalion of fresh silverware and steak knives with curved black handles and sharp carbon-steel blades.

Then the food came. And came. And came.

Raw oysters served with a pungent ponzu sauce. Tiny braised wild partridges seasoned with juniper berries on a bed of cabbage laced with tiny cubes of foie gras. Sautéed rapini and black-walnut-filled Seckel pear and cipollini coulis. Saffron-buckwheat crepes with a ragout of lobster and chanterelle mushrooms. Saddle of venison stuffed with quince. Ya de ya de ya.

Of course, I didn't know what half the stuff was, so I studied the menu like a lost tourist clutching a street map. I was full before the main course, and I didn't even know what the main course *was*.

At the foot of the table, Bo Lampack, the guy who looked like Mr. Clean, stood up and cleared his throat. The hubbub didn't subside until he clinked on his water glass for a good fifteen seconds.

"I don't know, think there's enough food here tonight?"

he boomed. "Might have to go out to McDonald's for a Quarter Pounder later on, huh?"

The laughter was boisterous.

"Oh, yeah, *right*. No restaurants around here for a hundred miles. So I guess you better eat up, folks. Hey, I'm Bo Lampack, from Corporate Teambuilders. Your team-building coordinator. As most of you remember, since I worked with most of you adventurers before." He paused. "Then again, alcohol does kill brain cells."

More raucous laughter.

He looked sternly around the table. "And after that banquet on the last night . . ." He paused again, and let the guffaws crescendo. ". . . I'm surprised you gentlemen have any brain cells left."

He surfed the waves of laughter like a pro. "Looks like we got some ladies with us this year, huh? Two beautiful ladies. You ladies think you can keep up with all these tough guys?"

I stole a glance at Cheryl. An enigmatic smile was frozen on her face like a mannequin's. Ali smiled bashfully, nodded.

"Actually," Bo said, "maybe the real question is, can you tough guys keep up with the ladies? See, in case you guys are thinking you're old hands and you got a head start on the ladies—sorry. Doesn't work that way. Because I always like to shake things up. Get you out of your comfort zone. So we're going to be doing some new things this year. Some fishing—only not the kind you're used to. Some kayaking. A great new GPS scavenger hunt. Even extreme tree climbing—and lemme tell you, it ain't like when you were a kid."

Kevin Bross grinned.

"Right, Kev? You've done recreational tree climbing,

haven't you? Rope-secured, with harnesses and cara-
biners and all?"

"Got certified in Atlanta," Bross said.

"Why does that not surprise me?" said Lampack.
"How about you, uh, Upton? It's wild, isn't it?"

Upton Barlow shook his head. "Haven't tried it yet,
but I'm looking forward to it," he said. Obviously he
wasn't happy that Bross knew a sport he didn't. "We
doing the fire walk again this year?"

"Uh, we've stopped doing the fire walk," Lampack
said. "Insurance problems."

Some nervous titters.

"Guy from Honeywell got hurt pretty bad, few
months back."

"I guess he wasn't a positive thinker," Bross said.
"It's all about mental concentration, you know."

"Tell that to the guy from Honeywell with third-
degree burns on the soles of his feet," said Lampack.
"Had to have skin grafts. See, this isn't all fun and
games, kids. Now, this year's program is called Power
Play, but it's not going to be like any play you've ever
done before. You're all going to have to sign liability
waivers as usual. There are dangers. We don't want any
of you executives falling off tightropes in the ropes
course and bashing your heads and delaying the launch
of your new plane or anything."

There was a weird, hostile edge to Lampack, I was
beginning to see. Like he secretly resented the corporate executives he worked with and took a kind of sadistic pleasure in taunting them.

"I won't lie to you," he said. "There's gonna be scary
moments. But it's moments like that that tell you who you
really are. When you're thirty feet off the ground you learn

what you're really made of, okay? You learn to confront your fears. Because this is about personal growth and self-discovery. It's about breaking down inhibitions. Knocking down those office walls so we can *build team spirit*."

He reached down and picked up a large reel of rope. He pulled out a length: half-inch white rope, blue threads woven through it. "You know what this is? This is not just your lifeline. This is *trust*." He nodded solemnly, looked around. "When you're walking across a cable thirty feet off the ground and someone's belaying you, you've got to trust him—or her—not to drop you, huh?"

He set the spool down. "You'll be challenged mentally and physically. And you're all going to *fail* at some point—our courses are designed to make you fail. Not our rope, though. Hopefully." He chuckled. "These tests are some of the most brutal trials you'll ever go through." He paused. "Except maybe one of Hank Bodine's PowerPoint presentations, huh?"

Bodine clicked a smile on and off. No one laughed.

"See, I'm going to get you all out of your comfort zone and into your *learning zone*."

A sudden explosion came from somewhere outside: the loud pop of a gunshot.

But it made no sense. This wasn't a hunting area. Everyone turned.

Lampack looked both ways, shrugged. "Guess a grizzly must've got into someone's garbage."

"Really?" Ali said.

"Happens all the time. Tons of grizzlies and black bears in the woods. Not supposed to shoot 'em, though people do. Get up early in the morning, and you might even see one washing himself down by the shore. Just leave 'em alone, and they'll leave you alone." He nodded sagely. "Now, we'll be evaluating the progress of your team development at the end of each day using the Drexler/Sibbet Team Performance Model—"

Another loud pop, then a door banged: the front door of the lodge, it sounded like.

A large man in a hunting outfit, camouflage shirt and matching pants, and a heavy green vest, traipsed into the room. He was well over six feet, wide and heavyset: a giant. He was around forty, with a powerful build that had gone somewhat to fat. He had short jet-black hair that looked dyed, dark eyebrows, a neatly trimmed black goatee. *Mephistopheles,* I thought. There was something satanic about his short black goatee, his jutting brow.

He stopped in the middle of the room, looked around with beady dark eyes, then approached the dining table.

"Man oh man," he said. "What do we got here?" His teeth were tobacco-stained.

Lampack folded his arms. "Private party, friend. Sorry."

"Party?" the hunter said. "Jeez Louise, don't it look like a party, though. Ain't you gonna invite me in?"

He spoke with a Deep South accent so broad and drawling he sounded like a hillbilly, some backwoods rube. But there was something cold in his gaze.

He took a few steps toward the sideboard, where some of the serving dishes had been placed, his brown smile wider, greedy black eyes staring. "Christ, will you *look* at that spread."

"I'm sorry, but you're going to have to leave," Lampack said. "Let's not have any trouble."

"Chill, Bo," warned Bross quietly. "Guy's probably drunk."

The hunter approached the table, arms wide as if

awed by the opulence of the spread. "Man, looky here. Christ on crutches, look at all this *food.*"

He shoved Ron Slattery aside and grabbed a partridge right off his plate with grimy hands. Slattery's eyeglasses went flying. Then the intruder stuffed the partridge whole into his mouth and chewed open-mouthed. "Damn, that game bird's *good,*" he said, his words muffled by the food. "No buckshot in it, neither. Do I taste a hint of garlic?"

Grabbing Danziger's wineglass, he gulped it down like Kool-Aid, his Adam's apple bobbing. "Mmm-*mmm*! Even better than Thunderbird."

Hank Bodine said, "All right, fella. Why don't you just go back to your hunting party, okay? This is a private lodge."

Bo Lampack folded his arms across his chest. "If you're hungry, I'm sure we can get you some food from the kitchen."

The giant leaned over the table, reached for Cheryl's plate. He dug his soiled stubby fingers into the mound of porcini-potato gratin.

"Oh, God," Cheryl said in disgust, closing her eyes.

"Mashed potatoes, huh?" He made a shovel out of his forefingers, scooped up a wad, and eyed it suspiciously.

"The hell's all these black specks doing in it? I think the potato mush is rotten, folks. Don't eat it." He cackled, crammed it into his mouth. "Not half-bad, though. Dee-*lici*ous."

"Where the hell is the manager?" Cheryl said.

From the far end of the table, Clive Rylance said, "All right, mate, just get on your way, now there's a good fellow. This is a private dinner, and I'm afraid you're outnumbered."

Inwardly I groaned. *Outnumbered.* Not the right thing to say. The hunter gave Clive a stony look. Then a slow grin.

"You a Brit, huh? Limey?" He leaned over between me and Upton Barlow, jostling us aside. He smelled of chewing tobacco and rancid sweat. Grabbing a crepe from Barlow's plate, he said, "You folks eat flapjacks for supper, too? I love flapjacks for supper." Then he took a bite, immediately spit it out onto the tablecloth. "Nasty! Jee-*zus,* that ain't syrup, that's for damned sure."

Barlow's face colored. He pursed his lips, exasperated.

"Will someone get the manager already?" Cheryl shouted. "My God, are you men just going to *sit* here?"

"You folks having fun? Celebrating something, maybe? Way out here, middle of nowhere?"

Another door slammed. It sounded like it came from somewhere in the back of the lodge.

A second man now entered the great room from a side hallway. This one was maybe ten years younger, also tall and bulky. He, too, wore a camouflage outfit, only the sleeves of his shirt had been sloppily ripped off, exposing biceps like ham hocks, covered in tattoos. His undersized head was shaved on the sides, a blond thatch on top. He had a big, blank face and a small, bristly blond mustache.

"Wayne," the first hunter called out, "you ain't gonna believe what kinda situation we just lucked into."

The second one smiled, his teeth tiny and pointed. His eyes scanned the table.

"Get your butt over here, Wayne, and try one of these here game birds. But stay away from the pancakes. They're nasty."

"Bo," Cheryl said, "would you please get Paul Fecher

right this instant? We've got the cast of *Deliverance* here, and the man's nowhere in sight."

Obviously she didn't see what it meant that the manager still hadn't emerged. When the waiter had spilled wine on Barlow, he'd popped out of the kitchen like a jack-in-the-box. He had to have heard this commotion; the fact that he wasn't here meant that something was very wrong.

"We don't need to shoot no deer," the goateed hunter said. "Never liked venison anyway."

Bo, relieved to get out of there, ran toward the kitchen.

"Hey!" the goateed guy shouted after him.

With a shrug, he turned to his comrade. "Wait'll he meets Verne."

The blond guy snickered.

Bodine rose slowly. "That's enough," he said.

I whispered, "Hank, don't."

The goateed giant looked up at Bodine, and said, "Sit down."

But Bodine didn't obey. He walked down the length of the table slowly, shaking his head: the big man in charge. He could have been running a staff meeting, that was how confidently he asserted his authority.

"Back to your seat, there, boss man."

As Bodine passed me I reached out and grabbed his knee. "Hank," I whispered, "don't mess with this guy."

Bodine slapped my hand away and kept going, a man on a mission.

Lummis muttered to Barlow, "Gotta be a hunting party that got lost in the woods."

"We're in a game preserve," Barlow replied, just as quietly. "Great Bear Preserve. Hunting's against the law."

"I don't think these guys care about the law," I said.

24

BODINE STOOD MAYBE six feet away from the black-haired guy, his feet planted wide apart, hands on his hips, obviously trying to intimidate him.

"All right, fella, fun's over," Bodine said. "Move on."

The goateed guy looked up from the food and snarled, mouth full, "Siddown."

"If you and your buddy aren't out of here in the next sixty seconds, we're going to call the police." Bodine glanced over at the rest of us. He was playing to the crowd. This was a man used to being obeyed, and there really was something about the sonorous authority of his voice that made most people want to do whatever he told them to do.

But the black-haired hunter just furrowed his heavy brow and gave Bodine a satanic smile. "The po-lice," he said, and he cackled. "That's a good one." Then he looked over at his comrade, potato mush on either side of his mouth. "You hear that, Wayne? He gonna call the po-lice."

The second intruder spoke for the first time. "Don't think so," he said in a strangely high voice. His eyes flitted back and forth. His arms dangled at his side, too short for his bulky torso.

Everyone had gone quiet, staring with frightened

fascination, as if watching a horror movie. I said, "Hank, come on."

Without even looking at me, he extended his right arm and waggled his index finger dismissively in my direction, telling me without words, *Stay out of this. None of your business.*

From the kitchen came a cry. A man's voice.

I saw the realization dawn on people's faces.

Bodine moved just inches away from the goateed man. He was doing what he must have done hundreds of times: invading an adversary's personal space, intimidating him with his height, his stentorian voice, his commanding presence. It always worked, but right now it didn't seem to be working at all.

"Let me tell you something, friend," Bodine said. "You are making a serious mistake. Now, I'm going to do you a favor and pretend none of this happened. I'm giving you an opportunity to move on, and I suggest you take it. It's a no-brainer."

Suddenly the man pulled something shiny and metal from his vest: a stainless-steel revolver. The table erupted in panicked screams.

He took the weapon by the barrel, and slammed the grip against the side of Bodine's face. It made an audible crunch.

Bodine let out a terrible, agonized yelp, and collapsed to his knees.

Blood sluiced from his nose. It looked broken. One hand flew to his face; the other flailed in the air to ward off any further blows.

The reaction around the table was swift and panicked. Some seemed to want to come to Bodine's assistance but didn't dare. Some screamed.

Cheryl kept calling for the manager.

If he could have come, he would have.

"God's sake, somebody *do* something!" Lummis gasped.

I sat there, mind racing. The second hunter, the one with the blond crew cut, hadn't moved. He was speaking into a walkie-talkie.

The goateed man, muttering, "Call me a goddamned no-brainer," held the weapon high in the air. It was, I noticed, a hunter's handgun, a .44 Magnum Ruger Super Blackhawk six-shooter. Gray wood-look grips and a barrel over seven inches. A big, heavy object. I'd never used one: I didn't like to use handguns for hunting.

Then he slammed it against the other side of Bodine's face. Blood geysered in the air.

Bodine screamed again: a strange and awful sound of vulnerability.

He fluttered both of his hands in a futile attempt to shield his bloodied face. He cried hoarsely, "Please. *Please.* Don't." Blood gouted from his nose, seeping from his eyes, ran down his cheeks, spattering his shirt.

I wanted to do something, but what? Go after the guy with a steak knife? Two armed men: It seemed like an easy way to get killed. I couldn't believe this was happening; the suddenness, the unreality of it all, froze me as it must have done everyone else.

"Buck!"

A shout from the front door. The black-haired man paused, handgun in the air, and looked. A third man entered, dressed like the other two, in camouflage pants and vest. He was tall and lean, sharp-featured, a strong jaw, around forty. Scraggly dark blond hair that reached almost to his shoulders.

"That's enough, Buck," the new man said. He had a deep, adenoidal voice with the grit of fine sandpaper, and he spoke calmly, patiently. "No unnecessary violence. We talked about that."

The goateed one—Buck?—released his grip on Bodine, who slumped forward, spitting blood, weeping in ragged gulps.

Then the long-haired guy pulled a weapon from a battered leather belt holster. A matte black pistol: Glock 9mm, I knew right away. He waved it back and forth at all of us, in a sweeping motion, from one end of the table to the other and back again.

"All right, boys and girls," he said. "I want all of you to line up on that side of the table, facing me. Hands on the table, where I can see 'em."

"Oh, sweet Jesus God," Hugo Lummis said, his voice shaking.

Cheryl said imperiously—or maybe it was bravely— "What do you want?"

"Let's go, kids. We can do this the hard way or the easy way, it's up to you. Your choice."

25

"WE GONNA DO this the hard way?"

Dad's shadow fell across the kitchen floor. He loomed in the doorway, enormous to a ten-year-old: red face, gut bulging under a white sleeveless T-shirt, can of Genesee beer in his hand. "Genny," he always called it, sounded like his mistress.

Mom standing at the kitchen counter, wearing her Food-Fair smock, chopping onions for chili con carne. His favorite supper. A snowdrift of minced onion heaped on the cutting board. Her hand was shaking. The tears flowing down her cheeks, she'd said, were from the onions.

I didn't know how to answer that. Stared up at him with all the defiance I could muster. Mother's little protector.

"Don't you ever hit her," I said.

She'd told me she'd slipped in the shower. The time before that, she'd tripped on a wet floor at the FoodFair supermarket, where she worked as a cashier. One flimsy excuse after another, and I'd had enough.

"She tell you that?"

Blood roared in my ears so loud I could barely hear him. My heart was racing. I swallowed hard. I had to look away, stared at the peeling gray-white paint on the doorframe. It reminded me of the birch tree in the backyard.

"I told him it was an accident." Mom's voice from behind me, high and strained and quavering, a frightened little girl. "Stay out of this, Jakey."

I kept examining the peeling-paint birch bark. "I know you hit her. Don't you ever do that again."

A sudden movement, and I was knocked to the floor like a candlepin.

"Talk to me like that one more time, you're going to reform school."

Tears flooding my eyes now: Not the onions. What the hell was reform school?

"Now, say you're sorry."

"Never. I'm not."

"We gonna do this the hard way?"

I knew what he was capable of.

Through eyes blurry from tears, I examined the ceiling, noticed the cracks, like the broken little concrete patio in back of the house.

"I'm sorry," I said at last.

A few minutes later, Dad was lying back in his ratty old Barcalounger in front of the TV. "Jakey," he said, almost sweetly. "Mind fetching me another Genny?"

SLOWLY WE ALL began to gather on one side of the table. Except for Bross and Rylance, I noticed. They both seemed to be edging away, as if trying to make a sudden break.

"Where's Lampack?" Slattery said.

"Let's go, kids," the long-haired man said. He pointed the Glock at Bross and Rylance. "Nowhere to run, *compadres*," he said to them. "We got all the exits covered. Get over there with the rest of your buddies."

Bross and Rylance glanced at each other, then, as if by unspoken agreement, stopped moving. I looked for Ali, saw her at the far end of the table. She appeared to be as frightened as everyone else.

Was this guy bluffing about having the exits covered? How many of them were there?

And what were they planning to do?

The man took out a walkie-talkie from his vest, pressed the transmit button. "Verne, you got the staff secured?"

"Roger," a voice came back.

"We got a couple of guys itching to make a run for it. You or Travis see 'em, shoot on sight, you read me?"

"Roger that."

He slipped the walkie-talkie back into his vest, then held the gun in a two-handed grip, aiming at Kevin Bross. "Which one of you wants to die first?"

Hugo Lummis cried, "Don't shoot!" and someone else said, "Move, just *move*!"

"Don't be idiots!" Cheryl shouted at the two men. "Do what he says."

"Makes no big difference to me," the long-haired man said. "You obey me, or you die, but either way I get what I want. You always have a choice." He shifted his pistol a few inches toward Rylance. "Eeny, meeny, miney, mo."

"All right," Bross said. He raised his hands in the air; then he and Rylance came over to the table.

"What do you want from us?" Cheryl said.

But he didn't reply. He wagged his pistol back and forth in the air, ticking from one of us to the next like the arm of a metronome. He chanted in a singsong voice: "My—mother—told—me—to—pick—the—very—best—one—and—you—are—not—*it*."

His pistol pointed directly at me.

"You win."

I swallowed hard.

Stared into the muzzle of the Glock.

"It's your lucky day, guy," he said.

My reaction was strange: I wanted to close my eyes, like a child, to make it go away. Instead, I forced myself to notice little things about the gun, like the way the barrel jutted out of the front of the slide. Or the unusual keyhole-shaped opening machined into the top.

"Huh," I said, trying to sound casual. "Never seen one of those up close."

"It's called a gun, my friend," he said. His eyes were liquid pewter. There seemed to be a glint of amusement in them. "A semiautomatic pistol. And when I pull this little thing here, which is called a trigger—"

"No, I mean I've never seen a Glock 18C before," I said. "Pretty rare, those things. Works like an automatic, doesn't it?"

Humanize yourself. Make him see you as someone just like him.

He smiled slowly. He was a handsome man, except for those eyes, which were cold and gray and didn't smile when his mouth did. "Sounds like you know your weapons." He kept his gun leveled at me, aiming at a spot in the middle of my forehead.

"Of course, seventeen rounds on auto won't last you very long," I said, then immediately regretted saying it.

"Well, why don't we find out?" he said in a voice that, in any other context, you might describe as gentle.

Everyone was quiet, watching in mesmerized terror. The air had gone out of the room.

"Do I get a choice?" I asked.

26

HE LOOKED AT me for a few seconds.

Then he grinned and lowered the gun. I exhaled slowly.

"All right, boys and girls, here's the drill. I want all of you to empty your pockets, put everything on the table right in front of you. Wallets, money clips, jewelry. Watches, too. Got it? Let's go."

So it was a holdup. Nothing more than that, thank God.

"Buck, some backup over here," he said.

"Gotcha, Russell," said the goateed guy, taking out his .44. I noticed he was no longer speaking in that hillbilly accent. He'd been putting it on.

"When these folks here are finished emptying out their pockets, I want you and Wayne to search 'em. Pat 'em down."

"Gotcha."

Buck began orbiting the table, watching everyone drop wallets and money clips onto the table. Ali and Cheryl unclasped their necklaces and bracelets, took off their earrings. The men removed their watches.

Hugo Lummis, next to me, unbuckled his watchband

and slipped it into the back pocket of his pants. I wondered if anyone else had seen it. I didn't think so.

I whispered to him, "Careful. They're going to search us." But he pretended not to hear.

Russell holstered his gun and began strolling nonchalantly around the room, picking up objects, examining them with idle curiosity, then putting them down. He walked with the loose-limbed stride of someone used to a lot of physical activity. An ex-soldier, I thought, but of an elite sort—a Navy SEAL, maybe, or a member of the Special Forces. There were crow's-feet around his eyes and deep lines etched in his leathery skin: He'd spent a lot of time in the sun. Not, I suspected, on the beach.

He stopped at a long table on which one of the hotel staff had stacked blue loose-leaf Hammond binders. He picked one up and leafed through it for a minute or so.

His two men were preoccupied, too—Buck was making a circuit around the table, his back to me, and Wayne was frisking Geoff Latimer. So for a moment, no one was watching us. I moved my hand slowly across the tablecloth, grabbed the handle of a steak knife, slid the knife along the table toward me.

Then I lowered it to my side, held it flat against my thigh.

I gripped its smooth black handle and ran my thumb along the knife edge. It would slice through human skin as easily as it dissected saddle of venison. Against a handgun it wouldn't do much, but it was the only weapon I had.

Russell ripped out a sheet of paper from one of the notebooks, folded it neatly, and put it in his vest pocket.

Hank Bodine was now struggling to get to his feet. His face was slick with blood; he was badly wounded.

"You can just stay put," Russell told him. "I don't think you're going to get up and dance anytime soon." He grabbed a handful of linen napkins from the table and dropped them in front of Bodine. They fluttered to the floor like birds' wings. Bodine looked at them dully, then squinted his bloodied eyes at Russell, not understanding.

"You got a choice, too," Russell said. "You can try to stop the bleeding or hemorrhage to death. All the same to me."

Now Bodine understood. He took a napkin, held it to his nose, moaned.

I flexed my left knee and brought my leg up behind me. Moving very slowly, I slid the knife carefully into the side of my shoe.

Barlow turned to look at me. I glared back as I lowered my foot to the floor.

The lights flickered for a second.

"What the hell's that?" Russell said.

No one answered. Had one of his guys hit some central switch by accident?

"It's the generators," Kevin Bross muttered.

"What's that?" Russell approached Bross.

"This place is powered by generators," Bross said. "One of them's probably failing. Or maybe the system just switched over from one generator to another."

Russell looked at Bross for a few seconds. "You almost sound like you know what you're talking about." Then he turned to Upton Barlow. "I like your wallet."

Barlow just stared back, his expression fierce but his eyes dancing with fear.

"Guy gives you a compliment, you say 'Thank you,'" Russell said. "Where's your manners?"

"Thank you," Barlow said.

"You're quite welcome." Russell picked up the wallet, flipped it open. "What's this made out of, alligator? Crocodile?"

Barlow didn't answer.

"I'm going to say crocodile." Russell peered closely at the wallet. "Hermes," he said.

"Air-*mez,*" Barlow corrected him.

Russell nodded. "Thank you. Why, look at this." He pulled out a black credit card. "Bucky, you ever seen one of these? A *black* American Express card? I don't think I've ever seen one before. Heard about 'em, but I don't think I've ever actually seen one up close and personal."

Buck approached, looked closely. "That can't be real," he said. "They don't make 'em in black." Now that he'd dropped the phony bumpkin accent, he spoke with the flat vowels of a Midwesterner.

"Sure they do," Russell said. "Friend of mine told me about it. It's one step higher than platinum, even. You can buy anything with it, I heard. Sky's the limit. Yachts, jet fighters, you name it. But you can't apply for this, my buddy told me. You only get one if you're important enough. If you're a big cheese. You a big cheese, uh—" He looked closely at the card. "Upton? That your first name, Upton?"

Barlow just stared.

Suddenly Russell had his pistol out and was pointing it at Barlow's heart.

"No!" Barlow cried. "Christ! Yes, *yes,* that's my first name."

"Thank you," Russell said. "Upton Barlow. Hammond Aerospace Corporation. You work for Hammond Aerospace, Upton?"

"Yes," Barlow said.

"Thank you kindly." Russell reholstered the pistol. "I've heard of Hammond Aerospace," Russell said. "You guys make airplanes, right?"

Barlow nodded.

"Probably flown in some of them," Russell said. "You make military transport planes, too, don't you?"

No one spoke.

"Been in one of those for sure. Never had one crash on me, though, so you must be doing your job. Good work, Upton."

He chuckled, low and husky, and advanced along the table to Kevin Bross. He leaned over, picked up Bross's watch. "Good God Almighty, look at this thing, Buck," he said. "Ever see a wristwatch like that?"

"Ridiculous piece of crap," Buck said.

Bross was gritting his teeth, breathing in and out slowly, trying to maintain control.

"Well, I kind of like it," Russell said.

"It's a replica," Bross said.

"Could have fooled me," Russell said, dropping it into a pocket in his vest. "Thank you, kind sir." He picked up Bross's wallet. "This isn't a . . . *Hermès*," he said, pronouncing it right. He shook it, scattering the credit cards across the tablecloth, and picked one up. "This guy only gets a platinum," he said. "Kevin Bross," he read. "Hammond Aerospace Corporation. You all with the Hammond Aerospace Corporation, that right?"

Silence.

"You all must be here for some kind of meeting. Right?"

No one said anything.

"I saw those notebooks on the table back there," he went on. "Said something about the 'Executive Council' of the Hammond Aerospace Corporation. That's you guys—excuse me, you ladies and gentlemen—right?"

Silence.

"No need to be modest, kids," he said. "Bucky, I think we just hit the jackpot."

The lights flickered again.

PART TWO

27

THE OTHERS HAD no idea what kind of trouble we
were in.

I'm sure they figured, like I did at first, that this was
just rotten luck: a rowdy bunch of hunters, lost and hungry and larcenous, had stumbled upon an opulent lodge
full of rich businessmen, miles away from anything
else, no cops around to stop them.

But I was sure this was something far more serious.
At that point, of course, I was going on nothing more
than vague suspicions and instinct.

Still, my instinct hadn't failed me yet.

Russell, the ringleader of the hunters, ordered the
crew-cut one, Wayne, to go upstairs and search all the
rooms. "I have a feeling we're gonna find laptops and
whatchamacallits, BlackBerrys and all that good stuff
upstairs," he said. "See what you can find. Anything
that looks interesting."

"Yup," Wayne said. He clumped across the floor and
thundered up the stairs.

"Bucky, will you please make sure none of our executives here . . . 'forgot' . . . anything in their pockets? Now,

I read something about opening remarks by the Chief Executive Officer. That's the boss, right? Which one of you's the boss?"

He looked around the table. No one said anything. Buck started at the far end of the table, frisking Geoff Latimer.

"Come on now, gotta be one of you guys."

Silence.

Then Cheryl spoke up. "I am."

"*You're* the Chief Executive Officer?" He looked skeptical, took a few steps in her direction.

Cheryl swallowed. "That's right."

"Chick like you? You're the boss?"

"Chick like me," she said. Her mouth flattened into a straight line. "Strange but true." The slightest quaver.

"A lady CEO, huh?"

"It happens," she said, a little starch returning to her voice. "Nowhere near often enough, but it happens. How can I help you, Russell?"

"So all these guys here work for you? A woman orders them around?"

Her nostrils flared. "I lead," she said. "That's not quite the same as ordering people around."

Russell grinned. "Well, that's a good point, Cheryl. A very good point. I have the same philosophy. So maybe you can tell me, Cheryl, what you're all doing in this godforsaken fishing lodge in the back of beyond."

"We're on an offsite."

"An *offsite*," he said slowly. "That's like—what? A meeting, sort of? Chance to get out of the office and talk, that it?"

"That's right. Now, may I say something?"

"Yes, Cheryl, you may."

"Please, just take whatever you want and leave. None of us wants any trouble. Okay?"

"That's very kind and generous of you, Cheryl," Russell said. "I think we'll do just that. Now may I ask *you* something?"

She nodded. Her bosom rose and fell: She was breathing hard.

"A lady CEO gets the same money as a man?" he said.

She smiled tightly. "Of course."

"Huh. And I thought I read somewhere how women CEOs only get sixty-eight cents for every dollar a man CEO gets. Well, live and learn."

Cheryl looked momentarily flummoxed. "They pay me quite well. Not as much as some other CEOs, it's true."

"Still, it ain't chump change. Bucky, what do you take home on your welding job?"

Buck looked up. "Good year, maybe thirty-eight grand."

"You make more than that, Cheryl?"

She exhaled slowly. "If you want me to apologize for the inequities of the capitalist system, you—"

"No, Cheryl, not at all. I know how the world works. I've got no beef with the capitalist system. I'm just saying you might want to spread some of that around." Now he was standing directly in front of her, only the table between them.

"Our corporate charitable contributions last year totaled—"

"That's awful nice, Cheryl. But I think you know that's not what I mean."

She looked exasperated. "I don't carry much cash, and you're taking my jewelry."

"Oh, I'll bet you got plenty more."

"Not unless you plan on leading me to a cash machine at gunpoint so you can empty out my checking account. But I don't think you're going to find an ATM very close by."

Russell shook his head slowly. "Cheryl, Cheryl, Cheryl. You must think you're talking to some rube, huh? Some ignorant bubba. Well, don't misunderstand me. You run a very big company. Makes a lot of money."

She pursed her lips. "Actually, we haven't been doing all that well recently. That's one of the reasons for this meeting."

"Really? Says in that book there you have revenue of ten billion dollars and a market capitalization of more than twenty billion. Those numbers off base?" His thumb pointed at the long table stacked with loose-leaf binders.

She paused for a few seconds, caught by surprise. "That's not *my* money, Russell. The corporation's assets aren't my own personal piggy bank."

"You telling me you can't get your hands on some of that money? I'll bet you can make one phone call and send some of those . . . assets . . . my way. Right?"

"Wrong. There are all sorts of controls and procedures."

"But I'll bet you've got the power to do it with one phone call. You're the CEO. Right?"

"It doesn't work that way in the corporate world. I'm sorry. I sometimes wish I had that kind of power, but I don't."

He slid his pistol out of its holster and pulled back the slide. It made a *snick-snick* sound. He raised it, one-handed, leaned across the table, and pointed it at her left eye. His index finger was curled loosely around the trigger.

She began blinking rapidly, her eyes filling with tears. "I'm telling you the truth."

"Then I guess you're of no use to me," he said softly.

"Don't!" Ali shouted. "Don't hurt her, please. *Please!*"

Tears trickled down Cheryl's cheeks. She stared right back at him.

"Wait." A male voice. We all turned.

Upton Barlow.

"We can work something out," he said.

Russell lowered the gun, and Cheryl gasped. He turned to Barlow with interest. "My friend Upton, with the good taste in wallets."

"Let's talk," Barlow said.

"I'm listening."

"We're both rational men, you and I. We can come to an agreement."

"You think so?"

"I know so," Barlow said. "I have no doubt we can work something out to your satisfaction."

"Kind of a win-win situation," Russell said.

"Exactly." Barlow smiled.

"So you're the go-to guy. You're the man."

"Look," Barlow said, "I just hammered out an offset deal with South Korea on a fighter plane. A coproduction agreement. Everyone said it couldn't be done."

I remembered that offset arrangement. Basically he arranged for Hammond to transfer billions of dollars in avionics and proprietary software to Seoul so they could build our fighter jet for us. Which meant we gave the

Koreans everything they'd need to build their own fighter jet in a few years. It was a monumentally lousy deal.

"You sure you got the juice to make it happen?" Russell said. "Your boss says she doesn't, but *you* do?"

"There's always a way."

"I'm liking the sound of this, Upton."

"And in exchange, you and your friends will agree to move on. Fair enough?"

"Now we're talking."

"So let's get specific," Barlow said. "I'm prepared to offer you fifty thousand dollars."

Russell gave that low husky chuckle again. "Oh, Upton," he said, disappointed. "And here I was thinking you were the man. Guy who makes things happen. But we're not even talking the same language."

Barlow nodded. "Do you have a figure in mind? Why don't we start there?"

"You think you can get us an even million, Upton?"

Barlow examined the table. "Well, I don't know about that. That's a huge amount."

"See, now, that's too bad." Russell strolled along the table, head down as if deep in thought. When he reached the end, he circled around behind me, then stopped. "What if I kill one of your friends? Like this fellow right here? You think that might get us to 'yes,' Upton?"

I felt the hairs on the back of my neck go prickly, and then I realized he'd put the gun against the back of Hugo Lummis's head. Lummis started breathing hard through his mouth. He sounded as if he were about to have a heart attack.

"Put that gun down," Cheryl said. "Aren't you the one who was talking about 'no unnecessary violence'?"

Russell went on, ignoring her: "You think you can dig up a million bucks, Upton, if it means saving Fatso's life?"

Droplets of sweat broke out on Lummis's brow and his big round cheeks and began dripping down his neck, darkening his shirt collar.

"Yes," Barlow shouted. "For God's sake, *yes*! Yes, I'm sure it can be arranged if need be."

But from my other side came Ronald Slattery's voice. "No, it can't. You don't have signing authority for that kind of money, Upton."

"Signing authority?" said Russell, keeping the barrel of the Glock against Lummis's head. "Now, that's interesting. What's that mean? Who has signing authority?"

Slattery fell silent. You could tell he regretted saying anything.

"For God's sake, Ron," Barlow said, "the guy's going to kill Hugo! You want that on your conscience?"

"You heard the man, Ron," said Russell. "You want that on your conscience?"

"Give him the goddamned money," Lummis pleaded. "We've got K&R insurance—we're covered, situation like this. Good God!"

"All right," Barlow said. "Yes, I'm sure we can arrange that. We'll make it happen somehow. Just—please, just put down the gun and let's keep talking."

"Now we're cooking with fire," Russell said. He never raised his voice, I noticed. He seemed supremely confident, unflappable.

He lowered the gun. Walked up to Upton Barlow and stood behind him. "This is starting to sound like a productive conversation. Because if you can get me a million dollars, company like yours, you can do better."

After a few seconds, Barlow said, "What do you have in mind?"

"Upton!" Cheryl said warningly.

"I'm thinking a nice round number."

"Let's hear it."

"I'm thinking a *hundred* million dollars, Upton. Twelve of you here, that's"—he paused for maybe two seconds—"eight million, three hundred thousand bucks and change per head, I figure. Okay? Let's get to 'yes.'"

Ali looked at me, and I knew she was thinking the same thing I was: This nightmare was only beginning.

28

THE STUNNED SILENCE was broken by Ron Slattery.

"But that's—that's impossible! Our K&R insurance coverage is only twenty-five million."

"Come on, now, Ronny," Russell said. "Aren't you the CFO? The numbers guy? Read the fine print, bro. Gotta be twenty-five million per insuring clause. Twenty-five million for ransom, twenty-five million for accident and loss coverage, twenty-five million for crisis-management expenses, another twenty-five million for medical expenses and psychiatric care. That's a hundred million easy. Did I add right?"

"This is ridiculous," Cheryl said. "You're dreaming if you think our insurance company's going to write you a check for a hundred million dollars."

Russell shook his head slowly. "Oh, no, that's not how it works, Cheryl. The insurance companies never pay. They always insist that *you* folks pay, then they pay you back. Legal reasons."

"Well, we don't have access to that kind of money," she said. "No one does."

Russell sidled up to her, his head down. "Cheryl," he said softly, "Hammond Aerospace has cash reserves of almost four billion dollars. I just read it in your note-book over there."

"But those funds are tied up, impossible to access—"

"You know what it said, Cheryl? Said 'cash and mar-ketable securities.' I'm no money guy, Cheryl, but doesn't that mean it's liquid?"

"Look," said Ron Slattery, turning around to look at Russell, "even if we *could* somehow access that kind of money, how the hell do you think you're going to get it? Cash, unmarked bills, all that?" His slash of a mouth twisted into a sneer. "I don't even know where the near-est bank is."

"Turn around, Ron," Russell said.

Slattery wheeled around quickly.

"Now, you see, Ron, you're talking down to me, and I don't like that. Obviously I'm not talking about stacks of bills. I'm talking about a couple of keystrokes on the com-puter. Click click click. Electronic funds transfers and all that. Takes a few seconds. I do know a thing or two."

"Not as much as you seem to think you do," Slat-tery said.

Russell gave a sly smile.

"We have controls in place," Slattery said. "Security codes and PIN numbers and callback arrangements. Things you can't even begin to imagine."

"Thing is, I don't *need* to imagine it, Ron. I've got you right here to explain it all to me."

"And which account do you imagine this hundred million dollars would go into? Your checking account? Or your savings account? Do you have any idea how fast you'll have the FBI up your ass?"

"What I hear, the government doesn't do so good with offshore banks, Ron."

Slattery was quiet for a few seconds. "You have an offshore account," he said. A statement, not a question.

"Anything can be arranged," Russell said. "If you know the right people."

"Please." Slattery smiled. "Setting up an offshore account is a complicated legal process that can take days, if not weeks. And it's certainly not something you can do from here."

"Ronny, you ever heard of something called the Internet?"

Slattery's smile began to fade.

"These days, Ronny, all you need's a laptop. There's websites out there that wanna sell you ready-made shell companies, incorporated in the Seychelles and Mauritius, places like that. Couple hundred bucks. You pay an extra fee, you can get the whole thing done in a day." He shook his head. "You mean I know more about this stuff than a professional money guy like you?"

"Well, be that as it may," Slattery said, "it's all theoretical anyway. We don't have the authority to move money like that."

"You don't?" Russell took a folded piece of paper from a pocket in his vest and held it up. "Says here you folks are the 'Executive Management Team' of Hammond Aerospace. CEO, CFO, Treasurer, Controller, blah-blah-blah. All the top guys in the company. You're all here. You telling me you guys—and gal, excuse me—don't have the 'authority' to transfer corporate funds? I don't buy it."

Slattery shook his head. His bald pate had begun to flush.

"Russell." It was Upton Barlow.

Russell turned. "Yes, Upton?"

"What you're really asking for is ransom, isn't that right?"

"Ransom? I don't know whether I'd call it that, Upton. I'm just looking to make a business deal here. Call it a transaction."

"Well, call it ransom," said Barlow, "and all you've got to do is call our headquarters in Los Angeles and make a demand. We have kidnap-and-ransom insurance. The company will have no choice but to pay you the money, then you can be on your way, simple as that. Everybody wins. Except maybe Lloyd's of London."

Ali and I exchanged glances again. She seemed to be as astonished as me that one of our own would actually *suggest* a ransom. But then, as I knew well, fear could do strange things to people.

"Well, Upton, I do appreciate the suggestion," Russell said pensively, as if he were a fellow executive helping to hash out the details of some complicated marketing strategy. "But kidnap-for-ransom, as I see it, is for amateurs. Or banditos in Mexico or Colombia. That might work in some foreign country where you've got the cops in on it with you, taking a piece of the action. But it never works here."

"But the difference is, we *want* to cooperate with you," Barlow said.

What an idiot, I thought.

Ali rolled her eyes.

"Sorry, Upton, but I won't play that game," he said. "I don't really feel like having this beautiful old fishing lodge turned into—what was it?—Waco or Ruby Ridge. You think I want me and my buddies trapped in here with SWAT teams all around, shouting at us through megaphones, using us for sniper practice, helicopters circling and all that? Uh-uh. No way, José. That's for idiots, Upton, and I'm not an idiot."

Barlow seemed momentarily stymied.

"No need for all that drama," Russell went on. "Not when we got all the players here who can make our little deal happen."

"I told you, we can't do that!" Cheryl said.

"Now, see, Cheryl, I'm not talking to you. You and Ronald, you seem to be the naysayers around here." He raised his voice, addressing all of us at once. "Okay, kiddies, here's the deal. I'm gonna make a call to an old buddy of mine—a guy who knows how all this stuff works. Meanwhile, Upton, why don't you and your Executive Management Team have a little powwow? A little . . . offsite, right? Figure out how you guys are gonna get me that money. Hey, Buck, do you think you guys can clear your schedule for a couple of days?"

"Shee-et, I dunno, I'm a busy guy," Buck said. He was using his redneck *Deliverance* accent again. It must have been some inside joke among the hunters, or whatever they were. "Hain't even finished worming the hogs."

"Want something done, ask a busy man to do it," Russell said. "So why don't you and Wayne check your Filofaxes and see if you can block out a little time for me, could you, please?"

Buck cackled. "Soon's I finish cooking the roadkill beef jerky, boss."

"When you're done searching everybody, I want you to tie 'em all up at the wrists. Hands in front of 'em so they can use the john if they have to." He took out his walkie-talkie and pressed the transmit button. "Verne, you and Travis bring the staff in here, please."

"Roger," a voice said.

"There's no need to tie anybody up," Cheryl said. "Honestly—where the hell do you think we're going to go?"

"Well, Cheryl," said Russell, "you sound very reasonable, the way I'd expect a CEO to sound. But you folks might be here a little while, see, and I never like to take chances." He had the pleasant, confident voice of an airline pilot announcing that we'd just encountered a little "heavy weather" and telling us not to worry about it. "All right, boys and girls, my buddies here will take good care of you. By the time I get back, I'm hoping and expecting we'll all be ready to rock 'n' roll." He smiled and nodded. "Gonna be a kinda carrot-and-stick approach, whatever you want to call it. You cooperate, we do our deal, and me and my buddies pack up and move on."

"What's the stick?" asked Slattery.

"You," said Russell. "We'll start with you. Thanks for volunteering." He was talking to all of us now, his eyes hooded, nonchalant. "You folks give me any problems, I'm going to kill my little friend Ronald. Call it a penalty for nonperformance, isn't that what you guys say? So I'm hoping you guys do some real creative thinking, okay?"

Slattery went pale as Russell stowed his walkie-talkie, then gazed around the immense room for a few seconds. "I want everyone on the floor where we can see 'em," he ordered his men.

"What do you want us to tie 'em up with?" said Buck.

"Jesus." Russell shook his head. "They're supposed to be doing something called 'ropes courses' tomorrow, whatever the hell that is. Just a wild guess, here, but I'm thinking it might involve rope, Bucky, what do you think?"

Buck gave Russell a look of irritation.

"Well, there you go," Russell said, pointing at the big wooden reel of climbing rope that Bo Lampack had held up at dinner. "And listen, Buck. Pay careful attention to that young guy." He jabbed a thumb in my direction. "I get a bad feeling about him."

29

"WATCH OUT FOR this guy, Glover," the guard said, smiling.

My first day at the Glenview Residential Center. Juvie. My home for the next eighteen months.

"Yeah, I see what you mean," said the second guard. "Better warn Estevez. He's gonna shit in his pants."

Their laughter rang in the cinder-block hallway. The first one said something in a low voice to the second, something I didn't catch. Handed him a clipboard with forms on it. The intake forms I'd had to sign at the bottom of every page.

I looked around, dazed. But watchful: Everything here looked strange, yet familiar. The walls painted a sickly institutional green, the ancient linoleum tiles on the floor, black squares alternating with white, scratched and grooved yet waxed and buffed to a high sheen.

Floor's probably polished by the kids, I thought. *The other prisoners.*

That sharp, high smell of pine disinfectant everywhere, which would forever summon a cataract of bad memories.

The first guard—I never caught his name—had brought

me over from the main administration building, a beautiful redbrick Georgian manor house. With its rolling,
manicured two-hundred-acre campus, the place could
have been some New England college, or at least as I
imagined a college would look.

Except for the discreet sign on the lawn: GLENVIEW
RESIDENTIAL CENTER. And the chain-link fence topped
by concertina wire. And the guard towers.

I'd been fingerprinted, stripped naked, made to sit on
a bench for an hour. Pictures were taken. They sheared
off my long hair, gave me a buzz cut. I was issued a set
of prison clothes: khaki pants with an elastic waistband,
red T-shirt, dark blue sneakers. Everything had my
name already stenciled on it. They'd been expecting me.

Glover, the chief guard of D Unit, was a burly blond
guy around forty, pale as an albino, white eyelashes.
And, I was convinced, bourbon on his breath.

He said only, "Tough guy," and escorted me to the
dayroom to meet the other kids.

They stared as I entered. My age, but not my size.
Most of them were bigger, tougher-looking: kids sent
up from the boroughs of New York City, gangbangers
with gang tattoos.

I looked away, scared shitless.

First mistake, I soon learned. Inside juvie, someone
stares at you, and you fail to meet his eyes, they assume
you're weak, scared, an easy mark.

Glover took me to my room. In the hall on the way a
kid about twice my size "accidentally" bumped into me.

I said, "Hey," and stiff-armed him.

The kid smashed a fist into my face. I tasted blood,
fell over backwards, cracked my head on the floor. The
kid kicked me in the stomach.

Glover stood, watching. Other kids began to gather, laughing excitedly, cheering like spectators at a prize-fight.

The kid kicked me in the head. I tried to shield my face with my arms. Desperately looked at Glover, expecting him to stop the assault. He was smiling, his arms folded across his big gut.

I tried getting up to fight back, but the big kid kept kicking and punching until I could barely see: Blood trickled into my eyes.

"Okay, Estevez," Glover finally said. "I think that'll do it."

The other kids complained but began clearing out. Glover watched me struggle to my feet. "That's Estevez," he explained, matter-of-fact. The walls swam around me. "He's the captain of D Unit."

He led me down the hall to my room. "Welcome," he said.

The steel door clanged behind him as he left.

30

THE MANAGER, PAUL, and his son, Ryan, were the first to enter the great room. Both of them were grim-faced. Paul's face was bruised, and he was limping. The reading glasses around his neck were bent, the lenses shattered. He must have put up a struggle. His lodge: He felt protective. Behind him followed the rest of the hotel's staff—the waiters who'd served us dinner, a pudgy guy with a mustache and glasses I recognized as the handyman, the two Bulgarian girls who did the cleaning, a few others who I assumed were kitchen staff. Then Bo Lampack, a long red welt across his fore-head and right cheek.

Behind them came two men with guns. One was like a younger version of Russell, only not as tall and with a weight lifter's build. *Prison muscles,* I thought. Instead of Russell's long hair, his head was shaved. Had to be his brother. He was in his mid-twenties, with intense greenish eyes. His face was soft, almost feminine, but that delicacy was counteracted by a fierce scowl. The edges of what appeared to be an immense tattoo peeked out of the crew-neck collar of his shirt and ran a few inches up his neck.

The other, probably fifteen years older, was scrawny and mangy-looking, with dirt-colored hair that stuck up everywhere on his head. His face was pitted with pock-marks and cross-hatched with scars that were particularly dense below his left eye, which was glass. Under his good, right eye, three teardrops were tattooed. That was prison code, I knew, meaning that he'd killed three fellow inmates while he was inside. His glass eye told me he'd also lost a fight or two.

Hugo Lummis saw the two scary-looking guys. He slowly removed the watch from his pocket and placed it on the table.

Russell briefed the two of them. The young guy he called Travis; the older jailbird was Verne. Then, taking a compact satellite phone from a black nylon sling, he went out the front door.

Verne, the one-eyed man, took turns with the hunters I now knew as Wayne and Buck cutting lengths of rope, frisking and tying people up, then moving them one by one over to the wall on either side of the immense stone fireplace.

"Palms together like you're praying," Verne ordered Cheryl. He wrapped a six-foot piece of rope several times around her wrists.

She winced. "That's way too tight."

But Verne kept going. He moved with quick, jerky motions, blinked a lot. He seemed to be on speed or something.

Even before Verne got to me, I could smell him. He gave off a nasty funk of alcohol and cigarettes and bad hygiene. I gave him a blank look, neither friendly nor confrontational.

He gave an alligator smile. His teeth were grayish

brown, with tiny black flecks. Meth mouth, I realized. The guy was a tweaker, a methamphetamine addict. "Much rather be frisking that babe down the end," he said as he set to work patting me down. He didn't seem to be a professional, but he knew what he was doing.

I said nothing.

"Save the best for last," he said to Buck, and they both leered at Ali.

The steak knife I'd concealed in my shoe had become uncomfortable, even a little painful. I wondered whether there was a visible lump in the shoe leather, but I didn't dare look down and draw his attention to it.

On the one hand, I was relieved that I hadn't left the knife in my pocket, where Verne would have found it right away. But now I wished it were someplace I could get to more easily. As Verne's hands ran down my chest and back, I held my breath so I didn't heave from the smell. My eyes scanned the dining table. The closest steak knife was in front of Cheryl, just a few feet away, but as soon as I made a grab for it, Buck—standing behind me with his revolver at the ready—would kill me. He wouldn't hesitate.

And even if I managed to grab the knife and use it on him, it was still only a knife. A knife at a gunfight, as the old saying goes.

Verne felt each of my pockets and seemed satisfied that they were empty. I didn't have a choice but to let him tie me up.

Now his hands moved down my pant legs, down to my feet.

I held my breath.

All he had to do was to slip his fingers into the tops of my shoes, and he'd discover the knife handle.

And then, if Russell's threat was serious, Buck would shoot. I didn't feel like finding out if Russell meant it.

What had I been thinking?

Once my hands were tied, the knife wouldn't do me any good. It was useless to me. I'd risked my life for nothing.

Verne's hands grasped my ankles. I looked down. His fingernails were dirty.

I tensed. A few drops of sweat trickled down my neck, coursed down my back, under my shirt.

"See that guy over there?" I said.

"Huh?" He looked up at me. "Don't try anything."

"The silver-haired guy with the bloody face. He needs to be taken care of."

He sliced a long piece of rope into smaller sections, using a serious-looking tactical knife. "I look like a doctor to you?"

"You guys don't want to lose him. Then you'll be facing a manslaughter charge on top of everything else."

He shrugged.

"I know first aid," I said. "Let me take a look at him before you tie me up."

"Uh-uh."

"Your friend Buck has a gun pointed at me. I don't have a weapon, and I'm not stupid."

"Let him," Buck said. "I'll keep watch."

"Thank you," I said.

Bodine was sitting with his legs folded. His face was battered and swollen. He looked up at me, humiliated and angry, like a whipped dog. I sat down on the floor next to him. "How're you feeling?" I said.

He didn't look at me. "You don't want to know."

"Mind if I take a look?"

"Lost a couple of teeth," he said, pushing out his lower lip with his tongue. I gingerly felt his face, under his eyes. He winced. "Jesus, Landry, watch it."

"You might have a broken cheekbone," I said. "Maybe a fracture."

"Yeah? So what am I going to do about it now?" he said bitterly.

"Take some Tylenol. Or whatever pain meds we have."

"Not going to happen with these assholes," he said quietly.

"We can try. You think your nose might be broken?"

"Feels like it."

"If we can get some Kleenex or some toilet paper, you should stuff some up your nose. Just to stop the blood flow."

He didn't say anything.

"You got a headache?"

"Wicked."

"What about your vision?"

"What about it?"

"You seeing double?"

"How'd you know?"

"That means he might have fractured the—I forget what it's called, the bone around the eye. The orbit, I think. Anyway, your vision should go back to normal in a day or so. You're going to be okay, but we've got to get you medical attention."

Bodine gave me a fierce look. "Yeah? When?"

"Soon as we can. Soon as this is over."

"When's that going to be?"

He didn't expect an answer, but I was surprised he'd said it. It was a sign of how far he'd fallen, how demoralized he was. Hank Bodine was always in charge.

Buck yelled to me, "Time's up. This ain't a church social."

I said softly to Bodine, "Depends on how we play it."

Bodine nodded once.

I said, "There's blood and stuff all over your pants. Let me see if they'll get you another pair from your room. Least they can do."

Bodine had pissed himself during the attack. I could see the large wet area and smell the urine. I felt a pang of embarrassment for him, and I didn't want him to know that I knew.

He watched me as I got up.

"Hey," he said after a few seconds.

"Yeah?"

"Thanks."

31

THE WHOLE PLACE smelled of cigarette smoke: Verne was chain-smoking at the other end of the room as he frisked Ali, taking his time of it. I had a feeling he was maybe paying a bit too much attention to areas on her body where she wasn't likely to hide a weapon. Her back was to me; I couldn't see her face, but I could imagine the look of grim resolve.

The middle of the room was a chaotic jumble of furniture: tables on their sides, chairs upended on top of sofas. Russell's men had shoved the furniture away from the wall on either side of the great stone fireplace to make room for the hostages.

We sat on the wideboard floor on either side of the fireplace, in two groups. On the other side—which might as well have been miles away—were the manager, the other lodge staff, and Danziger and Grogan. All the lights were on, giving the room a harsh, artificial cast.

Verne had wound the ropes around my wrists a little too tightly, before tying the ends expertly with a couple of overhand knots. "There we go," he'd said. "Try and get out of that. Harder you pull against it, tighter it gets. Give yourself gangrene, you're not careful."

Geoffrey Latimer, next to me, tried to shift his hands to get them more comfortable. "I wonder if I'm ever going to see my wife and daughter again," he said softly. He looked ashen. His face was flushed, and he was short of breath.

Cheryl said, "This damned rope is too tight. I'm already losing circulation in my hands." She looked weary, suddenly ten years older. There was what looked like a dirty handprint on her long, pleated skirt, as if one of Russell's men had pawed her. Without her big earrings and necklace, she looked somehow vulnerable, disarmed.

"I wish I could help you," Slattery said. "But my hands are tied."

If that was his attempt at black humor, no one laughed.

I said, "You want me to call one of them over here to retie you?"

Cheryl shook her head. "The less we have to do with them, the better. I'll get used to it. Hopefully this isn't going to be too long." She paused, looked at me, spoke quietly. "How's Hank?"

Bodine lay on the hard floor, dozing. His closed eyes were bruised and bloodied, his face a patchwork of red and white: Travis, who I had become more and more certain was Russell's younger brother, had thoughtfully taped up some of the more serious wounds with strips of white adhesive tape and a variety of Band-Aids he'd found in a first-aid kit.

I doubted she actually cared, but I said, "He might have a concussion. A broken nose. Maybe a broken cheekbone, too."

"My God."

I smelled her perfume, strong and unpleasantly floral, like a funeral home.

"Could have been a lot worse."

"We have to get the word out," she said. "Somehow we have to tell the outside world what's going on."

I didn't think our captors could hear us. Russell was outside somewhere, and his brother, Travis, was patrolling the room, his gun at his side, a good distance away. The blond crew-cut lunk was upstairs grabbing loot. The other two—Buck, the vaguely sinister black-goateed one, and Verne, ex-con and speed freak, were at the far end of the room.

"How?" Kevin Bross said. "You have a sat phone you're not telling us about?"

Cheryl glared at him. "No, I don't have a satellite phone. But the manager has one. He keeps it locked in his office. I know, because I've used it." She glanced at the stone wall that made up one side of the fireplace. "Maybe one of us can sneak over there."

Bross snorted.

Upton Barlow straightened his shoulders. "Now, isn't that interesting," he said with heavy sarcasm. He'd eased one of his shoes off with the other. I could see his Odor-Eaters insole. "And I thought we were all supposed to be 'offline,' as you put it."

"One of us had to be reachable, Upton," Cheryl said icily. "I am the CEO, after all."

"Hmmph," Barlow said. One little syllable conveyed so much—ridicule, skepticism, condescension.

Cheryl turned slowly to face him. "I wouldn't get too high-and-mighty if I were you, Upton," she said. "Wasn't it you who made Russell an offer—put the whole ransom idea in his head? Brilliant."

"That idea was already in his head," Bross said. "He and his thugs broke in here to rip us off."

"Forgive me for my clumsy attempt to save your life," Barlow said, his syrupy baritone dripping with contempt. "Or maybe you've forgotten that he was pointing a gun at your face at the time? I should have let him pull the trigger."

"Cheryl," said Lummis, "he *was* about to kill you and me both."

"And wasn't it *you* who told him about our K&R insurance?" Cheryl turned to face Lummis. "In violation of our strict secrecy agreement with Lloyd's of London? Do you realize the policy becomes null and void if you reveal its existence to anyone outside the executive council?"

Lummis's plump, pink cheeks were slick with sweat. "Good God Almighty, I'd say this qualifies as a situation of extreme duress."

The fact that we had a kidnap-and-ransom insurance policy was news to me, too, but I didn't get what the big deal was about revealing its existence. So what? Would knowing about it encourage potential kidnappers to escalate their demands? Hammond Aerospace was a multibillion-dollar company with very deep pockets anyway; who cared whether some insurance company paid us back?

"Hey, folks, let's all just count to ten," said Bo Lampack. The red mark across his face had begun to fade. "I know tempers are short, but we need to work together as a team. Remember, if we all row together, we'll get there faster."

"Oh, Christ," said Kevin Bross. "Where'd this knucklehead come from?"

Lampack looked bruised. "Hostility's not productive."

"In any case," Cheryl said, "it would be grossly negligent of me as CEO to allow us to give in to this extortion. I have a responsibility to protect the corporation."

Lampack, ignored by everyone, now just watched in sullen defeat.

"You have a responsibility," Barlow said, "to protect our *lives*. The lives of the people who run this company."

"We wouldn't be in this position if it weren't for your negligence," Bross said to Cheryl.

"What the hell is that supposed to mean?" Cheryl snapped.

"You know exactly what I mean," Bross said.

I caught Ron Slattery giving Bross a quick, furtive look. Annoyed, maybe, or warning: It was hard to tell. I wondered what it meant.

Then Slattery said, in a reasonable voice, "Cheryl, you know, we lost a whole lot more than that last quarter on the telecom satellite we're building for Malaysia, right? If we have to take a hundred-million-dollar charge for an extortion demand, or ransom, or whatever we call it—"

"Which I'm sure is covered by our K&R insurance anyway," Lummis put in.

Cheryl was shaking her head. "This is not how it works, Ron. You should know as well as anyone here. In Latin America, when the *secuestradores* kidnap an American executive, they never get more than thirty percent of their initial ransom demand. It's expected. If you pay them any more, they'll think they didn't ask enough."

"Well, Danziger handles all the special risk coverage for me," Slattery said. "I don't really get into the weeds."

"The point is, this guy's demanding a hundred million dollars—now," she said. "But the moment we go along with him—the moment we agree to wire out a hundred million dollars—he's going to think, Well, why stop now? If a hundred million was that easy, why not a *billion*? Why not *four billion*? Why not demand every last goddamned dollar we have in our cash reserves? And *then* what do we do?"

I nodded; she was right.

"We don't know that, Cheryl," Slattery said. His glasses were smudged, the frames slightly askew. "He's not necessarily going to escalate his demands. I don't think we have any alternative but to give him the hundred million and take him at his word."

She shook her head. "No, Ron, I'm sorry, but one of us has to say no, and that's got to be me. We're going to hang tough. Refuse to give in to his demands."

A panicked expression flashed across Slattery's face, then disappeared. But he said nothing. You could see his loyalty warring with his survival instinct. Russell had promised that he'd be the first to be killed if we didn't cooperate. Yet he was Cheryl's man, the only one here who owed his job directly to her. Her only ally on the executive council. Except for maybe Geoff Latimer; but Latimer seemed to be the sort who was quite careful not to take sides.

"She's going to get us all killed," Bross said, shaking his head.

"How easy it must be for you to issue orders," said Upton Barlow. "After all, you're not the one he's going to shoot first if we don't cooperate." His eyes shifted from Cheryl to Slattery. He'd sensed Slattery's panic the way a dog smells fear. He'd seen daylight between Cheryl and her toady, and he was determined to widen the crack.

"Oh, come on," Cheryl said. "These buffoons aren't actually going to kill anyone. They're trying to scare the hell out of us, and I can see it's working like a charm on you men. But Russell's not going to carry out his threats."

"Oh really?" Bross said. "And what makes you so sure of that?"

"Human nature," she replied brusquely. "I can read people. They may be thugs, but they're not murderers."

"Oh, Jesus Christ," Bross snapped. "These are a bunch of trigger-happy outlaws with guns. You are so out of your league here, Cheryl."

I agreed with Bross, but I wasn't going to say so. I didn't particularly like the woman, but I sure wasn't going to join the other piranhas circling her because they smelled her blood in the water.

"They're hunters who got lost," Cheryl said. "They're tired and hungry and all of a sudden they see this lodge, and they get the big idea to try a holdup. See if they can pull it off. If it wasn't us, it could have been a convenience store. These men aren't actually going to do anything so stupid as to kill one of us."

"They look mighty serious to me," Lummis said.

"There's a bright line between trying to bully a bunch of unarmed businessmen and cold-blooded murder," she said. "And they're not going to cross that line. They're hunters, not hired killers."

I couldn't hold back any longer. "I don't think they're hunters," I said softly.

"Why don't we find out what your CFO has to say

about this?" Barlow said with a malevolent smile. "You feel like staking your life on Cheryl's ability to read people, Ron? You're the one who gets his brains blown out first."

Slattery looked at Barlow, that panicked look returning, but he didn't reply.

Bo Lampack was trying to get everyone's attention, so we stopped and looked at him.

"If I may say something?" Lampack said. There was silence, so he went on. "Let's face it—a gun is really a phallus. Men like these who insist on waving guns around are really just waving their dicks around. They're compensating for their inadequacies. To challenge them outright is to emasculate them, which could provoke a really hostile and defensive reaction—"

"Will someone tell Russell to get in here and shoot this guy?" said Bross.

Lampack looked around for support, and when no one came to his defense, he sat back, looking deflated.

"They're not hunters," I tried again, a little louder.

Finally, Cheryl looked at me. "What makes you so sure of that, Jake?"

"For one thing, they're not equipped like hunters."

"And you know this how?"

"Because I hunt. I shoot."

"You shoot?" Bross said. "What, paintballs?"

"You want to hear me out or not?"

"Not especially."

"Let the kid talk," Barlow said wearily. "I've got to get to the john before my bladder bursts."

"Start with their outfits," I said. "The camouflage."

"Plenty of hunters wear camo," Lummis pointed out.

I nodded. "But they're not wearing the kind of camouflage you get at a hunting store," I said. "It's old military-issue." The pattern was the old six-color chocolate-chip camouflage, which the army had discontinued around the time of the first Gulf War. "They're also wearing genuine military tactical vests, with gear clips and mag pouches. Those sure aren't regular hunting vests." Hunting vests were normally made out of smooth acrylic so you didn't get snagged on brush or whatever.

"Well, so maybe they picked up their outfits at some Army-Navy surplus store somewhere," Cheryl said.

"That's possible," I said. "Sure. But they're carrying banana clips on their vests. I've never heard of a legit hunter carrying a banana clip. And that gun that Russell was waving around was a Glock 18C."

"Yeah," Bross said with heavy sarcasm. "We were all impressed by your knowledge of firearms."

"Excellent," I said. "That was my whole point—to impress you, Kevin. Then again, maybe I was trying to figure out how much he knew about it. Maybe even where he might have gotten it." I said to the others: "See, the Glock 18 is banned for sale to anyone who's not in law enforcement or the military."

"What—what are you saying, they're soldiers?" Slattery said. "Ex-soldiers?"

"Were you in the Army?" Barlow asked.

"The National Guard Reserve for a year. But my dad was a Marine," I said.

"Maybe they're one of those homegrown militias," said Slattery. "You know, those crazy survivalist gangs that turn up in places like Michigan and Kentucky?"

"*Jesus,* I've got to take a leak," said Barlow.

"A couple of them also look like they've done time in prison," I said.

"I wonder if they're fugitives of some sort," Geoff Latimer said. "Who maybe pulled off a bank robbery, and they're on the run. Remember that old Humphrey Bogart movie called *The Desperate Hours*? These escaped convicts are looking for a place to hide, and they break into this suburban house and they hold the family hostage—"

"What difference does it make who they are?" Cheryl said. "Their threats are hollow."

"You're partly right," I said. She gave me a wary look. "It doesn't really make a difference who they are or where they're from. But their weapons tell me two things. One is that Russell knows what he's doing. He's no amateur."

"More speculation," Cheryl said.

"And what's the other thing?" Slattery asked.

"That these guys aren't here by accident," I said.

32

A LONG TIME ago I'd learned that you can pretty much get used to anything.

There was no privacy at Glenview, even at night, in your own room: a surveillance camera mounted near the ceiling, its red eye winking in the dark. No doors on the toilet stalls. But you got used to it.

You learned to create your own zone of privacy, hide your emotions behind a mask of stoicism. To show emotion was to show weakness, and weakness got you hurt.

You can get used to pretty much anything if you have to. The food was inedible—rubbery fake scrambled eggs, bright artificial yellow, sometimes with a coarse human hair coiled around one of the curds; unsalted boiled potatoes with dirt-crusted peel mixed in; slices of stale white bread; rancid bologna, slick and green-tinged—until the hunger pains grew too strong.

If you needed to piss at night, you had to knock on your door until a guard came. Sometimes he'd come, sometimes not. You learned to pee into a towel in the corner of the room.

You learned to fight when challenged. Which happened over and over until your place in the hierarchy was established, until the other kids learned to leave you alone.

But you also learned to respect the natural order.

In the chow hall one day, Estevez "accidentally" bumped into me. I ignored him, kept moving. A mistake: Estevez took it as a sign of fear. But I was hungry, and they only gave you twenty minutes for lunch, which included waiting in line and bussing your tray.

He bumped me again. My orange plastic tray went flying, spilling brown gravy and gristle and peas everywhere.

This time I didn't wait. I drew back and slugged him in the mouth so hard that he actually rose a few inches off the floor. My fist throbbed in pain: A tooth was lodged between two knuckles.

Estevez crashed against one of the stainless-steel tables, spitting teeth. I saw my opportunity, went after him again, and then my lower back exploded in pain.

Someone had hit me from behind. I sunk to my knees, gasping.

Glover was swinging his baton. "Go back to the dayroom and wait for me," he said.

I sat on the bench in the deserted dayroom and waited.

When Glover arrived, ten minutes later, he approached me slowly, as if he were about to confide something. Instead, he grabbed my hair, gave me a hard backhand slap on one side of my face, then the other. Rhythmic, almost: *one two.*

"Hey!" I yelled.

"How's that?"

He kept at it, one side, then the other. *One two.* "How's that? How's that feel?"

"I didn't start it," I croaked.

"I want to hear you cry, bastard," he said.

His fist crashed into one side of my face, then the other. *One two*. Blood seeped into my eyes, from my nose.

"Cry, bastard," he said.

But I wouldn't.

One two. One two.

I knew what he wanted, even more than he wanted me to cry. He wanted me to hit him back. That would get me confined to solitary for three months. But I refused to give him the satisfaction.

"I'm not stopping till you cry, you bastard."

I never did.

33

"WHAT DO YOU mean?" Slattery said. "You think they planned—"

But then we fell silent as Verne brought Ali over. He held a gun on her: a stubby little stainless-steel Smith & Wesson with a two-inch barrel. She sat, looking angry and remote.

"I enjoyed that, sugar tits," Verne said with a manic leer. "Let's do that again soon without our clothes, huh?"

Ali gave him a glacial stare. Under her breath, she said, "I'm not really into short-barreled weapons."

He heard it, though, and he hooted. "Whoa, that chick's got a *mouth* on her! We'll see what you can do with that mouth later."

"Yeah," Ali replied. "I've also got sharp teeth."

He hooted again.

"Hey, Verne," I said.

He turned, eyes wild.

"You touch a hair on her head, and I'll take out your good eye."

"With what?" He smirked. "You can't even take a piss unless I say so."

"Hey," Barlow called out. "Speaking of which, I need to take a leak. Badly."

"So?"

"What the hell am I supposed to do?"

"Wet yourself for all I care," Verne said with a cackle.

"I'm serious," Barlow said.

"So'm I," Verne said.

Barlow gritted his teeth. "This is *torture*. I'm not going to make it."

I gave Ali a questioning look: *Are you okay?*

She smiled cryptically, maybe thanking me, maybe chiding me. She seemed more angry than frightened, which wasn't surprising. That was Ali: She was a fighter, not easily intimidated. Maybe that was the legacy of her Army-brat upbringing. I'm sure it was also something Cheryl had recognized in her immediately, a trait the two women shared.

"Excuse me," Latimer called out. He looked haggard. "I need my . . . insulin."

"Your what?" Verne said.

"There's a kit upstairs in my room. In my dresser. With syringes and a blood test kit and some vials of insulin. Please. Just let me go up and get it."

"You're not bringing a bunch of needles in here. Sorry, guy. Deal with it."

"But if I—please, if I don't get my insulin, I could go into a coma. Or worse."

"Hate to lose a hostage," Verne said, swiveling away.

"At least could I get something to drink, please? I'm dehydrated."

Verne was out of earshot.

"I didn't know you were diabetic, Geoff," Cheryl said. "How serious is this?"

"Hard to say. I mean, it's serious, but I don't have any symptoms yet. Just really thirsty."

"You're late with a shot?"

He nodded. "I usually give myself an injection before I go to bed."

"Did you mean it about going into a coma?"

"If too much time goes by, it can happen. Though I think I'll make it for a couple more hours. If I drink a lot of water."

"*Damn* them," Cheryl said. She turned around and yelled, "Someone get this man a glass of water *now*! And his *insulin*!" Her voice echoed.

Hank Bodine stirred, his eyes fluttering open. He looked around groggily, groaned, then shut his eyes again.

Travis came over, gun leveled. "What's the problem?" he said, scowling.

"Get this man some water," she said. "He's a diabetic, and he needs water immediately. He also needs his insulin shot."

"And I need to use the restroom," Barlow added.

Travis looked at her, at Latimer, and said nothing.

"And will you get Mr. Bodine a pillow, please?" she said. She pointed toward the jumble of displaced furniture. "A sofa pillow, at least."

"That's up to Russell," Travis said. "I'll see." Looking uncomfortable, he turned, crossed the room toward the dining area, and began speaking to the crew-cut guy, Wayne.

"Thank you," Latimer said. "Even if they won't get my insulin, the water should help."

"Will you please not mention water?" said Barlow.

"I still haven't heard why Landry thinks this whole thing was planned," Slattery said.

"Who cares what he thinks?" said Bross. "He's not even supposed to be here."

"Let's hear him out," Cheryl said.

"They're wearing the wrong brand of hunting vest," Bross went on. "A big fashion 'don't' in your world, that it?"

I refused to let him get to me. "They came in here knowing exactly where to go and what to do. They weren't stumbling around. These guys know too much. They knew where everything was the second they arrived—the kitchen, the front door, the upstairs. They knew which exits to cover. As if they'd scoped the place out in advance. It just feels too well planned to be a coincidence—too well *coordinated*."

"Right," Bross said, heavy on the irony. "This whole thing was planned. Get real. They didn't crash in here demanding a hundred million bucks, did they? That was only *after* Russell discovered who we are. At first they only wanted our *wallets,* for Christ's sake."

"And our watches," I said. "Don't forget the watches, Kevin. Even the 'replicas.'"

Bross glared.

"I think they were trying to make it *look* like a random, unplanned break-in," I said. "Which, in itself, is interesting."

"Why?" said Cheryl.

"I don't know," I admitted. "But I'll figure it out."

"I think Jake may be right," Ali said. "Look at who comes here—mostly rich people and corporate groups. Who else can afford it? All these rich folks out here in total isolation. Sitting ducks. If you're a bad guy looking to make some quick money, you can't do better than this."

"Russell knows too much about Hammond," I said. "All that stuff about our cash reserves—I doubt he figured that out tonight, on the spot, by looking at a balance sheet. He already knew it ahead of time."

"It's all out there on the public record," said Barlow.

"Sure. But that means he did research on Hammond before coming here. Right?"

For a few seconds, everyone was silent.

Then Slattery said: "But how'd he know in advance that *we'd* be here?"

"You guys come here every year around the same time," I said. "It's no secret."

"Then they must have had a source," Latimer said. "One of the lodge staff, maybe."

"Or they've been here before," I said.

"Excuse me," Bross said. "I don't even know why anyone's listening to you. Did anyone ask you for your opinion? You're not even a member of the executive council, or have you forgotten that? You're a substitute. You're nothing more than a ringer."

Amazing: Here we were, held hostage at gunpoint, and all Kevin Bross wanted to do was one-up me. With Hank Bodine at least temporarily incapacitated, he probably considered himself the reigning Alpha Male. And I was a threat.

"I got news for you, Kevin," I said. "There's no more executive council. Not anymore. Not now. Your life is no more important than mine or anyone else's. Neither is your opinion. We're all just hostages now."

I heard a groan, then a familiar rumbling voice. "Well put, Landry," Hank Bodine said. "When the hell's that pillow getting here?"

34

BODINE'S SILVER HAIR was mussed, clumps of it standing on end. His eyes had all but disappeared into the swollen mass of his cheeks. White strips of adhesive tape crisscrossed his face.

"There he is," Bross said. "How're you doing?"

"What do you think?" Bodine tried to sit up. "What's this, they tied me up, too? The hell they think I'm gonna do?"

Bodine's mere conscious presence had reordered the group like a magnet waved over iron filings. You could tell it rankled Cheryl. She needed to take charge. "The issue isn't who they are or how they got here," she said. "The issue is how we're going to deal with it. That's the only thing that counts at this point."

"Tell me something," Lummis said. "Do we even have the ability to do this—to make a funds transfer from here—if we wanted to?"

No one replied for a few seconds, then Ali said: "I'm sure he knows about the Internet connection in the manager's office."

"That's not what I mean. Can it be done from here? Can we really transfer a hundred million dollars out of the corporate treasury to some offshore account, just using the manager's laptop?"

More silence. Cheryl looked at Slattery: She didn't seem to know the answer either. I assumed that the only ones who really knew how the system worked were Slattery, Danziger, and Grogan—but Danziger and Grogan were on the other side of the fireplace, out of range.

"I could transfer funds out of one of our accounts from a laptop at Starbucks," Slattery said wearily, taking off his glasses and running a hand over his forehead. He closed his eyes and pushed against them with a thumb and forefinger, as if trying to massage a headache away.

"You're kidding," Lummis said.

"No, unfortunately, I'm not," said Slattery.

"Hold on a second," Kevin Bross said. "Are you telling me that any lunatic could just put a gun to your head and empty the company's treasury? We don't have any security procedures in place? I don't believe it."

There was something about Bross's tone—he sounded incredulous, but in an exaggerated way—that made me suspicious. Then there was the look of irritation that Slattery gave him in response. Bross, I realized, already knew the answer. He gave a quick, furtive glance at Bodine, seemed to be performing for him. Bodine's eyes were open, but the lids were drooping.

"It's more complicated than that," Slattery said.

"Yes or no?" Bross demanded. "Do we or don't we have at least some kind of security measures?"

"Ron," said Cheryl, "you don't need to get into this. It's beside the point."

"Well, I want to hear it," said Bross. "It's very *much* the point."

"Don't even dignify that, Ron," Cheryl said.

"The fact is," Slattery said, "the bank's computers don't know if they're talking to a computer inside Hammond headquarters in L.A. or at a laptop in a Starbucks or some old Macintosh in a fishing lodge in British Columbia."

"How is that possible?" said Bross.

"Well, it's—anytime you log on to our system from outside the headquarters building, you're creating a virtual tunnel into what's called the VPN—the Hammond virtual private network. All the bank computers see is a Hammond IP address. An outbound gateway. For all the bank knows, it's getting a message from my office on the thirty-third floor on Wilshire Boulevard."

"Can we move on, please?" said Cheryl. "This is irrelevant."

"Even when we're talking about a hundred million dollars?" Barlow said.

"Doesn't make a difference how much," said Slattery. "It's just a little more elaborate."

"Ron," Cheryl said, "*enough.*"

But Slattery kept going. "For large, sensitive transactions the bank requires two authorized users to make the request. Then on top of that, there's dual-factor authentication."

"Which is?" Barlow said.

"Forget it," said Cheryl. "We're not making any transfer."

"Sounds to me," Hank Bodine suddenly said, "like you're trying to shut him up. I want to hear this."

Cheryl just shook her head, furious. She did seem to want to keep Slattery from talking.

"You enter a user name and password as usual,"

Slattery said, "but you also have to use a secure ID token. Which generates random, one-time passwords—six-digit numbers—every sixty seconds. You take the number off the token and enter it on the website."

"So, if we don't have one of those doohickeys with us, we can't do the transfer," Barlow said. "Simple as that. I'm sure you don't carry one around with you, right?"

"It's on my key ring, upstairs in my room," Slattery said. "But Russell's probably got it by now."

"These fellas aren't going to know what it is," Barlow said.

Slattery shrugged. "If they know what they're doing, they will. The bank logo's printed right on there."

"Anyone else have a token like that?" asked Barlow. "*I* don't."

"Just the ones who have signing authority."

"Signing authority," Barlow repeated.

"The ability to authorize a financial transaction greater than, I think, fifty million dollars. Authorized users."

Cheryl turned slowly to Ron Slattery. "I don't believe I have such a token," she said.

"That's because you don't need to dirty your hands with all that financial . . . plumbing work. It's just for the guys like me who have to, you know, roll up our sleeves and do the operational stuff."

"Such as?"

He hesitated. "You know, the corporate officers who're involved directly with the finances."

" 'Authorized users,' as you put it."

"Basically, yes. Officers who have signing authority at that level." Slattery was starting to sound evasive.

But Cheryl was unrelenting. "Such as? Who has the signing authority at that level? Besides me, I mean."

Slattery gave a tiny shake of his head, as if silently cuing her to stop asking.

"What are you telling me?" she said.

"I mean—well, actually, you don't."

"I don't what?" Cheryl said.

"Don't have signing authority," Slattery said. "Not at that level. Not for a one-off cash transaction of that magnitude, anyway."

Cheryl's cheeks immediately flushed. She pursed her lips. "I see. Then who does?"

"I do, of course," Slattery said. "And the Treasurer. The General Counsel, and the Controller. Latimer, Grogan, and Danziger."

"And Hank, I assume."

He nodded.

"Anyone else?"

"No."

"I see," Cheryl said.

"Did I just hear what I thought I heard?" Bross said, his mouth gaping. "You actually don't even *have* the power to stop us from wiring out the funds, do you? Since you don't have the power to authorize it."

Cheryl looked at him for several seconds, her nostrils flaring. "Perhaps not. But I'm the CEO of this company, Bross. And if I hear any more of your insubordination, you're going to be cleaning out your office."

"If any of us survive," Barlow said.

"We're not wiring a hundred million dollars to these criminals," Cheryl said. "It's as simple as that. Whether or not I have the technical authority to sign off on a payment of that size, the fact remains: *I will not allow it.*"

"Cheryl, please," said Slattery. "We all know what he's going to do if we refuse. *Please.*"

"Once we give in to this extortion, it'll never stop," she said. "I'm sorry."

"You know," Barlow said, "I don't think you have the power to stop us. Am I right, Ron?"

Slattery glanced anxiously from Cheryl to Barlow, then back again.

Cheryl examined the rope around her wrists. "Ron," she said in a warning tone, without looking up.

"Cheryl," Slattery said. "I—" Then he met Barlow's hard gaze, his raisin eyes. "Yes," he said. "Basically that's right."

Still studying the rope, Cheryl said softly, "I expect more than that from you, Ron. I expect your complete support."

Slattery turned to her, but she didn't look up. "I'm—I'm sorry, Cheryl. Forgive me. But this is just—this happens to be the one case where we disagree. We really have no choice but to give the guy the money he wants. But—"

"That's enough, Ron," Cheryl said, cutting him off. You could almost see the icicles hanging down from her words. "You've made yourself clear."

I saw the tears in Ali's eyes and felt the bad wolf start to stir.

35

"CORRECT ME IF I'm wrong, Cheryl," Kevin Bross said, "but aren't you the *reason* we don't have a choice?"

Cheryl gave Bross a quick, cutting glance, then looked away. "I think we're done with this discussion," she said.

"We've just begun," Bross said. "Tell them, Ron. Tell them about the security measures you were pushing for. Which Cheryl turned down."

Slattery's sallow complexion immediately colored, but he said nothing.

"Oh, really," Cheryl said.

"Ron?" Bross prompted.

Slattery blinked rapidly, remained silent.

"Go ahead, Slattery," Hank Bodine said. "Let's hear it."

Slattery looked first at Bodine, then at Cheryl, and he said, "It's just that—I had my team draw up a plan to implement much stronger security on the company's website. I was concerned about, you know, hackers from Lithuania or Ukraine being able to get in and do all kinds of damage. Or steal code and blackmail us. This kind of thing happens to U.S. companies all the time now."

"Are we seriously going to rehash all of this now?" Cheryl said. "This is neither the time nor the place—"

"I think this is the perfect time and place," Bodine said, cutting her off.

"I wanted us to install a multilayered access platform," Slattery said. "Change the whole access infrastructure so we had the ability to turn off most functions for anyone who accesses the Hammond system remotely. Especially treasury functions."

"Plain English, please," Bodine said. "You're losing us."

"As I told you then," Cheryl said, "we have executives all around the world who need constant access to our entire system."

"They still could have had access, Cheryl. I wanted the ability to block the finance portals to outside access. All treasury information, all code repositories. No movement of money off campus."

"This is past history," Cheryl said. "We went back and forth on your proposal, and in the end I decided it was too complicated and too cumbersome to implement. And too expensive."

"So you killed Ron's plan in order to save money," Bross said. "And now look at how much money we're about to lose because of you."

Cheryl gave Bross a poisonous look. "Not because of me," she said. "I want to be on the record here—I'm absolutely opposed to giving in to this extortion."

"If it weren't for you," Bross said, "we wouldn't even be *able* to give in to the extortion. This whole nightmare didn't have to happen."

Cheryl looked down, shook her head. She looked as

if she was doing everything she could to restrain herself from lashing out.

"Does the board of directors know about this?" Barlow said.

Slattery was silent.

"They will," Bross said. "They're going to hear about how your mismanagement not only cost the company a hundred million dollars but put the lives of every single top executive at risk. I'd call this an egregious breach of fiduciary duty. Hank?"

"As soon as this is over," Bodine said, "they're going to hear all about it. And then it's not Kevin Bross who'll be cleaning out his office. It's gonna be a no-brainer."

36

"HANK," I SAID, "how about we spare the office politics and concentrate on trying to get out of here alive?"

Cheryl ran a fingernail back and forth in the gap between two floor planks. Ali tried to hide a smile. A couple of the others sneaked glances at me—admiring glances, I thought: No one ever expected me to talk back to Hank Bodine.

I didn't know how he'd react, and at that point I didn't particularly care. But after a few seconds he said, "We don't have a choice but to pay the goddamned ransom."

"I'm not sure that's true," I said. "Cheryl's right: If we give in too easily to Russell's demands, there'll be no reason for him not to keep jacking the price up. If I were in his position, I'd probably do the same thing."

She glanced up at me warily. Her long coral fingernail had dislodged a tiny gray burrow of dust and earth.

What I didn't say, of course, was that I didn't really care how much money Hammond Aerospace paid out in ransom.

"Yet we can't just say no. Because whoever these guys are, you don't carry weapons like that if you're not prepared to use them."

Cheryl arched a quizzical eyebrow. "So what are you suggesting?"

I turned to Slattery. "What's the account number?"

"Which account number?" Slattery said.

"If you want to access our cash management accounts at the bank, you've got to know the account numbers, right? Or at least one of them. You have them all memorized?"

Slattery looked at me as if I'd lost my mind. "Of course not. I keep a list in my office . . ." His voice trailed off as it dawned on him. "But not here. Yes." He nodded.

"There you go. You need to call in to the office to get those numbers. Right?"

"Excellent," Cheryl said.

"You think he'll let me make a call?" Slattery asked.

"If he wants his money, he will."

"What good does that do us?" Bross said. "That buys us maybe five minutes. That's pathetic."

"It gets him on the phone with one of his assistants or his secretary, Kevin. And then maybe Ron can communicate that everything's not okay here."

"Oh, sure," Bross said. "Right. Russell's going to just stand there while Ron asks his secretary for our bank account numbers, and says, 'Oh, by the way, I've got a gun to my head, so you might want to notify the police.'"

"There's something called a duress code," I said to Bross. I kept my tone calm and reasonable—but condescending, as if explaining to a particularly slow child. "A distress signal. A word or phrase that sounds perfectly normal to Russell but actually alerts whoever he's speaking to that something's wrong. It's like a silent alarm."

"You got a better idea, Bross?" Bodine said.

"Yeah," Bross said. "Keep it simple. These are hicks with guns. All we do is tell him we can't wire money from any computer outside of Hammond headquarters. The way it should be. The way it was *supposed* to be."

"No," I said. "You don't want to bluff him like that. If he's done his homework, he'll know that's not true."

"Most of *us* didn't know if we could or not," Barlow said. "Why should he know any better?"

"And what if he has a source inside the company?" I said. "We sure as hell don't want to get caught lying to him. Do we, Ron?"

Slattery didn't reply. He didn't have to.

"Let's not find out the hard way what he knows and what he doesn't," I said.

"Then we just pay it," Bross said.

"And after we pay the ransom," I said quietly, "what makes you think these guys are going to just let us go?"

Bross started to reply, but stopped.

"They're not wearing masks or hoods," I said. "For all I know, they're using their real names. They're not concerned about being identified. Why do you think that might be?"

"Oh, Jesus," said Barlow, realizing.

"There's only one possible reason," I said. "They don't plan to leave any witnesses."

Cheryl's fingernail came to a stop. Lummis exhaled audibly, tremulously.

"I don't have any duress code worked out with my office," Slattery said.

"Just say something unexpected," I said. "Something *off*. Something that might alert someone who knows you well enough that you're in trouble."

"But what about Grogan and Danziger?" Slattery turned to me. "For all I know, one or both of those guys has our account numbers memorized. They might think they're being helpful and volunteer the information to Russell, then there's no phone call."

I nodded. "We have to get to them, that's all. Make sure they know the plan."

Grogan and Danziger were sitting on the other side of the river-stone fireplace, twenty or thirty feet away. The fireplace jutted out a good six feet. They were so far away that we couldn't even see them.

The only way to speak to them was actually to get up and move around the fireplace to the other side. But the moment one of our kidnappers saw anyone attempting that . . .

"This is idiotic," Bross said. "All this 'duress code' crap. It'll never work."

"If you have another idea," Slattery said, "let's hear it."

Then the front door banged, and Russell entered.

37

A FEW MONTHS after I got to Glenview, a new boy
was admitted to D Unit. He was a scrawny little kid
named Raymond Farrentino, in for dealing drugs. He
was fifteen but looked twelve, and his voice hadn't even
changed yet. He looked like a girl: long eyelashes, a
delicate nose. He spoke with a stammer. His laugh
sounded like a cartoon woodpecker.

Someone gave him the nickname Pee Wee.

I became his protector, for no reason except that he
had no one else, and I felt bad for him. He was easy
prey. He couldn't fight. I knew how that used to feel.

But Pee Wee returned the favor many times over. He
was smart and clever, and he quickly had the place
wired. He figured out how to defeat the electronic door
locks on the cells so we could get out at night. He studied the guards' schedules and knew when the halls of D
Unit were unwatched, when they went out for a smoke.
He devised a method to get drugs inside: He convinced
one of the kids to get his brother to stash drugs inside
tennis balls and toss them over the fence into the
wooded area near the carpentry shop, where they
could be retrieved easily. If you wanted to get or hide

contraband, like cigarettes or booze, you'd turn to Pee Wee for advice.

It took him a few months, but he found his place in the hierarchy. He became respected for his expertise. He began to smile from time to time. Even, once in a while, to laugh.

One day, though, he started acting different. He became subdued, withdrawn. I couldn't figure it out. I began to notice long, deep slashes on his face, which he refused to explain. After a while, his face became seamed, crisscrossed with angry red scars.

Finally I confronted him, demanded to know who was doing this to him. I told him I'd take care of whoever it was.

He showed me his bloodstained undershorts, told me that Glover, the chief guard on D Unit, was coming into his room at night. He'd switch off the surveillance camera and do things to him that he couldn't talk about.

He said he was thinking seriously of killing himself, and he knew how to do it. Then he showed me the loose steel coil he'd removed from his mattress and sharpened on the concrete floor of his room. He admitted that he was slashing his own face.

He didn't want to look pretty anymore.

38

"WHO'S BEEN SMOKING?" Russell said.

He sniffed the air, turned toward the dining table. "Verne, that you?"

"What about it?" Verne said.

"I don't want to be breathing secondhand smoke. You take it outside next time."

"Sorry, Russell. Okay if I go out for a smoke right now?"

I had a feeling he was going to do more than smoke a cigarette.

"Make it fast," Russell said. He clapped his hands. "All right, let's get down to business. Where's my little buddy Ronald?"

He crossed the room to our side of the fireplace. "How're you doing there, little guy?"

Slattery nodded sullenly. "Fine."

Upton Barlow said, "I need to use the bathroom."

Russell ignored him. "You have a family, Ronald?"

Slattery hesitated.

"Three daughters, right?"

Slattery looked up suddenly. "What are you—?"

"Divorced, that right?"

"We're—separated. How do you—?"

"You cheat on your wife, Ronald? Is that what happened?"

"We're separated, I said. Not divorced."

"You cheat on her?"

"I don't have to answer this."

Russell patted his holster. "No, you don't," he said. "You always have a choice."

"No," Slattery said. "I'll—I'll answer. I didn't start seeing anyone until after our marriage pretty much—"

"Ronald," he interrupted, shaking his head and making a tsk-tsk sound. "If a man can't live up to his marital vows, why should anyone trust his word? You love your daughters, Ronald?"

"More than anything in the world," Slattery said. His voice shook, tears flooding his eyes.

"How old are they, your daughters?"

"Sixteen, fourteen, and twelve."

"Aw, that's nice. That's sweet. But girls can be difficult at that age, am I right?"

"Please," Slattery said. "Please don't do this."

"Am I right?"

"I love them with all my heart. Russell, *please.*"

"No doubt you do. But they don't live with you, do they? You're probably too busy to have a houseful of teenage girls."

"No, that's not why. My wife and I agreed the girls should live with their mother."

"So Daddy's free to screw chicks in his bachelor pad, huh?"

"That's not it at all—"

"I'll bet their dad's an important figure in their lives anyway."

"Very," Slattery managed to choke out.

"Gotta be tough on the girls not to have a dad around the house. Especially at such an important time."

"For God's sake," Barlow broke in, "will you let me go to the john?"

"They spend every weekend with me," Slattery said, "and every—"

"That the best you can do, Ron? Weekends? But I guess it's better than nothing, right? Better to have a weekend dad than no dad at all."

"Please," Slattery said, "what do you want?"

"I'm counting on you, Ronald. To make sure everything goes smoothly."

Slattery nodded frantically.

"I need to take a goddamned *piss*!" Barlow shouted abruptly. "I'm about to *explode*. You want me to do it right here on the floor?"

"Upton, please. I'm speaking with Ronald."

"This is cruel and inhumane," Barlow said.

Russell smiled. "No, Upton," he said patiently. "If you want to see cruel and inhumane, I'd be happy to demonstrate the difference." He raised his arm, flipped his fingers. "Buck, please escort poor Mr. Barlow to the head."

Buck sauntered over at a leisurely pace.

"You doing okay, there, Hank?"

Bodine stared at him and didn't reply.

Russell grinned. "Upton, sounds to me like you've got an enlarged prostate gland. Guy your age ought to be taking saw palmetto extracts. Pumpkin seeds, too. It's the only body you got. You really should take care of it."

"For Christ's sake," Barlow said.

Buck grabbed Barlow roughly by the arm.

Cheryl said, "I'd like to use the restroom as well. I'm sure others do, too."

"Thank you for the suggestion, Cheryl," said Russell. "Anyone else needs to use the facilities, my team will be happy to assist you, one at a time. Now, Ronald, have we figured out how we're going to make this transaction work? Everything clear?"

Slattery swallowed hard, nodded.

"Look," Bross said, "let me tell you something that everyone else is afraid to tell you. We simply don't have the ability to make a bank transfer from here."

"No?" Russell said.

Bross nodded. "No. Online bank transfer requests can only originate from computers inside Hammond headquarters."

Russell looked at him curiously for a moment, tipped his head to one side. "Tell me your name again."

"Kevin Bross."

"Bross," repeated Russell. "Bross balls, huh? Well, Bross Balls, maybe you can explain that to me a little more." He was speaking in that fake-innocent way I'd begun to recognize. I waited for the sting in the tail. "Use small words, please."

"See, every computer has what's called an IP address," Bross said. "And the bank's computers won't talk to another computer unless it has the right IP address."

"Really?" Russell said. "Gosh, that's bad news."

Bross nodded. "I'm sorry to break it to you, but that's just the way it works. Believe me, if we could do it, we would. So if there's some other arrangement we can make—"

"This is interesting," Russell said. He reached into his pocket, and we all froze.

He pulled out a small gray plastic object a few inches long and held it up. At its round end was the bright green logo of our bank; at the narrow end was a digital LCD readout.

"Because when I called your bank about setting up a corporate account, they said I could initiate a wire transfer from anywhere in the world, no problem. Any of your corporate customers can do that, they said. Just a wild guess, Bross Balls, but I'm thinking this here might be an RSA SecurID Authenticator."

Bross licked his lips. "Right, but Hammond Aerospace has a whole system of security protocols in place, Russell—"

"I thought you were just telling me how the bank's computers won't recognize an unauthorized IP address, Bross," Russell said softly. "We weren't talking about your internal security procedures, were we?"

Bross faltered for a few seconds. "I'm telling you everything I know, to the very best of my knowledge—"

"You know something, Bross? I'm disappointed in you. But I guess I should have expected you'd try to pull a fast one. Executive Vice President of Sales and all— you probably think you're good at the sell. So now we're gonna have a change in plans. I'm going to have a little talk with each one of you separately. One on one. You're each gonna tell me *privately* everything you know about how to transfer money out of Hammond. That way I'll know if anyone's trying to pull a fast one on me. See if there's any contradictions. Anyone lies to me, we're gonna have some immediate layoffs. A little downsizing, you might say. Oh, and one more thing. The price just went up. Teach you kids a lesson. It's five hundred million now. Half a billion."

I turned to look at Ali, but all at once the lights went out, and we were plunged into darkness.

39

A SHAFT OF sunlight neatly bisected the office of the Assistant Clinical Director of the Glenview Residential Center, Dr. Jerome Marcus. Dust motes hung suspended in the air. The room was surprisingly small, not much larger than a broom closet, choked with stacks of paper. Something in Dr. Marcus's face hinted at a secret resentment that a man so important would occupy an office so small. The corners of his small oak desk—*a child's desk,* I thought—were splintered.

"This is highly unusual," he said. He had a gentle voice, a kindly expression. "It's not the standard grievance procedure."

I nodded, swallowed, told him about Pee Wee Farrentino.

Dr. Marcus was a tall, round-shouldered man with a large, prominent forehead, neatly parted gray hair, rimless glasses that sometimes seemed to disappear. His blue button-down shirt was heavily starched and perfectly pressed.

He listened with growing dismay, fingers steepled. He asked me a lot of questions, took notes for a report.

He said it was an outrage, that behavior like that must never be tolerated.

As he spoke, I examined the books on the shelf behind him. Titles like *Encyclopedia of Criminology and Deviant Behavior* and *Encyclopedia of Crime and Justice* and the *Physicians' Desk Reference*. Thin blue loose-leaf binders whose browned labels curled out from their spines.

The bad wolf was urging me to go after Glover, choke the life out of him. The good wolf kept reminding me that if I did, I'd be sent to the hole for months on end. Or worse: Though I couldn't imagine what could be worse.

"You've done a brave thing," he said. He thanked me for coming to see him. His bottom lip, I noticed, was chapped.

Late that night the door to my room opened, and Glover and two other guards came in with batons.

"I know what you're doing to Pee Wee," I said.

"Don't leave any marks," Glover told the others.

40

"WHERE'S THE MANAGER?" Russell called out.

"Over here." A voice from the other side of the fire-place.

The clear night sky was filled with stars, and the moon was full. The room was bathed in pale gray-blue light. My eyes quickly adjusted. Russell went to the other side of the fireplace.

"What the hell's wrong with your power?"

"I don't—I don't know," the manager said. "Must be the generator."

"Well, who does know? Who fixes stuff around here?"

"Peter Daut," the manager said. "He's my handyman."

"All right, Peter Daut," Russell said. "Identify yourself."

"Right here." A muffled voice.

"What's the problem?"

More muffled voices. The handyman seemed to be talking to the manager, but I couldn't make out what they were saying. Then I heard the manager say, "Yes, Peter, please."

"You want to cooperate, Peter," Russell said. "No power means the satellite modem won't work, which

means I don't get what I want. Which means I start elim-
inating hostages one by one until I do."

"The generator blew."

Peter the handyman, I assumed.

"Water in the fuel filter. Happens a lot. The diesel's
always absorbing water out here, and I can't drain the
tanks, so I just keep changing out the filters. I was
gonna do that in the middle of the night tonight, because I have to shut down the generator engines while
I—"

"Where's the remote start switch?" Russell said. "I
know there's one inside here."

"That won't do it," the handyman replied. "The fuel
filter needs to be changed, out at the shed."

"Wayne?" Russell said.

From the far side of the room came Wayne's high-
pitched voice. "Yo, Russell."

"Please take this gentleman outside so he can fix the
generator."

While Wayne lumbered over, Russell returned to our
group. "Ronald, you're my first interview. Come with
me, please."

Slattery struggled to his feet. With his hands tied, it
wasn't easy. "Would you mind if I use the restroom
first?" he asked.

"When Upton gets back. One at a time. Okay, Travis,
Ronald and I are going to have a talk in the screened
porch down at that end." He pointed in the direction of
the dining table. "Keep a watch on our guests, please."

IN THE SHADOWS I could make out Travis striding
along the periphery of the room, a compact stainless-
steel pistol at his side. He'd removed his long-sleeved

camouflage shirt and wore only a sleeveless white tee.
But his arms were so densely tattooed, mottled and
greenish, that at first it looked like he was still wearing
camouflage. At the back of his arm, by his elbow, was a
tattoo of a spiderweb: another prison tattoo.

"Nice job, Kevin," Ali whispered to Bross. "That
was a great bluff. Really genius."

"I didn't see anyone get killed, did you?" Bross said.
"He didn't take out his gun. I tried, and it didn't work—
big deal. I'm still here."

"You don't get it, do you? Not only did you get the
ransom jacked up, but now we're totally screwed. He's
going to question everyone separately, and we didn't
even get a chance to talk to Danziger and Grogan."

"Go ahead," he said. "Why don't you just walk over
there and tell them yourself?"

"You'd like that, wouldn't you?" Ali said. "Have me
get shot? And what was your big strategy? That line of
crap you gave Russell, which he saw right through?
Didn't you listen to a word Jake said? We all agreed to
tell him we don't have the account numbers."

"Hey, I didn't agree to anything," Bross said. "And
we all know why you're defending this loser."

"Because he obviously knows what he's doing. And
you don't."

"The only thing that's obvious is that you two used to
sleep together."

Ali was silent for a few seconds. I didn't have to see
her face to know it was flushed—with embarrassment
or with anger or both.

"I don't think you want be too high-and-mighty
about office *romances,* Kevin," she said, biting off the
words. "Or should we ask—"

"Ali," I said.

"Landry?"

"Never let an asshole rent space in your head. The guy's not worth your time. We've got to get to Grogan and Danziger now. Before Russell does."

Bross made a *pffft* sound. "Who's going to do that, *you*?" he said.

I didn't answer.

41

I WATCHED TRAVIS, trying to get a fix on his rhythm. I was beginning to think that he hadn't just done prison time; the way he walked convinced me that he'd also served in the military, maybe the Army or the National Guard. He had that soldierly cadence. He'd been broken in by a drill sergeant and done long tedious hours on night patrol.

He was also taking his job seriously. Any of the other hostage-takers would probably have sat in a chair, watching us. But maybe that was a good thing. It meant his back would be turned toward me for at least sixty seconds at a stretch. Given how dark it was in here, Travis could hardly see us: a great stroke of luck. But he'd surely hear and sense any sudden movement.

And for the moment he was the only guard in the room. Wayne was outside with the handyman, would probably be for a good while, until the power was up and running again. Verne had just gone outside for a smoke—and a toke, or a snort—and might be back in a minute or two, even five, if I got lucky and he took his time. Buck would return from the bathroom with Upton Barlow at any minute, depending on how long it took for a middle-aged guy with prostate problems to empty his bladder. I had no idea how long Russell would spend with Slattery. Ten minutes? Half an hour?

So if I was going to get to Grogan and Danziger, it had to be done right away.

THE FUNNY THING was, I didn't think twice about doing something so insanely risky. I just did it.

Maybe it was all about the look in Ali's face at the moment she saw me start to move, a look I'd never seen before: part terror, part admiration.

Or maybe it was because I knew no one else would. And if I didn't warn the two men not to remember the Hammond account numbers, my plan was doomed to fail.

Not that it wasn't doomed to fail already. Too many things could go wrong with it. Russell—too canny, too suspicious—might not fall for the phone call thing. He might simply scare the information out of someone at gunpoint: your company's money or your life. I knew what I'd choose.

He might not pick Slattery to do the transfer, especially if he knew that there were five executives—Grogan, Danziger, Bodine, Slattery, and Latimer—who also had the power. Whoever he did pick could easily screw it up, not figure out a way to communicate duress without Russell picking up on it. And whoever was at the other end of the phone might not get it.

And what if he already knew the account numbers?

So the odds of it working, the more I thought about it, were pretty damned slim.

Here I was, risking my life for a gambit that was likely to fail anyway. A gambit that, the more I mulled it over, was already starting to shred like wet tissue paper.

But to do nothing, I was certain, was to ensure that some of us, maybe even all of us, got killed.

Russell was wrong: You don't always have a choice.

THOUGH THE TWO men were only maybe thirty feet or so away, on the other side of the enormous fireplace, it might as well have been a mile.

I waited until Travis had completed a circuit, did his military-style about-face and passed us. And then I tried to get up.

But rising from the floor with your hands tied together, palms in, wasn't easy. I had to swing my knees over to one side, then lean my torso all the way forward. Extend my hands as if I were salaaming. Then I pressed the back of one of my hands against the floor and pushed myself up and to my feet.

It took almost five seconds. Which was way too long.

By the time I was standing, Travis had almost reached the end of the room. There was no time for me to run around the fireplace to the next alcove before he turned around.

Now what? I asked myself. *Do I sit back down, wait until Travis's next circuit?*

Then a screen door slammed. Not the front door: Verne, back from his cigarette break.

42

I NO LONGER had a choice. I had to *move*.

I took long, loping strides, as fast as I could, yet at the same time treading as lightly as possible. A matter of a couple of seconds, but it felt like forever.

All the while my eyes were riveted on Travis.

He came to the end of his circuit and turned just as I sank to the floor next to the manager's son, Ryan. He— and everyone else around him—looked in astonishment. I gave a quick headshake to tell them to be quiet.

Travis glanced over but maintained his steady pace. He hadn't noticed.

Verne entered from the back hallway, walking quickly, sniffing, swinging his arms jerkily, humming some tune, amped. When he was out of range, Ryan Fecher said, "What the hell—"

I put a finger to my lips, slid across the floor.

Alan Grogan and John Danziger were seated next to each other.

"Are you out of your freakin' mind?" Danziger said. I noticed the large bald spot under his fine blond hair. His light blue alligator shirt looked as if it had been ironed. He was one of those preppy guys whose clothes always fit perfectly, who had a certain natural, aristocratic ease and economy of motion.

"Yeah," I said. "I must be."

I quickly explained. As I did, he and Grogan exchanged looks—of disbelief, then skepticism and apprehension.

"I don't have the account numbers with me, either," Danziger said. "Why would I?"

"Well, I do," said Grogan. "In my head."

"Figures," Danziger said with feigned disgust. He turned to me, and said, with obvious pride, "Grogan's a USA Math Olympiad gold medalist. Even though he'll never admit it."

Grogan glared at Danziger. "Thanks, pal." The moonlight caught the network of fine lines around his hazel eyes.

"Hey," Danziger said, "if that's the only dirty little secret about you that comes out here, you're lucky."

"Very funny," Grogan said, sounding almost peeved.

"Russell doesn't know you have those numbers memorized," I said. "So you don't say a word. We clear?"

Both men nodded.

"If anyone tells him different," Danziger said, "we're in deep shit. The guy's already made it clear he doesn't want to be lied to. And what the consequences will be if anyone does."

"Right," I said. "But if we all agree, then it's the truth. Right?"

Grogan and Danziger looked less than convinced.

"Having a gun pointed at you does funny things to people," Grogan said. "We don't know what the others might do if Russell threatens them."

"That's a risk we're going to have to take," I said.

We sat in silence for half a minute or so while Travis passed by. Then Danziger whispered, "Listen, there may be something else."

I looked at him.

"When you mentioned a duress code—it jogged my memory. You know, I set something up with the bank a while ago, but we never had an opportunity to use it. Never came up. It's sort of a silent alarm—an electronic duress code."

"Electronic? How does that work?"

"It's just a variant authentication code. If you enter a nine before and after the PIN, it trips a silent alarm. Tells the bank officer that the transaction is fraudulent, probably coerced."

"Then what happens?"

"Well, first thing, they freeze the account. Then a whole emergency sequence gets triggered—calls are made to a list of people. My office, the CEO's office, the director of corporate security. Telling them something's wrong: Someone's probably forcing a company officer to access the bank accounts."

"But are they going to know where it's happening?"

"Sure. Our own corporate security people can dig up the IP address we logged in from—where the duress code originated. That'll tell them exactly where we are."

I nodded. "So corporate security or whoever can alert the Canadian authorities. Yes. But would Russell know we tripped an alarm?"

"Not at all. He'll see a false positive response. He'll think the transaction was successful."

"He'll know it wasn't as soon as he checks his account balance."

"True. No way around that."

"So when he sees that the wire transfer didn't go through," I said, "we'll just tell him it must have gotten intercepted along the way. Maybe at some higher level at the bank. Or by U.S. banking authorities. Some line of bullshit—he's not going to know the truth. But by then, the word will be out that we're in trouble."

"Exactly."

"Could work," I said.

"Maybe."

"Right now," I said, "it's all we have."

43

THE MANAGER'S SON, Ryan Fecher, made a *psst* sound and slid over toward me.

"I recognize a couple of those guys," he said, so softly I could barely hear him.

"From where?"

"From here."

"When? Which ones?"

"Last week, I think it was. We didn't have any corporate groups, just separate parties. That guy—Russell? The leader? And that guy who keeps bringing people in and out?"

"Travis."

"I think they're brothers," he said.

"I think you're right. What'd they do here?"

"They kept to themselves, didn't socialize with anyone. Didn't want to do any of the normal stuff like fishing. They mostly hung out here, took a lot of pictures."

"Of what?"

"The inside and outside of the lodge, the grounds, the dock, all that. They said they were into architecture and they'd heard about this place. Wanted to know how many staffers we had and where they lived. If we had Internet and if it was wireless and if it was in all the guest rooms or not. Whether we had landline phones or satellite phones, and whether guests could use the sat phone. How we got supplies like food and stuff and how often we got deliveries and mail. And they wanted a tour of the lodge."

"Inside and out?"

"Everything. Even the basement, but I got busy—we were pretty short-staffed last week—so I just told them to look around themselves."

"They didn't seem suspicious to you?"

"Well, there was the architecture thing—I mean, this *is* one of the oldest lodges in Canada—and they said they were thinking of opening their own fishing lodge in Wyoming. Which I guess *was* kinda weird, since they sure had no interest in fishing, you know?"

"You never told me this," his father said.

"I never gave it any thought until now," Ryan said. "Why would I?"

If Russell and his brother had come to the lodge a week earlier to scope it out, they'd been tipped off by somebody.

I asked the manager, "Who knew we were coming?"

He looked puzzled, then defensive. "Who knew—? I'm not sure what you're getting at."

"These guys knew the top officers of the Hammond Aerospace Corporation were going to be staying here. This whole thing was planned. That means they had a source. An informer. Maybe even a member of your staff. That's what I'm wondering."

He scowled. "Oh, come on. You think one of my people was involved? That's just . . . *insane.*"

"Not necessarily involved. Just talked to someone. Maybe without even knowing who he was talking to."

He was indignant. "The only ones who get the booking schedule in advance are me and my son."

"People have to order supplies."

"I do the ordering. There's no one else. What makes you so sure this was planned?"

"A bunch of things," I said. "How do you get supplies in here?"

"We've got a contract air service out of Vancouver that does a supply run every three days."

"When's the next one?"

"Not until Saturday."

I nodded, wondered whether Russell knew that, whether it figured into his timing. "How'd they get here, do you think? Through the woods?"

He shook his head. "No way. The woods are way too dense. Had to be a boat."

"There must be old hunting trails."

"They're all grown over. No one hunts around here anymore. Haven't for years."

"Since it's been made a wildlife preserve?"

"Before that, even. There's really nothing to hunt. I mean, there's always going to be people who'll break the law if there's something to catch. But the deer are way too small. A long time ago people used to trap beavers. Used to be a grizzly hunt, once, a while back. But not in forever. Years ago the Owekeeno Indians cut trails through the forests, but they're all grown over, too."

"How far's the nearest lodge?"

After a few seconds, he said, "Kilbella Bay, but it's a ways."

"Can you get to it on land?"

"Nah, it's across the inlet."

"So these guys must have taken a boat or a seaplane."

"Would have had to. But . . ."

"But what?"

"I didn't hear anything. I always hear boats passing by on the inlet, or coming in, and I didn't hear any motors. And I sure would have heard a plane."

"You were busy in the kitchen."

"I woulda heard it, believe me. Always do."

"So maybe they rowed in."

"Maybe. Or took a motorboat in partway, then cut the engines and rowed the rest of the way in."

"Which would mean they probably left their boat down on the shore, right?"

He shrugged. After a moment, he said, "I did hear a gunshot."

"We all did."

"Come to think of it, I haven't seen José."

"Who's José?"

"One of the Mexican kids. I told him to hose out a couple of the boats earlier tonight, but . . ."

"Around the time these guys showed up?"

"It would be, yeah."

"He probably ran into the woods," I said.

Paul glanced at me, looked away. "Yeah," he said. "Probably."

I began sidling away, when he stopped me. "This lodge is my whole life, you know."

I nodded, listened. He wanted to talk, and I let him.

"I mean, when it was built, a century ago, it was sort of a madman's folly. A crazy rich guy came out here when there was nothing else around except a couple of salmon canneries and decided to build this huge, beautiful fishing lodge." He shook his head, smiled sadly. "I'm not even the majority owner. He's in Australia, in Canberra. Only comes up here when we have celebrities visiting—movie stars and tycoons. He likes to schmooze with them. I put in the sweat equity. Even in the off-season, I'm always working, doing the hiring, repair work." He closed his eyes. "My wife left me. Couldn't stand the isolation. So now it's just me and my son, and he wants out, too."

"That's not true, Dad," Ryan said.

"This is a time for complete honesty," Paul said to his son. To me, he continued: "You know, my chief pleasure in life is when guests leave happy. I know, you probably don't believe that, do you?"

"I do."

"Or when they write me or e-mail me to say what a good time they had. It makes me feel like a host at a great dinner party. And now . . . this."

"Some dinner party."

"I don't know what I could have done differently."

"There's nothing you could have done," I said.

He seemed to consider that for a few seconds; he looked unconvinced. "Once he gets the ransom . . . We're not getting out of here alive, are we?"

I didn't reply.

He closed his eyes. "Dear God."

"That doesn't mean we can't try to do something."

He nodded for a long time. "You know any Hindu mythology, Jake?"

"I'm afraid not."

"There's a story. A Hindu myth. About a king who's given a curse. He's going to die in seven days from a snakebite. And you know—when he hears this curse, he feels . . . serene. Joyful."

"Oh yeah?"

"See, he knows he's got seven days to live. Seven days to prepare for his death. To devote to the contemplation of Krishna. To prepare for his departure for the spiritual world. He's filled with joy, Jake, and you know why? Because we're all under a sentence of death, and none of us knows when death will come to us. But he knows, you see. He *knows*. He knows he's going to die, and he's accepted it."

I paused just long enough for him to think I was mulling all this over. "No offense," I said, "but I'm not a Hindu."

I WAITED FOR Travis to pass by again.

A thought had occurred to me, and I shifted around to Danziger.

"If we have kidnap-and-ransom insurance," I said, "doesn't that mean we have some firm on retainer that specializes in rescuing hostages?"

Danziger smiled: rueful, not condescending. "That's only in the movies. In the real world, very few risk-management firms actually do retrievals. They do hostage negotiation with the kidnappers and make the payment arrangements. But this isn't a ransom situation. Russell's too smart for that. He knows what he's doing." Danziger paused. "He does seem to know an awful lot about how this all works."

"So do you."

"It's part of my job. At Hammond, the controller is also what they call the 'risk manager.' That means I work with Ron Slattery and Geoff Latimer to arrange for all the special risk insurance coverage. Told you I'd put you to sleep if I told you too much about what I do." He seemed distracted, looked at Grogan. "How does he know so much about K&R, do you think?"

"I've been wondering the same thing," Grogan said. "You remember when Latimer told us about this security firm in California he thought we might want to have on retainer? Some law school classmate of his founded it or ran it, maybe?"

"Right!" Danziger said. "They did recovery and retrieval, not just hostage negotiation. A lot of child abduction cases, I remember—divorces and such. One of their employees got arrested in South America on a child recovery case he was working, charged with kidnapping under the international treaty agreements. Did a couple years in prison in the U.S. That pretty much cooled me on them."

The two men exchanged glances.

I said, "You think that's Russell? That guy?"

Danziger shrugged. "How else could Russell know so much?"

"What do I know so much about?"

A voice with the grit of fine sandpaper.

Russell.

I looked away, stared at the log walls. I didn't want to catch his eye. Didn't want him to notice that I'd moved.

My heart hammered.

"I know a lot of stuff," he said. "Like the fact that you were sitting over there before."

I looked at Russell, shrugged nonchalantly.

"I think you and I need to have a talk, Jake," he said. "Right now. Where's the cook?"

A small woman with a big mop of unruly curly hair,

who'd been dozing against the stone side of the fire-place, looked around and said, "I'm the chef."

"Man, I never trust a skinny cook," he said. "How's your coffee?"

"My coffee? We have Sumatra and Kona—"

"How about java? You got java? I'd love a big pot of coffee. Nice and strong."

She looked at the manager, frightened. He nodded.

"He's not the boss anymore, babe," said Russell. "I am. Now, my friend Verne is going to take you into the kitchen while you make us some coffee."

"How do you like it?" she said. "Cream? Sugar? Splenda?"

"Now you've got the right attitude. I like it black. Those artificial sweeteners will kill you."

44

AFTER I'D BEEN at Glenview a few months, Mom was allowed to visit.

She looked like she'd aged twenty years. I told her she looked good. She said she couldn't believe how I'd changed in a few short months. I'd gotten so muscular. I'd become a man. It looked like I was even shaving, was that possible?

Most of her visit we sat in the molded orange plastic chairs in the visitors' lounge and watched the TV mounted high on the wall. She cried a lot. I was quiet.

"Mom," I said as she was leaving. "I don't want you to come here again."

She looked crestfallen. "Why not?"

"I don't want you to see me in here. Like this. And I don't want to remember why I'm here. I'll be out in a year or so. Then I'll be home."

She said she understood, though I'll never know if she really did. A month later, she was dead from a stroke.

45

THE SCREENED PORCH was cool and breezy. It had a distinctive, pleasant smell—of mildewed furnishings, of the tangy sea air, of the oil soap used to wash the floor. It was obviously not a place that saw much use.

"Come into my office," Russell said. He'd taken off his tactical vest and had put on a soiled white pit cap that said DAYTONA 500 CHAMPION 2004 on the front and had a big number 8 on the side.

The moon, fat and bright, cast a silvery light through the screens. The sky glittered with a thousand stars.

He pointed to a comfortable-looking upholstered chair. A glider, I found, when I sat in it. He sat in the one next to it. We could have been two old friends passing the time in relaxed conversation, drinking beers and reminiscing.

Except for his pewter gray eyes, flat and cold: something terribly detached about them, something removed and unnerving. The eyes of a sociopath, maybe; someone who didn't feel what others felt. I'd seen eyes like his before, at Glenview. He was a man who was capable of doing anything because he was restrained by nothing.

I felt a cold hard lump form in my stomach.

"You want to tell me what you were doing out there?" he said.

"Trying to help."

"Help who?"

"I was passing along word from the CEO."

"Word?"

"To cooperate. Telling the guys not to cause trouble. To just do whatever you say so we can all get out of here alive."

"She told you to walk over there to tell them that?"

"She prefers e-mail, but it doesn't seem to be working so well."

He was silent. I could hear the waves lapping gently against the shore, the rhythmic chirping of crickets.

"Why'd she ask you?"

"No one else was crazy enough."

"Well, you got balls, I'll give you that. I think you're the only one out of all of them who's got any balls."

"More balls than brains, I guess."

"So if I ask Danziger and Grogan what you were talking about, they're going to tell me the same thing."

The hairs on the nape of my neck bristled. "You're good with names, huh?"

"I just like to come prepared."

I nodded. "Impressive. How long have you been planning this?"

I registered a shift in his body language, a sudden drop in the temperature. I'd miscalculated.

"Am I going to have trouble with you?" he said.

"I just want to go home."

"Then don't be a hero."

"For these guys?" I said. "I don't even like them."

He laughed, stretched his legs out, yawned.

I pointed to his cap, and said, "I saw that race."

He looked at me blankly.

"That's Junior, right?"

"Huh?" It took him a few seconds to remember he was wearing a NASCAR cap.

"Dale Earnhardt Jr.," I said.

He nodded, turned away, looked straight ahead.

"Junior crossed the finish line a fraction of a second ahead of Tony Stewart," I said. "Yeah, I remember that one. Seven or eight cars just wiped out. Michael Waltrip's car must have flipped over three times."

He gave me a quick sidelong glance. "I was there, man."

"You're kidding me."

"Also saw his daddy get killed there three years before."

I shook my head. "Crazy sport. I think a lot of people tune in just for the crashes. Like maybe they'll get lucky and see someone die."

He gave me a longer look this time, didn't seem to know what to make of me. One of the snotty rich executives who followed NASCAR? It didn't compute. I guess I was doing a decent job pretending to care.

"Nothing like the old days," he said. "NASCAR used to be like bumper cars. Drivers used to race hard. A demolition derby. The old bump-and-run."

"Reminds me of that line from a movie," I said. "Rubbin's racin'."

"*Days of Thunder,* man!" He was suddenly enthusiastic, his smile like a child's. "My favorite movie of all time. How's it go again? 'He didn't slam you, he didn't bump you, he didn't nudge you—he *rubbed* you. And rubbin', son, is racin'.' That's *it,* man."

"That's it," I said, nodding sagely. *Bond with the guy. Connect.* "Sometimes a driver's just gotta shove another car out of position. Spin the other guy out. Wreck his car. Trade a little paint. But that's all changed now."

"Exactly. Now you race too hard, they sock you with a penalty. Everyone's got to stay in line."

"NASCAR got sissified."

"They turned it into a corporation, see."

"Damn straight."

He gave me another quizzical look. "How come you're so much younger than the rest of the guys?"

"I just look younger. I eat right. Saw-tooth palmetto."

A smile spread slowly across his face. "Saw palmetto. You someone's assistant or something?"

"Nah, I'm just a ringer. A substitute."

"That why you're not on the original guest list?"

So he does have a guest list. From Hammond? It could just as well be someone who works at the resort. Someone who doesn't have the most up-to-date information.

No, it had to be a source inside Hammond: How else could he know so much about Ron Slattery's personal life?

He has an inside source: but who?

"I was a last-minute replacement."

"For Michael Zorn?"

Interesting, I thought. *He's keeping track.* "Right."

"What happened to Zorn?"

So his information was at least a day or two old. Also interesting: He knew a lot about money laundering and offshore banks, about kidnap-and-ransom insurance, yet he didn't know everything about Hammond's finances. Not, at least, what he needed to know.

"Mike had to go to India for some client meetings," I said.

"So how'd they choose you?"

"I have no idea."

He nodded slowly. "I think you're full of shit."

"Funny, that's what my last quarterly performance review said."

He smiled, turned his penetrating gaze away.

"But if I had to guess, it's because I know a lot about our newest airplane."

"The H-880. You an engineer?"

"No, but I think I met one once."

He chuckled.

"I'm the assistant to the guy who's in charge of building the SkyCruiser. I'm like a glorified traffic cop. Actually, forget the 'glorified' part."

"Any of that traffic include money stuff? What do you know about the payments system—how money's moved in and out of the company?"

"I know that my paycheck gets deposited into my bank account every two weeks. That's about it, though. As much as I need to know. I'm the low man on the totem pole here."

He thought for a while. "That doesn't mean what you think."

"What doesn't?"

"'Low man on the totem pole.' The lower part of a totem pole is actually the most important part, see, because it's what most people look at. So it's usually done by the chief carver. He has his apprentices do the top part."

"Thanks," I said. "Now I feel better about it."

"Of course, the other guys don't know about totem poles. So they treat you like shit."

"Not really."

"I see things."

"I guess I don't. Though they do like to rub it in about how much money they have. Fancy restaurants and golf-club memberships and all that."

"That's 'cause they're not men. They're soft."

"Or maybe it's just that they know I just don't come from their world."

"Well, it's pretty obvious you're nothing like them. They're all a bunch of pussies and sissies and cowards."

He was playing me, too, but why?

"Not really. Some of them are serious jocks. Pretty competitive—Alpha Male types. And they all make a lot more money than me."

He hunched forward in his chair, pointing a stern finger. He spoke precisely, as if reciting something he'd memorized. "Someone once said that the great tragedy of this century is that a man can live his entire life without ever knowing for sure if he's a coward or not."

"Huh. Never thought about that."

He glanced at me quickly, decided I wasn't being sarcastic.

"You know what's wrong with the world today, bro? The computers. They're ruining the human race."

"Computers?"

"You ever see elks mate?" Russell said.

"Never had the pleasure."

"Every fall the female elk releases this musk in her urine, see. Tells the bull elks she's ready to mate. The bull elks can smell the musk, and they start fighting each other over the female. Charge at each other, butting heads, locking antlers, making this unbelievable racket, this loud *bugling,* until one of them gives up, and the winner gets the girl."

"I've seen bar fights like that."

"That's how the females can tell which bulls are the fittest. They mate with the winners. Otherwise, the weak genes get passed on, and the elks are gonna die out. This is how it works in nature."

"Or the corporate world."

"No. That's where you're wrong." The stern lecturer's finger again. "My point. Doesn't work like that with humans anymore. Used to be, a human who was too slow would get eaten by a saber-toothed tiger. Natural selection, right?"

"Didn't the saber-toothed tiger go extinct?"

A darting look of irritation. "These days, everything's upside down. Women don't mate with the better hunter anymore. They marry the rich guys."

"Maybe the rich guys are the better hunters now."

He scowled, but I had a sense that he didn't mind the fencing. Maybe even liked it. "It's like Darwin's law got repealed. Call it the rule of the weak."

"Okay."

"You think women can tell which men are the fittest anymore? They can't. You see a guy who's really cut and buff and wearing a muscle shirt to show it off, and you can figure he spends all his time in the gym, but you know something? Odds are he's a faggot."

"Or a WrestleMania champ."

Another flash of annoyance; I'd gone too far. "I mean, look at these guys." He waved at the wall, at the hostages on the other side. "This country was made by

guys like Kit Carson, fighting the Indians with knives
and six-shooters. Brave men. But that's all gone now.
Now, some pencil-neck geek sitting at a computer can
launch a thousand missiles and kill a million people.
The world's run by a bunch of fat-ass wimps who only
know how to double-click their way to power. Think
they should get a Purple Heart for a paper cut."

"I like that."

"Their idea of power is PowerPoint. They got head-
sets on their heads and their fingers on keyboards
and they think they're macho men when they're just
half wimp and half machine. Nothing more than
sports-drink-gulping, instant-message-sending, mouse-
clicking, iPod-listening, web-surfing pussies, and God
didn't mean for the likes of them to run this planet on
the backs of real men."

A knock at the door, and Verne came in with a mug,
which he handed to Russell.

"Finally. Thank you, Verne," Russell said.

"Now they're all bitching and moaning about how
they can't sleep on the floor," Verne said, shrugging and
twitching.

"Tell 'em this ain't the Mandarin Oriental. Who's
complaining—the boss lady?"

"Yeah, her. And some of the guys, too."

"Pussies. All right, look. No reason to keep 'em
there, with the hard floor. I *want* 'em going to sleep.
There's a room with a big rug, off the main room. The
one with all the stuffed deer heads on the wall. The
game room."

"I know it."

"Move 'em all in there. Tell 'em to stretch out and go
to sleep. Easier to keep watch."

"Okay."

"Close and lock the windows."

"Gotcha," Verne said, and he left.

He folded his legs, leaned back in his chair. "Aren't you the one who told Verne you were going to gouge out his good eye if he touched your girlfriend?"

"She's not my girlfriend."

He surprised me with a half smile. "You do have balls."

"I just didn't like the way he was talking to her."

"So how come you know about the Glock 18?"

"I did a year in the National Guard after high school." When no college would accept me.

"You a gun nut?"

"No. But my dad sort of was, so some of it rubbed off."

Dad kept trophy hand grenades around the house, a veritable arsenal of unregistered weapons: "Gun nut" didn't really begin to describe him.

"You a good shot?"

"Not bad."

"I'm guessing you're probably a pretty decent shot. The good ones never brag about it. So you got a choice here. You're either gonna be my friend and my helper, or I'm going to have to kill you."

"Let me think about that one."

"Guy like you could go either way." He shook his head. "I still get a vibe off you like you might try to be a hero."

"You don't know me."

"Thing is, I don't hear the fear in your voice. Like maybe there's something missing in you. Or something different."

"That right?"

"Haven't figured it out yet."

"Let me know when you do."

"I'm thinking you might try something reckless. Don't."

"I won't."

"What I got going here is too important to get screwed up by a kid with more testosterone than brains. So don't think you're fooling me. Don't think I'm not on to you. Someone's gonna have to be the first to get shot tonight, just to teach everyone a lesson. Make sure everyone gets it. And I think it might just be you."

46

IF HE MEANT to scare me, it worked. I refused to let him see it, though. I paused for a second or two, then affected a lighthearted tone.

"Your call," I said, "but I'm not sure you want to do that."

"Why not?"

"You think I'm the last guy you can trust? Consider maybe I'm the *only* one you can trust."

He sat back, folded his arms, narrowed his eyes. "How's that?"

"You said it yourself, Russell. Of all the guys here, I'm the peon. I don't get a bonus. I don't get stock options. I really don't *care* how much money you take from the company. A million, a billion, it's all the same to me. Doesn't affect me in the slightest. I don't care how much money Hammond makes or loses. I didn't even want to come here in the first place. Most of *them* didn't want me here."

"You telling me you don't really care one way or another if something happens to any of those guys? Sorry, I don't believe you."

"Don't get me wrong, I don't want to see anyone get hurt. But it's not like any of them are friends of mine.

They may be worth more, but their lives aren't worth any more than mine."

"You'd care if something happened to your girl-friend."

"She's a friend. Not a girlfriend." I hesitated. "Yeah, I'd care if anything happened to her. I'll admit that. But I'm cooperating. I want this to be over. I just want to go home."

"Well, a man's gotta do what a man's gotta do. Anything could happen."

"Like I said, I'm cooperating."

His pewter eyes had become dull, opaque, as if someone had switched off a light. "Sounds to me like maybe we're on the same side here."

He didn't mean it, and I knew better than to agree. "I don't know about that," I said. "But I get it that you're not kidding around. So I'll do whatever I can to help you get what you want."

"That's what I like to hear."

"So what are you gonna do?"

"What am *I* gonna do?"

"Half a billion dollars, huh? That's a shitload of money. What are you gonna do with it?"

His stare pierced through me as if he had X-ray vision and was examining my insides to see what made me tick. "Don't worry. I'll figure something out."

"Half a billion dollars," I said. "Man. Know what I'd do? If it was me?"

A long pause. "Let's hear it."

"I'd take off to some country that doesn't have an extradition treaty with the U.S."

"What, Namibia? Northern Cyprus? Yemen? No thanks."

So he had looked into it. Most people wouldn't know the right countries unless they were serious.

"There's other places," I said.

"Such as?"

Was he still sizing me up, or did he really want to know? "Costa Rica, I think," I said.

"Forget it. That's like trying to disappear in Beverly Hills."

"There's this place in Central America, between Panama and Colombia I think it is, where there's no government. Ten thousand square miles of real outlaw country. Like the Wild West in the old days. Kit Carson stuff."

"You're talking about the Darién Gap." He nodded: You couldn't tell him anything. "No roads. Mostly jungle. Full of Africanized honeybees. I hate bees."

"There's gotta be decent countries in the world that haven't signed extradition treaties—"

"Signing an extradition treaty is one thing. *Enforcing* it's another. Plus, there's a difference between extradition and deportation, buddy. Sure there's plenty of decent places. You can get lost in Belize or Panama. The Cubans won't deport you to the U.S. if you know who to pay off. Cartagena's not bad, either."

"You've done your homework."

"Always. I hope you learn that sooner rather than later."

"Sounds to me like you've been planning this for a while."

A slow, lethal grin. He said nothing.

"I hope you've taken precautions to cover the money trail, too," I said. "You steal half a billion dollars from one of the world's biggest corporations, you're gonna have an awful lot of people trying to track it down. Track *you* down."

"Let 'em hunt all they want. Once it moves offshore, it disappears."

"You know, our bank's not going to authorize a transfer of five hundred million dollars to the Cayman Islands or whatever. That'll just raise all kind of red flags."

"Actually, I was thinking Kazakhstan."

"*Kazakhstan?* That sounds even more suspicious."

"Sure. Unless you know how often Hammond wires money to a company in Kazakhstan."

"Huh?"

"It's all there on the Internet. On some—what is it?— Form 8-K on file with the Securities and Exchange Commission. Seems Boeing buys their titanium from Russia, so you guys buy it from Kazakhstan. One of the largest titanium producers in the world."

"That right?" I'd never heard this. I wondered if he was making it up; I didn't think he was.

"Titanium prices keep skyrocketing, so you guys like to stockpile it. Hammond's got a ten-year contract with some company in Kazakhstan, name I can't remember, for over a billion dollars. So every year you wire hundreds of millions of dollars to the National Bank of Kazakhstan."

"We wire money to Kazakhstan, huh?"

"Not directly. To their correspondent bank in New York. Deutsche Bank."

"How do you know all this?"

"Like you said, Jake, I do my homework. So let's say I set up a shell company in Bermuda or the British Virgin Islands or the Seychelles and gave it the name of some made-up titanium export firm in Kazakhstan, right? Your bank wires it to this fake company that has an account at Deutsche Bank in New York—they're not going to know any better."

"I thought the Germans cooperate with the U.S. on money laundering."

"Oh, sure. But Deutsche Bank isn't going to have it for more than a second or two before it goes to the Bank for International Settlements in Basel. And from there—well, just take it from me. I got this all figured out."

He really did. He wasn't making it up—he seemed to know too many details. "I'm impressed."

"Never underestimate me, buddy. Now, a couple of questions for you."

I nodded.

"That lady CEO," Russell said. "Cheryl Tobin. Most of these guys don't like her, huh?"

"I like her okay." What did he care?

"Well, you're low on the totem pole." A sly smile. "I'm talking about the senior guys."

"Most don't," I admitted.

"How come? Because she's a bitch?"

I paused for a second. Some guys use "bitch" interchangeably for "woman." Men like Russell, I figured. I wasn't going to teach him manners. "Yeah, they're probably not comfortable having a woman in charge. But the fact is, like it or not, she's the boss."

"Boss may not always be right, but she's still the boss, that it?"

"Like that."

He shook his head. "I think it's because they don't want her investigating them. They're scared she might find something. Like a bribe, maybe."

"News to me." Had Slattery told him about the internal corporate investigation? Or someone else—his inside source? "Wouldn't surprise me, though. She's a real stickler for rules."

"They'd love to get rid of her."

"Maybe, some of them. But the board of directors hired her. Not them."

"And she doesn't have the power to fire any of them, does she?"

"Never heard that before."

"There's a lot about your company I know."

"I can see that." And I wondered how.

"She's holding out on me."

"That's her job. Someone has to, and she runs the company. But she'll come around."

"Maybe I don't need her."

"Maybe you do. That's the thing, Russell. You gotta keep your options open. Anyone who has signing authority is someone you might need around. The point is for you to get your money. Not prune the deadwood."

"But she doesn't have signing authority, does she?"

"That's way above my pay grade, Russell."

"Interesting, isn't it?"

"If true. You get all this from Ron Slattery?"

"I have my sources." He winked. "Gotta know who I need to keep alive."

"You never know who you might need."

"Only need one."

I shook my head. "Don't assume that. The amount you're talking, the bank's probably going to require the authorization of two corporate officers. That means user IDs and passwords and who knows what else."

"Once I get the user IDs and the passwords, I don't need 'em anymore."

"Russell," I said, "let's be honest: You're talking about shooting someone to put the fear of God into the rest of us, right? But the thing is, you don't know which names the bank has on their list. What if they insist on a call-back?"

"A callback?"

"A phone call to verify the transaction."

"Not going to happen that way. It's all going to be done over the Internet."

"Right, but look at it this way. A request for half a *billion* dollars e-mailed from some computer outside the country—that's bound to raise all kinds of questions at the bank."

"Not if we're using the right authorization codes."

"Maybe," I said. "Or maybe not. Let's say the wire request goes to some pain-in-the-ass bureaucrat at the bank. Some low-level employee in the wire-transfer room who's seen too many TV shows about Ukrainian bank fraud and doesn't want to lose her job. She calls back the number on file for the Hammond treasury operations office or whatever it's called, but nobody at Hammond headquarters has a record of any transfer request."

"The top guys are all here," he said. He sounded a little less sure of himself.

"So someone at headquarters says, Gosh, I don't know anything about that, but here's the phone number of the lodge where all the honchos are. The bank lady, she's thinking she's being such a good doobie, she's gonna get a promotion for sure, maybe even be made deputy assistant supervisor of the wire room, and she calls the number here. Which happens to be the only telephone in the whole place—the manager's satellite phone. Maybe you answer the phone yourself. Whatever. But she asks to speak to someone whose name's on her list."

"They'll talk to her, believe you me."

"And maybe the protocol is, she's got to talk to *two* senior officers. An amount that size."

"Maybe."

"So you want to have at least two of them around to answer the phone and say, Yeah, it's cool."

"She's not going to know who she's talking to. Shit, Buck could pretend he's Ronald Slattery, comes to that."

I shrugged. "And if they have voiceprints? Half a billion dollars, you never know what sort of security precautions they might take."

"Still only need two of them."

"Thing is, Russell, you don't know for sure which names are on the bank's list."

"Huh?"

"Look, I don't know how this works. But what if the bank has a list of two or three names you've got to call if a request comes in for a transfer over, I don't know, fifty million or a hundred million bucks. You're not going to know who's on that list."

He was silent for five, ten seconds. Looked around the porch. Moths fluttered outside. Some big insect—a june bug, maybe—kept colliding with the screen. The crickets seemed to be chirping louder and faster, but maybe that was just my imagination. It was brighter outside than in here: I could see the glimmering of the moon on the waves, the silvery wooden dock, the boulders and rocks of the shore.

"You're pulling all this out of your ass, aren't you?" he said.

"You bet."

He nodded, smiled. Then his smile faded. "Doesn't mean you're wrong, though."

"And another thing? One of the hostages needs his insulin."

"That guy Latimer."

"He could go into a coma. He could die. You don't want that."

"I don't?"

"He's the General Counsel. He might have signing authority, too. Don't dynamite any bridges you might need to cross later on."

He nodded. "Why're you being so helpful?"

"Maybe I want to save my ass."

"If you're trying something, I'll know."

"I told you. I just want to go home."

We looked at each other for a few seconds. It felt like an hour. The roar of the ocean, the lapping of the waves against the rocks on the beach.

"Stay on my good side," he said, "and you'll make it out of here alive. But if you try anything—"

"I know."

"No," Russell said. "You don't know. You think you know what's happening here, dude, but you really have no idea."

47

RUSSELL'S WORDS ECHOED in my head as Travis followed me out of the screened porch and through the great room.

You think you know what's happening here, dude, but you really have no idea.

He took me to another room I hadn't seen before, some kind of parlor or reading room with antlers and moose heads mounted on the walls. The floor was covered with a large Oriental carpet, where some of the hostages were stretched out or curled up, and others sat in clusters, talking quietly. For a moment it reminded me of kindergarten, when all the kids would lie down on little rugs at naptime.

A Coleman lantern on a trestle table near the door gave off a cone of greenish light. Nearby, two guards on duty, sitting near each other in railback chairs, murmuring to each other: Buck, the one with the black hair and goatee; and Verne, the ex-con with the teardrop tattoos.

Only one door, I noticed. There were windows, but they were shut and, I assumed, locked.

I wondered how long they'd keep us here. It was early Thursday morning already. I assumed that Russell would be interrogating people throughout the night: the large pot of black coffee.

Travis shoved me to the floor. Then he called Geoff Latimer's name. Latimer was lying on his side, pale and exhausted.

"You're in luck," Travis said, helping Latimer to his feet with a gentleness I didn't expect.

"Thank God," said Latimer.

Travis and Latimer left the room, and the two guards whispered. Verne, twitchy, jiggled his foot up and down. They obviously weren't worried about us—unarmed, our hands bound.

The room was mostly quiet. Bodine and his guys were speaking in low voices. A few of the hostages whispered to one another—Bodine, Barlow, and Bross, the Three Musketeers, off in one corner, conspiring. I noticed that Ron Slattery had joined them.

Others had fallen asleep already, worn out by the stress and the long day and the late hour. A few snored.

"Jesus, Landry."

Ali was sitting ten or fifteen feet away with Cheryl and Paul Fecher, the manager, and the manager's son. I looked over at the two guards at the other end of the room, their faces half washed out by the lantern's light, half in shadows. I couldn't tell how closely they were watching us, whether they were really paying much attention.

Slowly, I slid across the rug.

"We were worried about you," Ali said.

"It was fine."

"When he caught you on the other side of the fireplace—"

"It was a little tense," I said.

"What'd he want to know?" Cheryl asked.

"Well, he figured out pretty quickly I didn't know anything useful. Mostly he seemed to be sizing me up. He asked about you and . . ." My voice trailed off. The manager and his son were sitting near Ali, watching us talk, but no one else from Hammond was within earshot. "He knew about the investigation."

Her eyes widened for a fraction of a second, then narrowed. "How in God's name? Why would anyone tell him?"

"I'm pretty sure he has a source inside Hammond."

Cheryl nodded. "He knows too much, that's for sure. Danziger also thinks he may be a professional, in the K&R business."

She glanced over her shoulder. Danziger was lying on his side by the wall, asleep. "He also briefed all of us on the duress code."

"Much better than my original idea," I said.

"At least you had a plan," she said. "I owe you an apology."

"Why?"

"I misread them. You had them pegged. And the way you stuck up for me—I won't forget it." She seemed embarrassed. "This isn't easy."

"This isn't easy for any of us," I said.

The door opened. Travis entered with Latimer, then called out Danziger's name. Latimer sat near us. He looked much better, now that his diabetic crisis had passed.

He smiled, mouthed *Thank you.*

I just nodded.

Suddenly the lights in the room went on, as abruptly as they'd gone off. Lamps and wall sconces blazed to life. A number of people woke up, looked around.

"Guess the generator's fixed," Latimer said.

I nodded.

"You know, what you did before—getting over to the other side to talk to Grogan and Danziger?"

"Stupid, huh?"

"Brave, Jake. Guys with guns strutting around here. You could have gotten yourself killed."

"I don't think so."

"You're a brave guy, Jake."

"Just a survivor."

"More than that."

"Well, you know, a wise man once said that one of the great tragedies of our century is that a man can live his whole life and never know if he's a coward or not." I smiled, held up a forefinger. "Russell told me that."

"You know what the definition of a coward is?" he said. "A coward is a hero with a wife, kids, and a mortgage."

"So maybe that's it," I said. "No wife, no kids. And I don't have a mortgage. I rent."

There was a noise at the far side of the room. Wayne, the crew-cut one, entered with Peter the handyman, a small, pudgy man with a bushy gray mustache, receding gray hair, and thick aviator-frame glasses. He was sweating profusely.

Wayne whispered to the other guards for a few minutes, then led the handyman to the back right corner of the room.

A minute or so later, Russell and his brother entered, John Danziger in front of them.

Danziger looked terrified.

Russell cleared his throat. "Excuse me, ladies and gentlemen," he announced. "We have a little business to transact." He unholstered his Glock.

"Some of you guys apparently think you're gonna be clever," Russell said. "Try to throw a little sand in the gears. Try to screw things up for everyone else. Like I'm not going to find out." As he was talking, he popped out the Glock's magazine and held it up, scanned it to see if it was full. It seemed a strange thing to do. He must have known the gun was loaded. "Didn't some guy say that we all gotta hang together or we'll hang separately? Like, George Washington or one of those guys?"

"I believe that was actually Benjamin Franklin," Hugo Lummis said.

Russell looked at Lummis blankly for a moment. "Why, thank you, Hugo." He nodded. "Not many of you got the balls to correct a man with a loaded gun."

"I'm not correcting you," Lummis said hastily. "I'm just—"

"Quite all right, Hugo," Russell said. "I like learning stuff. Not everyone does, though. People get ideas stuck in their heads. That's why you're all gonna have a little lesson right now. A *seminar.* Shouldn't take too long, though." He seated the magazine back in the butt of the pistol with a quiet click.

"John," he said gently, "could you please kneel right here? Yes, that's right. Right there. Not on the rug—on the wood. That's good."

"Please, don't," Danziger said. He knelt, his eyes darting around the room, his face frozen.

"Now, John," Russell said, "you and I are going to give

all your colleagues here a lesson they're never going to forget. See, the best lessons, I figure, the teacher learns right along with the students. So even though I'm teaching this lesson, we're all gonna learn something. Everyone but you, John. I'm thinking it's probably too late for you. You're just gonna have to be the demonstration."

"Please," said Danziger. He knelt on the wooden floor, facing us, his torso perfectly erect, his hands bound in front of his flat belly. He could have been in church. His light blue alligator shirt had big dark sweat stains under the arms.

Russell strode up to Danziger at an angle, like a veteran teacher approaching a blackboard. His Glock was in his right hand.

On Danziger's other side stood Travis, also holding his gun.

Danziger's eyes moved frantically. For a brief instant he looked into my eyes.

Russell's voice was calm and quiet. "So, John," he said, "what's a duress code?"

48

WE WATCHED IN terror.

"A 'duress code'?" Danziger said. "You mean, like a burglar alarm, when—"

"I don't think we're talking about a burglar alarm, are we, John?"

"I told you, I don't know what you're talking about," Danziger said.

"You did, didn't you? So I guess you really can't help me." Russell lifted his pistol and placed it snugly behind Danziger's right ear. He snapped back the slide.

I shouted, "Russell, don't do it!"

Someone—Lummis, maybe?—screamed, "No!"

There was a sudden commotion: Alan Grogan struggling to his feet. "Please!" he called. "I'll talk to you. I'll tell you anything you want."

"Is that Alan?" Russell said without even turning to look.

I watched, riveted and angry, my mind spinning. Russell wouldn't actually pull the trigger. Especially not after the talk we'd had.

But if he really intended to, there was no way to stop

him. Not with my hands bound, not sitting this far away. And not with four other armed men nearby.

Grogan zigzagged across the carpet, around the other hostages. He tripped over something but got right back up, with a jock's agility. His face had gone crimson.

"You don't need to do this," Grogan said.

Travis raised his gun and aimed it at Grogan, then the other two did the same.

"Alan," Danziger said, "sit down! You've got nothing to do with this."

Russell turned to Grogan, a cryptic half grin on his face. "You wanted to tell me something? Try and save your friend?"

"Anything you want to know," Grogan said. "Just put the gun down."

"Alan, sit *down*," Danziger said. "You don't know anything about this."

"I think he wants to help you, John," said Russell. "He doesn't want me to blow your brains out."

"John, just *tell* him!" Grogan shouted. "*Please.* It's not worth it. Please."

"It's not worth it, John," Russell said. "Do you know what's going to happen when I pull the trigger?"

"*Don't,*" Danziger whispered. "Please. I'll tell you everything I know about the duress code. Anything you want to—"

"It's not pretty," Russell went on. "It's not like on TV. A nine-millimeter bullet has a muzzle velocity of, like, a thousand feet per second. First thing it does is punch out a round piece of skull, see? Drives the bone fragments right into your brain, okay? Then, at the same time it opens up a nice big cavity in your brain.

Like a cave. Builds up pressure inside there. Your brain actually explodes, John."

"Russell," Grogan said, coming closer, "you don't have to do this. He'll tell you everything you want to know, and so will I. No one's going to use any duress code, I promise you. That was just an idea, we talked about it, but it's *not going to happen*!"

But Russell would not stop his sadistic monologue. "Where I'm aiming, see, the bullet's going to travel right through the brain stem. Kill you instantly. For you, it's lights out. But for everyone else, it's grisly, I gotta tell ya."

Danziger was talking, trying to talk over him. "The duress code is nothing more than a couple of numbers," he said. "You type in a nine before the—"

"They're gonna see blood and tissue," Russell went on, "little gobs of gray matter, spurt out the exit wound. Might even see something called backspatter, contact wound like this. The gray matter shoots out the entrance wound, too. It's not pleasant. Not for me, anyway. I might get some of your brain tissue on my clothes."

Danziger was shaking, sobbing silently. Tears were streaming down his face. Sweat had soaked most of his light blue shirt.

"Stop!" he shouted. "I'm *telling* you! *Please!*"

"Russell," Cheryl called out, her voice trembling, "do *not* do this. You do not want to face murder charges. There's no reason to do this. No one's going to try to stop the wire transfer. You're going to get everything you want."

"He's *telling* you!" cried Grogan. "Listen to him. What else do you *want*?" He, too, was weeping now.

"Alan, I want you to stay right where you are," Russell said. "Don't come any closer."

"Russell, please listen to me." It was Bo Lampack. He struggled to rise, fell to his knees, then rolled upright. "Help me help *you*." He stood tentatively, walked toward Russell. "I'm Bo," he said.

"Sit down, Bo," Russell said.

Yet Bo kept approaching. "I want you to know that we're all on the same page. All of us. We all want to resolve this. We all want to give you what you want."

"Don't come any closer, Bo," Russell said, staring him down.

"I'm just saying," Bo went on, coming still closer, "that you should understand that you're completely in control. And we, all of us, have the deepest respect for you. We understand completely that you're a human being with needs just like all of us—"

Russell swiveled, slammed his pistol against Bo's face. Bo screamed and fell over backwards, his face bloodied.

Then Russell placed the Glock back behind Danziger's right ear. "Do you want to tell me what happens after you type in that duress code?" Russell said very softly.

Danziger closed his eyes. "It triggers a silent alarm," he said, his voice trembling. "It tells the bank that the transfer request is being made under compulsion."

"Okay, good," said Russell. "Now, John, tell me something. Is there any other *duress code*? Besides the nine, I mean."

Danziger mouthed the word *No* but no sound came out.

"I can't hear you," said Russell.

"No," Danziger gasped.

"No other way for someone to sneak in a *duress code*?"

"No. Nothing else."

"That's it? No other tricks that you know of? Nothing else your buddies might try to screw this up?" Russell twisted the Glock, swiveling the muzzle on that same spot behind Danziger's right ear.

Danziger's face was contorted and dark red. "I—can't think of anything else," he whispered.

"You'd be the guy who'd know, isn't that right?"

"Yes," Danziger said. "There's no one else who . . ." His voice was choked by sobs.

"Who what?"

"Who knows the—the systems—"

"So that's it, then?" Russell said. "No other tricks?"

"Nothing. I swear to you."

"Thank you, John," Russell said. "You've been very cooperative."

Danziger gasped for air, nodded. He closed his eyes, looked drained.

"Thank you," he whispered.

You could almost feel everyone breathe a collective sigh of relief. Russell was a sadist, but not a murderer. He had tortured the information he wanted out of Danziger, so there was no need to kill him.

"Oh, thank God," breathed Grogan. Tears were streaming down his face as well.

"No," Russell said softly, "thank *you*. Good-bye, John."

He squeezed the trigger and the gun jumped in his hand and filled the room with a deafening explosion.

Danziger slumped to one side.

The gunshot seemed to echo for an instant, though it was merely an auditory illusion: My ears rang with a high-pitched, wavering tone. I stared, unable to fully comprehend what I'd just seen.

Then the silence was broken as someone let out a gasp.
People began to scream, others to cry.

Someone vomited.

A large chunk of the right side of Danziger's head
was missing.

Russell wiped his left hand over his face to smear off
the red spatter. Verne let out a loud whoop and pumped
his fist.

"Yeah!" he shouted. "You see *that*?"

A number of people dove to the floor. Some tried to
cover their eyes with their forearms, ducked their
heads. Ali buried her head between her legs.

I wanted to shout, but I couldn't. My throat seemed
to have closed.

Russell stood up, lowered the Glock to his side,
backed up a few steps. Travis stared furiously at his
brother.

Over the cacophony, the shouts and the keening, I
heard Russell tell his brother, "A man's gotta do what a
man's gotta do."

Hank Bodine bellowed, *"Goddamn you!"*

In all the chaos, my eyes were drawn to Grogan. He
was on his feet, stumbling forward to Danziger's body.
His face was red and crumpled, and he was crying, his
head shaking. He knelt next to Danziger's body, reached
with his unsteady fettered hands to lift his friend's
ruined head, trying to cradle it.

His mouth was moving as if to speak, but no words
came out, just deep gasps, like hiccups. Blood oozed
between his fingers.

A slick of blood and something viscous had pooled
on the floor next to Danziger.

Then Grogan leaned over and kissed the dead man's lips, and suddenly everybody understood.

I couldn't see Grogan's face. I could only see his shoulders heaving.

He lowered Danziger's head gently to the floor and knelt there for several seconds as if praying. Slowly he rose to his feet as a terrible anguished scream welled up from his throat, and he staggered toward Russell, his face contorted with rage and grief.

"You goddamned son of a *bitch*!" he shouted, spittle flying.

He lunged at Russell, jabbing his tethered hands at Russell's face as if to throttle him. *"God damn you to hell, you goddamned son of a bitch!"*

"Alan?" Russell said in a matter-of-fact voice as he stepped to one side, out of the way.

"Why?" Grogan gasped. "Why in God's name—?"

"You, too," Russell said, and he fired one more time.

PART THREE

49

PEE WEE FARRENTINO'S delicate, feminine face had become monstrous: a welter of angry red cross-hatched scars. Ugly, just the way he wanted.

But it hadn't stopped Glover's midnight visits. Neither had my meeting with Dr. Jerome Marcus, the Assistant Clinical Director of Glenview, who'd followed the bureaucratic imperative not to rock the boat. He buried his report. He wanted a larger office.

Pee Wee's eyes had gone dead. He'd given up.

One morning, he wasn't at inspection. The morning guard, Caffrey, went to his room and found him.

He'd torn strips from his bedsheets and fashioned a noose, lashed it to the old iron radiator, managed to twist his body into the right position to strangle himself. Only Pee Wee could have done something that clever.

Caffrey, stricken, described it to us: We weren't allowed to look.

The bad wolf took me over. I felt myself propelled into a dark tunnel, no way out but forward, no turning back.

During outdoor exercise period, I made the first move. I lunged at Glover, wrested the baton out of his hands, my strength almost superhuman. The high-octane fuel of rage.

As he tried to grab it back, I slammed it against the back of his knees. Just as he'd done to me so many times.

He lurched, sprawled to the ground, roared that I was going straight to the hole. He yelled for Caffrey.

But Caffrey stood and watched.

Glover—cowering, his lip split, his eyes leaking blood—hollered for Estevez.

I slammed my fists into his face, *one two one two,* until I felt hard bone go soft.

One two one two.

I'd made myself Raymond Farrentino's protector, and I'd failed, and this was the only thing I could do.

He roared, an enraged beast, throwing his fists at me blindly, trying to block my punches. He caught me on the side of my face with a right hook so hard it should have knocked me over. But it didn't. I was in the zone. My rage was both a force field and anesthetic. His head jerked from side to side to dodge the blows. He snarled, his teeth bloody.

Even in my madness, my temporary insanity, I knew that beating Glover to a bloody pulp would solve nothing. It would only get me in the most serious trouble. But it felt too good to stop.

I kneed him in the stomach, and his eyes rolled up into his head for an instant. He sagged, and I slammed a fist into the underside of his jaw, heard something snap. He swayed backwards, tipped over, his head smashing into the ground.

Then something remarkable happened. Estevez, then Alvaro and a few of the bigger kids, began swarming around Glover and me. Some had homemade brass knuckles or sharpened mattress coils: an homage to Pee Wee.

We could all see the fear in his pale dull eyes. A spell had been broken. Only later did I wonder how many of them had also been Glover's victims.

As the others pummeled him with their fists and slashed with their mattress coils, knocking me aside, guards began streaming out of D Unit and the adjoining cottages, batons and Mace at the ready.

They began pulling the kids off Glover, stopping them from crossing the line, going one step too far.

A lockdown was ordered. Anyone who didn't return to his room at once would be placed in the Special Handling Unit. The word got around quickly that the punishment would be severe: transfer to what they called gladiator school—a maximum-security penitentiary for violent offenders, even worse than Glenview.

I was sent to solitary, informed that I would be brought up on charges of assault and battery. I'd be tried as an adult. Instead of getting out when I was seventeen, I wouldn't see the outside world until long after my twenty-first birthday—if, that is, I even survived.

And that was when a second remarkable thing happened: a posthumous gift from Pee Wee, his final clever move.

The lockdown wasn't even an hour old when someone found the note he'd left for me.

A few nights, pinned against the wall of his room, he'd found himself staring at the red pinpoint of light on the surveillance camera. Glover sometimes forgot to turn it off.

For Pee Wee it was simple to break into the D Unit command center, where the tapes were recorded and stored, where there was equipment to make copies. He'd sent tapes to the Division of Youth Services, the local newspapers, the local TV station. Smuggling out had been even easier, for him, than smuggling in.

That evening, I stood on my bed and watched through the tiny square of wire-reinforced glass as two police cruisers and one TV van pulled up the long driveway. Twenty minutes later, a couple of handcuffed figures emerged in the glare of the xenon arc TV spotlights. One was a gray-haired man with rimless glasses and a perfectly pressed shirt. The other was Glover, almost unrecognizable, unable to walk. He was carried by three policemen.

50

WAYNE CAME IN with a mop and a bucket full of suds. The two frightened cleaning girls—Bulgarians who'd come here for the summer to work—dutifully mopped up the blood. Russell had ordered them to the front, and Travis had untied their restraints, and at first they'd stood there shaking and weeping, probably thinking that they were next. Russell pointed out a dark red blood splatter on the rug and told them to clean that up, too. As if he didn't want to leave the place a mess when all this was over.

By now the hostages had settled down into a dazed, terror-stricken stupor, almost a trance state. No one spoke. No one even whispered. Ali was crying softly, and Cheryl stared grimly into space.

"What do you want us to do with the bodies?" Wayne asked in an unexpectedly soft voice, as he and Travis lifted Grogan.

"Take 'em out in the woods," Russell said. "Maybe the grizzlies will eat 'em."

Travis glanced furiously at his brother but said nothing.

Russell reached down, took Danziger's arms, and tried

to pull the body up—I guess he was going to attempt a sort of fireman's carry—but then suddenly let go. Danziger's body slid to the floor while Russell wiped his hands on his pant legs: There was blood everywhere.

Then he grabbed Danziger's ankles and dragged him across the floor.

It left a long red smear.

At the threshold of the room he stopped. "Was my lesson clear enough?" he said.

No one answered.

ONLY ONE OF the kidnappers remained in the room now: Buck, the one with the black hair and goatee. He sat slumped in his chair, looking pensive. His .44 Magnum lay on his right thigh, his right hand on top of it.

The manager was crying silently. He was lost in grief and shock, along with so many others in the room.

Cheryl was the first to speak. "Someone told him," she whispered.

Silence.

"Was it you, Kevin?" she asked softly.

"How *dare* you—" Bross erupted, spittle flying.

"He could have gotten it out of Danziger himself," I said. "That's the point of all these 'interviews'—playing us off against each other."

Lummis was gasping for breath, wincing, his face deep red.

"Hugo, for God's sake, what is it?" said Barlow.

"I'll be—fine," Lummis gasped. "Just—need to—to try to calm down."

Buck looked up, stared for a few seconds, then seemed to lose interest. Muffled, angry voices came from the next room: Russell and his brother, I guessed, arguing in the screened porch.

I cleared my throat, and the manager looked up at me with red-rimmed eyes.

"We need to get help," I said.

He blinked away tears but said nothing.

It was obvious, to me at least, that cooperating with Russell and his guys would only get us killed. We had to contact someone, anyone, in the outside world. Even if no one else would do anything, at least I would.

"Where do you keep your sat phone?"

It took him a few seconds to respond. Clumsily, he tried to wipe the tears from each eye with the backs of his bound hands. He looked hollow. "My office," he whispered. "But that crazy guy—Verne?—asked me about it and made me give him my office key."

"That's not the phone that Russell was using, was it?"

He shook his head. "Mine's an older model. He just must have taken mine so no one else could use it."

"Your office—you keep it locked?"

He nodded. "But they took the key, I told you—"

"I understand. What happens if you misplace your key?"

"You mean, do I hide a spare somewhere?" He nodded. "Under the base of the lamp on the legal bookcase outside my office door. An old skeleton key. Opens every damned door in this old place—real high-security, huh? But I told you, he took the sat phone."

"That's all right. There's other ways."

Ali, watching us talk, said: "The Internet."

"Right. They obviously haven't cut the line if they're planning on using it to do the wire transfer."

"Landry, you see that guy in the front of the room?

There's like five guys with guns out there. You've really lost it."

I looked toward the window.

Two silhouetted figures in the silvery moonlight struggled with a body, moving in the direction of the forest.

"But Russell—"

"I have a feeling that Russell told his brother he was only going to put a scare into Danziger and Grogan. Not bullets in their heads. As long as we can hear them arguing, we can count on them being distracted in the screened porch."

"And this guy?" She glanced at Buck.

I explained.

"Are you out of your mind?" she said.

51

"YOU LOST YOUR mind?" Dad said.

"I don't know what you're talking about."

"Trying to rip me off? You didn't really think you could get away with it, did you?"

Suddenly he had the crook of his arm around my neck and was squeezing hard. I could smell his Old Spice, his boozy breath.

"Hey!" I felt the blood rush to my head, bright spots swimming. "Cut it out!"

"We can do this the hard way or the easy way. Up to you. Which it gonna be?"

I tried to pry his arm loose, but he was much stronger. I was thirteen, tall and scrawny. Everything was bleaching out.

On the bulging muscle of his upper arm, the Marine Corps tattoo: an eagle, a globe, an anchor, a circle of stars, "USMC" in Old English lettering. I noticed the imperfections, the fuzzy lines, the blotches of green-black ink.

"You know how easy I could break your neck?"

"Let go!"

"Either you're gonna give me back the fifty bucks, or I'm gonna break your neck. Which it gonna be?"

I'd taken the money from the cigar box in his dresser to buy a bus ticket and get the hell out of the house. A cousin was at college in Bellingham, Washington. I figured the fifty dollars would get me at least halfway across the country, and I'd beg or borrow or steal the rest. Once I showed up at Rick's apartment, he wasn't going to turn me away. The worst thing was leaving Mom alone there with Dad, unprotected, but I'd pretty much given up on her. I'd begged her to leave, and she wouldn't. She wouldn't let me say anything to Dad. "Just stay out of it, sweetie," she'd said. "Please, just stay out of it."

Finally, I gasped, "All right!"

Dad loosed his grip, and I sank to the floor.

He held out his hand, and I fished the crumpled bills from the back pocket of my jeans. Tossed the wad onto the wall-to-wall carpet.

He smiled in triumph. "Didn't I teach you nothing? What kind of pussy are you, can't defend yourself?"

"I'm telling Mom."

He just snorted.

"I'll tell my guidance counselor what you did."

"You do that, and I'll tell the cops how you been stealing money from your parents, and you know what's gonna happen to you? They'll send you right to the boys' home. Reform school. That'll straighten you out."

"Then I'll just take one of your guns and steal the money."

"Hah. You gonna rob a bank, Jakey? Or the 7-Eleven?"

I sat there on the carpet, head spinning, as he went

downstairs to the kitchen. Heard the refrigerator door open. The hiss of a pop-top: a can of Genny.

Mom was standing at the top of the stairs in her Food-Fair smock, tears in her eyes. She'd seen the whole thing.

"Mom," I said.

She gave me a long, imploring look, and for a moment she looked like she was coming to give me a consoling hug.

Instead, she gave me another sad look and went down the hall to the master bedroom to change out of her work clothes.

52

I LAY ON my side as if asleep and drew my left knee up to bring my foot closer to my roped hands.

I'd lost a little feeling in my fingers, not because the ropes were too tight but because my palms had been clamped together in the same position for so long. They felt prickly and thick and useless.

But I was able to extend my hands and, despite the limited range of motion of my fingers, grasp the blade of the steak knife. And fumbling with my leaden fingertips, I got hold of the handle and pulled it slowly, carefully, from my shoe.

Meanwhile, Cheryl was talking to Ali in a low, soft murmur. "What just happened—it puts all these petty games into perspective, doesn't it? One minute I'm vowing I'm going to take this fight to the board of directors and outmaneuver Hank, and the next minute I'm wishing I could call my children and tell them I love them."

"How old are they?" Ali asked.

"Oh, Nicholas is a sophomore at Duke, and Maddy's living in the West Village. They're not children. They're grown. They're in the world. They don't need me. But . . ."

Now that the thing was out of my shoe, I realized how much low-level discomfort it had been causing me. I'd almost gotten used to it, as if a sharp stone were stuck in there. To get it out was a relief.

"I feel like we've just come out the other side," Cheryl said. "Got through the hard part. Both of them, we had such a difficult relationship for so long. Maddy dropped out of Hampshire and stopped speaking to me for, oh, it must have been three years or more. Nicholas still resents me for sending him away to prep school so young. He's convinced I wanted him out of the house so I could concentrate on my career."

Ali looked uncomfortable hearing her boss speak so openly. She studied the carpet. Then she said: "He's young. He'll come around."

I turned my head to make sure Buck couldn't see me. He seemed to be dozing.

Keeping my back to him—and to Cheryl and Ali as well—I positioned the knife blade up and began moving it back and forth against the rope.

The blade was razor-sharp, but it was the wrong tool. Great for cutting aged prime steak, maybe, but not so great with synthetic kernmantle. This was a high-quality climbing rope woven from twisted strands of polyester around a nylon core. It was made for rappelling, so it had a high tensile strength. It was made to be abrasion-resistant. In other words, it wasn't supposed to cut easily. A coarser knife-edge would have had more bite. A serrated edge would have been best of all.

But what I had was a steak knife, and the wrong kind.

So I kept sawing away.

"No, he's right," Cheryl said. "I couldn't be mom and corporate executive at the same time, and I knew it."

"You needed a wife," Ali said.

"Or a stay-at-home dad. But they didn't even have a dad at all for most of their childhoods. After Bill ran off with some chippy." She sniffled. "So this is what I screwed up my kids for. So I could spend half my time trying to keep Hank Bodine from stabbing me in the back."

Once I'd pierced the outermost polyester sheath, the strands began to fray, then splay outward. The process started getting easier, until I'd got halfway through the first rope. They'd wound the rope around my wrists three times, but of course I'd only have to cut through in one place to get it off.

"I bet Hank's kids are screwed up even worse," Ali whispered. "Only he probably doesn't even care."

Upton Barlow noticed what I was doing, and he stared in astonishment. Then, to my surprise, he smiled and nodded.

"And then die in this godforsaken fishing lodge in the middle of . . ." Cheryl's voice got high and thin and constricted, then stopped.

I went back to sawing at the rope.

"Didn't think you'd ever see a CEO cry, right?" Cheryl said.

"Cheryl," Ali said gently.

"You know what they say—when a man's tough, he's decisive. When a woman's tough, she's a controlling bitch." She sniffed again. "That's okay. I knew that when I started. Back in the day. When all women in business were legally required to wear those stupid floppy bow ties with every blouse. At least it'll be easier for you. The clothes aren't as bad."

Finally, I was down to the last strand, and the blade broke through.

My hands were free.

But Barlow was looking at me with a different expression: alarm. His eyes darted up and to the side repeatedly, signaling something to me.

I heard the floorboards squeak.

Others were now looking around, seeing the same thing that Barlow was looking at.

I froze. It had to be Buck, and judging from the sound, he was standing just a few feet away.

Slowly, very slowly, I lowered my hands to my chest.

Tried to wind the rope back around my wrists, keeping my movements small, imperceptible from behind.

I sank to the floor, closed my eyes, feigning sleep. The carpet had that farmyard smell of wet wool.

I waited.

Buck cleared his throat. "You ladies keep it down," he said.

Then I heard his footsteps recede. I waited twenty seconds, then a minute, before opening my eyes.

Barlow nodded.

I sat up slowly. Ali, then Cheryl, saw, and their eyes widened.

"Oh, my God," Cheryl said.

53

I GAVE ALI a quick nod.

"Excuse me," she called out.

Buck looked around. I held my breath.

"Excuse me," she said again.

Buck came over, scowling. His jet-black hair looked stringy and unwashed.

"The hell do *you* want?"

"I need to use the bathroom."

"You can wait," he said, turning away.

"No, I can't," Ali said. "It's—look, it's a woman problem, okay? You want me to explain?"

Buck stared, shook his head slowly. He didn't want to hear details. Men never do.

"It's gonna have to be quick," he said at last.

She held up her hands, and he yanked her to her feet. "Move it," he said.

She walked, and he followed. Before they left the room, he slowly looked around. "Anyone moves an inch," he said, and he unholstered his gun. "You saw what happened."

I waited for a few seconds, then slipped my hands free of the rope and stood up.

Then I trod quickly along the carpet. Behind me, I could hear faint rustling, soft whispers. I turned around, held up a hand to silence them.

A low voice: "You're a goddamned idiot, Landry."

I didn't even have to look to know it was Bross.

"I hope they catch you."

"Kevin," said Bodine. "Not another word."

"Shut the hell up, Bross," Cheryl whispered.

"No way," Bross said, not even bothering to keep his voice down. "I'm not going to sit here and let this kid get us all killed."

I was just about out the door when I heard the squeak of floorboards.

"I thought I heard something," boomed a voice from the corridor.

Buck leveled his giant Ruger .44 at me. With his other hand he clutched Ali's neck.

She watched me evenly, her face a mask of calm.

Buck shook his head, cocked the revolver. "Russell warned me you might be trouble."

54

I PUT MY hands up in surrender.

"Jesus, Landry," Ali said. "I thought Russell cut him in."

Remarkable how calm she sounded—annoyed, even.

"Not in front of the others," I said. Her poise steadied me.

"Don't move," Buck said.

I ducked my head, said quietly, "You telling me Russell didn't let you in on our deal?"

"I told you, don't move."

I took a step forward. We were now maybe six or eight feet apart. "Can we take this out in the hall?"

"Maybe Russell wanted to cut him *out*," Ali said. She winced involuntarily as he squeezed her neck.

I was close enough now to smell his oniony foulness, the wood fire on his clothes. "I really don't want to talk in front of the others."

"The hell you talking about, cut me out?" Buck said.

"Why the hell do you think they even brought me here?" I said.

Another step. I looked up. "Because I'm the treasury guy. The operations guy. Hammond Aerospace is a com-

pany with billions of dollars in cash, and I'm the only guy
who can tap into it. That's why Russell told his brother to
cut me loose. He didn't fill you in? Unbelievable."

"Russell—?" That giant steel cannon of a gun was still
pointed at the middle of my chest. Buck was listening
now, but he was also prepared to shoot at any moment.

I took another step closer.

"I don't know how much they're paying you, Buck,
but it's chump change compared to what Russell and
his brother are taking."

His expression was guarded, but you couldn't miss
the glimmer of interest, of greed.

"It's not just that you're getting the short end of the
stick," I said very quietly. "You don't even know how
long the stick really is."

"What're they getting?" he asked.

One more step. We were right next to each other
now, so close that I could smell his chewing-tobacco
breath. "This has got to stay between you and me," I said
in a voice that was barely audible. "I mean it." My head
was down, my chin on my chest. I noticed the dried mud
on the laces and the soles of his boots.

"What kinda money we talking?" Buck demanded.
"I want to know."

I dipped my knees slightly, but not so much that he'd
notice. My back was rounded, my stomach muscles
contracted.

"Why don't you tell *me*?" I whispered.

I didn't care what he said, just so long as he opened
his mouth, parted his jaws.

"Tell you—?" he began, and then I uncoiled, exploded upward, the top of my head slamming under his
chin with a sudden violent force.

His teeth cracked together so loud it sounded like the snapping of bone. He made a weird *uhhh* sound as he tumbled backwards, sprawled onto the floor with a loud thud. His Ruger crashed to the floor alongside him.

The impact had sent a jolt of pain through my skull, but it was surely nothing compared to what Buck felt the instant his teeth smashed together.

Ali gasped as she pulled free of his grip. Someone behind me cried out, then a few more. Buck was unconscious. That I hadn't expected: I'd thought I might knock him off-balance long enough to grab his gun. Maybe my skull had struck some bundle of nerves underneath his jaw or in his throat.

"My *God,* Landry," Ali said. "Where the hell did that come from?" She was looking at me with a peculiar combination of gratitude and respect and, I think, fear.

"I was just about to ask you the same thing."

"But what you did just now—how did you—?"

"I don't know," I said.

But of course I did.

55

A FEW WEEKS after I'd finished serving out my sentence at Glenview, I appeared before the Family Court judge, at the advice of my Legal Aid lawyer, to request that my records be sealed. Otherwise the crime would follow me for the rest of my life.

The Honorable Florence Alton-Williams regarded me over her tortoiseshell half glasses. "Well, young man," she said in her stern contralto. "Your record at Glenview was impeccable. The warden's report on your conduct was simply glowing."

Of course it was. Neither he nor the superintendent wanted trouble from me; they didn't want any more details about Pee Wee's death to see the light of day.

"Looks to me like the right wolf won," she said.

I didn't reply.

SWOOPING DOWN TO retrieve Buck's stainless-steel Ruger, I tucked it into the waistband of my pants. Then I turned around to face the roomful of my fellow hostages. Everyone was awake now.

"You goddamned *idiot*," Kevin Bross said, even before

I could speak. "As soon as Russell sees this, he's going to start picking us off—"

"That's why I need help moving this guy," I said.

Some looked at me blankly; some looked away.

"Come on. *Anyone*. Upton, you're a strong guy. I'll cut you loose."

"I'm sorry, Jake. Those guys are going to be back any second," Barlow said.

"Come on, Landry, let's go," Ali said. She stood at the edge of the room, held her hands out to me. "Slice these ropes off me."

"No. They'll notice you gone right away. Someone else. Paul, you know the layout of this place better than anyone. You'll know where to stash this guy."

"I'm in no shape," the manager said.

"How about your son? Ryan?"

Ryan shot me a frightened look, but his father spoke up for him: "It's a suicide mission."

"This asshole's going to get us all killed," Bross said.

"How about you, Clive?" I said.

Rylance shook his head. "It's madness, Jake."

"Come on," I said to the rest of the room. "Someone? Anyone? Do I have to do this myself? *Any* of you guys?"

Silence.

"*Damn* it," I said, and turned to deal with Buck's body myself.

"You got yourself into this," I heard Bross say. "Try and get yourself out of it. What the hell did you think you were going to do—sneak out of here? Save your ass?"

I turned slowly. "Trying to save all of our asses, Kevin," I said. "Because if you think just sitting here and being good boys and girls is going to save us, you're wrong. We have to get help."

"That's exactly what got Danziger and Grogan killed."

"Wrong. Russell killed them because they'd figured out who he is. Somehow he found that out—they could identify him. And I'll tell you something else: Grogan was the only one who knew our bank account numbers. Which means Russell's not going to get his money. And you want to guess what Russell's going to do when he doesn't get his money, Kevin?"

Bross's crooked mouth hung open in disgust. "Why is anyone even listening to this moron? He's got his head up his ass."

"No," said Cheryl quietly. "He's got guts. Unlike some of us here."

"Jake," Barlow said, "we're totally isolated here. There's no way to reach anyone anyway."

I shook my head. "There's a couple of possibilities. But I really don't have time to explain. I have to get this guy out of here. So all I ask of the rest of you is to cover for me. When they ask what happened to Buck, all you know is that he said something about being freaked out by the shootings, how he didn't want to go to jail for the rest of his life. You don't know anything more. And if they notice I'm gone, too, I said I had to take a piss, and I couldn't wait. That's *all* you say, okay? Nothing else."

I looked around the room. "But it only takes one of you to say something different, and we're all going to pay the price." I looked directly at Bross. "So even if you think I have my head up my ass, don't screw it up for everyone else. Including yourself, Kevin."

Bodine was nodding. So was just about everyone else, except Bross, who scowled furiously.

"No one's going to screw it up," Hank Bodine said. "Not if I have anything to do with it."

"Thank you."

"No, Jake," he said. "Thank *you*."

"All right. Is no one going to help me move this body?"

Silence.

"Me," came a voice from the far back corner. It was one of the Mexican waiters. The one I'd talked to at dinner.

Pablo, I remembered his name was.

"I help you," he said.

56

PABLO WAS SMALL and skinny, with short dark hair and widely spaced brown eyes; for an instant I thought of Pee Wee.

But they looked nothing alike. This kid was slight of build, but scrappy, not fragile. And something else I'd glimpsed at dinner, as he apologized for spilling the wine: Behind the innocent eyes loitered a hell-raiser. A kindred spirit.

It was surprising how much easier it was to cut someone else loose than it had been to free myself. A couple of quick slashing motions using the heel of the blade, and the fibers began to give way, the strands splaying.

"There's no closet in this room, right?" I sliced through the ropes and tugged them off, jammed the two pieces of rope into my back pockets with the others.

"No closet."

"Out there?" I jerked my head toward the door as he clambered to his feet, ran behind me.

"For the table linens," he said. "But basement is closer."

No movement in the windows, no silhouetted figures. No screen doors slamming, no footsteps in the hall; not yet.

The entrance to the fitness center, in the basement, was next to the screened porch. Too close to Russell and his brother.

"How do we get down there?"

"I show you."

He knelt at one end of Buck's unconscious body, grabbing under the arms, his chest pressing against the back of Buck's neck.

The eyes came open just a bit, exposing little white crescents, and for a second I thought he might be regaining consciousness.

Turning around, I squatted between Buck's legs, grabbed his knees, leading the way out of the room.

Two hundred and fifty pounds or more of unconscious man was even heavier than I'd expected. Dried mud crumbled from the traction soles of his combat boots.

The great room was dark and still smelled of dinner. *How many hours ago was that? Five, maybe six? No more: yet the other side of a chasm.*

We threaded carefully among the jumbles of haphazardly stacked furniture.

"Where kitchen is," he said, directing me with his eyes. We struggled to balance the body between us, keep it from sagging.

"If they come in," I said, "we drop him and run, understand?"

He nodded, strain contorting his face.

"There," he whispered.

I steered Buck's knees toward the kitchen door. The small round inset pane of glass was black, opaque. That meant, I assumed, that no one was in the kitchen.

The floorboards creaked.

I pushed against the door, swinging it open into the dark corridor. The cellar door, on the left, was sturdy oak.

"There," Pablo said again. "Switch is on the wall."

I let go of Buck's right knee to grab the big black iron knob. His right leg dangled, then his boot thumped loudly against the floor.

Somewhere a screen door banged.

I gave Pablo a look, but he already understood. We were moving as quickly as we dared with our ungainly burden.

The cellar door groaned open, rusty hinges protesting. I found the light switch on the wall, flicked it up, and a bare bulb came on, illuminating a narrow, steep stairway. The ceiling was low and sharply canted.

"Careful," Pablo whispered. "The steps—no backs."

I saw what he meant at once: The wooden steps were open, had no risers. A trip hazard, particularly since we couldn't easily look down.

The steps squeaked as we descended into dank cold air, the faint odor of mildew.

The cellar was dark, seemed to go on forever. Presumably, it followed the footprint of the lodge. The concrete floor, fairly recent, had probably been poured over the original packed earth.

A new cinder-block wall ran along one side, partitioning off the fitness center, a recent addition, from the rest of the basement. Against the wall was a line of old black steamer trunks, wooden crates, neat stacks of cardboard boxes. A facing row of metal shelving displayed miscellaneous junk: old lamps, cardboard boxes of lightbulbs, an antique Waring blender. An open pantry on the other wall was stacked with burlap sacks of rice and canned beans and giant tins of cooking oil.

"We need to tie him up to something that won't move," I said. "Where's the boiler?"

"Maybe something else," Pablo said. He jerked his chin to the left.

We carried Buck's body along a narrow aisle between tall steel shelves of laundry detergent and bleach and floor wax. Now, I figured, we were directly under the great room and the front porch. Oddly, the concrete walls sloped inward to what looked, at first glance, like the floor-to-ceiling bars of a prison cell. The light from the stairwell was too distant; I couldn't make out what it was.

Pablo gently set down Buck's head; I dropped the legs. Then he located a light switch mounted on a steel column and flipped it, lighting a line of bulbs on the ceiling.

Behind the steel bars, I could see, was a room whose walls and low, barrel-vaulted ceiling were built from weathered red brick. The floor was gravel. Plain wooden racks held hundreds of dusty wine bottles.

The wine cellar.

"Yes," I said, grasping a bar and tugging. "Good."

I pulled the two lengths of rope from my pockets, held them up. "We're going to need some more rope."

"Rope? I don't think down here . . ."

"Anything. Wire. Chain."

"Ah, maybe . . ." He turned slowly and headed back the way we'd come.

The wine cellar's grate was made of stout iron bars, the finest jailhouse construction. The Château Lafite wasn't going anywhere, and neither was Buck.

A guttural moan.

I spun around, saw Buck starting to sit up.

57

HIS LARGE HANDS pushed against the cement slab floor. I sidestepped around behind his back, then lurched forward, hooking my right elbow under his chin. The bristles of his hairy neck felt like steel wool against the crook of my arm. When I had his throat in a vise grip, I grabbed my right hand with my left, clasped them together, and squeezed.

Adrenaline coursed through my bloodstream.

He struggled mightily to free himself from the jailer's hold, flung his hands upward, twisting and torquing his legs around.

My arm muscles trembled from the exertion. In ten seconds or so he'd gone limp. The carotid arteries on either side of the neck supply blood to the brain. Compressed, they don't.

Dad had taught me the blood choke. He'd actually demonstrated it on me once until I passed out.

Pablo rushed toward me, ready to help, then watched me set Buck's head on the floor. He held up a tangled mess of brown lamp cord.

"Perfect." I handed him the steak knife and asked him to cut off pieces a couple of feet long.

In Buck's tactical vest I found a black nylon sheath, out of which I pulled a knife. This was no steak knife, either. It was just like the one I'd seen Verne take out earlier—a Microtech HALO, a single-action front-opener. I could tell right away from the logo, a white claw in a circle set against the matte black, anodized aluminum handle. At Glenview one just like it had sent a kid to the hole for six months.

I pressed the titanium firing button, and a lethal-looking blade shot forward. It kicked in my hand. A four-inch blade, partially serrated. I didn't need to touch the spearpoint to know it could take off a fingertip.

I handed it carefully to Pablo.

"*¡Dios mío!*" he breathed. He had one gold tooth: lousy Mexican dental care.

"Be careful."

While he sliced lamp cord, I took out the Ruger, thumbed the cylinder release, saw it was loaded. Several of his vest pockets were stuffed with .44 Magnum cartridges; I grabbed a handful. There was a flashlight in one of his vest pockets, and I took that, too: an expensive-looking tactical flashlight, the kind you see SWAT teams use to temporarily blind suspects at night.

When Pablo was finished, he handed the knife back to me awkwardly, blade out. He didn't know how to use it. He watched as I pulled back on the charging lever to retract the blade.

I looped some lamp cord around Buck's wrists, and we used it to pull him upright. Then we shoved him against the iron grate and secured him, spread-eagled, in a standing position. Pablo wrapped cord around his ankles while I searched the dusty floor and finally found an oil-stained rag in a corner, stiff and covered

with dirt, and stuffed it into Buck's mouth, in case he
came to again soon.

"I need to go back upstairs," I said. "To the manager's office."

"But is not safe to go up there."

"I don't have much choice. Is there any other way
upstairs besides the way we came in?"

"No."

"Not a bulkhead?"

Pablo didn't know what the word meant, and I didn't
know the Spanish. "A delivery entrance?"

He looked blank.

"La entrada de servicio," I said. *"Ya sabes, el área
dondese carga y descarga, por donde se meten las cosas
al hotel."*

"Ah." He nodded, thought for a moment. "Yes, but
not to upstairs."

"So there *is* another way out?"

"To the water only."

I didn't understand.

He went over to the iron bars, pointed out the gate in
the center that I'd noticed earlier. Mounted on the gate's
frame just to the left of Buck's lolling head was an old
push-button mechanical combination lock. He punched
in three numbers, turned a knob. Then he slowly pulled
the gate open. It looked heavy, though it was surely a lot
heavier with Buck lashed to it.

"In here," he said.

I followed him into the wine cellar. He pointed to an
arched section of the brick wall that had no wine rack in
front of it. "The old delivery entrance."

The arched entrance had obviously been bricked in a
long time ago. "That doesn't really help us," I said.

"No, no, look. Is where Mr. Paul hides the very expensive wines and things."

He reached behind a wine rack and pulled out a long metal rod, then poked it into a crack in the mortar between two bricks.

A clunking sound, and the entire arched wall jutted forward.

Not a wall: a brick-and-mortar door.

"What the hell—?"

Behind the brick-paved door was a small room. A few wooden wine racks, randomly placed, held maybe a few dozen dusty bottles. A small stack of plastic file boxes, probably Paul's private records.

And a second iron gate. This chamber was actually, I saw, the mouth of a long tunnel.

"This goes right down to the dock, doesn't it?" I said. "Under the dock, in fact."

Pablo nodded. "When they built the lodge a long time ago, all the deliveries came by sea. They used to bring all the things in through this tunnel. But not for a long time. The old owners, before Mr. Paul, they closed it off."

And they'd taken advantage of the renovation to build a hidden wine cellar for the good stuff. Or a hidden storage nook. "Is this gate locked?"

"No more."

"Everyone who works here knows about this?"

"No, just . . ." He was suddenly uncomfortable. "José and I—sometimes we smoke, you know, the *mota*."

"Weed."

He nodded. "Mr. Paul, he fire us if he know. So José found this place under the dock."

"I'm going to try to get upstairs to the office. I want

you to go down to the water," I said. "And look for a boat."

"Which?"

"Any one that has a key in the engine. Or a rowboat, if you have to. You know how to use a boat?"

"Yes, of course."

"When you get out there, move slowly and quietly, and don't start up the motor until the last possible minute. Take the boat to the nearest lodge and wake them up. Get help. The police, anyone. Tell them what's going on. Okay?"

"Okay." He seemed to hesitate.

"You're worried about the noise from the boat's engine, aren't you?"

"They have guns. They shoot."

"But you'll be far from the lodge."

A sudden static burst came from Buck's two-way radio: "Buck, come in."

The voice echoed in the low-ceilinged chamber. I couldn't identify it.

I returned to the outer gate, pulled the radio from Buck's belt: a Motorola Handie-Talkie.

"Buck, it's Verne," the voice said again. "Where the hell are you?"

"Maybe they look for you now," Pablo said. "Is not safe for you up there."

It all depended, of course, on what Ali and the other hostages told them. I switched off the HT. "You go," I said. "Get help. Don't you worry about me."

58

AT THE TOP of the stairs, I switched off the light, stood in absolute darkness.

Quiet.

Then again, the cellar door was two inches thick, and then there was the kitchen door: a lot of wood between me and anyone who might be searching for me. I turned the knob, pushed the cellar door open slowly. The hinges squeaked no matter how slowly I opened it.

A few steps into the dark hallway, I stopped again to listen.

Voices now.

From the great room. I sank to my knees, out of sight, and listened.

Two voices, hushed and urgent. One was Verne's, manic, rising and falling, speedy and loud. The other was Wayne's oddly high alto. The tattooed ex-con conferring with the crew-cut blond lunk.

Scraps of argument, some words and phrases more distinct than others.

". . . heard him saying he was going to bolt." That was Verne.

"To who?" Wayne, now.

"—said he changed his mind. Got spooked after Russell killed those guys. Didn't want to go to jail for the rest of his life."

"He told you that?"

". . . the chick said."

"What chick?"

"I don't know, whatever her name. Paris Hilton, how the hell do I know? The babe."

Something I couldn't hear, and then Verne saying, "I'll take his cut." A sniggering laugh.

Something else, then Wayne: "Where the hell's he gonna go?"

"Out there somewhere. Russell wants you to get your ass out there and look for him."

"The hell's he gonna go? Not the Zodiac—"

"They got other boats down there."

". . . cut the spark-plug wires, so what's he gonna do, swim to Vancouver?"

Wayne said something else I couldn't quite make out, and then Verne said, "Christ's sake, then look in the woods."

"Can't go more than twenty yards in that forest without getting stuck. You saw that."

"You saw the guy in the jungle in Panama—he's an animal."

"And if I find him?"

"Waste him, Russell says. Can't trust him anymore."

"I'm not going to waste Bucky for taking off. That's whacked, man."

"You don't do it, buddy, Russell's gonna grease *you*. You know he will. He's not taking any chances. Not when we're this close to the big score."

The jungle in Panama. Special Forces, then. Military,

anyway. At least these guys and Buck, probably Russell, too.

So I'd learned a couple of other things as well. The cover story about Buck had worked. They weren't looking for an unconscious comrade but a defector. They weren't looking for me, either; they hadn't yet realized I was missing.

That meant they'd search outside, not inside. I could hide here until they were gone and get to the office without being spotted.

Other, crazier ideas came to me. Fire a few rounds at those two, right through the door. The .44 Magnum rounds would penetrate the hardwood, no problem. But without accuracy: I didn't know their position. Not without looking through the round window—which would expose my location.

Sure, I might get lucky. But the odds were that I'd hit neither. Maybe wound one of them. They'd grab their weapons, and it would be two against one. And as soon as Russell and his brother heard the shots, it would be four against one.

Trying to shoot these two was insanity. Yet until they moved, I couldn't get to the manager's office.

By then, Pablo was on his way to the water. Maybe, depending on how easy it was to move through the old tunnel, he was already outside, under the dock. Even at the kidnappers' Zodiac.

Then the voices stopped. Retreating footsteps, then a screen door opening and closing. One of them—was it Wayne?—had gone outside to search for Buck.

I slid across the floor, paused to listen again.

No one out there now.

I pushed the kitchen service door from the bottom, just a few inches.

Then a few inches more.

The Ruger tucked into my belt: I needed both hands free.

Then, rising slowly, I sidled through the doorway and eased it closed behind me.

59

LOOKING LEFT, THEN right, I surveyed the room, satisfied that no one was in sight.

Through the cavernous shadowed room slowly, cautiously, footsteps soft. I was afraid I might trip over something. But as my eyes adjusted, I was able to zigzag without tipping over a vase or a wineglass.

Past the staircase landing, then into the hallway that led to the side entrance, the bathroom, the manager's office. Three identical wooden doors off the hall: dark-stained, five horizontal raised panels. All with black iron knobs and locksets that opened with the same skeleton key, Paul had said. First was the bathroom, the next two unmarked, the fourth had a small brass plaque that said MANAGER.

Just as Paul had promised, a legal bookcase stood outside his office door. Squat, dark-stained quarter-sawn oak, glass-fronted. The sort of gloomy semi-antique furniture you might find in the courthouse office of a public defender in a small town in upstate New York.

On top of the bookcase, a brown ceramic lamp. I lifted it, spotted the skeleton key.

The manager's office door was locked, but the old

key fit snugly in the lock. It turned with a satisfying click.

I pulled the revolver from my belt, held it in my right hand as I turned the knob and opened the door with my left.

The room was small, windowless, absolutely dark. It smelled of old wood and damp paper. I pocketed the skeleton key, then shut the door behind me.

I paused for a moment, considering whether to lock the door or not. Was it more important to keep the bad guys out or be able to make a quick escape? Impossible to know.

I decided not to lock it.

Then I pulled out Buck's tactical flashlight, pressed the tailcap switch to pulse the beam on for a second. In one freeze-frame I could make out a small, rolltop desk, stored its location in my memory. On top of it, an Apple iMac computer, the one-piece model with the flat screen and spherical base that was popular a few years ago.

I had an Apple computer at home. When you pressed the power switch, it chimed like the opening chord of a Beethoven symphony. Unless the volume was turned down. But you didn't know until it was too late.

Even turning it on was a risk, but wasn't everything just then? I found the power button by feel on the back side of the base and pressed it.

In a few seconds it chimed. Loud.

I sat in an old rolling office chair and watched the screen light up and come to life, listening for footfalls in the hall.

And suddenly I changed my mind, got up, and locked the door. At least if someone came by to investigate, I'd hear the doorknob rattle and have just enough time to take aim.

The screen flashed the Apple logo. Its hard drive crunched and crunched, and I waited. It seemed to take forever. If Paul had installed a password to keep out unauthorized users, he hadn't bothered to mention it.

But no, a swirly blue pattern came right up. A row of icons on the right: Internet Explorer and the Safari browser. I double-clicked Safari and waited for it to load.

And waited.

Jesus, I thought, *this is slow.*

For God's sake, hurry. I found myself talking to the computer, all the while listening for footsteps, knowing that at any minute I might be discovered.

But all I got was a big white box, a blank screen.

Then a few lines of text, not what I wanted to see:

YOU ARE NOT CONNECTED TO THE INTERNET.

Safari can't open the page http://www.google.com/ because your computer isn't connected to the Internet.

I quit Safari and reloaded it, and got the same error message. I clicked on the "Network Diagnostics" button and got a pane with a row of red dots and more dismaying news:

Built-in Ethernet—failed

Internet—failed

Either the modem was down or the satellite Internet connection wasn't working.

Shit.

Switching on the flashlight, I traced the modem cable to a closet. The door was unlocked, and the modem was right inside, bracketed to the wall.

Its power light was on, but the receiver light was off. That told me it wasn't getting any satellite signal. So I did what we've all learned to do in this age of balky technology equipment: I shut the modem down, waited a few seconds, then powered it back up.

No change. Nothing different.

The problem wasn't with the modem or the computer. Someone had cut off Internet access. There was no way to e-mail out.

Or wire money out, either.

60

THAT WAS THE puzzling thing.

It could hardly be a coincidence that the Internet connection was down. Russell's men must have done something. After all, once they'd grabbed the sat phone, the only way for their hostages to transmit a distress message was via the Internet.

Yet without it, there'd be no half-billion-dollar ransom. So barring some accident during the takeover, they must have dismantled it. Not in here, though, or I'd have seen it. Somewhere outside.

I had to get out there and try to restore the link.

The summer after I'd got out of Glenview and before I joined the National Guard, I'd gotten a job as a cable TV installer. Before the summer was over I quit, but not before I'd acquired a few useless skills, like how to splice coaxial cable.

Maybe not so useless.

But if the line had been cut, it would take me a long time to repair it without the right tools—a crimper and some connectors and other parts that I doubted Peter the handyman kept around. When the satellite went down, they probably called the satellite company. Chances were, Peter didn't do those repairs himself. That was a fairly specialized skill.

I waited at the door, didn't hear anyone walking by. Holding the Ruger in my right hand, the key in my left, I unlocked the door, pushed it open a few inches, looked out.

No one in the hall that I could see.

As I crept along the dark hall, I glanced out a window. No one out there. Maybe Wayne was still trudging through the forest, looking for Buck. Maybe he'd gotten caught in the underbrush.

I kept looking, trying to locate the satellite dish. I vaguely remembered seeing one somewhere behind the lodge, mounted on top of an outbuilding. Which made sense: The dish didn't fit in with the rustic décor.

Sure enough, it was where I remembered: on top of a shed about two hundred feet from the lodge. The cable that ran from the lodge to the dish would be buried, of course. If it had been cut, there were only two places it could have been done: at the shed, or on the exterior of the lodge.

Gently nudging the screen door open, I stepped out onto the soft earth, then pushed the door closed behind me so it wouldn't slam. The pneumatic closer hissed in annoyance. Pine needles crunched underfoot. I inhaled the delicious cool air. It smelled of salt water and pine. It was a relief.

For a moment, I allowed myself to enjoy the illusion of freedom.

But of course I wasn't free. Not as long as Ali and all the others were trapped inside.

Just keep going, I told myself. *Don't overthink.*

Self-doubt could be crippling.

I walked slowly along the log siding, looking for a cable stapled to the concrete foundation. The wall outside Paul's office was the most logical place to find it. I couldn't risk switching on the flashlight; fortunately, the moon was bright.

In a few minutes I found it: a loop of cable sprouting from the concrete, a few inches above the ground.

One end of the cable dangling loose.

It had been unscrewed from its connector. That was how they'd cut off Internet access. Quick and easy. Above all, easy to screw back in when they were ready to use it.

Except for one little thing.

The connector was missing.

A little piece of precision-machined, nickel-plated brass. An F-81 barrel connector, it was called. Used to join two pieces of coaxial cable. I'd spent much of that summer fumbling with the damned things, losing them in people's basements and on their lawns.

I quickly searched the ground, just to be sure, but I didn't need to. I knew what Russell had done. Simple and clever. He'd removed that tiny, but crucial piece, to make sure no one could get on the Internet to send out an SOS.

I was impressed by Russell's thoroughness.

It also gave me an idea.

I raced over to the generator shed, where the satellite dish was bolted to the roof. At the back of the small, shingled building, I found where the cable came out of the ground and ran up the outside wall to the dish.

Kneeling, I took out Buck's knife, pressed the trigger button to eject the blade.

With one quick motion, I sliced through the cable.

If I couldn't use the Internet, then neither could Russell. I doubted he or his men knew the first thing about how to splice coaxial cable, which sure wasn't like electrical wire.

I did, though. Those few weeks of tedium suddenly seemed less pointless.

Now I had something he needed.

But as I turned to head down to the shore, I heard a voice.

61

IT HAD COME from the front of the lodge.

A shout, quick and sharp: "Stop right there."

Pablo had been spotted; it could be nothing else.

I turned toward the shore, taking long, silent strides along the side of the building.

Down the hill a few hundred feet a bulky silhouette descended the wooden steps of the dock. An arm extended: a weapon.

"I'm not going to tell you again."

Pablo was standing on the beach, hands at his side. He was torquing from one side to the other, as if trying to decide which way to run. Behind him, floating in the water, the black hulk of an inflatable craft moored to the dock.

I watched with a feeling of desperate helplessness. Pablo had volunteered to help, and implicit in that deal was that I'd be his protector.

Some protector.

Wayne wasn't going to shoot the kid, I was certain—not without Russell's approval, anyway. They'd bring him in, interrogate him, force him to tell them how he'd managed to escape. And where I was.

In the meantime, I'd have to grab a boat and summon help, but the time would be even shorter, and the likelihood of successfully rescuing the other hostages would have plummeted.

Would Russell then decide to make a "lesson" out of some lowly lodge staff member? There'd be no reason for him to do it, not after Grogan and Danziger. But with Russell, you never knew.

Wayne descended a few more steps, then stopped, raising his other hand to steady his grip. From here, his gun looked larger, longer than it had before. An optical illusion, maybe.

Pablo gave a high, strangled yelp, his words obliterated by the crash of the surf.

Wayne was much closer to the shore now than to me.

Torn by indecision, I raised my gun, lined up the sights. His body was a distant blur.

No. I couldn't bring myself to fire at Wayne. Besides, at this distance, I had little chance of hitting the target. And once I pulled the trigger, whether I hit him or not, everything would change at once. They'd hear the gunshot, know I was out here.

If I fired, I'd surely miss—and I'd become a fugitive.

I had to help Pablo escape. That was all I could really do now.

So I did the only thing I could think of to distract Wayne, get him to turn around, divert his attention and give Pablo the chance to run. I picked up a rock.

No way would I hit him at this distance: the greatest pitcher in baseball couldn't have beaned the guy from here. But at least the sound of the rock hitting the ground might break his concentration, cause him to turn. That was something.

Pablo raised his hands in surrender, walked slowly toward Wayne, who said something I couldn't hear. Then Pablo did something bizarre: He clapped his hands, then put his arms behind him and clapped again.

What the hell was he doing?

I hurled the rock as hard as I could, and at that precise moment, Wayne fired.

Three shots in quick succession.

He probably never even heard the hollow *pock* of the rock hitting the wooden step.

I saw the muzzle flash, but the shots were distant, muted pops, masked by the sound of the ocean.

Pablo twisted, jerked forward, crumpled to the ground, a small dark shape on the beach. He lay still, obviously dead. He could have been just another rock, another boulder, a pile of debris.

62

MOM'S VOICE WOKE me, high and keening, from the kitchen downstairs: "Please! That's enough! That's enough!"

Something hard crashing. My digital clock said two in the morning.

Dad, thundering, "You goddamned bitch."

I lay in bed, not moving, heart racing.

Mom's voice, hysterical: "Get out of here! Get out of the house! Just leave us!"

"I'm not leaving my house, you bitch!"

He'd lost another job. As scary and foul-tempered as he usually was, when he got fired, he drank even more; he hit Mom even more.

Another crash. Something thudded. The whole house seemed to shake.

Silence.

Terrified, I leaped out of bed, vaulted down the stairs to the kitchen. Mom was lying on the floor, unconscious. Eyes closed, twin streams of blood running from her nostrils.

Some protector I was.

"Get up, you bitch!" my dad screamed. "Get the hell up!"

My blood ran cold. He'd gone berserk.

"What'd you do to her?" I shouted.

He saw me, snarled: "Get the hell out of here."

"What did you do to her?" I lunged, hands outspread, shoved him against the stove.

At fifteen, I was as tall as my dad and starting to get some muscles on me, though Dad was still far beefier and more powerful.

For a second, his face went slack in surprise: I'd just done the unthinkable.

Then his face went deep red. He turned, grabbed a cast-iron frying pan from the stovetop, whacked it against the side of my head. I'd backed up out of the way, but not in time. The pan clipped my ear, the pain unbelievable.

I yowled, doubled over, my ear ringing.

"We gonna do this the hard way?" he shouted, and he swung the frying pan again.

This time, instead of backing up, I shot forward, pushed him hard, everything a blur. His sour perspiration smell, his beer breath, the gray-white of his T-shirt spattered with Mom's blood.

A flash of black, the frying pan, as he pulled it back to swing again. Mom's cry: She'd regained consciousness.

Everything was happening at once, and nothing made sense, nothing but the anger inside me that had finally boiled over, the pumping adrenaline that gave me the strength to overpower the monster, to smash him back against the upper kitchen cabinet, the one with the glass windows in it and the neatly stacked dishes. To keep him from hitting me again, to stop him from hitting Mom again.

To be a protector.

The back of his head cracked into the sharp corner, where the wood veneer had peeled off, and he'd never gotten around to repairing it.

He roared, "You son of a bitch, I'm going to kill you!"

But the anger and the adrenaline and all those years of storing it inside made me stronger than he, at least for the moment. And maybe he didn't expect it from me, and maybe he was just too drunk.

My hands clutched the sides of his head, the way you'd hold someone you were about to kiss, only I shoved his head against the corner of the cabinet again, and again, and again.

He bellowed low and deep, like a beast. Blood roared in my ears. Snot ran down my nose. His eyes bulged, looking shocked and disbelieving and—was it possible?—afraid.

I didn't stop. I was in that dark tunnel now, had to keep going. Kept smashing his head back against the sharp corner. Felt something in his skull go soft. I had a fleeting thought, in the red haze of my madness, that it was like a hard acorn squash that had suddenly turned into an overripe zucchini. The awful bellowing finally stopped, but his eyes bulged.

I finally heard my mom's voice shrilling: "Jakey, Jakey, Jakey, stop it!"

I stopped. Let go. Dad toppled, then slumped to the floor.

I stared.

"Jakey, oh my God, what have you done?"

My legs buckled. An icy coldness in my stomach, icy fingers clutching my bowels, my chest. And at the same time, something else, too.

Relief.

63

I STOOD IN the cool breeze and the dusky moonlight for what felt like a whole minute. It might have been only a few seconds, though: Time had slowed.

Pablo was unarmed, no threat; he'd obeyed orders, had done what he'd been told to do.

He had put his hands up. He'd surrendered. There was no reason to kill him.

Wayne's gun had looked longer because it was longer: He'd screwed on a sound suppressor. Probably so as not to tip off Buck, who he thought was out here.

Grief hollowed me out, and into that hollow place rushed a far more familiar emotion. Loosing the bad wolf, giving in to the rage: There was something strangely comforting about it.

It fueled me, propelled me, focused my mind, sharpened my senses.

I knew now what I had to do.

WAYNE LUMBERED DOWN the dock steps to the beach. Maybe he wanted to make sure Pablo was dead. Maybe he wanted to move the body somewhere, hide it or dispose of it. Or maybe he simply wanted to check the Zodiac to see if it was okay.

The hiss of the pneumatic closer.

I peered around the corner of the building, saw Verne emerge from the side entrance. He took something out of his pocket that glinted. The flick of a butane lighter, a puff of smoke. He held the flame to the bulb end of a glass freebase pipe, sucked in the smoke, held it in his lungs until he coughed it out.

I dropped to my knees, crawled along the front of the lodge. The porch was as long as the building's façade, raised about five feet above ground level. I moved quietly, staying close to the wooden skirting, struggling to maintain my balance. The slope down to the shore was steep.

It wasn't easy, given the sharp incline from the shore to the lodge. When I reached the wooden walkway that connected the porch to the steps that wound to the pier, I stopped.

Wayne wasn't looking up at the lodge, though I didn't think anyone inside had heard the silenced gunfire. The great room remained dark. The only light spilled from the windows of the enclosed porch at the northwest corner.

I resumed crawling, went under the walkway, which was elevated a few feet about the steep hillside, shimmied through the narrow gap between creosote-treated timber pilings, then back along the porch skirting until I was beneath the screened porch.

Once I reached the west side of the lodge, I figured I should be able to crawl the short span to the woods unseen. That was the only way to reach the shore, and the boat, without being seen, but getting through the dense forest, though—

Voices.

I sank as low to the ground as I could.

Russell was saying something, in a calm voice, that I couldn't make out. Then came a reply, and I recognized Travis: ". . . ain't what we were hired to do."

Their voices got softer, more conversational, and as much as I strained to hear, I couldn't.

I wondered how long it would take for Wayne to return to the lodge and report that he'd just killed a young Mexican, a member of the lodge staff—and a hostage. The first question would be how one of the hostages had escaped. There'd be a head count. They'd quickly realize I was missing, too.

Which would surely trigger further reprisals. More "lessons."

The ground was earthen and soft, but here and there were buried surprises, rocks and twigs that bruised my kneecaps. The narrow strip of lawn lay just ahead, and beyond it, the forest. The only way down to the water, the boats.

And then Travis's voice, whining, almost pleading: "—hundred million. Not five hundred million, man, come on, what are we doing here? Jesus, Russell, man, that's like a whole new level of, of—"

Russell murmured something lulling.

Travis spoke, but just a fragment floated through the air: ". . . your cellie from Lompoc."

Lompoc, I thought. That was a prison somewhere. A federal prison. Russell's cellmate from Lompoc prison, it had to be.

John Danziger: *One of their employees got arrested in South America on a child recovery case he was working, charged with kidnapping under the international treaty agreements. Did a couple years in prison in the U.S.*

Now Russell raised his voice. "No, Travis, you listen to me very carefully. All he cares about is getting the goddamned ninety-seven-point-five million dollars in his goddamned account in Liechtenstein by the close of business today. He gets that, he's cool, he's off the hook."

Who was "he"—Russell's prison cellmate?

Travis interrupted him, but I couldn't hear what he was saying.

My scalp prickled.

Ninety-seven-point-five million.

Off the hook.

Liechtenstein.

Close of business today.

So this wasn't just a clever heist dreamed up by a gang of ex-soldiers. They'd been *hired.*

I sat up, keeping my head just below the porch floor. I waited, listened harder, finally gave up. Then, my heart knocking, I rose slowly and raced toward the edge of the forest.

64

FOR A MOMENT, hidden in a dense stand of pines, I looked back at the lodge.

A tall, lanky figure stared out the porch window: Russell.

Maybe he was simply impatient, wondering what was taking Wayne so long. He had a schedule to keep, after all.

I began scrambling down the steep hill toward the shore. Coniferous forest, especially virgin, primitive woods like this, could be like Amazonian jungle. I found myself climbing through hellish, thorny under-brush, thickets of ancient, moss-covered spruces and giant Douglas firs, tendrils of protruding tree roots. Twisted, gnarled pines with boughs so densely grown together I couldn't see more than a few feet in front of me. Branches whipped against my face. The forest canopy was so thick overhead that it blocked the stars.

As I stepped over a drift of leaves and pine needles, my foot struck something.

It swung forward and grasped my shin, and when I saw what it was, I had to stop myself from screaming.

A well-manicured hand. Through the blanket of

leaves that had been strewn over Danziger's body I could make out the light blue sleeve of his alligator shirt.

Next to it was another drift of leaves: Alan Grogan.

And a third body concealed by leaves and twigs. With the toe of my shoe, I cleared away just enough to see a dark-skinned young man in jeans and sweatshirt. José, I knew at once. Pablo's friend. The first one they'd killed, when they first arrived: the gunshot we'd all heard at dinner. He'd probably seen them come ashore when he was cleaning out the boats.

Undone by what I'd just seen, I kicked free of the dead hand, lurched forward, and tripped on a root; tumbled headfirst, then cracked my forehead against a craggy rock outcropping.

For a few seconds I breathed hard, allowed the pain to suffuse my body. When that didn't work, I bit my lip, tried to will the pain away.

Head throbbing, I scrambled to my feet. My face, scratched and scraped from the branches, stung.

The roar of the waves told me I was close now.

The terrain had become so steeply pitched that I couldn't keep myself from sliding downhill. Only by grabbing at the branch of a downed tree was I able to stop just before plummeting off a scrabbly ledge into the ocean.

There was no shore here; the ledge was far too narrow. But the water was shallow, and it was the only way to the dock. Slowly, I lowered my feet into the surf, braced for a cold shock, relieved to find it wasn't too bad.

I waded along the shoreline, careful not to let the water reach my waist. Buck's revolver was in my pocket, and I wanted to keep it in operational condition.

The shoreline wound past the trees to the small beachfront. The water had gotten steadily colder, or maybe it had been deceptively warm at first; my legs were getting numb. My pant legs chafed my crotch.

There, out in the open, I could be seen from the lodge. I looked up, saw no one.

Wayne was gone. I assumed he'd made his way back to the lodge while I was climbing through the woods.

The Zodiac floated in the water, hitched to the dock.

On the sand nearby lay Pablo's body.

THE ZODIAC WAS a classic military inflatable, a commando boat with a skin of leathery black synthetic rubber. The Army donates them to fire and police departments, and sometimes they turn up on the black market.

Around twenty feet long; probably seated fifteen people. Mounted on the black plywood transom board at the stern was a twenty-five-horsepower Yamaha outboard motor. A good, light engine, powerful enough but not too loud. A pair of aluminum oars rested in brackets: much quieter.

As I approached, though, I realized that the boat wasn't just tied up. It was locked. A cable connected the Zodiac to a steel horn cleat bolted to the dock. It was a strong cable, too—thick twisted-steel wire, coated in clear plastic, its ends looping through a sturdy brass padlock.

I tried to fight back the surge of desperation.

Was there some way to get the cable off? Hoisting myself out of the water, I climbed onto the dock, then immediately lay flat on the splintery planks so I wouldn't be easily spotted from the lodge. I leaned over, tugged at the cleat to see if I could pry it loose.

A sulfurous smell rose like marsh gas, assaulted my nostrils. As I grappled with the cleat, the metal cold and slick in my hands, I heard the splash of the water, surging and boiling against the dock's wooden posts, dark and ominous.

But the steel cleat was too secure, and the cable was too sturdy. The boat wasn't going to move anywhere. I'd have to clamber back up the hill through the forest and look for a cable cutter. Maybe in the maintenance shed up the hill.

That meant exposure, more time. Could I risk it? If I had to . . .

Discouraged, I arose.

And felt a hand on my shoulder.

65

EVEN BEFORE I turned around I knew whose hand it was. I hadn't heard Wayne's approach: I'd been distracted, and the surf had masked the heavy tread.

Now I found myself looking into the little black hole at the end of the sound suppressor threaded onto his black SIG-Sauer.

You don't put a silencer on a gun unless you mean to fire it.

"Boy, you're full of surprises, aren't you?" he said. "Nowhere to run, you know."

Buck's revolver was in my pocket, if I could get to it in time. But an unsilenced gunshot would draw notice from the lodge, attention I didn't want. The knife would be a better idea.

If I could pull it out without him seeing and killing me first.

I took a long, slow breath. "Who says I want to run?"

"Just put your hands up, Jake," he said, "and come back inside. I don't want to hurt you. I really don't."

He didn't know I'd seen him pull the trigger.

I reflexively glanced at Pablo's sprawled body, on the sand behind him.

His eyes remained locked on mine; he knew what I'd seen.

"Come on, now, let's go," he said. "Hands up, Jake, and you won't get hurt. I promise."

I'd barely heard him talk before. The man who'd just killed Pablo had a surprisingly gentle manner. His piping voice was almost melodious.

And he knew my name, which was interesting.

I'd killed once before and thought I'd never have to do it again.

I didn't want to.

Don't make me do this.

"Jake. You see, you really don't have a choice."

"No, I really don't."

"All right," he said. "Now we're talking."

I bowed my head as if considering my options, and my right hand felt unseen for my back pocket, very slowly pulling out the knife.

Pablo had died because I couldn't bring myself to kill for the second time in my life.

It really was that simple. Not just that I'd misjudged Wayne, though I had. But that I couldn't do it.

I could now.

Nodding, I thumbed the trigger button and felt it jolt in my hand as the blade ejected.

And then I lunged at him.

The man who'd just killed Pablo. I saw him as if through fog.

My heart raced. A quick upward swipe against his throat, and his mouth gaped in surprise, exposing the tiny jagged teeth of some feral woodland creature.

His knees buckled, and he toppled backwards. The

dock shook. His pistol clattered, slid almost to the edge of the dock.

Now I had the knife against his throat, my knees on his chest. The blade caught the moonlight. It glinted and sparkled. Blood ran from a gash just below his neckline.

"You know what this knife can do," I said. "Answer a couple of questions, and I'll let you go."

He blinked a few times, and I saw, out of the corner of my eye, his right hand start to move. I pressed the blade against the skin. "Don't."

"What do you want to know?"

"What happens after you get your money?"

He was blinking rapidly: nervous. His eyes shifted up and to his right, then back. "I can hardly breathe, you know. Your knee—"

"What happens to us?"

"Don't worry, Jake," he said. "We're not leaving anyone behind."

I studied his face, saw the very beginning of a smile, no more.

"What's that supposed to mean?" I said, though I knew.

He didn't answer. I slid the blade lightly against his throat. A fresh line of blood appeared.

"Hey!"

"Who hired you?"

"You did."

I slid the blade again, a bit harder this time.

"You don't get it, do you? We're just employees like you. Just doing a job. Come on, Jake. Seriously, now. There's no need for violence."

I gritted my teeth; my hand trembled. He probably thought I was frightened.

I wasn't, not anymore. "Tell that to the kid on the beach over there."

"I saw that. It's a shame."

"I saw it, too," I said. "Watched you put three bullets into him. One more question, Wayne. What did you say to him at the very end?"

Now he was unable to stop his smile. "I told him to dance the *cucaracha*."

Tears blurred my vision.

Wayne took a deep, labored breath. "He looked like a puppet, didn't you think?"

Blood roared in my ears, and I was in the dark tunnel, speeding along, no exit.

This time I slashed without holding back, and a geyser spewed from his neck, spilling over his camo shirt and vest. He made a choking, gagging sound. His right hand grasped the air, the fingers twitching.

With both hands, I gave his body a hard shove. It made a great splash.

66

THE ADRENALINE BEGAN to ebb from my blood-stream, leaving me rubber-limbed, feeling played out.

I stood, though my knees were barely able to support me. Wiped the blood off the knife, then retracted the blade and slipped it into my back pocket. I fought off a wave of nausea. Then I remembered Wayne's SIG-Sauer, picked it up from the edge of the dock, slipped it into my waistband.

Tried to summon the strength to climb back up the hill, through the tangled underbrush, to go to the tool-shed and try to find a pair of bolt cutters.

And then, from somewhere up the hill, came a high-pitched cry.

A female cry, quickly stifled.

Coming out of the eastern side of the lodge, the area where Verne took his smoking breaks, were the silhou-ettes of two people, one shoving the other.

It was Verne, and he had a woman with him.

I RACED UP the wooden steps, right out in the open, no longer caring whether Russell or anyone else was watching.

As I approached, I heard scuffling. For a few seconds I couldn't comprehend what was happening, why Verne was kneeling on top of Ali, pinioning her down, why something had been stuffed into her mouth and her skirt was pulled up and her soft vulnerable flesh was exposed, but the moment, the very second I understood, my brain stopped working.

67

I WAS IN that strange and familiar place where my pulse pounded steadily and the anger shot through my veins like high-octane fuel. I was possessed by a single-minded purpose. I was in a trance, in a tunnel. The whole world had collapsed to just him and me.

Verne looked up, startled, as I rushed up to him, but it wasn't easy for him to move. Not with his pants pulled down that way, his discolored white jockey shorts down around his knees, his engorged phallus a beet-red upturned thumb sprouting from a mop of mossy brown pubic hair. Not while he was struggling to hold Ali down with both hands and feet.

She was writhing and bucking against him, trying to free herself with all her strength, but her hands were roped together, and she was far overmatched in any case. Her face was red from exertion. Her cries were muffled by the panties he'd stuffed in her mouth.

Then, scowling at me, still kneeling on Ali's thighs, he lifted his right arm, swung it behind him to grab for his holster, entangled in his trousers.

I had Buck's gun in my pocket and Wayne's pistol in my waistband, but in my adrenaline haze I'd forgotten about both of them. I reared back and drop-kicked him, hard, in the throat. Something in there crunched and gave way.

Verne made an *ooooof* sound, then emitted an enraged, animal-like growl. He wobbled, knocked off-balance, but quickly righted himself, got back up on his knees and tried to stand as he grabbed his pants to hitch them up.

Ali twisted away. Her face was scratched and her lipstick was smeared and her eyes leaked tears. Her blouse was ripped, exposing her bra.

He seemed to have given up on his gun, for the moment. Instead, as he propelled himself up from a squatting position, he grabbed my foot, twisted it, and slammed his other fist into my solar plexus. I doubled over, staggered backwards, the wind knocked out of me.

My entire world had one single purpose: inflicting a very personal violence on that monster.

Back on his knees, he had his revolver out now and was aiming at me. He shuddered and twitched, his gun hand shaking. His eyes danced. The meth might have speeded up his reaction time, but it had also fried his nervous system; he couldn't hold the gun steady.

I grabbed his gun hand at the wrist with one hand, twisted the gun in my other, and jerked it backwards. His finger had gotten stuck in the trigger guard, as I expected it would, and as I wrenched the gun out of his grip, his trigger finger bent way out of joint, obviously broken.

Then, flinging his gun out of the way, I slammed my elbow into his face. He went *uhhhh,* toppled backwards. He groaned, struggled up to a sitting position, gasping for air.

I flashed on that image of Ali trapped beneath his knees and arms, her nakedness exposed, her beauty and vulnerability, and what little restraint I had was gone.

Grabbing his sleeves from behind, I slammed the entire weight of my body against the back of his head, lifting my feet off the ground, throwing all my weight into it, forcing his head down. His throat gurgled. His neck bent all the way forward until his chin nuzzled his chest, and I felt his head jolt forward, then he made a short, sharp gasp as his neck audibly snapped.

For a few seconds, I lay on top of him. Then I rolled off him, heart racing, panting and heaving.

I rose, went over to Ali, lying exhausted on the lawn, and knelt and pulled out the gag. I threw my arms around her, squeezed hard. Her face was hot and wet against my shirt.

I held her for almost a minute. She'd begun to sob. I held her tight and waited. When her sobs slowed, I let go, took out the knife, and slashed through the ropes to free her hands.

68

"WE NEED TO get him out of here," I said, picking up the rope I'd just cut off her and jamming them in my pocket. "And we've got to get *ourselves* out of here, too. Before someone comes looking for him."

"Landry," she said, rising slowly. Her voice shook. "What you just did—"

"Later," I said. "Come on, help me." Verne's little stainless-steel revolver lay on the grass. I grabbed it, and slipped it under my belt.

I grabbed Verne's legs, and she took his arms. She looked dazed but kept moving. He was lighter than Buck had been, but still Ali struggled. Her strength had been sapped.

The edge of the forest was just a few feet behind the shed. We'd only gone a few feet through the dense underbrush when she dropped his arms. "I can't," she said, panting.

"This is far enough." The body couldn't be seen from the house, with the shed in the way.

Then I began rummaging through his vest, grabbing all the spare ammo I could find. He had an extra couple of magazines in one of the pockets, already loaded.

We stood behind the shed. Her face was shadowed.

Her lipstick was smeared and her face was scratched and tear-stained. It broke my heart. Gently, I put a hand up to her face and wiped away her tears, the smudged makeup. I wanted to feel the satin skin of her face. She closed her eyes, seemed to respond to the consolation in my touch.

"Are you okay?"

She nodded, began sobbing again.

"Ali." I stroked her hair.

"Who the hell are you, Landry?" she whispered.

69

"THERE ISN'T ANY time," I said. "Any second, Russell's going to realize we're both missing. If he hasn't already. We'll talk some other time. Right now I need your help."

SHE ASKED ALL sorts of questions, her mind firing on all cylinders.

" 'Close of business today' has to refer to close of business in Europe," she said. "Liechtenstein. Which is, if I remember correctly, next to Switzerland. Nine hours ahead of us. If their banks keep the same hours as our banks, that means Russell probably can't transfer funds after seven in the morning here."

"Did you notice a clock in the game room?" I asked.

"No. But sunrise here is around five A.M. this time of year—I remember going over the schedule. So it's maybe four thirty. The other thing is that he has to wait for our bank in New York to open. Around nine, I'd guess—six o'clock here. So he has one hour to make everything happen."

"And we have about an hour and a half."

"You know what's strange about this whole thing?" she said at last.

"What?"

"Think about how well briefed Russell seems to be. How well prepared. How much he knows about the company."

"He has a source inside the company," I said. "Has to be."

"But do you think it's possible he's actually *working* for someone inside Hammond?"

I was silent for a moment. "That's what that guy Wayne said, only I didn't quite get what he meant. I asked him who hired them, and he said, 'You did.' Meaning Hammond, I'm guessing."

"Someone here?"

"Possibly."

"But for what?"

"Good old embezzlement, maybe."

"Not so easy these days," Ali said. "Not since Enron, anyway. Too many people looking at the books."

"So if you want to steal a load of money, you've got to get creative, right?"

"I suppose so. Not my area of expertise. But why do something like this—a kidnapping? Why hire Russell and his men to try to pull off something so big and messy and downright *risky*?"

I nodded. "Only one reason, I figure. If you're trying to make people think it's something it's not."

"I don't follow."

"That's the thing that's been bothering me about this kidnapping—how obvious it feels. How . . . I don't know, almost *staged*."

"Staged?"

"You ever hear of something called an *autosecues-tro*?"

She shook her head.

"Happens in Latin America from time to time. It's a staged kidnapping. A *self*-kidnapping. People fake their own kidnapping, to raise money from insurance companies or employers. Even from their own family members."

"A hoax, then."

"Of a sort."

"But . . . what kind of massive greed would make someone do something so insane? All this *bloodshed*."

"Maybe the murders weren't supposed to happen. Maybe Russell's just out of control. And maybe it's not greed."

"Then what?"

"Maybe desperation."

"Huh?"

"Look at all the guys on our management team— they're not reckless types, right? Greedy, sure, some of them. No doubt. But they're not motivated by the big score."

"So what would drive them to do something like this?"

"Fear."

"But *who*?"

I shook my head.

"Maybe the question to ask is, who had the chance to meet with Russell privately?" she said.

"We all did, right? When he did his 'interviews.'"

"But when problems came up, when decisions had to be made—whoever hired Russell would have had to talk to him in private. So he'd need a way to do that without the rest of us noticing. An excuse."

"Anyone who asked to use the bathroom could have talked secretly with Russell, and we'd never have known it."

"And Upton Barlow asked a bunch of times," I said. "Because of his prostate problem. And Geoff Latimer, with his diabetes."

"Did you know he was diabetic?" she said.

"I never met the guy before today. Though I did see syringes in his suitcase."

"The weird thing is, when I was working in HR, I never saw any medical claims from Latimer that had anything to do with diabetes."

"Geoff Latimer? Get real. Of all the guys here, Latimer strikes me as the least likely to do something like this. And besides, who's more loyal to Cheryl?"

"And she's loyal right back. Like that crap that Bodine's threatening to bring before the board about how Slattery was pushing to strengthen computer security and she turned it down?"

I remembered Slattery saying he could wire as much money as he wanted to out of Hammond's treasury from a laptop at a Starbucks. "What about it?"

"You saw the way she took the fall for it."

"Took the fall? I thought it was her fault."

"That's Cheryl. 'The buck stops here' and all that. She was persuaded *not* to implement Slattery's plan— by one of her most trusted advisers."

"Geoff Latimer," I said, and stopped.

70

THE NIGHT SKY was still blue-black and clear and crowded with stars, but a pale glow shimmered at the horizon.

We raced around the back of the lodge, staying low to the ground. Ali took Verne's stubby little Smith & Wesson revolver because it was small and fit her hand, and she was frightened of semiautomatics. I kept the Ruger.

I stashed the SIG-Sauer to use as a backup, just in case we needed it.

Tucked away in the trees behind the lodge was the maintenance shed. It was a rustic old structure, weathered and shingled. The paint on its door was peeling. An ancient brass padlock on a rusted steel hasp secured the door. It was unlocked, though; it came right open, just as the manager had said it would.

Inside was the overpowering odor of oil paint and insecticide and gasoline.

The floor was old plywood. I closed the door behind her, clicked the flashlight on, and set it down on a bench. It illuminated a circle against the shelving on one wall, casting the cramped interior in a dim amber light.

I unclipped Buck's Handie-Talkie from my belt and switched it on, dialed up the volume. It was still on channel 5, the one Russell's men had been using.

But channel 5 was silent, transmitting only a thin static hiss.

"They could have switched channels, right?" Ali said.

"Or they're not using it. I want you to monitor this, okay? Listen for anything that might tell us what they're doing. And keep that gun in your hand."

"Where are you going?" She sounded alarmed.

"I want to see where Russell and his brother are."

"Why?"

I gave her a level glance. "If they're in the screened porch, I might be able to take them by surprise."

"Take them . . . ?"

"Shoot them, Ali. Take them down. One or both."

"Jesus, Landry!"

"Will you be okay in here?"

"You're worried about *me*?"

"Can you fire the revolver if you have to?"

"I know how to use a gun."

"I know you do. I'm asking if you can bring yourself to do it."

She inhaled deeply. "If I have to," she said. "I think so."

THE FIRST SURPRISE was the porch: No one was there. It was dark and empty.

The second surprise was the game room, where the wooden blinds had been drawn. They'd been open all night, though the windows had been shut. With the blinds down, I couldn't risk firing.

That meant they knew we were out here. They'd taken precautions.

Dropping to the ground, I waited about a minute, listening for any movement, waiting to see whether I noticed anyone looking out. When I was fairly certain I wasn't being watched, I got to my feet and ran back to the shed.

Standing outside the closed door, I said in a low voice, "It's me."

The door came open slowly. Ali stood there, revolver in her hand, looking like a natural. Her eyes were questioning, but she said nothing.

I went in, shut the door behind me. "They know," I said.

"They know what?"

"That I'm out here. Maybe that you are, too, by now."

"How can you be sure?"

I explained.

"So what does that mean?" Ali said. "What are we going to do?"

"We go to Plan B. I'm going to shut off the generator. Which will do two things."

"They can't wire the money without power," she said.

"Exactly. *And* unless I splice the cable back together. Which means they're going to have to cooperate if they want the funds. It'll also disorient them. And in the confusion, I'm going to try to get back inside without being noticed."

"*Inside?* For what?"

"To get the others out. Meanwhile, I want you to stay here and see if you can find a heavyweight bolt cutter."

"For the Zodiac," she said.

I nodded.

"If there was a bolt cutter here, you'd have grabbed it already, Landry. I know what you're doing. You want me to stay here."

I hesitated for barely a second. "Right," I admitted. "I don't want you out there if they start shooting."

"Yeah, well, I'm not staying inside here. I want to do what I can."

"The best thing you can do is stay alive. If anything happens to me, maybe you can get help. Maybe there's a rowboat down there you can take."

"Don't lie to me, Landry. If there were a rowboat, you'd have mentioned it already."

She knew how my mind worked, of course. "All right," I finally said. "But at least wait here until the power goes out. Keep a watch on the house." I edged the door open a bit and looked out. A faint glow was visible in the kitchen window. "When you see the generator shut down, run over to the kitchen entrance."

Then I thought of something. I swept the walls with the flashlight. Tools hung in perfect rows on Peg-Board or on hooks on the wall. Cans of paint and paint thinner and plastic bottles of garden chemicals and hose-end sprayers lined the narrow wooden shelves. Motor oil and dry gas and spare spark plugs on another shelf. Piles of stuff on the floor, the only thing out of place.

Neatly folded on a shelf next to the paint cans, I found something that would work: a canvas drop cloth. I shook it open, then took out Buck's knife and sliced a long rectangle.

"Could you lift up your skirt?" I said.

She looked at me curiously, then got what I was doing. She pulled up her skirt. I positioned the little Smith & Wesson revolver on her thigh, then wound the canvas strip around both the gun and her thigh, just tight enough to secure the weapon in place: a decent makeshift holster.

"I wouldn't mind an explanation," she said.

I pulled the skirt back in place. The gun was still visible through the fabric, so I made a few adjustments, repositioning the revolver closer to the inside of her thigh, where it no longer protruded.

"Element of surprise," I said. She nodded.

"Try it," I said. "Make sure you can do it fast if you need to."

While she practiced, I ran the flashlight up and down the walls, shined the beam on the piles on the floor.

Noticed the crates that didn't belong here.

A cache of spare ammo, it appeared. Russell's men had brought the crates in with them and stashed them out of sight. No firearms that I could see, though.

Then my eyes were caught by several red cylinders about the size and shape of Coke cans. Black markings on them: AN-M14 INCEN TH.

"This stuff is theirs?" she asked.

"Right."

"So what are they?"

"Thermite hand grenades."

"Hand grenades?"

"Thermite. Incendiary."

"What for?"

"The Army uses them to burn things down fast. Much faster than splashing gasoline around, and a whole lot hotter."

"My *God*. You think that's what they're planning to do before they leave? Toss in one of those? Burn the lodge down with everyone inside?"

"That's my guess, yes. But not until the funds go out."

"Which he can't do until the power goes back on. And you fix the satellite cable."

"Exactly."

"Landry," she said. "These grenades. Are they something—we could use?"

"Maybe." I was quiet for a few seconds while I thought about it. And then I explained how.

"I'm going out," I said. "You sure you want to do this? If you're at all—"

"Of course I'm scared," she interrupted. She attempted a brave smile. "But don't worry about me. I'll deal."

"You always do," I said, and turned to leave. "I'll meet you at the back of the lodge. As soon as you see the lights go out."

"Landry," she said. "Make sure you come back."

71

THE DOOR TO the generator shed was unlocked, of course. Inside it was hot, smelled of machine oil; the floor was a concrete slab.

I panned the flashlight across the gray sheet-metal acoustic enclosure around the generator: a Kubota eighteen-kilowatt. It ran quiet, with only a muffled thrumming.

I flipped open the generator's control panel door and studied the array of knobs. There was a power knob, a fuel valve, various gauges and digital indicators.

The two-way radio, clipped to my belt, chirped.

I froze, listened. Heard nothing.

Turned the volume up.

That was the sound of someone pressing the transmit button. But no voice followed. As if someone had started to transmit, then changed his mind. Or maybe hit the button by accident.

I turned back to the control panel. Just shutting the power off wouldn't do much good. It might throw Russell and his brother into momentary confusion, maybe even flush them out of their sheltered positions.

But just as likely it would heighten their paranoia.

Russell would summon Peter the handyman, who'd try the remote start switch inside the lodge. Which wouldn't do it.

The fuel knob, though: There was an idea. Turn off the power, let the engine die, then close the fuel valve and wait a minute or two. When the power switch was turned back on, the fuel valve, too, everything would look normal. But the generator still wouldn't work.

They'd flip the remote start switch, and the generator's starter motor would turn over and over like an old car on a subzero morning. Maybe Russell would send the handyman out to deal with it. Probably accompanied by Travis, to make sure the handyman complied. Travis, of course, would be armed—they knew I was out here, too.

It would take the handyman a long while to figure out what I'd done—he'd check out the control panel, find all the knobs on, everything in the right place. A bafflement. And meanwhile, Russell would be desperate: No power meant no way to get what he'd come for.

The radio chirped again. I stopped.

"Jake."

Russell's voice, tinny and flat from the transmission.

"Time to come back inside," he said.

I stood still. *Don't answer, don't let him know you can hear him.*

In the background, frenzied shouts.

But Russell's voice remained calm. "I know you're out there, Jake. You really should come back. Your girlfriend's worried."

72

I SWITCHED OFF the flashlight. Turned the HT's volume down, not off. The generator remained on.

I pushed the shed door open slowly, looking to either side.

No movement out there as far as I could see.

Keeping in the shadows, I crept along the perimeter of the yard, around the back toward the maintenance shed, where I'd left her.

Even in the gloom, at a distance, I could see the shed door open, the light on inside.

She wouldn't have left the door open and the light on. She wasn't that careless.

I took a few more steps, scanning side to side, alert for any movement.

The shed was empty. Ali was gone.

The radio chirped. "It's over, Jake. She's right here. Hey, remember that Glock 18 you know so much about? Well, she's about to learn even more about it. Firsthand. The best way."

A second or two of silence, then a female voice, a torrent of words, loud and frantic and distorted.

"DON'T DO ANYTHING HE SAYS STAY OUT

THERE STAY SAFE DON'T DO WHAT HE
SAYS—"

I almost didn't recognize Ali's voice. I'd never heard
that kind of fear in her voice before.

I grabbed the Motorola, but at the very last second
willed myself to stop.

Don't answer.

*He won't do anything until he knows I can hear him.
Otherwise, for all he knows, he's talking to dead air.*

Don't answer.

Russell's voice cut off her cries. "You don't want to
test me, Jake. You know what I'll do. All I want is for
you to come back inside."

He paused. I kept silent.

"Once we do the transfer, you and your girlfriend
and all your colleagues here can go home," he said.
"But if you don't get back in here—well, it's your
choice. Like I say, you always got a choice."

73

THE SCREEN DOOR hissed as I pulled it shut.

The hall was dark, but light poured out of the open door of the manager's office.

I approached silently. Even before I saw who was sitting at the desk, I caught the faint sweet trace of his Old Spice.

Geoff Latimer looked up, startled, then his face slackened in astonishment.

"Roomie," I said.

"Jake!" he said. "You—were you able to get word out?"

I came closer to the desk. Saw a list of numbers printed on a sheet of paper next to the keyboard: Hammond's bank accounts. "Couldn't get the Internet to work," I said. "You having any luck?"

He shook his head, eyes guarded.

"It must have been awkward for you," I said quietly, "when Cheryl asked you to run the internal investigation."

"Awkward?" He looked even paler than usual.

" 'Who will guard the guards?,' right?"

"I don't understand."

"Stand up, Geoff," I said.

"You shouldn't be here. Russell told me to do the funds transfer, and he's going to be back—"

"Where do you inject yourself?"

"Where do I *what*?"

"The insulin. For your diabetes. Where do you inject it?"

"Jake, you're not making sense."

"Only three places a diabetic normally injects insulin," I said. "What's your place?"

"My—my stomach—but we don't have time for this, Jake."

I grabbed his shirt, yanked out the tails.

His smooth, pale belly. Not a mark.

His eyes were keen.

I dropped the shirt. "You told Russell to kill Danziger, didn't you?"

He swallowed. "What the hell are you talking about?"

"John *knew*. He'd figured out you contacted Russell through some old buddy of yours who ran a security firm Russell used to work for. So Danziger had to die, isn't that right, you son of a bitch? Grogan, too."

He glanced at the door. Maybe he was expecting Russell or Russell's brother to save him. Turning back, he said, "Jake, this is insane. I'm trying to *help* us. You're wasting time we don't have."

"That's true," I said, and I took out the revolver and placed it against his forehead.

"*Jesus!*" he gasped. "What the hell is this? Put that thing down *now*!"

"All to get rich, huh?"

"Jake, where'd you get that gun? Get that damned thing *off* of me!"

I pressed the end of the gun barrel harder into the pasty skin of his forehead. I could see the red mark it left. His eyes welled with tears.

"But I'm thinking it was more complicated than that. You stole money from the company, put it in some 'special purpose entity' offshore. But then the investment tanked, right? And you had to cover the loss, fast. Something like that?"

"Will you please put that gun down?" he whispered. "That thing could go *off* if you're not careful! Are you crazy? I'm trying to get us *help,* Jake."

"You needed to come up with a hundred million dollars somewhere. You were desperate."

"Who is putting these insane ideas in your head? Is it Bodine? Slattery?"

"I don't think you meant for things to happen the way they did today," I said. "You didn't hire Russell to hold the company up for half a billion dollars, did you? That was his idea. You were totally clear in your instructions, I'm sure. A hundred million, right? You told him to make sure it looked like he and his guys were just some backwoods hunters who got the bright idea to take a bunch of businessmen hostage, hold them up for ransom."

He stared at me, frantic. His eyes were brown, trusting: child's eyes.

I jammed the end of the barrel harder against his temple, and he gasped. "You knew Russell had a lot of experience in situations like this, but you didn't do your due diligence, did you?" Then, even more softly: "You didn't want people to die, did you, Geoff? Tell me that wasn't part of the plan."

Tears spilled down his scrubbed red cheeks.

"No," he whispered. His face seemed to crumple. "It wasn't supposed to happen like this."

"How was it supposed to happen?"

But Latimer didn't answer. He closed his eyes. His lower lip trembled.

"What's that you like to say—pigs get slaughtered?"

"No!" he cried. "It wasn't for me! I never made a *dime*!"

"So how *was* it supposed to happen?" I whispered. "Russell's guys would hold the company up for a hundred million dollars, then let us all go free? They'd get their cut, and you'd cover your loss? And no one would find out about the money you embezzled from Hammond? Was that how it was supposed to go down?" I grabbed his bony shoulder, shoved him toward the door.

"Please, Jake, do you think I had any *idea* what was going to happen?"

"Thing is, Geoff, you still don't," I said as I pushed him down the hall.

I SHOVED LATIMER into the great room, the revolver at his back.

Russell stood behind Ali, an arm around her neck, his Glock to her temple. He didn't need to say anything: He had a gun to Ali's head and wouldn't hesitate to kill her if it suited his purposes.

I had Latimer, the man who'd hired Russell, but he was only useful if Russell still needed him at this point. And that I didn't know.

I noticed Travis standing about ten feet to the side of his brother, his gun aimed directly at me. The room blazed with light, every lamp switched on. I wished I'd taken the time to shut off the generator, as I'd planned to before Russell had seized Ali. The cover of darkness could have been useful just then.

I tried to calculate the geometry of the situation, but there were too many unknowns. This much I knew for sure: It was two of them against me, and the only thing between Ali and her death was the twitch of a trigger finger.

Something struck my lower back, a supernova of pain exploding and radiating and doubling me over. I sprawled to the floor. For a moment, everything went white. I gasped, rolled over on to my side, saw who had kicked me from behind.

That jet-black hair and goatee, that towering physique, the pinkish face abraded and badly bruised. But otherwise the man wasn't much worse for wear.

"Well, what do you know," Buck said. "I had a feeling I'd be seeing you again."

74

"LET HER GO, Russell," I said as I struggled to my feet, still clutching the Ruger.

"That your big idea, swapping Latimer for your girlfriend?" Russell said contemptuously. "Come on, buddy. I really don't care what happens to him at this point."

But Latimer had broken free anyway. He now stood between Travis and Buck, his bodyguards. His face was flushed, his eyes furious.

"You know, I really should have killed you first," Russell continued.

"That's all right," Buck said. "I'll do it for you. Happy to oblige."

Ali was staring at me. She seemed to be communicating silently; but what, if anything, was she trying to say? I saw the fierce resolve in her eyes: Maybe she was simply telling me not to worry about her, that she was fine, she was strong. But I already knew that.

Or maybe she was waiting for me to give her a signal, to tell her what to do.

I didn't know what to do.

I raised the pistol, moving it from man to man to

man, aiming at each, one at a time. But Russell knew I'd never risk a shot at him. Not while he had his gun on Ali: his human shield. Even if my aim were perfect, it would take no more than a jerk of his finger on the trigger at the instant of his death, and she'd die, too.

"You have to take him out," Latimer said, his voice echoing. "He's the only one who knows anything now."

"I don't work for you anymore, Geoff," Russell said.

Both his brother and Buck had guns pointed at me. I wondered whether Travis would actually pull the trigger if Russell ordered him to. I had no doubt that Buck would.

"Actually, Russell, I don't think Geoff's really thought this through," I said. "See, you need me alive."

"Do I?" Russell sounded almost curious.

"If you want the Internet connection to work, anyway," I said. "You do want your money, don't you?"

"Ah." Russell nodded. "I see. Well, it's all hooked up now."

"No, Russell, it's not. One of your guys must have screwed up—cut the line."

Russell smiled.

Buck said, "Guy's bluffing, Russell."

"Don't take my word for it," I said. "Ask Geoffrey."

"How's the satellite working, Geoff?" said Russell.

Latimer hesitated a few seconds. "Something's wrong with it. I couldn't get connected. He must have done something."

"Should have brought your A team on this job," I said. "Sloppy. You see, Russell, I worked as a cable installer once for a couple of months. Not one of my favorite jobs, but I guess you never know when a skill might come in handy."

I waited a beat, but Russell didn't reply. "Call me crazy, but I've got a feeling you're not really an expert in splicing RG-6 coaxial cable."

Silence.

"How about you, Buck?" I said. "Or you, Travis?"

Silence.

"Didn't think so. The handyman sure isn't. Ask him. Guy can probably do anything with a boat or a generator or a busted dishwasher, but when the satellite goes down, I'll bet you the manager gets on the sat phone and calls the satellite company. You planning on calling the cable company, Russell? Ask for a service call, maybe? Wait a couple days for them to get all the way out here?"

"We don't need him for that, Russell," Latimer said. "Even if he's telling the truth, we don't need him to fix the line. I'm sure the handyman can figure it out. The main thing is, there's only one person who *knows* about all this. You have to take him out right now."

Russell glanced at Latimer. Smiled again. "You know, Geoff," he said, "I think you're right." In one swift, smooth movement, he removed the Glock from Ali's head. I swung the Ruger around to aim at the center of his chest, gripping it with both hands, and in the instant before I could pull the trigger to take him down, an explosion rang in my ears.

Latimer slumped to the floor. Ali screamed, jumped, but Russell's arm held her tight against his body.

I stared, at once relieved and horrified.

"Now, Jake," Russell said calmly as he replaced the gun against Ali's temple, "my brother's going to escort you outside and watch while you repair the line. I know you care whether your girlfriend lives or dies, so I'm sure you won't try anything stupid."

"I'll take him outside," Buck said.

"Thank you, Buck," Russell said, "but I don't think that'll be necessary. Jake's going to return your gun to you. He'll be unarmed. Jake, place the Ruger on the floor. Slowly."

I paused. Breathed out slowly.

Russell jammed the Glock into Ali's temple, and she gave a cry.

"All right," I said. "But here's the deal: As soon as I fix the cable, you let her go. I'll signal you when I'm finished, and you can check. Confirm the Internet connection's working. If I keep my end of the bargain, you keep your end. Okay?"

Russell nodded, smiled. "You don't give up, do you?"

"Never," I said.

75

TRAVIS KEPT HIS distance, his weapon trained on me.

I knelt at the side of the shed where I'd cut the cable, and held up one end for him to see. A glint of copper in the moonlight.

"Can I have a little light here?" I said.

With his left hand, he took out his flashlight and switched it on, blinding me.

"Out of my eyes, please."

He shifted the beam toward the ground, shined it on the loops of cable coming out of the earth against the shed's concrete foundation, then at the severed ends.

I said, "You do this, Travis?"

"What?"

"One of you guys must have cut this."

Travis sounded surprised to be asked, even irate. "No."

"I'm going to need some stuff. A crimping tool, a couple of F-type male connectors, and an F-81 connector. And a cable cutter and a pair of pliers. A toggle strip tool, if they have one."

Travis shuffled a foot on the gravelly sand. "I don't know what the hell you're talking about."

"If they have it, it's going to be in the toolshed. If

they don't, I'm going to have to wing it. We need to find
out, fast."

"How the hell do I know what they have?"

"You don't. I'll have to look."

He shined the flashlight into my eyes again. I
shielded my eyes with a hand.

"I'm going to have to ask Russell."

"You check with your brother every time you wipe
your ass? If they have anything, it'll be right here, in the
shed." I touched the shingled wall. "Let's take a look.
You guys don't have time to screw around."

He hesitated. "All right."

The diesel engine inside was chugging away. Didn't
he wonder why the tool shed had a generator inside?
But he didn't seem to know one outbuilding from another, and he probably wasn't thinking too clearly. He
was intent only on keeping me from going anywhere or
doing anything.

Instead of coming around to the front to the shed
door, I rounded toward the back.

"Hey! Door's over here."

"Yeah, and the key's hanging on a hook back here," I
said, and kept going. I muttered, "Or do you want to call
for Big Brother and ask him for permission to get it?"

He followed, still trying to keep a distance, his gun
on me, the beam in my eyes.

"Will you point that flashlight over here, please?" I
said, not indicating anything. "And not at my eyes?"

"Where?"

"Shit," I said, stopping by a gnarled old pine whose
branches raked the shed's low roof. "It's not here. You
see it anywhere?"

The cone of light swept up and down the shingles:
quick, jerky movements, impatient.

"Shit," I said. "We're going to have to get the handyman out here to open up the shed."

He moved the flashlight beam from the ground up to
the shed's low roof, then down again. I could see him
hesitate, trying to figure out how to get out his two-way
while keeping the gun on me and putting the flashlight
away. As he did so, I stepped closer to him, pretending
to search for the missing key. He clicked off the flashlight, jammed it in a vest pocket, and felt for his HT.

"Wait," I said. "I think I found it. Sorry about that."

Wayne's SIG-Sauer nestled in a crook of the old
pine's tree trunk. I grabbed it, swung it around, and put
it against his ear.

"One word," I said, "and I'll blow your brains out."

He hesitated just long enough for me to grab his gun
hand at the wrist and twist it, hard. He was amazingly
strong: all that prison muscle. But finally I was able to
wrench it out of his hand.

His left fist crashed into my cheek. He didn't have
room to maneuver, to aim his punch or get a decent arc,
but still the blow was incredibly powerful. A jagged
lightning bolt of pain exploded in my eyes, my brain. I
tasted blood.

But that didn't stop me from thrusting my knee into
his groin. He expelled a lungful of air through my fingers. The whites of his eyes flickered briefly, and he
grunted, looked sick.

I shoved the gun into his ear, but before I could say
anything, his fist smashed into my temple, so hard that
pinpoints of light danced before my eyes.

Don't give in to it.

I kneed his groin again, slammed his head into the tree trunk, then swung the pistol against the side of his head with all of my strength.

He went right down.

Slumped against the tree and slid to the ground. His eyes were open just enough to see the whites.

But he was out.

I TIED HIM up with some of the rope I'd cut off Ali, then popped out the magazine of his Colt Defender, checked to make sure it was loaded. It was. The SIG was down at least three shots, so I jammed it into my back pocket as a backup. Then I headed to the other shed.

MY FATHER HAD what he called a "toy box" of war trophies and deactivated training grenades he'd brought home from Vietnam. When I was maybe six he explained to me what an incendiary grenade was. A little later that afternoon, as I ran circles around him trying to get him to play hide-and-seek, he hurled one at me.

To teach me a lesson.

Only after I stopped crying did he explain, with a hearty guffaw, that you had to pull the pin first or it wouldn't detonate. I'd always assumed it was a dummy grenade, but with my father you never knew.

The stash of weapons and supplies was still in the shed.

There were four thermite grenades, but I only needed one.

Five minutes later, when I'd finished my prep work, I returned to the lodge.

RUSSELL'S EYES NARROWED. He knew something wasn't right. He didn't even have a chance to ask where his brother was.

"We got a problem," I said.

"What problem?"

"You," I said, and I held up the grenade for a second, just long enough for it to register.

I grasped the pull ring, tugged it out, and then I hurled it at him.

"You crazy son of a bitch!" he screamed, diving out of the way.

Ali shrieked and jumped free, and Buck leaped away, too.

The confusion gave me enough time to pull the Colt Defender out of the waistband of my pants and squeeze off two shots. Russell was a blur. When the bullet struck his shoulder, he roared, then crashed into the over-stuffed sofa, his gun dropping from his hand, sliding a good ten feet or more.

Buck canted to one side. A crimson starburst appeared on his shirt just above his vest.

Muffled screams from somewhere close by: the game room?

Russell, back on his feet, hesitated for an instant, as if deciding whether to reach for his gun.

The fury in his face told me he now understood that I'd removed the primer from the grenade; he was not a man who enjoyed being duped.

I aimed the pistol and fired another round, but then something moved in my peripheral vision.

Buck, summoning a final burst of malevolent strength, had somehow managed to raise his gun. He fired. I glimpsed the tongue of flame at the end of the muzzle, felt a fireball of pain explode inside my right thigh.

The floor came up to hit me in the face.

My forehead and cheekbone felt broken, the pain ungodly. Everything was spinning. I struggled to get upright, finally managed to stagger to my feet, then Russell swooped at me, kneeing my solar plexus.

I sagged, fell backwards, retching, the gun dropping to the floor. I couldn't catch my breath. He grabbed my hair, jerked my head upward, slammed it back down against the floor.

Blindly, I swung at what I thought was his face but connected with something softer: muscle.

I tried to lift my torso at the same moment that he jammed his knee into my wounded thigh, and everything went white and sparkly.

The room and everyone in it danced and jiggered before my eyes, turned liquid. I could see Russell, purple-faced, reach back to slip something out of somewhere (was it his boot?)—

and in his fist something glinted: a blade, a long-handled knife, the point of a spear—

and he drew it back in his fist with a guttural, bestial roar, aiming directly at my heart, and I was paralyzed, watching Russell in his animal rage, the silvery gleam of the knife blade, and I was too numb to fully grasp that he'd finally won.

I thought: *This is the bad wolf.*

I tried to plead, but only a grunt came out, and I was slipping away, no longer had the strength to grab the gun out of my pocket, to do anything but—

The top of his head came off.

Red mist. The blast numbed my ears.

He toppled, blood everywhere.

Ali held the Smith & Wesson in a perfect two-handed grip, shoulders forward, an ideal stance.

Her hands were shaking, but her eyes were fierce.

AFTER

78

THE CANADIAN POLICE kept us in Vancouver for almost four days.

There were a lot of legal matters to deal with, an investigation to conduct. The two surviving kidnappers were immediately arrested by the Major Crime Unit of the Royal Canadian Mounted Police, who actually turned out not to ride horses or wear those funny-looking red uniforms or the silly wide-brimmed Stetson hats.

Buford "Buck" Hogue was evacuated by helicopter to Royal Columbian Hospital in New Westminster, where he died in surgery. Travis Brumley was placed in a detachment cell at Port Hardy, then brought before a judge for arraignment.

I felt strange telling the police investigators that, of all the hostage-takers, Travis seemed the least violent and therefore the least guilty. As far as I knew, he hadn't killed anyone. He'd even tried to stop the bloodshed. But as they kept pointing out, Travis was still the perpetrator of a violent crime. He'd be charged with murder, no question about it.

Then again, these were Canadians. I didn't know

what Canadians did with murderers. Maybe gave them a very strict talking-to.

The bodies of the victims and the hostage-takers were all airlifted to Vancouver for autopsy. All the rest of us were subjected to some pretty lengthy questioning by the Major Crime Unit team, no one longer than I, after my wounds were bandaged up in the hospital.

ONCE THE EXUBERANT relief of our rescue had worn off, the exhaustion set in. We were all pretty traumatized. In between police interviews and statutory declarations in front of justices of the peace, we slept a lot, talked, called our families and friends.

I couldn't help noticing that Clive Rylance and Upton Barlow and even Kevin Bross were a lot friendlier to me. I suspected it wasn't simple gratitude for what I'd done. These were men who could smell power shifts from miles away, and they all knew that Cheryl had big plans for me. I had become someone they needed to cultivate. They wanted to stay on my good side.

But something seemed wrong with Ali: She'd become quiet, withdrawn. On the second day, I finally got a chance to talk to her alone. We were sitting in a waiting room of the RCMP's E Division headquarters outside Vancouver, a depressing room with linoleum floors and ratty couches and that pine smell of disinfectant I loathed.

"It's eating me up inside," she said. Her eyes were bloodshot.

"What?"

"What I did."

I drew closer to her on the couch, took her hands. "You saved my life."

She stared at the floor, unable to meet my eyes. "I keep replaying it in my head. I'm not like you, Jake. I don't think I'll ever shake it."

"You never will," I said very quietly. "I understand, believe me. More than I ever wanted to tell you."

And then, taking a deep breath, I told her everything.

ON OUR LAST morning in Vancouver, I was having breakfast by myself in the restaurant of the Four Seasons when Upton Barlow approached my table.

"Mind if I sit down?" he said.

"Not at all."

He noticed the bandage on my face. "You okay?"

"I'm fine."

"I underestimated you, my friend," he said.

I didn't know how to respond, so I didn't.

"I still find it hard to comprehend that Geoff Latimer embezzled from the company. And on such a scale at that. Just goes to show, you never really know people."

I looked up from my coffee, saw the anxiety in his face. "I think it was more complicated than that."

"Well, no doubt," he said, feigning an offhanded tone. "What—what did he tell you at the end?"

Of course, that was what he really wanted to know: Had Latimer revealed everything? As far as Barlow knew, Latimer had spilled his guts to me. "A lot," I said.

Barlow's cheeks flushed. "Oh, yeah? Do tell."

I leaned close to him. "See, Upton, here's the thing. There's going to be a lot of changes at the top, as I'm sure you know."

He nodded, cleared his throat. "What do you know about these—changes?" He must have hated having to ask me that.

"I know this much: Cheryl's going to look a lot more favorably on those who cooperate."

"Cooperate?"

"You have something Cheryl wants."

He nodded, cleared his throat again.

"Some people will get thrown to the wolves," I said. "You have to decide if you're going to be one of them."

IN EXCHANGE FOR Cheryl's guarantee not to hand him over to the Justice Department, Upton Barlow said he'd be only too happy to tell her everything.

About how her predecessor, James Rawlings, had asked his trusted General Counsel, Geoff Latimer, to set up an offshore partnership in the British Virgin Islands.

It was Hank Bodine's idea, actually, but then Rawlings—a shrewd but aggressive investor—decided he wanted to triple the pot within a year and replace the funds in the company's coffers before they were discovered missing. Turn fifty million into a hundred fifty. The ever-cautious Geoff Latimer had warned his boss that trading on margin like that was terribly risky.

But Jim Rawlings was willing to take the risk in order to amass enough untraceable cash for what he liked to call "offsets"—facilitation payments, success fees, whatever. Barlow preferred to call it by its true name: a slush fund for bribes.

To give Jim Rawlings his due, there was a reason why Hammond's foreign business was so strong during his tenure.

It wasn't just the lousy four hundred thousand bucks that Hank Bodine had told Geoff Latimer to wire to an offshore account he'd set up for the Pentagon's Chief

Acquisitions Officer. No, it was the millions and millions that Bodine had dispensed to foreign ministers and third-world dictators the world over. Those guys didn't sell out as cheap as U.S. government bureaucrats.

Jim Rawlings never expected the fund to go belly-up, of course. He never expected to put Latimer in the desperate position of having to come up with a hundred million dollars to pay off a margin call when the investment collapsed. Had he lived, Rawlings would have taken care of things.

Then again, he never anticipated an outside investigation whose unblinking, ceaseless scrutiny made it impossible for Latimer to dig up the money somewhere in the Hammond treasury.

"If Rawlings hadn't dropped dead playing golf at Pebble Beach, none of this would have happened," Upton Barlow told Cheryl later. "I never liked golf."

79

I ALMOST DIDN'T make the flight home.

I had the dubious honor of being interviewed personally by the head of the RCMP Major Crime Unit, a dour and weary-looking homicide investigator named Roland Broussard with a black mustache and a uni-brow. Sergeant-Major Broussard was said to be their most skilled interrogator.

Midway through his interrogation, he got a copy of my juvenile arrest record—yeah, sure, they promise you that your records are "sealed," but they never really are—and from the way he started crunching his breath mints I could tell he was excited. He seemed to have decided that I was like an arithmetic problem that never added up the same way twice.

But finally he excused me, after everyone else had boarded the Hammond jet. They held the flight for me, though.

I limped up the metal steps and entered the main salon. As I walked in, my eyes getting used to the dim light, I looked around for a seat.

There were a number of empty ones.

I'd forgotten how ludicrously opulent the company

plane was, all the wood paneling and the Oriental rugs
and the marble tables and the leather recliners.

Someone clapped, and then a couple of people, and
before long there was a smattering of applause, which
sounded strange in the sound-deadened cabin. I smiled,
shook my head modestly, plopped down in the nearest
seat, which happened to be next to Hank Bodine.

He was talking on his cell phone, and as soon as he
saw me, he rose and found another seat, off by himself.
For the first half hour of the flight, he made call after
call, and I could see him getting more and more frus-
trated.

Then Cheryl summoned me to her private cabin.

ALI LET ME in but immediately excused herself. She
went to a fancy mahogany desk in the corner and
tapped away at a laptop. Cheryl was sitting in one of the
overstuffed off-white chairs, her feet up on an ottoman,
and she, too, was talking on a cell phone.

I took a seat on a couch facing her, picked up a copy
of the *Wall Street Journal,* skimmed the movie review,
and pretended not to listen in on Cheryl's conversation.

"Jerry," she was saying, almost coquettishly, "you
know I've been chasing you for years." She gave a lilt-
ing laugh. "Oh, you'll love Los Angeles. I'm sure of it.
Don't you get tired of all the *rain*? I did. All right, then.
Good to reconnect, and I'm glad we could come to
terms. I'm *thrilled.*"

She snapped her cell phone shut and looked up at
me. She seemed to be in a giddy mood. "You—" she
began, but then the door to the cabin flew open, and
Hank Bodine stormed in.

"What the hell is going on?" he yelled.

"Pardon me, Hank?" said Cheryl.

"Every time I call my office, I get some damned recording saying I've reached a 'nonworking extension at Hammond Aerospace.' I can't even reach my own admin."

"Gloria Morales has been reassigned, Hank."

"*What?* You have no right to do that without my sign-off!"

Ali approached Cheryl, handed her a burgundy leather pad with a single sheet of paper on top of it. "Thank you, Alison," Cheryl said. She picked up a large black fountain pen from the marble end table, took her time uncapping the pen, then dashed off a bold signature at the bottom of the page. She held the paper up and blew on it to dry the ink. Then she gave it back to Ali, who wordlessly took it over to Bodine.

"What's this?" he said warily. He snatched the paper from Ali's hand and stared at it, his eyes steadily widening. " 'Violation of fiduciary duty of loyalty' . . . What the hell do you think you're doing?" He shook his head. "Nice try, Cheryl, but you don't have the power to fire *anyone*."

"Really?" Cheryl inspected her fingernails. "You might want to ask Kevin Bross about that. I'm sure you've noticed he's not on board. Try him on his cell— he's still in Vancouver. I didn't think he merited a ride on the company plane."

Bodine emitted a single sharp bark of laughter. "You'll never get this past the board of directors. They specifically took away your power to hire and fire. You can write all the letters you want, but they don't mean a damned thing."

She sighed. "The executive committee of the board

of directors met this morning in special session, Hank," she said patiently. "Once they had a chance to read the e-mails that Upton kindly provided, they realized they had no choice."

"Upton!" Bodine said.

"They quickly realized how far-reaching the legal consequences will be. And, of course, none of them wants to be hit with a lawsuit *personally*. They simply wanted me to clean up the mess you made. Which I was happy to do. As soon as they restored my power to do so. Quid . . . pro . . . quo."

Bodine's face had gone beet red.

"From their standpoint, of course, it was . . ." Cheryl paused, pursed her lips as if savoring a delectable chocolate, then smiled, ". . . a no-brainer."

80

AS THE METAL steps rolled up to the plane, I looked out the window and saw a crowd of photographers and television cameramen and reporters.

When the plane door opened, a roar came up from the crowd, and the reporters closed in, shouting questions. Cheryl was the first to exit, then Ali, then me, and finally the rest of us.

It was a bright, sunny, perfect California day. Suddenly something streaked out of the crowd, fast as a rocket, tracing frenzied circles on the tarmac.

"Gerty," I yelled. "Come!"

She ran toward me, her leash flying behind her, and vaulted into the air. Her tongue swiped my face. Then she bounded away and knocked a photographer's very-expensive-looking camera out of his hands. The poor dog was crazed with joy and relief.

Zoë shouted an apology to the photographer, tried to nab the dog, then gave up.

ALI BECKONED ME over to Cheryl's limousine.

"Jake," Cheryl said. "Ride with us."

"Thanks, but I can't," I said. "My car's parked here."

"Well, we have a lot of work to do when we get back to the office. Quite a few senior positions to fill. There'll be a number of vacant offices on the thirty-third floor, and I'd like you to take one of them. As one of my special assistants."

"Thanks," I said. "I appreciate it. But I'm not really cut out for the thirty-third floor. I'll mix up the salad fork and the fish fork. I'll drink out of the finger bowl. You never know what I might blurt out. You know me by now, I think—it's just not my scene."

She looked at me for a few seconds, her eyes gray ice. Then her expression softened. "Actually, I could use some more straight talk on the thirty-third floor."

"Thing is, I can't let Mike Zorn down." I smiled sheepishly. "Gotta deal with the whole chicken-rivet thing."

After a few seconds, she said, "I understand, I guess. But I'm sorry."

"Anyway," I said, "I called a couple of engineers from the plane. They've got a possible solution they want to explore. I'll keep you posted."

AS I HEADED toward the parking lot, Gerty straining at the leash, Ali called out to me.

I stopped, looked around.

"Did I just hear you turn Cheryl down?"

"It's nothing personal," I said.

Gerty was whining and scrambling and jumping all over Ali, and I tried to pull the dog back.

"Guess I shouldn't be surprised," she said. "It's that whole change thing, huh?"

I shrugged. "I just like being good at what I do."

She shook her head and smiled. "Maybe someday I'll figure you out." She caressed Gert's head.

"When you do," I said, "fill me in."

She leaned over, began massaging the dog's neck, running her fingers through the silky ruff, saying, "Pretty," and "What a good doggie." Gert's tail wagged like crazy. She shimmied and wriggled and tried to swipe her big tongue all over Ali's face.

"So this is the dog-wife, huh?"

I nodded.

"She's beautiful. I think she likes me."

"She likes everybody."

Ali glanced back at the limousine. "You still live in the same apartment, right?"

"Of course."

"Mind giving me a ride to my place?"

"Sure," I said. "But I gotta warn you—there's dog hair all over the car."

"That's all right," she said. "I can deal."

ACKNOWLEDGMENTS

COULD IT HAPPEN?

Even though this story is fiction, the premise—the kidnap-for-ransom of a major corporation's entire top leadership—is one of those scary possibilities that give corporate security directors insomnia. Or should. There have been a few, isolated cases of executives taken hostage: The best known is probably Thomas Hargrove, whose long captivity by guerrillas in Colombia inspired the Russell Crowe/Meg Ryan movie *Proof of Life*. But nothing like this, thank God, has ever been attempted.

Not yet, anyway . . .

As usual, I tried to get the details as accurate as possible, and as usual I couldn't have done it without my expert sources. Let me start with one man who did more than anyone to keep things real: Richard M. Rogers, the near-legendary former commander of the FBI's Hostage Rescue Team. Dick's willingness to run through scenario after scenario with me was an immense help; I can't thank him enough. Thanks to my friend Harry "Skip" Brandon, formerly of the FBI and now an international security consultant based in D.C., for introducing us.

On the secretive business of kidnapping and hostage negotiation and recovery, I was advised by Gary Noesner of Control Risks Group, Tom Clayton of Clayton Consulting, Frederick J. Lanceley of Crisis Negotiation Associates, Sean McWeeney of Corporate Risk International, and Dominick Misino, former hostage negotiator with the New York City Police Department. Greg Bangs, who runs the kidnap/ransom and extortion unit at the Chubb Group, explained K&R insurance to me. My invaluable team of security consultants included Roland Cloutier of the EMC Corporation, Jeff Dingle of LSI Security Services, and Mark Spencer of EvidentData.

On money-laundering, my experts included Matthew Fleming of Detica Inc; Thomas Erdin of EW Asset Management in Männedorf, Switzerland; David Caruso of the Dominion Advisory Group; Barry Koch, global head of anti-money-laundering for American Express; and, most of all, one alarmingly knowledgeable friend in London who wishes to go unnamed. Gary Sefcik of Mellon Global Cash Management, the financial journalist Danny Bradbury, and Tom Cimeno of the Boston Private Bank all briefed me on the intricacies of bank security and electronic funds transfers. Ernie Ten Eyck, a forensic accountant, helped structure Geoff Latimer's scam (and explained how it might be uncovered). My old friend and unindicted co-conspirator, Giles McNamee, of McNamee Lawrence in Boston, once again devised some really clever schemes.

A truly top-notch legal team guided me on internal corporate investigations and various corporate shenanigans: Paul Dacier, general counsel of the EMC Corporation; Jamie Gorelick of WilmerHale; Nell Minow of the Corporate Library; Craig Stewart of Arnold & Porter; and Judge Stanley Sporkin. But, most of all, Eric Klein of Katten Muchin Rosenman in L.A., who shared his wide-ranging expertise with great generosity. Peter Reinharz, former chief of New York City's Juvenile Prosecution Unit, told me how the New York State juvenile justice system works (and doesn't). I was particularly moved, and inspired, by Dwight Edgar Abbott's powerful account of his years in the California Youth Authority, *I Cried, You Didn't Listen.*

On the aerospace business, I got some excellent in-depth background from the CFO of the Lockheed Martin Corporation, Chris Kubasik. (Boeing flatly refused to cooperate—protecting their trade secrets against the threat of suspense fiction, I guess—with the sole exception of a spokeswoman, Loretta Gunter, who was nevertheless hamstrung in what she was allowed to tell me.) But I got plenty of insider detail from former Boeing execs who don't want to be named, as well as the veteran aerospace reporter Jim Wallace of the *Seattle Post-Intelligencer;* Ralph D. Heath, Lockheed's executive vice president for Aeronautics; and Greg Phillips, former senior air safety investigator for the National Transportation Safety Board. On the ways and wiles of the business world in general, I received astute advice from my friend Scott Schoen of Thomas H. Lee Partners; Joanna Jacobson (who shared some keen insights into the challenges of being a female CEO); and, once again, my friend Bill Teuber, the vice chairman of EMC.

Professor James H. Williams of MIT gave me an overview of the use of composite materials in airplanes (and how hard it is to know when they're damaged). Les Cohen of Hitco Carbon Composites explained how a composite vertical tail is manufactured; and Michael Bacal of the Hexcel Corporation and Bill Webb of Cytec Engineered Materials told me about adhesives technology. Thanks as well to Sara Black, technical editor of *High-Performance Composites* (a great name for a rock band, as Dave Barry would say). But no one was more unstinting with his time and expertise on this stuff than Dr. Seth Kessler, president and co-founder of Metis Design in Cambridge, who first told me about "chicken rivets." For that alone I owe the guy big-time.

RIVERS INLET IS a real place, a remote salmon-fishing paradise on the central coast of British Columbia. I thank Pat Ardley of Rivers Lodge and especially John Beath of Rivers Inlet Resort for helping me get it right, mostly. Thanks as well to Maciek Jaworski, head fly-fishing guide at King Pacific Lodge, Princess Royal Island, B.C.; Professor Henry Louis Gates Jr. of Harvard, for some great details. Ron MacKay, of Forensic Behavioural Analysis in Ottawa, told me about the Canadian RCMP. My thanks as well to Brick Ranson of Ocean Marketing in Guilford, Connecticut; John Harris of Harris Digital Networks; the forensic pathologist Dr. Stan Kessler; my fellow watch fetishist, the writer Paul Guyot; my firearms expert, Dr. Edward Nawotka; my Special Forces source, Kevin O'Brien; and my weapons and tactics adviser since my first novel, Jack McGeorge. Jack Hoban, expert in the Bujinkan method and former instructor in the Marine Corps Martial Arts Program, was Jake's trainer. My brother Dr. Jonathan Finder gave some useful medical advice, as did Dr. Tom Workman. For help with Spanish, my thanks to Marguitte Suarez and to Carlos Ramos of my Spanish publisher Roca Editorial.

For all those team-building offsite games that my guys didn't get to play, I got some great ideas from John Sargent, CEO of Holtzbrinck USA; his friend Tom Zierk; Richard Vass of Offsite Adventures; and David Goldstein of Teambonding. Ed Hurley-Wales of Workscape helped with Ali's HR career.

A couple of people made generous contributions to charities in exchange for the naming rights to some of my characters: Pamela Daut, who donated to California State University at Fullerton on behalf of her son, Peter Daut; and Deborah Yen Fecher, who contributed to the Center for Women and Enterprise on behalf of her son, Ryan Fecher.

I've come to consider my publisher, St. Martin's Press, my publishing family, and I'm grateful to everyone there for their constant support, from *Paranoia* on. Sally Richardson, president and publisher, has been the greatest cheerleader and advocate, as have Holtzbrinck CEO John Sargent; Matthew Shear, vice president and publisher of the paperback division; Matt Baldacci, VP and marketing director, editor in chief George Witte; and executive editor Jen Enderlin. And Publicity Director John Murphy, Alison Lazarus, Steve Kleckner, Merrill Bergenfeld, Jeff Capshew, Dori Weintraub, Andy LeCount, Brian Heller, Ken Holland, Tom Siino, Rob Renzler, Christina Harcar, Nancy Trypuc, Bob Williams, Anne Marie Tallberg, Sofrina Hinton, Ronni Stolzenberg, Esther Robinson, Steve Troha, Harriet Seltzer, Chris Holder, Craig Libman, and Gregory Gestner. At Audio Renaissance, publisher Mary Beth Roche and Laura Wilson. And the artists who come up with such great covers: Michael Storrings, Jerry Todd, and creative director Steve Snider.

I'm fortunate to have a couple of wonderful assistants: Sarah Blodgett, who runs my office and lets me write my books, and my web goddess, Ellen Clair Lamb.

My wife, Michele Souda, endured my long absences during the writing of this book with patience and constant encouragement. Our daughter, Emma, always knows how to cheer me up and restore my perspective. Special thanks to my brother Henry Finder, a brilliant editor, who gave generously of his limited time (since he does, after all, have a day job) and whose editorial advice I always value. Molly Friedrich is not just a terrific agent but also a trusted editor; her input on this book at a crucial point really got me back on track.

And what can I say about my editor, Keith Kahla, that I haven't said before? I lucked out, getting an editor like Keith. He really worked overtime on this book, completely transforming an early draft. There isn't an aspect of my publishing career that he doesn't care about. What success I've had in publishing I owe largely to him—for which I'm eternally grateful.